# A B(
## WITHOUT

# A Book Without Covers

## JOHN ANDREW STOREY

UPFRONT PUBLISHING
LEICESTERSHIRE

A Book Without Covers
Copyright © John Andrew Storey 2003

All rights reserved

ISBN 1-84426-108-5

First published 2003 by
UPFRONT PUBLISHING LTD
Leicestershire

Typeset in Bembo by
Bookcraft Ltd, Stroud, Gloucestershire
Printed by Lightning Source

# Acknowledgements

The author would like to thank the following copyright holders for permission to quote extracts

Melvin Powers, for permission to use extracts from *Think and Grow Rich* by Napoleon Hill.

Hodder and Stoughton and Nicholas Ellison Inc., for permission to use an extract from *Surfing the Himalayas* by Rama-Dr Frederick Lenz.

The Random House Group and the Paul Brunton Philosophic Foundation for permission to use extracts from *The Quest of the Overself* by Paul Brunton. More information about Paul Brunton can be found at www.paulbrunton.org

H J Kramer/New World Library, for permission to use extracts from *Way of the Peaceful Warrior* by Dan Millman.

As day dawns everything manifest
Emerges from the unmanifest;
As night falls it merges back
Into that same designated unmanifest.

*The Bhagavad Gita*

# DAY

# 20 December 1995: A Place to Begin

> I have been privileged in moments of great intimacy to
> witness the softening of voices to a sigh as if those voices came
> from deeper spirits in communion. It reminds me of the
> sighing of whales deep in the ocean.
>
> Now, after the experiences of tonight, which I cannot
> relate here, I feel that sighing as a kind of prayer – maybe the
> only true kind of prayer – capable of communion with other
> souls over vast distances.
>
> As the sigh of whales can carry across oceans, I feel the
> sighing of the human spirit carrying across the boundaries of
> this life into somewhere beyond, somewhere eternal.

This is not a literary device. It is real life, as best I can describe and
explain it at this time.

I wrote that passage for my own benefit quickly, after a long and
sleepless night. To my rational mind now, it looks obscure and
melodramatic. But it was heartfelt, and it was a feeling of the heart
that I was trying to catch.

Having written it, I closed my little black book, got showered and
dressed, and drove to work. It was only when I locked the car and
walked towards the door that it dawned on me. A journey had begun.

I knew it was coming too. It had started as a fleeting idea. For
several months I had been writing to a friend, Kate. I was writing
about myself and it suited her to listen. It was more emotional than
methodical. I was trying to explain my life, all its mistakes and all the
various conclusions I had reached and then changed over the years,
in the hope that Kate might get a perspective on her own situation. I
wasn't sure exactly how it was supposed to help her but, as I said, for
the time being it suited her to listen. And it helped me too. I got a lot
of new insights, and I reached a new understanding about my own
spiritual journey. So long as I was conscious of it, it never seemed to
end; there was always a search going on, even if the 'progress' I made
wasn't always apparent.

The time I am talking about, when my fleeting idea occurred,
was one of those times of 'no apparent progress' at the beginning of

1

this year. Every book I picked up at that time left me thinking: nobody is saying what I want to hear! I wanted to read that somebody else, just like me with my letters to Kate, was fumbling forward blindly, moment to moment, a real human being. So the seed of an idea was planted that such a book wasn't waiting on a shelf, but inside me.

Oddly enough, from that moment I began to find and enjoy books again. I took up ideas and used them. I began to see real progress. It is tempting to think now that I was preparing myself, but it was never so calculated, more a matter of immediate need and self-interest.

A month ago I awoke from a vivid dream. I lived in a community that depended for its existence on a rocky, potato-like substance. The production of this substance in turn depended on one man, a man who was dying and no longer able to do whatever was necessary.

The good days were gone when the community said, 'Our people used to talk to each other.' There was only a small amount of this substance left, throbbing and glowing at the bottom of a glass-lined circular chamber made for many times that quantity.

The dying man possessed no secret; he possessed a gift that had to be passed on before he died. This was a great sadness to him, because to pass on this gift was like asking the recipient to commit suicide, such was the sacrifice he would have to make of all normal life in order to give himself completely to this 'gift'.

The day came when a successor had to be chosen. I sat in the room where the decision was to be announced. I was sure that the choice would be me. Then the spokesman said, 'In the interests of safety, we have decided it should be James Bell.' That wasn't my name of course but, this being a dream, I still knew it meant me. I was sitting sideways on a sofa, my back against the armrest, and my knees tucked up in front of me to hold an exercise book which contained my own writing. I smiled as the choice was announced, and when the moment came to respond I remember as I awoke saying, 'I feel a great peace.'

I don't generally try to remember my dreams but this one was vivid and hard to forget. I tried to catch my intuitive feelings before the moment was lost. Only two things struck me: that the 'substance' represented love, and that the dream had much to do with why I am sitting here writing now. 'In the interests of safety'? I didn't know what that meant. Whose safety?

It is because of that dream that I thought of this as a moment of providence. My passing idea had almost reached the stage of a definite plan. I had a new sense of urgency, but I remembered that ever since I was a teenager I had entertained thoughts of writing, and I could always see, looking back, that I would have produced nothing worth reading. Why should now be any different? I didn't know; it just finally felt right. Since that dream it had even felt inevitable, the only remaining details being when and how.

Last Friday I had lunch with Irene, a dark-haired woman just a few years my junior, who can be intense and dismissive in turns, sometimes frustrated by events to the point of tears, and sometimes jovially detached. We became friends almost from her first day at work, and our routine allowed regular social contact. Mostly I listened. I asked the kind of questions that some would find uncomfortably probing. Irene welcomed the chance to be open and honest.

On Friday, after talking over several issues, Irene turned on me with a tone of mock accusation and said, 'Well, what about you?' as if all my questioning of her had been a deliberate distraction from the real agenda. 'Tell me about you for a change!' She reached across the table and prodded me playfully.

I said, 'I'm thinking of writing a book.' I looked sheepish, but she seemed to take me at my word.

'Oh, that's lovely! What's it about then?'

'Well, it's a spiritual journey,' I said, still sheepish. 'It's *my* spiritual journey, but it hasn't started yet, and when it does, I don't know where it'll lead. That's the whole point really, you see, that we are all on this journey and we need to share it somehow.'

I didn't explain myself very well. I felt wrong-footed, but Irene was interested nonetheless. She said that art, her own chosen means of expression, seemed a lot easier; there wasn't the need to 'think and confront yourself' so much.

Irene and I went to a Christmas party together that same evening, a work gathering. Irene was wearing a new black dress and looked particularly lovely, as many men seemed to notice. She told me beforehand that she couldn't dance, but she made a pretty good job of trying, and Sam, a normally pleasant man brooding through a haze of alcohol, saw fit to seize his chance as Irene and I left the dance floor. He strode forward purposefully and delivered a surprisingly strong blow to my chest with an open palm, simultaneously taking Irene by the arm and leading her back to the dance floor. I took a step back through the blow and laughed as I watched Irene being sped away.

I laughed because I knew exactly what was in Sam's mind: that he wanted to make a move on Irene and I was unwelcome competition. But I wasn't in competition; I wasn't even in the same game! I gestured with open palms and an expression of amused confusion. I knew Irene wouldn't be interested, but I also knew she was quite capable of telling him that for herself, and she really quite enjoyed the amorous repartee in between.

Irene, I thought, was especially good at relationships. Some months ago she taught me a lesson that seemed right and valuable but which I confess I had difficulty putting into practice. I told her of my reluctance to involve myself in trivial conversation, that my interest was never aroused until someone was willing to talk at a deeper or more emotional level. Irene, on the other hand, clearly had no difficulty in joining in and laughing along with any amount of trivia and gossip. She told me that it was important to establish the relationship first, at whatever level that took, and let something deeper develop from there. Without establishing a relationship first, we could miss out on any number of fulfilling friendships. I knew she was right. I had watched my father operate in just that way for so many years but I had not seen the strength of it.

While they danced, I looked around the room and saw Sarah. I walked over to talk with her. Sarah is a young woman, thin and a little girlish in her dress and in her smile, the way the edges of her mouth crease and her shoulders lift in a slight shrug. I worked with Sarah, but had very little contact with her. It was good to see her again. A change of hairstyle suited her and she looked altogether well.

It had been at this same annual party two years earlier that she had spoken to me properly for the first time. Before that we had never done more than acknowledge each other as we passed in the corridor. But at that party she had been unusually energetic and outspoken as I chatted to the general group of which she was a part. An hour later she was much more subdued. I stood by the dance floor and became aware of her coincidentally standing beside me. The music was loud but she kept shouting questions into my ear and I tried to answer as best I could. The conversation very quickly moved from trivial to personal and I sensed that she did not want any trite replies.

She was on the point of becoming upset. Although she was the one asking questions, my answers seemed more her business than mine. I suggested we move away from the dance area so that we might talk more easily. And that was what we did: a little friendship forged in thirty minutes of strong words and a few tears.

To this day I do not know why Sarah singled me out that night. She moved to another office shortly after, and our contact ceased until something triggered in her a surge of anxiety she could not explain, except that she was sure it concerned a past in which huge memory gaps had always privately alarmed her.

We resumed contact and spent many hours on the telephone over a period of four months. Sarah shared her weaknesses with me; I shared mine with her. At first, my motive had been to put her at ease, but once these things were brought into the swirl of our emotional exchange, I cannot say that support and comfort went only one way. In the event, she came through the worst of that and our contact was no longer a priority.

There had been a long gap until I saw her again at the party. After a brief exchange of pleasantries, it felt natural to sit down and talk together. We sat across a table holding hands with a warmth and openness which may have surprised onlookers. We talked of how we had lost touch since that time. I told her I had always thought it would be that way, that once she was feeling better in herself I would serve only as a painful reminder of less happy times. With a gentle smile and unexpected candour she said I was right: she didn't want to be reminded. She praised my wisdom while I stifled any look that might betray my feelings. There was a part of me that didn't want to be so easily brushed off.

We changed our timeframe from past to future. Sarah told me her plans and asked for mine. I was vague, even more vague than I had been with Irene. I said I was learning a lot of new things and the pace of this was growing rather than slowing down.

Sarah cautioned me, but I said she didn't understand the deep spiritual drive I felt inside. In Sarah's eyes that made matters worse. She gave me a look which told me I was toying with my sanity, that I should remember the delicate balance of my emotions and not precipitate crisis. Sarah didn't understand that I had changed. I was stronger now. She couldn't see the inner transformation that had taken place in the year since we had last spoken, and I had nothing to show for that change, nothing that could have convinced her there and then in that crowded room above the thumping music.

'This is my song!' she cried, switching her focus in an instant.

I followed her on to the dance floor to the strains of Abba's *Dancing Queen*, and felt drawn in by her unhindered exuberance. Sarah was a fine dancer; she had a way of moving that was unmistakably her own, and I told her so.

She smiled and shouted back above the din, 'Dancing is how I express myself!'

She certainly did seem freer at that moment than I had ever seen her before. She came forward to hug me and our dancing stopped.

As we left the dance floor she hugged me again and said, 'I wish you were ten years older, then you could be my dad.' I was not offended. No really, I wasn't. I did have that small part that wanted her, wanted anybody, to be attracted to me. But a bigger part saw the compliment intended.

Later, standing on the fringe of the dance floor, Irene's words from lunchtime kept coming back to me. I was alone but suddenly in need of solitude. I walked out of the room and sat on the steps for a while to cool off; it was the place where Sarah and I had eventually sat to talk two years earlier. I thought of Irene and her painting and Sarah with her dancing, and then me with my writing. I felt overawed with the enormity of what I had already undertaken, by writing down my thoughts daily, and by what I was about to take on. Of all means of expression, writing seemed to me the hardest at that moment. Out of all the ways of taking a journey, I had taken the one most obscured by fog, pitfalls and dead ends impeding my every step. I asked myself, 'Is this what I choose?' and finally I answered, 'Yes'. But even as I said it, I was aware of a paradox in my reply: I was making a free choice but it was the only choice I felt able to make.

In the early hours, Irene and I sat in the car talking. There was a strange atmosphere between us; it was very cold outside and the car should have – must have – cooled down to an uncomfortable degree, yet we were not cold. And there it was again, that sweet softening of voices …

All these memories and thoughts, the impressions of last night, hurried words on a private page. More and more as the months of this year have progressed it has come down simply to having a place from which to begin. But until this day and that sudden flash of realisation, I had never thought it should begin with death.

# *Grieving*

The little black book in which I had scribbled my thoughts, I only started that last September. I went to a weekend conference. The seminars and lectures felt valuable, even moving. So rather than socialise between each one, I kept rushing back to my room to jot down the main thing I had learned and any related thoughts. Sometimes I would sit there trembling as if I was doing something momentous, but I couldn't have put my finger on what it was and, anyway, I had the feeling that all the emotion was borrowed from other circumstances. My father had been taken into hospital and that day was to have an operation to remove a cancerous growth from his leg. Several times I had tried to ring home for news but nobody answered the telephone. Having no word, I kept unnecessarily absenting myself from company for the sake of those brief notes and treating them with uncommon reverence. But it brought me to a decision.

I was tired of learning valuable lessons and then losing them, relearning and losing them again. It always astounded me to discover that my most recent insight was the same insight I might have cherished ten or even twenty years earlier. I never knew how it was possible to lose something so precious and lose it so completely in between. I decided to start a notebook in which I could record each lesson, each insight, however small, so that I need never lose them again.

I put the plan into action within a few days of returning home. At the conference, however, it had been a passing thought of no great significance compared to thoughts about my dad. For the rest of the day I tried without success to get news.

Late in the evening I gave up the effort and ventured out. By that stage I had lost my companions to one of several functions, and I wandered around from one room to another looking so I could say I had looked, but still hoping not to find them. I preferred the company of my own thoughts, though standing on the edge of a dance floor made me self-conscious and I decided to dance. On a crowded dance floor, I figured that a lone dancer would be less conspicuous than a lone watcher. I closed my eyes and lost myself in the rhythm.

Somebody bumped me to the right. I shuffled over to the left, closed my eyes and continued. Another bump; I drew in my

7

elbows and carried on. Then a woman almost fell into the space in front of me, but it wasn't an accident. She asked if it was okay to dance with me. I nodded my acknowledgement, smiled politely and danced rather more reservedly until the song ended. Then I thanked her and left the dance floor alone; she seemed to be with a group of others.

I found a seat well back from the dance floor and settled down there to be quiet in the midst of the noise. The music had changed pace: Frank Sinatra singing *My Way*. It was a song I had found corny and profound in turns. That night I was thinking of my dad and the song *was* profound.

It must have been thirty years ago when he had adopted that song as his personal anthem. As a young boy in a big family, having a dad with one arm and no qualifications yet always feeling sure we would be provided for, I sensed even then that the song suited him well. I felt it all the more sitting in that darkened room contemplating the possibilities of his fight with cancer.

Another memory: in our single living room he had sung along with Gene Pitney as he brushed his teeth at the mirror. 'I'm gonna be strong!' he sang, and a sense of pride or something similar surged up his one good arm and the toothbrush broke in his mouth. We all laughed.

*My Way* was rising to a crescendo. My tears began to well in the darkness.

I became aware of somebody standing very close to my right, the same woman from the dance floor.

'Are you all right?' she asked. She couldn't see my face, and her tone told me that she was offering a general introduction rather than serious concern. I kept looking straight ahead across the dance floor and nodded by way of a reply. I seem to remember she tried to make small talk for a while but received no significant response from me. She fell silent and, shortly after, moved away.

By the end of the evening, I was feeling more composed, even benign. A shift of perspective had taken away my discomfort and granted a temporary acceptance of where I was and what I was allowed to know. The music had stopped and the lights had been switched on. I was standing by the door surveying the whole room with a new resolve to find my companions. I was gazing over people's heads when a voice spoke to me: the same woman again, now standing directly in front of me.

'I'm sorry for bumping into you on the dance floor,' she said. 'My friend wanted to meet you; I was supposed to draw you into our group.'

'That's okay,' I replied, still in my benign state. 'It was a nice dance. I enjoyed it.'

'He's over there.'

Her arm pointed across the room somewhere, but my eyes didn't follow. For a brief moment she seemed to be trying to read the lack of reaction in my face. Then she continued, 'But you're not gay, are you?'

'Actually, I don't think I have a gay bone in my body,' I said, and, if I had thought about it, that could have sounded like a very insensitive thing to say, but it came out in such a quiet, matter-of-fact sort of way that she saw no offence. We laughed at the misunderstanding and she told me how her friends had watched me dance and had speculated long and hard before finally deciding that no straight man would dance alone and especially not like that! I had to laugh again; what else could I do? We exchanged names – hers was Jane – and I did join her, and her friends.

Renewing our acquaintance the following evening, Jane and I talked about relationships and about love. I told her about my unusual corresponding relationship with Kate, and she said it was like I was dipping my toe in the water and did I really want to swim? The analogy confused me; I hadn't seen it like that and I couldn't really answer her question.

Then it turned into another one of those abstract conversations with a private agenda. Jane was recently divorced, and I remember her asking why it was that men cope with separation so much worse than women. I didn't know if that was true, but I offered an opinion anyway. I said perhaps it was because many women actually experience a break-up as a kind of liberation, allowing them to fulfil things in their lives from which they had been held back. In other words, they experienced a relationship as a constraint. Whereas men probably had plenty of freedom throughout the relationship and were more conscious of loss rather than gain when a break-up happened. I was speculating and I should probably have admitted that I didn't know, but it didn't matter; Jane had only ventured the question because she had a definite opinion of her own to express. She said that women did all their grieving during the relationship, in the course of it breaking down. Men, on the other hand, never saw it

9

coming – didn't look – and only started to grieve when the end actually came.

Maybe she was right. I didn't have any basis to debate it, and anyway my mind was still turning to thoughts of home.

As it turned out, Dad's operation had gone well. He had spent the weekend in comfort and, better than this, was in good spirits, laughing and joking with the nurses. When I finally got to visit him, things had taken an unexpected turn. Everybody was putting it down to withdrawal from the anaesthetic. I was gently forewarned in the waiting room. When I walked into his room, a side room off the main ward, my dad's expression was pained, he was uncomfortable and exasperated. And he was tearful. A false high induced by the anaesthesia had given way to a shock of post-operative pain, and then bad news had been heaped on bad news. There were complications, an unspecified infection in the wound which would need to be tested and treated, a huge hernia in his stomach – he had always known there was something there and it wasn't just fat – and blood tests had shown that he was diabetic.

He lay on his side, unable to choose any other position due to skin grafts on his back and both thighs. The leaden weight on his stomach was causing severe heartburn. He apologised for crying.

Things improved little over the following days; the infection was resistant to one antibiotic after another. A specialist bed was brought in to allow him to sit in a more comfortable position. The consensus was that it was just a matter of time before he would feel better. My dad subscribed to that view, at least in the attitude he expressed.

In calmer moments we talked of old times, times before I was born and things I had never heard about before. My grandfather, on my dad's side, had got into trouble when he came out of the army and had ended up in prison. But he had brought up seven children to be respectable people, brought them up through the depression years and another war. I marvelled at this and how my dad had gone on to father six children of his own and, with a physical disability and no advantage of education, had kept us warm, fed and, most of all, loved and cared for. I really hadn't always appreciated that. Looking back over those years was like looking at a microcosm of evolution in action, an unbreakable will to grow. I shouldn't even say he had a disability; he always insisted that losing his arm at sixteen had only worked to his advantage.

The day came when the doctor took my dad chapter and verse through the radiotherapy treatment he would be required to undergo. I don't know why it should have hit him so hard; it had always been something he had been led to expect. I imagine now that it was the prospect of a lengthy period of pain and discomfort when he hadn't yet cleared the first hurdle, but this is the benefit of hindsight and at the time I was not prepared for the depth of despair to which he sank.

I sat with two of my sisters, Anne and Kim. The conversation was general and Dad was clearly not able to rise from the pit of his own black thoughts to pay it much attention. When I asked how he was, he began to cry and again felt the need to apologise. He wished that his leg had been amputated; his crying intensified. I moved forward, knelt down at the side of his chair and put my arms around his shoulders. It was a move made on instinct, even while my head was thinking that my sisters really were the better ones to give this reassurance. In the background I could hear their wise words: to take things one day at a time, that things would look brighter once he was up and about. In the foreground Dad was telling me that if his quality of life was gone, there was no point in him going on; he wasn't going to face any more operations like this one.

'Is that how you feel, Dad?' I asked, looking directly up at him from my childish position.

I don't know and have never asked my sisters whether they heard those words, or heard them in the way that I heard them, but they seemed not to acknowledge it at the time. I had no way of knowing, then or now, whether he would survive this battle. But one day he would die, as we all must, and I told myself there and then that I had better find a way to come to terms with that knowledge.

Privately, I began to grieve. I took the woman's way, if such it was.

## 22 December 1995

No details are necessary, but the thing that finally sparked this off two nights ago was a moment shared with another person as she struggled to understand and come to terms with the sudden loss of her partner a few months earlier, around the same time that my own 'grieving' had begun. A personal inconsistency was brought more sharply into focus for me.

As a teenager I was rudely awoken to the fact that one day I would die, and I struggled with the idea of death for several years as if nothing else mattered. How could anything else matter if I was going to die? I took the stance of an atheist and peppered it with vitriolic challenges to God that he should show himself, prove his own existence.

One Sunday morning my challenge was answered. At least that's the way it feels, even now. The night before had been spent at a nightclub. Violence had erupted. I was a stranger there and the violence seemed indiscriminate. Yet the thing that stuck in my mind most was the sight of a couple leaning against a pillar in the midst of this mêlée, kissing. Their casual indifference to all that was occurring gave, to my inexperienced eyes, as sure a vision of hell as I could have imagined. Maybe I wouldn't see it so starkly now, but it is probably important that this was uppermost in my mind as I retired to bed that night.

In the morning, as I woke, I was instantly aware of a sense of peace. I was still sleepy and the awareness had no depth. When I got up, I began to notice that the house was beautiful, and the people in it radiantly so. A spontaneous love was reaching out through me to them – through me and not from me. I had no deliberate part in what was happening; it was a flow that I had not started, could not encourage, but – thank God – did nothing to prevent.

As the day drew on and this peace continued without decline, I began to grasp the extraordinary nature of what was happening. This is the best way I can think to describe it: it was as if the infinite span of the universe was matched by an infinity reaching inside me to a centre impossibly deep, inconceivably peaceful. The divine love which flowed through me like an underground river surging for the plain came from this peaceful centre and touched all things. The shimmering beauty surrounding me flowed, in turn, from outside, reaching deep inside to this same centre, an unbroken intercourse between infinite and infinite. I was a membrane, my consciousness wafer-thin, sublimely resonating, caressed.

I have a vivid memory as I walked out that night of a ramshackle wire fence whose beauty wavered softly before my gaze. I lay in bed that night in a serene contemplation until sleep filtered in. The next morning I woke and it was gone.

I have thought about that day in many different ways: that it was a vision of heaven, that I was touched by God. Those were the two ways I settled on most often.

Now this is the personal inconsistency which I mentioned. The experience of being 'touched' in this way left me with an acceptance – I might call it knowledge because it was surer than faith – of my eternal soul. I 'knew' that there was some existence before this life and there would be something after it, but at the same time I felt no need to concern myself with either of these things, what mattered being what I did here and now. I told myself that these details were unknowable.

In the face of grief – other people's, for I had never experienced my own – I could only offer a mute human presence as the griever stared into a void I did not perceive and could not share.

My dad's situation may have been there in the background two nights ago, but in the end it was something to do with that subtle softening of voices. I was transported into that void; it wasn't my own but the force of it struck me just as deeply as if it had been. Suddenly I wanted the vision to see beyond it, not for my sake but for the sake of another. I thought about all those 'unknowable' details and began to question whether they really were so unknowable.

I know this is serious. My level of understanding has, if nothing else, afforded me these many years a working relationship with life, a platform from which I could get on with the business of living. To question is to take away this platform. And without the platform everything built upon it has to be questioned anew.

And how is it possible to question the nature of death? I could read all manner of books and articles, listen to first-hand accounts, and they might all say the same thing, but even then how could I know it to be true? Nobody else could give me that knowledge, but how could I experience it for myself?

Thinking of Kahlil Gibran's words – 'For what is it to die but to stand naked in the wind and melt into the sun?' – I tucked myself away this afternoon in the smallest room of the house, closed my eyes and contemplated this vision of death. Unfortunately, tiredness overtook me before any kind of revelation. I began to doze in my upright position with my head lolling forward awkwardly. I don't know how many minutes that lasted, but as my awareness returned, I resumed the effort as if without pause.

In my mind's eye at that point I was no longer staring into the sun but into darkness, and before I could think to change this, I was mentally jolted into a different state. I saw and felt myself hurtling through a tunnel of purple tones for several minutes. Then the effect was gone. I opened my eyes and moved on.

Figuratively speaking, I shrugged my shoulders at this minor incident. I could not make sense of it. But there was a general feeling of relief afterwards. I had spent two days riding the swell of my own emotions in the aftermath of that moment of shared grief, and it had been with a degree of urgency that I had closeted myself away. In the process a balancing or levelling out had taken place. I didn't feel any longer that anxious need to focus, but rather an opening out of curiosity, a desire to take stock of new circumstances and consider options before trying to move forward.

Do I need a leap of faith at this time? I have lived so long with an inner certainty which had no need of it, and yet I have to concede that my certainty is only memory, however clear that might still seem. I have never again come close to the experience of that day I have described, but sometimes I think that everything I have thought and done since then has been an attempt, in whatever way, to return to that feeling.

## *Emptiness*

If this is a new stage of a lifelong journey, it probably began all those months ago when nobody was saying what I wanted to hear. As soon as the spark of an idea came to me that I should write it myself, then a series of little foundations started to fall into place. I have my wife, Julie, to thank for the first thing.

By all the cheap psychological tests designed for magazine entertainment, Julie and I should not be compatible, yet we have remained happily together for twenty-four years. By the same token, Julie shares none of my urge for spiritual 'growth' – sharing a birthday with my dad and possessing the same sense of consummate practicality with all things – yet from time to time, she will, by instinct, point me in directions I could not have discovered alone and which, in turn, profoundly influence my thinking. It was her instinct which brought me to the discipline of standing still.

The ancient Chinese martial art of Zhan Zhuang (pronounced Jan Jong and meaning 'standing like a tree') involves nothing more than standing still in certain set positions. The positions are designed to open up natural channels for the flow of chi, or life energy, around the body. It is a discipline unlike any Western notion of exercise, involving simultaneous exertion and deep relaxation of the muscles. Without complete relaxation, the exercise becomes an excruciating effort of will against a relentless build-up of lactic acid in the muscle tissue. With body and mind completely relaxed, the exercise is transformed into a blissful state of physical comfort and mental quiet.

Within days of trying out the exercise, my legs began to tingle, a feeling of circulation gradually returning, as though my limbs had been numb for some time without me realising it. Sitting in a lazy or awkward manner, this tingling stretched halfway up my calves. With my feet placed flat on the ground, the tingling surged all the way to my hips. By mental will, I could make it rise through my entire body. I had lost no circulation of blood, nor ever been aware of any other restriction of bodily wellbeing, but some kind of circulation was returning, something was coming alive. This was enough to convince me that perseverance in the exercise would pay.

The experience of standing still has affected my outlook. Each morning I feel a flowing energy running the length of my body. I speculate that this energy and my sensitivity to it are raised at such times, but also that I must be surrounded by the same energy at all other times, and so must everyone else. And I wonder what it would take to see the very thing that I can so clearly feel.

Another foundation came from a book, as so many of my influences do. After finding something to move towards, I very quickly discovered that some books were saying some very useful things. I found a book called *Mindstore* by Jack Black which introduced me to relaxation from another angle: as the best means of silencing negative self-talk, leaving a more empowered self to set goals and take action towards them.

Under the direction of this book I created my own inner landscape, a place of peace and renewal. This place also found a link with my new practice of standing still. I formed a goal of developing the discipline diligently and daily. As months passed I have to confess that I was less diligent in making or following any other goals, my ideas probably being too ill-formed at the time to have any compelling force. I might have given up on my new landscape but the practice of standing still became the means of maintaining it for the time being. Since both required relaxation it seemed natural to combine the two. I stood with my eyes closed taking an imaginary journey from the right bank of a river, across a meadow, treading a well-worn path up a rounded hill and finally traversing a garden to enter a red-roofed house. In this house – the House on the Right Bank – each room had a different purpose: a shower room where the negative thoughts of the day could be washed away and replaced with positive attitudes and expectations, a hallway with pictures to remind me of past success, an editing suite where I could play visions of whatever 'future history' I might choose. In the entrance, I had to place a symbol of my potential. I left this empty for some time, pondering what might be appropriate.

There was an emotional pain which had cast its shadow, first secretly then openly, over most of my life. I did not consider that it had anything to do with this new place I had created, but it had up to that time seemed beyond my power of control. The pain of a single incident of childhood abuse at the hands of a stranger had erupted into my consciousness at the age of thirty and had felt like an open wound ever since. Ten years on, I can concede that this was a good and necessary thing for the insight it brought. But the abiding remnant of every black period – which over the years I had learned to make less frequent, though never less intense – was emptiness, a complete purging of emotion.

One evening, at the time when I was considering what the symbol of my potential should be, I chanced upon a television programme about trees and fungi. I learned that fungi live as parasites on the trunk of a tree. The roots of the fungi burrow into the bark and feed on the wood within, slowly hollowing out the tree until there is nothing left for the fungi to feed on. Then the fungi naturally fall away from the bark, their life at an end, their spores cast adrift to begin the process elsewhere. As I listened to this description, I was appalled by the long and painful death I was sure the tree must endure.

I was wrong. The tree did not die. The only wood to be eaten away by the fungi was already dead and of no further use to the tree which, far from being dead itself, was stronger, healthier and better able to withstand the rigours of the weather. To illustrate the point, the presenter proceeded to climb up the inside of the trunk to the top of an ancient oak tree, the oldest tree of the forest and the most majestic.

As he climbed the smooth inner wood of the tree, I understood that it was time to turn my own emptiness into healing. I walked into my inner landscape and placed that empty tree in the entrance to my house: an empty tree, symbol of my potential.

I remember the day, several months later, when blossom first appeared on that tree. It had grown so large that I had to take away all the windows, leaving a cathedral-like lattice work of arched wooden beams through which the sun streamed and a gentle breeze wafted. My landscape had taken on a life of its own.

Later that morning at the breakfast table, Hayley, my elder daughter, was poking gentle fun at her grandmother for shouting the name 'John' over and over in her sleep. She did not know that John was the grandfather she had never known: Julie's father who had died when Julie was just fifteen. The unexpected jolt of memory left Julie's eyes brimming with tears. Julie fought with her feelings in silence and it was left to me to explain. When Julie left the room, Hayley's eyes filled up in sympathy. I felt their pain, and a pride for how they bore their emotions. Cathy, my younger daughter, looked on in silence. She often discovers the boundaries of acceptable behaviour from the passive observation of her sister's trials.

All in all these early steps brought together a practice of physical, mental and emotional discipline to which, I suppose, I am now seeking to add a spiritual dimension. I could call it a spiritual discipline, but in this area I am not sure what would pass for discipline. I know that what I am seeking is not a tidy compartment of an ordered life. It should be every part of life.

If I could use an analogy, the process of growth is like a game in which we have to haul several sandbags up a stepped hill. The sandbags are very heavy, so moving one bag up by one step is a tiring business and requires a certain amount of rest before the next push. Lifting one up by two steps at a time is so exhausting that we end up falling back and finding all our effort is wasted.

There are those for whom the effort required for a successful lift is psychologically too much – they give up and stay where they are, giving the occasional tug to remind themselves that it was too hard, and through this lack of effort they actually grow weaker. It is all too much. If they ever perceive the game for what it is, then they choose to lose, for the time being at least.

There are others who will select a favourite sandbag, the one that seems easiest to grab a hold of, and diligently lift this bag step by step leaving the others way behind. They haven't noticed that each sandbag is tied to all the others by an elastic thread, and that with each step, the pull from the deadweight below becomes stronger until no amount of effort will move that one bag any higher. By this stage, however, they may have become intoxicated by their elevated status. They may judge that it is 'beneath' them to go all the way back down the hill, especially when they rightly suspect that their favourite bag is going to start rolling down behind them, pulled by that elastic cord. They may not see the problem at all, having their eyes so firmly fixed on the top of that hill, and instead bemoan their apparent fate, being such spiritual and visionary souls and having to struggle through a mundane existence.

I am not talking of people, of course, but states of mind, which I recognise because I have entertained each one of those delusions. Now I find myself trying to play the game a little more intelligently, moving those sandbags a step at a time, one by one. And this is where the fiendish complexity of the game becomes apparent, because the steps are all higgledy-piggledy, the cords between some bags are much shorter or stronger than others, and just when you seem to be getting the hang of it, 'somebody' has added another sandbag down at the bottom of the hill when you weren't looking. All that subconscious baggage can be a real nuisance.

I'm trying to say that you can't be too simplistic about it. If there is a hierarchy of disciplines then flexibility has to come somewhere near the top. You have to be flexible enough to look around and notice that, even with the best intentions, you might be working against yourself.

And somewhere near the bottom comes emptiness because, when you fall flat on your face and all your best-laid plans slip straight through your fingers, your best plan is not to go firing off another knee-jerk reaction, but to sit there in that emptiness and get comfortable with it until you find a new kind of strength, one that will stand firmer than your previous best illusion.

## Proactivity and Mission

Maybe books are like angels, sitting there waiting for the moment when you are ready. Within a short time of finding Jack Black's book, I found *The Seven Habits of Highly Effective People* by Stephen Covey.

I eagerly read about the first habit of proactivity. Twenty years earlier I had read the books of Dr Frankl and become familiar with what he called the last human freedom, the one that nothing and nobody could take away: the freedom to choose how our circumstances would affect us, the freedom to choose our own attitude. And here he was again, quoted as a model of proactivity. That was the kind of lost lesson my little black book was meant for.

I took it all in for a second time. To be human meant having the freedom to choose how to respond to any situation, in short to be 'response-able'. And to be proactive meant exercising that 'response-ability' at every moment, choosing what to think, how to feel, what to do. If I failed to make those choices, I would be merely reactive, letting my thoughts, feelings and actions become conditioned until I was no longer living but being lived.

I agreed with all this so wholeheartedly, I told myself, that I had no need of the thirty-day test proposed at the end of that chapter. The purpose of the test was to exercise proactivity, positive thinking and emotional management every minute of every day as the highest priority, and to keep it up for thirty days. That would be enough to make proactivity a habit of mind, to give this attitude a momentum of its own.

That was in February.

Early in May a colleague pulled me over in the office to show me a 'joke' in a student magazine. The cartoon showed a man in the background and a small child in the foreground. The unspoken theme of the cartoon was that the child was a sexual plaything for the man, but more than that, the child was seducing the man, asking to be used for sex. My colleague was outraged. I was shaken to the core. It had hit me without warning. I was shunted back more than thirty years, back to that old childhood incident. Dad had told me many years later what the defendant's lawyer in court had pleaded, that I had been a willing party, a precocious child who had invited his sexual advance. Dad had jumped to his feet and protested. I remembered my puzzlement at being told that. How could he have said such a thing? I didn't even know what sex was.

In the weeks that followed my being shown that cartoon, I tried every coping strategy I knew. Finally, inevitably, I descended into a black depression and could only wait until it dispersed in its own time. It stayed with me for a week. I was back with that emptiness again, for the first time since placing the empty tree as a symbol of

19

my potential. When the depression finally cleared, I stayed with that feeling of emptiness, searching for a new lesson, a new way forward.

That's when the obvious answer finally struck me. I had not been proactive. Far from my perceived understanding, I had not grasped the concept at all. I went back to *The Seven Habits* and read that chapter all over again. This time, when I reached the end I took up the thirty-day challenge with a will. I watched my thoughts every minute of the day, challenging every negative thing that I found there. I watched my language, and every time I found myself saying or thinking 'I have to… ', I would change it again to 'I choose… '. I spent minimal time on problems and more time on solutions. For every worry, I analysed my circle of concern (the things that were affecting me but which I could do nothing about) and my circle of influence (the things I could change); I put my energy into the second and took appropriate action. Whatever I felt, I asked, 'Is this how I choose to feel?' If it was not what I would have chosen, I did not accept it. I reminded myself instead that feelings make good servants and poor masters, then I reasserted my control.

The first day of this test was easy – my motivation was high and novelty was with me. Soon after that I had to dig in. The rest of the week was hard, no question about it, but I had a lot of incentive – ten years' worth of it – to spur me on. If I woke up in the morning and found my attitude wanting, feeling the pressures of the day ahead, I would tell myself the most urgent thing to do was to change my attitude; everything else could wait. The second week got easier. The third week was easier still. By the last stretch of the thirty-day test I was coasting. The habit of mind had sunk in and was running itself.

I have, as they say, never looked back. I do not expect depression for any cause to affect me again. I also learned the crucial difference between intellectual understanding and real understanding.

Simultaneously, I felt ready to take the next step offered by *The Seven Habits*: to define my own life mission. At the suggestion of the writer, I imagined attending my own funeral and hearing eulogies from family, friends and work colleagues. I considered what I would want to hear, how I would want to have been for them, what I would have wanted to achieve. In this way I tried to define the values I wanted to live by, to begin with the end in mind.

It was no easy task. I really thought I had all this sorted. In my hierarchy of values I had placed love over everything, family before friends, friends before work. When I tried to put this hierarchy down on paper it was too simplistic by half. For three months I struggled with it and struggled against a little voice inside telling me that this was sad and pathetic, a forty year-old man sitting alone trying to define who he was. I tried to relieve this by talking to friends, but nobody could understand what I was trying to do or why. Much as I love Irene, her response was typical. 'Give it up,' she said. 'Relax. Stop trying so hard.' I didn't take her advice. I kept my own counsel and carried on.

First I mapped out what felt important for family, friends, work and my own development, but I found all the same values being repeated. So I turned it on its head and considered which values I should live by and how. I decided to begin with three ideas which had resonated most deeply with me over the ten years following my emotional upheaval. Each one had struck me with a force that felt like recognition.

The first came from a Roman Catholic abbé, whose books I had read avidly in the early months of this period. I had been trying to read the New Testament systematically, but the self-accusation I was reading into everything was tearing me apart. The abbé, Michel Quoist, offered a gentler interpretation. He said, 'We are made by love and for love.' When my systematic reading finally reached the letters of St John, I read, 'God is love.' I read it with the relief of someone reaching the end of a walk over hot coals.

The second idea came from *The Seven Habits* itself, a quote from Teilhard de Chardin: 'We are not human beings having a spiritual experience. We are spiritual beings having a human experience.' I can't exactly rationalise this, but when I read those words something leapt inside me and cried, 'Yes!'

The last idea was my own. I had attended a course on listening skills. It had felt like a minor revelation to me, not for the formal learning but for the moments in between, talking and listening to complete strangers, finding within minutes a depth of trust to be able to disclose anything, and parting as friends. I came away feeling that it had been as close to a vision of heaven on earth as anything I had ever witnessed, and furthermore, I had felt ever since a strong conviction that this was the 'atmosphere' I wanted to bring to anyone I should meet.

With these three values I had the why. The rest was just a matter of filling in the how. By August it was finished and set out in such a way as to fill an A4 sheet of paper which I could carry around in my wallet.

I AM MADE BY LOVE AND FOR LOVE.

I AM A SPIRITUAL BEING HAVING A HUMAN EXPERIENCE.

I AM HERE TO HELP MAKE HEAVEN ON EARTH.

THESE THINGS ARE TRUE FOR ALL HUMAN SOULS.

### By love and for love:

**I fulfil** myself and help others to fulfil themselves.
**I recognise** that interdependence is the true mark of emotional maturity.
**I am not** the sum of my feelings, thoughts, habits or past experience; the love that moves me and renews me is above these things.
**Whatever** my past experience, I use it to make me strong, to find wisdom and understanding, and to change me for the good.

### As a spiritual being:

**I recognise** that my purpose and talents are unique but can only be realised through self-searching, commitment and wilful application.
**My own** spontaneous and natural desires are not there to be sacrificed or subordinated to other things. They are to be nurtured and protected as my only sure guide to the many purposes of my human existence.
**To be** creative or receptive for a good and loving purpose, and in all things to show loving kindness: these are the measures for my daily achievements.
**Knowledge** gained, lessons taken to heart and honest self-examination in the spirit of constant change for the better: these are the measures of my daily growth.

### To help make heaven on earth:

**I reach** to touch the souls of other human beings and allow them to reach for and touch mine in an atmosphere of warmth, trust and complete acceptance. I seek to maintain and develop all relationships in a way that will allow this to happen.

**I cherish** the humility needed for true understanding and the courage needed to make myself understood.

**I value** and defend the freedom of everyone to find and fulfil their own purpose.

**I am open** to be influenced and ready to influence for the sake of a greater good to be found through the sharing of thoughts and feelings. Recognising my contribution towards the growth of others, I strive to share my own insight through creative and courageous self-expression.

**I do not** walk away from the suffering of a human being, or any other living thing, if there is a way for me to help. It is an integral part of my own fulfilment to search for and be mindful of the best help that I can give.

**To support these aims:**

**I commit** myself to healthy living and the beneficial exercise of mind and body to achieve a quality of life equal to these ideals.

**I make** myself a friend to money; I learn its ways and apply them well, suffering in myself neither fear of loss nor greed for gain, but seeking only to apply it wisely and with integrity.

**Life** should be joyful; if it does not feel joyful, I should look no further than myself for the changes that are needed.

For all my struggling I have to confess that when I had finally finished my statement, what pleased me most about its apparent blandness was the thought that I did not need any substantial change in my life to live up to it. I effectively filed it away and got on with living. I guess that was where the power of vision took over. Within a very short time of completing it, things did begin to change; I began to change.

It was on that weekend conference in September that I first understood what was happening. I had worked so hard to shape the vision – bring it into being – now it was shaping me, step by step, bringing me closer into line with my stated intent. The idea of writing down life's lessons might normally have been something I would have mused over and forgotten. Instead I greeted it with all the enthusiasm of an 'Aha!' experience. These lessons were the measures of my daily growth. Of course it made sense to record them.

Then the little 'holes' in my character began to bother me. I wasn't doing everything on that statement. Some things I did in abundance, like listening, but where was the courage to make myself understood, the creative and courageous self-expression? Those 'bland' generalities were teasing questions out of me all the time: how can I fulfil this vision? What do I need to do better? Several months on, it is probably the main reason I am now writing this and why my searching seems to have accelerated rather than settled down.

# 1 January 1996

Taking a week off work over Christmas I read Jack Black's *Mindstore* again in readiness for setting some goals, and also to recapture some of the excitement I felt on reading it at the beginning of the year. Setting a spiritual goal exercised my mind a great deal. Unlike other more worldly goals, I had no clear idea of what I was aiming for or where I was starting from.

For many years I had thought of the spiritual journey as a journey from one oasis to another, the way in between fraught with difficulty and lack of direction. It was small wonder, I thought, that so many looked across that wasteland and immediately took fright. If that first oasis was a childish, unchallenging sense of security, what would be the final destination? So often I had been inclined to see my wife, Julie, as one drawn back, in her own way, to that childhood sense of innocence, but after all, how did I know which side of the desert she was on? Did Jesus not say that whoever does not receive the Kingdom of God like a child will never enter it? My 'map' of the territory was too simplistic.

Then my dad was another case in point. On the approach to Christmas, he had to spend another period in hospital because radiotherapy treatment to his recently skin-grafted wound was causing increasing discomfort. Regular visits and discussions resumed and, despite Dad's serious situation, many of those discussions, at his own instigation, revolved around the share price movements of one company or another.

Coming back to my sandbag analogy, money is one of those sandbags that people typically pick up and try to run all the way up the hill with or resolutely leave at the bottom of the hill, insisting that it has nothing to do with anything. Either way their lives are pulled out of balance.

My dad never has any moral problem with money. Neither is he an overtly spiritual man, but he is a loving man and I don't know if there is a distinction. Maybe he just found our discussions a distraction from pain. I have been glad of those clinical figures myself from time to time, and last May sitting in my own emptiness, was one of them.

One evening when I visited, Dad wasn't there. I waited a while in the empty bedroom thinking he had gone to the toilet, but he hadn't. Eventually I asked the nurse and discovered that he may have gone to the hospital carol concert. I followed general directions until I was able to follow the sound of singing. I had to excuse myself to pass through a small crowd in the doorway. My dad was sitting at the front of the makeshift congregation in a wheelchair. My sister, Kim, was kneeling on the floor beside him holding his hand. He sang along though he did not know the words. There was a smile on his lips and a misty reverence in his eyes. The practical life he had always lived and extolled was not the whole story.

So I pondered the question of this spiritual goal while simultaneously setting some other practical goals, including financial ones. By New Year's Eve I felt I was ready to start 1996 with purpose. Before doing so, at the book's suggestion, it was appropriate to consider any lingering resentments and to forgive and release those concerned so that I might be freed from the past and better able to move forward.

I lost two friends of long-standing in the year just gone. Heather: well, I don't understand what happened there, I really don't. I have spent lot of thought and energy trying to figure it out but I never seem to get anywhere with it. When things are wrong between Heather and me, communication flies out of the window, and without communication, trying to track Heather's thoughts is like trying to hit a moving target in thick fog on a dark night: even if you hit it, you never have the luxury of finding out. But lately Heather seems happier to have placed some distance between us, and for all the energy I have needlessly spent, I have decided that I must forgive and release.

Matthew I can understand. Julie and I were family friends throughout the ten years of his marriage. Then his marriage broke up and he moved on to a new relationship. Julie and I were left to support his wife for two years until she found another relationship. Things should have settled down after that, but endless wrangling over the children and money made matters worse and worse. It reached a stage where we could not offer support to either one of them without seeming to undermine the other, and so we vacillated.

In November, after a gap in contact of six months, I tentatively rang to see how things were. Matthew was unquestionably angry with me, and when I broached the issue he told me so. He said I had not supported him. I knew from other sources that his wife, in the end, had felt unsupported also. We had tried to take a middle line, offering support as far as we could without judgement, but we had ended up alienating both of them. Matthew made it clear that our friendship was over. If he ever felt any differently, he said, he would ring me, but it was definitely one of those 'don't ring me, I'll ring you' scenarios. I did not express any resentment at the situation; I wanted to leave a channel open for that time in the future, however remote.

None of those details matter really, but the whole episode caused me to question the nature of friendship itself. I had not supported him, therefore our friendship was over. I could understand that certain things needed to be done, and certain things needed to be declared, for friendship to come into being. But given that our friendship existed and was real, the question I kept coming back to was: did I have to do anything to remain worthy of friendship? I still have no answer for this, or rather I have two 'obvious' answers which completely contradict each other. Firstly 'No', a friend should not have to do anything or be any particular type of person to remain worthy of my friendship. Then again 'Yes', for there would be no point in human connection at all if it wasn't undertaken in the sincere hope that it would, in some way, reduce the stock of our pain and add to the sum of our happiness.

Am I still looking at this at the wrong level? Do these contradictions agree at a different level? I don't have the answer to that as yet. Back in September when my dad was so upset, I had tried to tell him that his worth did not depend on what he could do for us: his worth was in who he was. And that's the same kind of contradiction really, one my dad was struggling with then, and probably is now.

As for Matthew and me, it all still seems like a whole mess of unresolved resentment. I didn't have any faith that a phone call would change it. So I decided that it was time to forgive and release.

Kahlil Gibran says, 'Let there be no purpose in friendship save the deepening of the spirit.' In our perceived betrayal of each other, Matthew and I may yet serve that higher purpose. For now, I forgive and release because I must move on.

I spent the evening of New Year's Eve at a family gathering. Dad was too uncomfortable to stay very long. I felt ashamed of the mixed feelings I had when he decided to leave early. Later on I had a general conversation with my elder brother, David, about plans for the future. David is the most successful person I know: strong in all subjects and all sports at school, achieving excellent qualifications, and apparently moving from strength to strength in his career, and this without detriment to his family life. But he said that he was still not really doing what he wanted. Though he had a general idea of what this might be, he had never actually set himself a goal. This was not because he lacked the time or imagination; he candidly confessed that he had not set a goal because he was afraid he would not achieve it.

It made me wonder to what extent in the past I might have succumbed to the fear of failure and its close relative, fear of success. I realised that if I was to set a goal, these twin fears would act as powerful forces in the wrong direction. I would not have befriended them at all had they not served some purpose, however obscure, but I had to believe that I had outgrown whatever need they once fed. It was time, once again, to forgive and release my past weaker self, and to move on.

Today I woke ready to set some new goals, practical, financial and spiritual. I wrote out each aim in detail and added to each an affirmation which was personal, positive and stated in the present tense. I then added a picture of what I was aiming for. It was a long process.

When it came to my spiritual goal, since I had no idea which way to go, I decided to make it my goal to find out which way to go. My description went as follows:

> I have a clear idea of what is there to be experienced of the higher spirituality of people (and things); I understand what I need to do to develop my spiritual power at this level and I am ready to commit myself to this task.

To support this I composed the following affirmation:

> I stand, here and now, on the threshold of a truth which connects all things; I am ready to take that step forward and turn my eyes to a greater vision, a further horizon.

I also wrote down the most compelling reasons I could presently find for maintaining desire, belief and certainty, and I drew an image. For want of any 'real' picture, I drew a stick picture of myself standing on the threshold between a monochrome world and one vibrant with colour, with people and trees surrounded by coloured auras.

I don't know how realistic or fanciful that image might be, but I just keep thinking there must be more to see, more to feel. In extreme circumstances we have probably all felt something. For example when two people have argued bitterly, we can walk into the room knowing nothing of what has occurred and yet instantly sense that something is wrong. We say we could 'cut the atmosphere with a knife'. But this is an extreme sign of something surely more subtle and always present. I wonder at the possibility of increasing our sensitivity to this atmosphere. But this is just speculation. As I come nearer to the threshold, I may need to abandon every preconception. It is only important now to begin from somewhere.

Finally, I set a date by which the goal should be achieved: 27 April 1996. There was no significance in this, except that it would be my birthday. And having undertaken this process for several goals, I settled down for the evening satisfied that I had made a positive start to the year. I watched a film with Julie: *Strictly Ballroom*. There was a central theme to the film, stated over and again by different characters:

**A life lived in fear is a life half-lived.**

It felt like providence was urging me on. I wrote the phrase down, ready for the days when I would need it.

# *6 January 1996*

On the morning of 2 January, I was due back at work after my period of rest and planning. I got up early to exercise, opened the windows to the dark frosty morning outside and took off my T-shirt. This is a strange procedure, I know, for an exercise which involves no move-ment, but my standing exercise is preceded by certain warm-up motions. These movements involve no strain, yet possess the curious ability to generate heat inside the body. When I had finished these movements, the winter breeze felt like a cooling spring waft for the remainder of the exercise.

Having 'warmed up', I let my body come to rest in a standing position with my knees bent and arms held out in front, like sitting on a big squashy ball and holding another against my chest. In this position I began the process of relaxation, bringing my attention to my scalp, forehead, eyes and working down each part of the body to finish with the soles of my feet. With eyes closed I conjured up my inner landscape: 'The sun is shining, the sky is blue, birds are singing in the trees. I feel the lush grass of the meadow beneath my feet and hear water rippling in the stream behind me.'

It always begins with the feeling of a breeze blowing through my hair. On this particular morning I stayed with that feeling and the image of the meadow for a little longer than usual. Then with no evident transition, I was sitting, in my mind's eye, at my bureau writing imaginary words for this book.

'We all have within us,' I wrote, 'something – someone – greater than the person we presently are.'

At the same time as writing I could hear the words being said in my voice, except that the voice was deeper, more resonant, carrying great authority and assurance.

It went on, 'I could explain this, but there is no need; you already know it is true.'

As those final words were uttered, my body was instantly engulfed in a sensation I can only describe as flames dancing three feet high above my naked skin. For several minutes – in truth I don't know how long – I stood motionless in a state of rapture.

How should I describe it? I was not Moses standing before the burning bush; I *was* the burning bush! Was it transfiguration? When it finally ebbed away I was neither burned nor changed, but the remainder of my exercise passed in a reverie of peace and wonder.

More prosaically, I wondered if this was the voice – the level within myself – to which I needed to connect in order to write this book at all. I tried to mimic the style, imagining what this Greater Self might say: thoughts of destiny, courage, breaking free from shackles and following guiding stars, that kind of stuff.

It wouldn't work. I couldn't keep it up. I couldn't recapture that extraordinary feeling, whatever it was.

'And anyway,' I asked myself, 'who am I?' To all outward appearance, I am a rational man grounded in practicality, but what is rational and what is practical? I search for what I do not know, knowing only that my progress will at best be disjointed, and may fall short of any firm conclusion. I do not, apparently, even speak with one voice.

I have no right to speak, save that all human beings must, in some unique way, bequeath their nature to the sum of humanity. What I say will be commonplace, even dreary to some, while possessing revelation for others. I have no way of knowing how these words will weigh in the hearts and minds they might reach. After all, my own understanding is a rich and complex mix of all that I read, see and hear, all that I experience, and all that I think, all of these impinging on each other, changing each other constantly. Nobody reading these words will have my understanding 'grafted' on to their own; in the time it takes for the words to pass from page to perception, they would already be different, already unique to the reader's own understanding. If any one of us should speak as of right, then we must know that we have no right to control, or even to discover, how far those words might reach or how they are received.

So the real question for now is a personal one. How do I find and follow my own Greater Self? Reason alone will talk me down from this ambition. It always has. The path of reason will always diverge from the path I seek because it can only use the past and present to work forward. It is never going to put more than a toe into the unknown. Reason is not a creature of destiny.

It was because of musings like this that I considered I should be reading some spiritual book for proper guidance. But having no suitable book to hand, I settled down instead, on the day after my burning bush thing, to read a book about money. After all, I had also made some financial goals.

I read these words:

Faith is the Head Chemist of the mind, when faith is blended
with thought, the subconscious mind instantly picks up the
vibration, translates it into its spiritual equivalent, and trans-
mits it to Infinite Intelligence, as in the case of prayer.

All thoughts which have been emotionalised (given
feeling) and mixed with faith begin immediately to translate
themselves into their physical equivalent or counterpart.

*Think and Grow Rich*, Napoleon Hill

My jaw dropped as a realisation dawned on me. Until reading those
words I don't believe I had ever really understood faith before. I was
reading a book about money and finding it to be quite the most spiritual book I could have imagined.

Faith, as presented by religion, had always seemed like blind
obedience, the message being that there is a force guiding our lives
so infinitely subtle that we can never see it directly, and so infinitely complex that we can never fully understand it. Yet we are
asked to have faith, not only that it exists, but that it possesses
certain qualities and works in certain ways. No matter how bad
things may seem, religion tells us, we must have faith that it will
work out for the best in the end. We have no control except to
earnestly and unselfishly beseech in prayer that power which does
control. That was the simplistic message I received at least, and
many others like me. If religious leaders of the present day
intended to convey a different understanding, then the message
was not coming across.

Meanwhile, these 'hard-nosed' businessmen embrace faith as a
fundamental building block – a commodity, even – shaping their
own lives and everything around them. Far from feeling down-
trodden, but believing that things will work out, they understand
that if this is how they feel then their own perception is at the very
root of the problem, and the first thing that must be addressed.
They are not powerless pawns in a larger game; control never
leaves their own hands. That is the way that faith actually
works.

I read on:

Not only thought impulses which have been mixed with
faith, but those which have been mixed with any of the posi-

tive emotions, or any of the negative emotions, may reach and influence the subconscious mind.

From this statement you will understand that the subconscious mind will translate into its physical equivalent a thought impulse of a negative or destructive nature just as readily as it will act upon thought impulses of a positive or constructive nature. This accounts for the strange phenomenon which so many millions of people experience, referred to as 'misfortune' or 'bad luck'.

There are millions of people who believe themselves 'doomed' to poverty and failure because of some strange force over which they believe they have no control. They are the creators of their own 'misfortunes' because of this negative belief, which is picked up by the subconscious mind, and translated into its physical equivalent.

It is essential for you to encourage the positive emotions as dominating forces of your mind, and discourage – and eliminate – negative emotions.

A mind dominated by positive emotions becomes a favourable abode for the state of mind known as faith. A mind so dominated may, at will, give the subconscious mind instructions, which it will accept and act upon immediately.

A light came on inside my head.

### We create our own reality

Thinking back over the past year, I have read many things which might have brought me to this conclusion, but the penny had never dropped until that moment. How many other times had the opportunity to understand faith been presented to me? In criticising the picture of faith apparently drawn by others, I presumed perhaps too little of others ability to teach, and too much of my own ability to learn. I did not understand until the right conditions had been created within me. As Jesus said, 'He who has ears to hear, let him hear.'

In this light, I wondered how my past looked. How did my misfortunes and pains appear? I realised I had to be ready and willing to look again as memories presented themselves. I could not allow myself the comfort of being a 'victim of circumstance', without the honesty of examining my own part in creating those circumstances. The prospect intrigued me, but I didn't want to force the pace. I was more concerned to look forward with this new revelation.

I diligently stuck to my exercise and the taking of my inner journey for the rest of the week. This morning, Saturday, was no exception. I looked forward to the lack of time constraint at the weekend. I had some music playing quietly in the background, a compact disc on a random setting. I took the journey through the meadow, up the side of the hill where I had placed my House on the Right Bank, finally crossing the lawn and stepping into the entrance and pausing beneath the boughs of my empty tree. Then a coincidence happened. A new track had been selected. It was a Cranberries song titled *Empty*. Before the empty tree, and all it had come to signify, I had celebrated through this song my own survival in the face of the emptiness which had periodically engulfed me. The song had therefore become intimately linked with my memories and the words had grown heavy with personal significance.

*I was a young boy again, naked on the dirty, musty floorboards of a derelict house. I could hear his breathlessness, feel his hands hurriedly pawing me. Where was the friend we were meant to be helping? How were we meant to reach him? The crack in the window was too small.*

As the song continued there were more associations, once scripted by a need to make sense of my emotional struggle but now triggering automatically.

*I was thirty. Crying, 'Dear God, it was the only truly Christian thing I ever did. Why do I suffer like this?' I had lost more than twenty years of memories; I could no longer remember how I felt, whether I had ever truly known happiness. I could no longer trust what I thought I had experienced and learned over all those years. I would look at photographs and wonder: who was that person?*

The song reached a crescendo, repeating the word 'empty', over and over again. A surge in the orchestration of the song was mirrored by a similar surge under my flesh.

I looked again at the empty tree, and a voice welled up inside me:

I AM MADE BY LOVE AND FOR LOVE.

I AM A SPIRITUAL BEING HAVING A HUMAN EXPERIENCE.

I AM HERE TO HELP MAKE HEAVEN ON EARTH.

And the flames rose again – briefly – then the song was over.

I had made a decisive mental shift – a decision – and moved on to the shower, letting the force of the water wash every negative sentiment of the past clean away. And still the sensations came. As I visualised sparkling particles of light, between the water droplets, penetrating my skin, cleansing the source of all negative emotions and replacing them with positive belief, it became a real feeling – not just an idea or an image. I felt this self, filled with sparkling light, growing and then breaking out as if my old skin was cracking and falling away. I felt my new body – new skin – tingling from head to toe, fizzing and popping.

At the end of my exercise I opened my eyes, exhilarated. Imagine such energy harnessed, imagine the ability to call on it at will! At the end of an eventful week it felt like every experience was propelling me higher.

But that was this morning, and I wouldn't want to feel my confidence was misplaced, but I discovered that I was not above mistakes. In the evening I visited Dad at home for the first time since New Year's Eve. He was no better, perhaps a little worse. He was not taking the doctor's advice. Although he had been told to keep his legs raised and to take plenty of bed rest, he said that he was most comfortable sitting in his chair in front of the TV with his feet on the floor. The result was that his legs had swelled with a build-up of fluid. He was depressed. My feelings were a mix of worry and impatience.

When he got up to walk around and ease his stiffness, I took the opportunity to follow and talk to him. He was very low and wanted to express how badly he was feeling, but I didn't listen. I tried to tell him what he must do to make himself better, to begin now to make plans for when he was well again. I told him to write down his plans. I even put the paper and pen in front of him but he was close to tears as he struggled in vain to be receptive. He was fighting against his own need to speak. And still I persisted, 'Dad, I know about this stuff. I've read about it. I know it works.' He was shaking his head and telling me about the terrible pains in his legs. Finally, I gave up and listened to his complaint. I did not try to offer any further solution.

Now at home, I feel confused. Nothing is served by trying to press my convictions on to another. I suspect my motives. Was I really trying to bolster my own faith by seeking acknowledgement from my dad? I should have the courage to live by my own belief.

Then again, if my motive was pure, why did I think it right this time to abandon my faith in the power of listening? Why did I resort to problem solving when I have seen, so many times, how fruitless this can be. It is just the urgency of the situation; that's all it is.

## *Listening and the Influence of Friends*

Ten years ago, my dad listened to me when everything inside must have been urging him to take a grip of my life and put it back on some sort of track. He listened to the dark feelings I had about my childhood abduction. He told me a few things I never knew about it, the things that were said in the courtroom while I sat alone in the waiting room outside, listening to a huddled group of policemen swapping jokes. What had been said by the defendant, the claims he had made for my willingness and sexual precocity, seemed quite ridiculous, but it was the sixties and things were very different then. My dad told me of his own anger and how he stood up in the gallery and voiced his protest.

He listened also to my religious confusion, though to have felt any confusion on such a subject must have seemed a baffling thing to him. I told him how I had read the parables of Jesus and found myself the foolish one in all of them, that I didn't know what I should do, only that I couldn't continue to be the person that I was.

I told him of my feelings for another woman, how my need to talk, my need to talk to her, had overwhelmed me, though I was sure it was friendship and not more.

It must all have been heartbreaking for him after the event, but at the time he showed only compassion. He listened without any solution to offer me. Strangest of all, he expressed pride in me. That didn't make any sense to me at the time, but I remember it felt much more than a word thrown away for want of something to say.

I became a 'natural' listener after those dark days and have attributed this to several qualities which I had not, until then, possessed. But it is only as I write this now that I begin to realise the influence of my dad's perfect example when I was most in need. I do not mean to lavish praise undiscerningly, for he was many times not a perfect listener, but in answering my need some power within my dad transcended every baser instinct that night, and for that, if nothing else, he must have wept humble tears. I know that I have wept many times since, when that same power has transcended my limitations for the sake of another.

A few weeks after that experience, I was back at work, sitting in a room alone, when a woman who had been no particular friend came in and engaged me in conversation. She asked how I was, and that was quite special because a lot of people had been avoiding the subject out of sheer embarrassment. In a low ebb of self-regard, I possessed an honesty which could be quite disarming to someone unused to it. In my own mind I had nothing to lose, nowhere lower to sink, and so nothing to hide – hiding is for people who still feel they have something left to protect. I really told her how I was. She responded with equal honesty about her own troubles, past and present. Pretty soon I was the one doing most of the listening, and in my utterly docile frame of mind I was accidentally making quite a good job of it.

I had for the time being lost the sense that I had any answers for my own situation, and I reasoned therefore that I had no answers for anybody else. So problem solving was not a temptation that troubled me; I just listened. Another accidental attitude was one of complete acceptance. I was, again in my own estimation, the lowest, most wretched, most unworthy human being ever to have lived. It was quite possible that I was beyond redemption, so far beyond in fact that my own fate was no longer of concern. No person's behaviour could make them worse than I, so how could I do any other than accept this woman, no matter what she had done?

The more I listened without judgement, the more she opened up. She told me of an affair she was having and how badly she felt about it. 'That's awful, isn't it?' she said, inviting me to agree. I said without hesitation, 'Human comfort is a wonderful thing', because I had learned that it was, and unwittingly I was doing something else right: I was acknowledging her feelings in all their unruliness, inconsistency and illogicality. In all the years since, I have never felt able to judge anyone who shared their feelings so openly.

I was forgiving sins and had no idea whether that was right. I kept thinking of the parable of the shrewd manager. He had wasted his master's money and was to be called to account for it. So that he might have a home when the master dismissed him, he called on all those in debt and invited them to rewrite their own accounts. He said to himself, 'When my job is gone, I shall have friends who will welcome me in their homes.' The parable ends with these words: 'As a result the master of this dishonest manager praised him for doing such a shrewd thing; because the people of this world are much more shrewd in handling their affairs than the people who belong to the light.' And Jesus went on to say:

> So I tell you: make friends for yourselves with worldly wealth, so that when it gives out, you will be welcomed in the eternal home. Whoever is faithful in small matters will be faithful in large ones; whoever is dishonest in small matters will be dishonest in large ones. If, then, you have not been faithful in handling worldly wealth, how can you be trusted with true wealth? And if you have not been faithful with what belongs to someone else, who will give you what belongs to you? No servant can be the slave of two masters; he will hate one and love the other; he will be loyal to one and despise the other. You cannot serve both God and money.

Sometimes I almost understood that parable; other times I didn't understand it at all. I tried to reason it out and kept meeting with a huge contradiction. Even so, in a metaphorical way I was forgiving debts and making friends, better friends than I had ever known before or had any right to expect. Listening – really listening – is a powerful affirmation of the human spirit, and it often puzzled me how anyone could have known that I was ready to give that much for their sake. I knew that sometimes it might just have been a matter of making the right responses, but at other times people talked when they couldn't possibly have judged how I might respond. Why, out of all the people in that noisy nightclub for example, had Sarah chosen me to speak to at such a vulnerable level? Then again, how is it that I instinctively know whether someone inquires of me out of genuine concern, or out of a thirst for gossip? Is it an instant response to a complex set of sensory stimuli, or is there a feeling coming across which is much simpler but altogether less tangible?

I was listening at first because I had lost all regard for myself; it was, if you like, a happy accident arising from despair. Later it became clear to me that this ability to displace one's own thoughts, feelings and concerns, and give whole, undivided attention to another, is the essence of listening. For this reason, if for no other, I came to see my darkest days as the seed of my salvation, bringing friendships and blessings into my life which never would have happened otherwise. It was that same growth and new life I later recognised in the empty tree.

And with friends came their influence, intangible but no less real, adding to the stock of my thoughts and ideas; adding to the stock of my nature.

Kate, my corresponding friend, is a case in point. The first time that I visited Kate, I was her manager. She had been absent from work for some time, suffering anxiety attacks, and I had heard that she was worried for her job. I wanted to offer some reassurance on that score at least. Our conversation was strained, with lengthy silences, though Kate seemed not to be aware of time passing. I had grown used to listening through silence and was not uncomfortable with it for I have found it has value. But Kate is a very beautiful woman, and I dared not trust the instinct that was telling me to stay. I asked if she wanted me to leave and reached for my jacket to affirm my willingness.

Kate said no, that was not what she wanted.

The hour of talking and listening that subsequently passed between us left me strangely lifted – a state from which I have not fallen in the years of our friendship since – as reticence and silent resignation slowly gave way to trust, and Kate shared with me the small secrets of her grief, things she had never cared nor dared to share before. I stayed much longer than I had expected; it was hard to take my leave and return to work. As she stood to see me to the door we exchanged a brief hug and she called me an angel. I have wondered since whether that was just an expression, or whether she saw something in me similar to the way I was feeling inside at that moment.

Our friendship did not develop in a predictable way. Shortly after that first visit, Kate's anxiety became so great that she was barely seeing anybody. To leave the house was a major ordeal, to receive visitors at home was little better. For a second time I doubted my motives and chose to fade quietly from her life.

The reason for Kate's anxiety was a bereavement as severe as any I had known or could imagine. Several years earlier she had lost her mother, step-father, brother, best friend and her best friend's baby in a single car accident. The shock had never left her, though at a practical level she appeared to cope well. The anxiety attacks which plagued her at the time of my visit were precipitated by the death of a close uncle, a significant emotional link to her mother. Lord knows I had no basis from which to offer solace. I had never lost a close relative or friend. I still haven't.

It was only a month or so after my visit that Kate's natural father died. She had only recently resumed contact with him. Kate had told her counsellor that she felt jinxed, that she lived with a sense of dread, waiting for the next bad news to strike. Her counsellor had said, very reasonably, that bad luck in the past didn't make bad luck any more likely in the future and she really must put unwarranted fears out of her mind. Kate had remained unconvinced. I could only guess at the appalling confirmation that this latest event offered her. I resolved to write a letter of condolence, as I imagined many friends and colleagues would. I truly cannot remember what that letter said, except that it was more emotional than formal. I wanted her to know that, although I had no place in her life, my heart nevertheless reached out to her. I neither asked for, nor expected, a reply.

Kate did write back. Her letter read like a plea from some distant, unreachable well of despair, and I was moved to tears. She asked that I should write again, because letters, for the time being, were less painful, giving her more time to compose her fragile feelings. I set about the task like a man with a mission. Having very little detail of her life, and no fitting experience of my own to relate, I told her candidly of my past and the life lessons that it had brought, while cautioning that she should take none of it as advice; it would be better by far for her to discover her own way forward by writing back and expressing her feelings.

Kate gave me much encouragement to keep writing, often saying that she read my letters open-mouthed with astonishment that my feelings should so closely reflect her own. Several weeks later she was well enough to return to work. I had changed jobs and was no longer her manager, but we would continue to see each other regularly around the workplace. Despite this, however, Kate asked that our letters should continue and so they did. Exchanging no more than the usual social conversation at work, we continued to relate as the closest of friends through our letters.

Week by week, for four months I wrote lengthy letters about my past life. After that time I felt I had exhausted every subject I could think of – I had come to a dead stop. I pondered what to do. Two or three weeks passed – an age compared to the frequency of earlier letters. Finally I wrote about the present, like any normal letter except that I was still delving into my deepest thoughts and feelings. In doing so I apologised to Kate. I felt it could not help her and that to write in this way was impossibly self-indulgent. Once again Kate encouraged me to keep writing.

Kate's letters in return were less frequent and less wordy. In recent times she has not written at all, but keeps promising that she will and keeps encouraging me to continue.

I understand that writing is not for everyone. I have some friends who can talk incessantly for as long as I have hours to listen, but with pen and paper their words are brief and to the point; any attempt at more is soon met with frustration. I believe this has much to do with the speed of thought. I am rarely the instigator of the kind of fast-flowing dialogue which tends to occur whenever my family get together. Sometimes I can chip in with off-the-cuff remarks which add to the general hilarity. Often, though, by the time I have thought of something to say, the conversation has moved off in a different direction entirely.

So I consider myself slow-witted in conversation. But writing is different; somehow writing matches more closely the pace of my own thought processes and I can savour a free flow of ideas. I can well imagine how the writing process could frustrate my quick-witted conversational friends whose thought processes move too rapidly for the hand to keep pace.

To return to Kate then, the recent fall in correspondence, though hard for me, is surely a good sign that her thoughts are returning to a normal pace.

Kate is, for the same reason, a perfect example of how a friend can add to one's own nature simply by being a friend. Even though the writing has come mostly – and in recent months entirely – from me, I have been aware throughout that it was very much a two-way process. The first letter I received from Kate changed the way that I wrote; there was a natural merging of styles. Reaching into myself for insight that might help Kate, I gained many fresh insights into my own problems. Encouraging Kate to feel a way through her despair galvanised a new determination in myself to rise above my own failings.

These are the things I can enumerate, but the influence of a friend shows in quite imperceptible ways too. As an adolescent my tastes for music, clothes, books, television programmes and all manner of other things were influenced by the prospect of sharing those tastes with friends. With Kate I found that many of my concerns, my ways of thinking, my sensibilities, were shifted in such a way as to bring our lives into closer orbit.

I am quite sure that these shifts take place for all friendships; the ability to be a friend is, I think, directly in proportion to one's open-ness in allowing this constant moulding of character. There is no way, and no need, to sum up the things Kate did for me. The person she was changed the person I was forever.

I want to mention Anya too, for the strange force which seemed to be at work again on our first meeting. Anya comes from Finland but is working in England. Through work, Julie met and became friends with her quite some time ago, but I met Anya for the first time last November.

A few weeks before our meeting I had had a dream which was still playing on my mind at that time. In the dream I was at a family gathering. I was talking to one of my sisters to my left, but aware of a stranger sitting to my right. I looked back to my right and found that the stranger was an old Native American woman, with dark leathery skin and long black hair pulled around her face into a ponytail behind. As I turned around to glance in her direction, I found that she was staring directly, and very purposefully, into my eyes. I looked back at her for a moment.

Then she said, 'You don't recognise me, do you?'

When I admitted that I didn't, she said, 'I used to look after you when you were young.'

As soon as she said this I realised that I did recognise her. I immedi-ately threw my arms around her, and she threw hers around me, with the kind of desperate warmth reserved for long-absent friends. As we hugged she told me of all the things we had done together, and with each event I simultaneously remembered it and saw it happening in my mind's eye. The need to be mothered by her seemed overwhelming.

I awoke with a full recollection; it was another of those vivid dreams that you just have to think about, and it was the mothering which bothered me most at the time. When I thought back, a desire to be mothered had been a feature of some relationships. Heather, the friend I forgave and released, had fitted the description of dark skin and long dark hair. I had certainly felt that need to be mothered by her, though it was a role she could not possibly have fulfilled. I knew that but still felt it. There was another woman too, who I met from time to time in my work. She fitted the same description, and many times I had gazed at her from a distance with that melting feeling inside, wanting to be close, to be hugged. But on the occasions when I did speak to her, this mirage evaporated before my eyes. She was just an 'ordinary' person, not particularly attractive, and the feeling was gone until the next time.

I wondered whether I had unconsciously been trying to meet and reunite with this Native American woman all along. But in my waking state I was sure that there had never been such a woman in my childhood.

Two weeks later, Anya and I had dispensed with pleasantries very quickly. In the space of Julie leaving the room to make a drink, our conversation had progressed from holidays and weather to reincarnation and astral flying. After our meal, Julie left to make another drink and I decided to tell Anya about my dream. I wanted to know what she would make of it. I don't know why it seemed right in Julie's absence, but I already had a feeling that the way Julie and Anya related, the way we related as a threesome, and the way Anya and I related were all different and quite distinct.

Anya and I were sitting a couple of metres apart. As I related the story I began to feel odd inside: my flesh turned to goose bumps and it felt like I was suddenly charged up with static electricity. When I described the woman in my dream Anya cried out, 'My God, my flesh has turned all goosy. What is happening?'

I immediately cried back, 'Mine too!'

We stared at each other; the whole atmosphere between us seemed to be powerfully charged. I moved to sit on the floor at Anya's feet. Our conversation was rising to a new level, but then Julie returned with drinks and the dynamic was subtly shifted, the moment gone. Even so, as Anya has said several times since, the moment was very special.

Over the weekend that followed, Anya told me her own thoughts about that dream, possibilities which I hadn't considered at all. I had taken it as a warning not to be too easily swayed by my desire to be mothered. Anya talked of spirit guides, of souls who will appear to young children to ease their transition into this world, of memories from other lives. I must have looked apprehensive about the idea of reincarnation, at least in my own life, because she then told me that Jesus himself had spoken of it but that all such references had deliberately been excluded from the Bible as we know it today. I had never heard of such a notion, though I tried not to appear too perplexed; I didn't want Anya to feel she needed to choose her words with circumspection.

I didn't reach any new and firm conclusions as a result of our discussions that weekend, but it is because of our friendship that my mind, ever since, has contemplated wider possibilities – I often find myself wondering what Anya would think of one thing or another – and who can say how this greater openness might tell on the course of my life?

The ways in which friends can influence my life are endless. They can cause a profound shift of character or utter one word that, in retrospect, caused a decisive change of direction. For this very reason I know that I must include the words and deeds of friends on this personal journey, and I am troubled by that. I do not wish to describe my friends any more than is necessary, or recount the circumstances of their lives, which are mostly told to me in confidence. My friends are real people (though the names I use here are of my choosing); even my kindest attempt to portray them would bear no comparison with their lives as they see them.

I will not subject them to that. Nor would I wish to convey the impression that their lives only have significance insofar as they revolve around mine. That is an unfortunate limitation from which the purpose of my writing does not allow me to stray. But there are no small people here, not like in the movies. Before I move on, I tender a heartfelt apology to all these friends for the injustice I am bound to perpetrate in mentioning their words, their deeds and their failings.

## 29 January 1996

In the days after that unfortunate conversation with my dad – when I had ineptly tried to have him set goals and to visualise them – my spirits were lower and self-doubt was on the rise. If we have a Greater Self to follow, it is probably just as true that we have a smaller self nagging to be noticed. I tried to deal with it in my inner landscape. Once I had relaxed and imagined myself standing in the meadow, I spent a little time listening to the disparaging remarks of this smaller self. I would look down and see, dancing around my ankles, an irritating goblin demanding that I follow him.

Then I would ask, 'Why should I?' and throw him over my shoulder into the stream behind.

By 11 January I was feeling ready to move forward again. As I 'programmed' my day, I imagined touring the bookshops at lunchtime and finding exactly the right book to push forward my spiritual goal. When the time arrived, I wandered from shop to shop with a sense of anticipation. In fact I found nothing in the spiritual and self-development categories. In the last shop, I had effectively given up the search and was making my way out past fiction when a book caught my eye: *The Celestine Prophecy* by James Redfield.

I cannot put my finger on it – the title was just one among many – but something drew me to it. I said in my little black book later that somehow I had felt 'guided'. With only a cursory glance at the cover I felt an urge not just to buy it, but to begin reading it straight away.

I did not feel disappointed. It spoke of the meaning of coincidence, the very kind that had led me to the book in the first place. It spoke of energy fields, confirming their existence and confirming too that they could be seen with practice, just as I had imagined.

All part of this chain of coincidence, the book said, is the people we meet. It suggested that we meet because we have a message for each other and because we might, if we are open, help each other's spiritual journey in some unique way. As I read of this and the visible energy fields, Anya kept coming into my mind. I was feeling two things: first, I must send to her a copy of this book – I had the feeling that I only needed to send it, and that no explanation was necessary; she would just know who had sent it and why – second, that she would be the one to help me see these energy fields.

A few days after buying the book, I tried to explain to Julie the process and the feeling that had led me to buy it, and the feelings I had concerning Anya. Julie was bemused by the whole thing. I surmised that being open wasn't the universal panacea I had expected, and that I'd better not be too public with my thoughts just yet. I didn't want to attract discouragement. In these early days I was avoiding any negativity that might dampen my enthusiasm. Nevertheless I deferred to Julie's opinion and included a letter of explanation to Anya when I posted a copy of the book to her.

And still the book carried me along. The whole of Einstein's life's work, it said, showed that what we perceive as hard matter is no more than a pattern of energy in empty space. This applies to our 'physical' presence as much as anything else. When we get down to the tiniest aspects of that energy, the elementary particles, and try to watch how they operate, the very act of watching alters the results. It is as if these particles are influenced by what the experimenter expects.

I copied out this passage with excitement, underlining that last idea for emphasis. Here was the beginning of scientific confirmation that we do indeed create our own reality.

I have to concede that much of my excitement in reading came from the feeling that each page was articulating and confirming the very ideas I had been wrestling with. It was as though my mind was just a small step ahead, anticipating each chapter, each insight. Maybe that is what always moves us best, when coincidence leads us to the words we are most ready to hear.

I have been talking about the influence of friends, and *The Celestine Prophecy* puts forward a certain view of human relationship: that there is an exchange of energy taking place in each interaction, a giving or a forceful taking, grabbing, even stealing of energy. When we don't know where this energy comes from, when we have no sense of its source, then we become afflicted with an attitude of scarcity. In human relationship this leads to strategies designed to preserve our own energy or take from others. I wondered at the ways I might have joined in this game.

If my close relationships are healthier now than they once were, it is because in the past I have recognised some damaging strategies of my own and finally worked to eradicate them. It took me a long time to see it, but I did use the circumstances of my childhood trauma as a kind of kick-start to a deeper level of friendship. It was a secret, always waiting to be given up at the right time, when the emotional impact could be fully appreciated. This moment of intimacy and sympathy in each friendship was a little pay-off I worked out for myself. In doing so I invested in the prolonging of the 'pain' I was going through. I also threw each of those friendships out of balance.

Friendship, for a time, became a sharing of weakness rather than strength. It brought a special brand of loyalty mixed in secrecy which kept each liaison peripheral to every other and peripheral to established social life. And the position of mutual need established within that relationship opened the way for subtle manipulation, bending one to the stronger will of the other for the sake of maintaining the exquisite imbalance.

Eventually I saw my play for sympathy for the destructive and self-perpetuating strategy that it was. I began to seek a way of relating which allowed emotional intimacy but from a position of respect for each person's inherent independence and integrity. This did not mean that I did not share my weaknesses any more. I did. But the purpose was different, and the result was different too. Perhaps this has something to do with that exchange of energy James Redfield speaks of. My actions hardly changed, but the resulting balance of energy in each relationship was radically different.

Of my old relationships, the ramifications of imbalance are still played out in my life from time to time. I became friends with Ayeesha at just such a time, and it had a decisive effect on the development of our friendship and the influence we have had on each other since.

In October 1994, when Kate was due to return to work, I had taken a week off. I was still writing to Kate very frequently at that time. I was also talking to Sarah – the expressive dancer – most evenings on the telephone. It was through her that I learned of malicious gossip, which had arisen at work, concerning myself and Ayeesha, even though my friendship with her had barely begun at that stage. It was the first time that the darker side of ruminations about my 'enigmatic' disposition had hit home. In our conversation, Sarah told me that Ayeesha had also heard these rumours and had decided to confront the people concerned. It seemed there was a stark division of opinion about me. Those that knew me in any depth counted me as nothing more or less than a trusted friend. They knew the basis of their own relationship with me, and found no reason to suppose that other relationships were any different. Those that did not know me saw a married man openly consorting with other women; no more proof was needed than that.

Ayeesha had only recently arrived at the workplace. For more than a month we had spoken very little to each other, except for my off-the-cuff remark about her unusual 'printed' hand-writing style. One day we had to travel together to a neighbouring town. The rapport was instant. Ayeesha was a natural talker, I was a natural audience; it was like a mortise and tenon, carved in separate cultures, now coming together by design. By the end of that day, Ayeesha had been surprised several times over at the comfort she felt in sharing

her life and thoughts. I should say our friendship had already established a firm foundation, though we would not have conceded the
point so readily.

After that day, Ayeesha would regularly come over to my desk
to talk. I should have known then that people were already speculating about the sudden rapport between us. One day when she was
bemoaning the lack of friends at work compared to her days at
college, I hesitantly suggested that we might have lunch together. I
was hesitant because of the large gap in our ages. Although it had
seemed like a proper and guileless thing to say at the time, I
inwardly cringed afterwards, thinking that it was totally inappro-
priate and may have made Ayeesha uncomfortable. To my relief,
she took me up on the offer a few days later, at least showing that
she had not felt the discomfort I had feared. It was the day before
my holiday, and it fuelled all the busy-bodying which took place in
my absence.

On the day of my return, I was relieved to be working in a private
room away from those who believed they had spoken without my
knowledge. Ayeesha came to see me. I did not waste words: I told
her that I was aware of what had been said and that I was sorry; she
did not deserve that kind of treatment. Ayeesha seemed taken aback
at first, but then she told me what had happened.

Having confronted three women whom she had heard gossiping
together, those women had taken her under their wing, so to speak,
and told her that she must be very careful because I was a dangerous
man. They proceeded to list my shady relationships. Ayeesha hadn't
known what to make of it; she didn't entirely trust them, but then
she didn't know me very well either. I did not try to defend myself.
Apologising to her again, I said I would quite understand if she
wanted to keep her distance. Our conversation was brief and she left
without any resolution of the matter.

Kate also came to see me. It was her first day back. That was when
she asked that I should keep on writing to her. I smiled and said that I
would, betraying nothing of what had transpired, but wishing, for her
sake, that she would leave soon and not become similarly tainted.

To my surprise, Sarah came to see me too. She wasn't even
supposed to be at work but she had called in and decided to pay me a
visit at the same time. I told her what I had learned from Ayeesha.

In a matter of fact tone, she said, 'Oh yes, that's what they said to
me, but I decided to ignore them in the end.'

Suddenly it was patently clear why there had been that gap of several months between our first talk and the disclosures that followed. Why had she eventually decided to trust me? I didn't know and didn't ask.

I was feeling angry inside, but I was also beginning to feel a tormenting self-doubt – at that time, self-doubt came easily and usually unchecked. Those busybodies were not right about me, but neither were they entirely wrong. In the early days of forming new friendship, I *had* allowed distinctions to become blurred. I had seen how sincere motives could turn selfish. I had also determined to draw back from that position, but there were plainly some dues still to pay. My self-doubt was telling me those dues were richly deserved. I worked on with a growing sense of shame and despondency.

Just before the day's end, Ayeesha came to see me again. She had some work-related excuse, but she didn't take long to get back on to the subject of my reputation. First of all she made light of it, saying I should be very proud and that most men would kill for a reputation like that. I said I wasn't proud, but I wasn't going to narrow my horizons to fit anyone else's ideas of propriety.

Ayeesha changed tack, becoming more serious. She said, 'You know, you should be careful. These people could do you a lot of harm.'

Despite her youth, Ayeesha was a very business-minded woman; she thought I should take more care for my career prospects. She didn't know how low that came on my scale of priorities. She didn't know that the collapse of my fragile world view had left me with only one abiding notion: that in all the world, in all existence, in all of time, there was only love and failing to love; nothing else mattered, or had ever mattered.

I replied to Ayeesha's practical advice in a grim tone.

'I have some friends who need a lot of help right now. I am not going to walk away from them for my own sake. I am not going to walk away from any friend for the sake of a damned career. I answer to my wife and I will answer to my friends. I am not going to answer to anyone else.'

I did not speak in anger, rather in resignation. I had always suspected, and now knew, that this kind of summary judgement was an inevitable corollary to the unconventional nature of my attachments.

Ayeesha tried to restate her position, as if I hadn't understood, but she was not trenchant. Some women are described as vivacious in their looks, which I take to indicate a certain liveliness of expression; Ayeesha was vivacious in her vocal expression. She could talk around a situation in many different ways and switch the mood with equal dexterity. While some people would push and push at an issue, trying to force their will upon it, Ayeesha would push, prod, cosset and tickle it just to see what would happen. She could see many sides to a situation and found no need to focus on any one. I had my nose pressed uncomfortably against what I took to be a view as plain as glass, while she was standing back and admiring the whole diamond.

The upshot of it all was that we determined to remain friends. Ayeesha gained my undying admiration for her independent spirit. I would like to think that my stubborn brand of loyalty gained her appreciation in turn, but it was probably more complex than that. Ayeesha sized up my several-sided character, and the delicate balance of her intuition fell in my favour.

I have since seen Ayeesha as beautiful. I don't mean I decided she was or that I started to feel a physical attraction for her; I mean I saw her as beautiful and that is something very special.

It all ties up with Irene leaving work and moving away at the end of last year, which was probably one reason why Irene and I hadn't wanted that night together in the cold car to end. I had made friends with Irene at roughly the same time as Ayeesha. They were quite separate friendships but, as it turned out, Irene and Ayeesha became friends too and the three of us could happily spend time together. That was a feature of the new balance in relationships which I talked about.

Because I was due to be off work over Christmas, Irene and I said our farewell on Christmas Eve. At first it was a fairly peremptory goodbye, in the knowledge that we would keep in touch. We parted in the middle of a busy shopping centre at midday. I walked only twenty paces and turned back to see Irene browsing inside a nearby shop. I walked back, tapped her on the shoulder and said, 'That goodbye didn't seem right somehow.'

She said 'No', and put an arm around my waist, leading me out of the shop for a proper hug. Before we reached the doorway Irene was crying.

I took on the decisive role and led her away for a drink of coffee. Once seated, we talked about exactly how we should keep in touch and made a definite date. Irene felt better. I felt better. This time we parted properly.

The following week – Irene's last week – I wasn't meant to be at work but I had some papers to return, so Julie and I called in on New Year's Eve. By chance, we met both Irene and Ayeesha and we all decided to go to lunch together. We walked out of the office and down the road, laughing at how certain people would have been mightily confused by the sight of all four of us together.

It was very pleasant that we could all be that way, and interesting how the topics of conversation could change according to the combination of people, as if by an unspoken agreement.

It was towards the end of that meal that I saw Ayeesha as beautiful. She flashed the briefest look in my direction. Our eyes met, and there was a subtle change in her expression, a sign of mutual understanding. At that moment she could have been any age, we could have been *in* any age. And that was it, a moment so brief I could not put a time duration upon it, and so special I could never forget. It is something I have glimpsed many times in Julie, and also in other friends. Like the softening of voices, it seems to come from an unfathomable connection which you just can't engineer or control.

Kahlil Gibran says, 'Beauty is life, when life unveils its holy face.' I guess the movement of that veil is another expression hinting at the 'truth which connects all things', that indefinable something I am searching for.

In *The Celestine Prophecy* there is a passage in which the 'hero' experiences being listened to intently by a woman, so intently that he finds he can relate his story in a surprisingly animated, clear-headed way. Later he is told by a friend that people can pour their energy into another quite voluntarily, and that this experience was just such an occasion. In other words, listening amounts to a gift of energy.

It made sense to me when I read this. There had been a number of times in the past when I had listened to somebody so completely that I had been aware of this sensation of pouring into the other person. Sometimes it was almost tangible; my whole identity seemed to be softening and melting into the other. For the time being, I no longer had a separate identity, but far from this being the complete submission that it sounds, it was a wonderful exploration.

In those moments, I tasted every nuance and tone of expression, living the story, feeling at first hand what it was to be this other human being. That is the best I can describe it. If I thought about it while it was happening, I am sure I would instantly be pulled back into my own skin.

Ayeesha said to me recently – before I had read this particular passage in the book – 'You know, John, when you listen, you listen with your whole body.' I wasn't sure what she meant. It certainly wasn't something I could consciously replicate. Maybe this was how she experienced this gift of energy.

This evening I rang Ayeesha – I rang her, so it can't be just a one-sided thing. She had a headache; I promised to be brief. Over an hour later Ayeesha declared that her headache had gone! This time she described the feeling of being listened to as making her feel lighter. I had not even discussed with her this theory of energy exchange; she was speaking from her own direct experience. I could only marvel that this should even happen down a telephone line. What is the nature of such an energy?

For the little I have spoken to Ayeesha of these ideas, she has influenced another step on my intuitive path. She was one of three people in a matter of days to compare my experience to Indian mysticism. I decided it was too much of a coincidence to ignore and, three days ago, set out to find an appropriate book, in much the same manner that I had found *The Celestine Prophecy*.

I browsed through a book on Hinduism. It mentioned Shiva a lot, and something about concentrating on the breath, on the space between breathing out and breathing in. It mentioned the mantra, a personal word or phrase used to invoke a state of meditation – enlightenment comes when the mantra continues without effort as you go about your day. In the end, I was put off by the profusion of Indian names and, instead, settled on an unashamedly populist book called *Surfing the Himalayas* – snowboarding through Buddhism, conversations with a saffron-robed monk named Master Fwap. It all provoked a 'reasonable' scepticism, but I decided to honour whatever inkling led me to it.

# 23 February 1996

If books enter our lives at the time when we are most ready to receive them, how much more true could this be of people? People, compared to books, enter our lives in such a fluid way, drifting in and out of our presence, responding with an independent will. It is easy to dismiss such interaction as a random exchange, having no particular significance for the most part. But what if this is not so? What if every encounter has a significance which we overlook only to the detriment of our own development?

The random flow of human interaction brought an old acquaintance back into my life, and if the opposite were true – that events have no more significance than we ourselves attach to them – then my acquaintance and I chose to treat our meeting as important.

Helen worked with me for several years. In the beginning, we worked closely and managed to marry a productive working relationship with an easy, unchallenging personal acquaintance. On one level Helen's personal life was an open book for all to view. I might have suspected there were other levels, but I did not probe for them, nor upset the balance by revealing my own.

She moved to a new office within the same building and our contact for a while was negligible until Helen's forthcoming marriage gave her the impetus to get fit, and therefore to accompany me on regular lunchtime exercise sessions. By that stage Helen was not happy with her working environment; she looked back on our time together and the team we were a part of as a 'golden age' when the work, and the people doing it, were treated with due respect. Friction at home was also taking its toll, and eczema, a persistent childhood problem, returned as a symptom and exacerbation of her distress.

We began to talk on a new level. In the end, our so-called exercise sessions were given over almost entirely to walking around the park and talking together. Only once did we drop the pretence of exercise so that we might have longer to talk. Even then, we did not drop the pretence of going for exercise, so far as those at work were concerned. This was an absolute must for Helen; the thought of being tainted by gossip, however unjustly, was something she would not face. But it went further than this. She could not let it be seen that she wished or needed to talk, at least not to another man.

When Helen left, our contact ended abruptly. Others at work were invited to her wedding; I wasn't. I knew her motives well enough, I believed, to understand why, but I felt some hurt nonetheless. It was not the first time – and I knew it would not be the last – that I would accept this as a consequence of listening to unhappiness: while ever that unhappiness remained beyond the pale of social acceptability, then I remained there too. Why I accepted this as my role – to the exclusion of any other purpose in relating – is another question.

Helen's leaving was intended as a career break, to take some much needed time for rest and contemplation, and to pursue other interests. The rules required that she return to work for a two-week period to keep in touch with the job. I was walking along a corridor going back to my desk when she opened the door directly behind me. I turned and immediately gave her a welcoming hug, which was a foolhardy thing to do. Firstly, she did not feel comfortable with such displays at the best of times; secondly, it was an acknowledgement of our friendship in front of others. Such was my own positive state of mind that I acted without pause for reflection. Helen was clearly feeling good too; she took my gesture in her stride.

We sat down and talked together in an animated fashion, she about aromatherapy and the counselling she had undergone, I about my standing exercise and new-found energy level. I told her that I only needed to think about it to be wrapped in this tingling sensation of flowing energy. And it was true: ever since my 'burning bush' experience, that was what I found myself able to do; it was even happening as I was telling her.

I told her also about *The Celestine Prophecy*. This is a weakness of mine – to go around recommending the latest book as if it were the be-all and end-all – but Helen had read an article about it and took my mentioning it as a sign that she must read it immediately.

The following morning, during exercise, I had the strange sensation of receiving a message, something I must tell Helen straight away. The message was, 'The very next thing you need to do is to open up to other people.' This was in the context of the counselling she had talked about, and the eczema which was still with her.

I felt awkward about passing on such a message. When we spoke briefly later that morning, Helen told me of the need she felt to protect herself in social situations, even at family gatherings. It gave me the opening I needed. I told her the message. It felt like another instance of strong and meaningful coincidence. Each time we met, we were buzzing and sparking off each other in this way. Our relationship had changed. We had parted and developed in our separate ways, and now, coming together again, we were repeatedly enriched by each other's enthusiasm.

This weakness I have – for recommending books – stems from a need to convince myself as much as anyone else. The truth is that I was still having days of feeling outside the flow of events, and procrastinating with my stated goals. Progress was elusive and the signposts of my way forward were ambiguous and confusing.

Determined that I should train myself to see energy fields, I believed that my plan had received a timely fillip when I was sent on a two-day course in a country hotel. My joining instructions included a brochure and photograph of the hotel gardens. It looked like the right kind of place for magic to happen. I imagined standing among those trees and shrubs in the early dawn and seeing the energy around them. When I arrived there, to my disappointment the grounds were much smaller than they had appeared; it would not have been possible to remain there for long without being acutely conscious of other residents puzzling over my behaviour. The shrubbery also seemed too well manicured by half.

For the first day, I sat in the training room with a group of strangers, watching each person intently as they spoke, against the plain background of the hotel wallpaper. I believed I could see an energy field around the heads of certain people; it seemed to be particularly wide around one man, whose intelligence had won my respect from the start. I detected a bluish tint. None of this was sufficiently distinct to feel sure. I had first learned to 'see' by gazing at my fingers against a darkened background. Moving my fingers in and out, I had gradually seen little bands of energy being squeezed and stretched like a sticky syrup which had no weight or density of its own. I was able to repeat that experiment until I was sure of what I was seeing, but in the hotel room my visions were too faint and fleeting to be sure of anything. I did not count it as the kind of breakthrough I was looking for.

In the evening I reluctantly set out for the pub with the rest of the group. We had not left the hotel grounds when one of the men told me of a glacial valley only a mile away, where, he said, the vegetation had remained undisturbed for five thousand years. I was seized with enthusiasm again. Surely this was the reason for my strong sense of purpose in being there. I rose early the following morning to leave time to exercise and arrive in the valley as dawn broke.

It was 1 February. It was cold and overcast, grey clouds behind a matted nest of branches. Stripped of foliage, the dominant colour was a greyish brown, relieved only by the muted greens of moss. On the ground, hardy leaf plants crouched flush to the soil. I wandered around for an hour and kept pausing to focus purposefully. I saw nothing, except perhaps that same bluish tint around some branches, but it was too difficult to be sure against the shifting background of the sky.

Arriving back in the hotel grounds, I noticed something around the ordered shrubbery. It had the appearance of a heat haze. I reached the breakfast hall as the others were close to finishing. They had clearly been having an entertaining conversation, a bonding experience from which I had absented myself deliberately and without warrant. I felt foolishly estranged.

When I returned home I tried to make sense of that experience. My expectations had been too high to be fully met. Maybe I had made a real beginning, but I felt that my intuition was not good enough to be trusted without question. A few days later I read in *Surfing the Himalayas* that, according to Buddhist teaching, after many years of meditation and quietening the mind, the 'third eye' may open to reveal a new insight and depth of experience. I could understand how this might happen suddenly, after a time of seemingly unfruitful effort. Part of my morning routine had been to bend forward and stretch my back muscles. I had spent months doing this with little, if any, progress. Then, one morning, my back had suddenly stretched much farther with apparent ease and had continued to do so ever since. I wrote in my book: it was as if we ask and ask in the certain knowledge that we will eventually be answered, but we have no control over when that answer might come.

No sooner had I expressed this idea than another thought occurred to me: Napoleon Hill, in *Think and Grow Rich*, placed great emphasis on being specific about the details of a goal, including the timeframe. I wondered if it was, after all, possible to seek even a spiritual goal by a definite date. Was it possible to set a specific date for enlightenment itself? I could only say I knew of no reason why not, but neither did I know yet what enlightenment was. As I neared the end of *Surfing the Himalayas*, I was beginning to feel disappointed that it was not going to tell me.

I had been introduced to meditation, the notion of chakras – the seven energy centres of the body – and the ego, and I had read that enlightenment could not be achieved without the guidance of an enlightened master. The resistance I felt to this was, no doubt, the resistance of my ego. As the book made clear, using the ego to achieve things is one possible way forward, but a very inferior way.

I noted down these points. I was conscious of my confusion and that I had presented myself so positively for Helen's benefit while privately feeling that I was fumbling in the dark. I had noticed before that this act of writing, posing questions and wondering last thing at night was apt to provoke an immediate response in the form of a dream, and that night it happened again.

The dream took the form of an old film starring James Stewart (a favourite of mine). He was driving along on the way to make his fortune and was obliged to stop by the people at a dilapidated roadside shack. He was anxious to get on his way, but somehow I already knew he would end up staying there. Three smiling locals were keeping him talking. Eventually he was persuaded inside the shack to taste some toffee from a tin on the table, a secret recipe of someone who had lived there before. He was so impressed by the taste that he decided to stay and make his fortune right there.

The film moved on; James had a wife and child and appeared to be living out of his vehicle while awaiting the delivery of a more comfortable shack. The nature of the business had also changed. He was now selling real estate. I knew, however, that the era of the Great Depression was about to start and that he would have to find some way to survive through it. He was living by a lake and I was thinking that he would have to learn how to fish.

At that moment the child walked along the road by the side of the lake. On the far side was a snow-capped mountain (the very mountain pictured on the front of my book, *Surfing the Himalayas*!). The child moved from the road to the lakeside. Ducks could be seen tail up, feeding. Below the surface I could see that the lake was teeming with fish. I awoke just as it began to dawn on the child that he should learn how to fish.

As I awoke, this saying was in my mind:

Give a man a fish, and you feed him for a day.
Teach him to fish, and you feed him for life.

I lay awake in the darkness catching my immediate impressions, which were that the dream had to be connected to the book. It had, I remembered, described the reality we see as the surface of a lake, and it went on:

Most of the water in a lake lies beneath its surface. In much the same way, only a small portion of life can be seen. The vast majority of life is nonphysical; it exists beyond the physical surface of life, in other dimensions. If you want to experience life in its totality, it is necessary to enter into Samadhi.

A second impression was that the dream concerned what the book called relational thinking, the kind of thought which occurs through meditation, something quite unlike rational thinking. In the dream, fishing signified meditation. It was telling me that I needed to learn how to do this if I am to live. It showed me how the lake – reality – teemed with life beneath the surface.

I remembered also the story of Jesus standing by the Sea of Galilee watching the disciples. They had been fishing all day without gain. Jesus said, 'Cast your net on the other side.' They did, and found so many fish that their net could barely take the strain.

The closest I have come to relational thinking is probably in conversation with friends. When somebody gives you that special quality of attention, you can find yourself telling things long forgotten. Sometimes I will stop, or my friend will stop and say, 'How did we get on to that?', and the string of association is so complex it can take an age to unravel. Sometimes I find myself expressing thoughts I didn't even know I had until that moment.

Irene and I honoured the commitment we had made to maintain contact. On one such evening, over dinner, Irene complained about the tiresome antics of her mother-in-law, who had interfered in her marriage from the very beginning. It was not the first time this complaint had arisen and Irene was clearly feeling quite bitter about the way things were going. By way of conclusion, however, Irene said that she could not be too critical because at least her mother-in-law was 'in therapy' for her problems.

It was then that I ventured, 'Maybe your mother-in-law is just using therapy as a part of her whole control drama.'

The idea was only just beginning to dawn on me. I continued to think aloud, 'It's as if she is saying to you, "Look, I'm doing as much as I can, now you people had better just tread carefully around me because I can't be expected to get better if you don't help. I might just go over the edge altogether!"'

Irene looked slightly puzzled at first, but then somehow hooked on to my train of thought. I do so admire her ability to do that. I can say challenging things and she never takes offence and never dismisses my ideas out of hand. Sometimes I am not challenging enough, and she will prod me and say, 'You have to be honest with me: tell me I'm talking rubbish!'

I try to reply convincingly to this by saying, 'Don't worry, when you are talking rubbish, I'll tell you!', but inside I am thinking that I don't know how to be so critical. I have spent so long listening without attempting any judgement that it is no longer a natural stance for me. I wonder why Irene looks for criticism in this way. Ever since it was apparent to us that we were becoming friends, she has insisted, 'We must be honest with each other', meaning critical, even to the point of brutality. Yet Irene has never been so critical of me. What has there been in Irene's past relationships for her to make such a point of this? Is my 'niceness' fundamentally dishonest? It's one of those things Irene makes me wonder about but about which I can't reach any conclusion.

Irene carried my new thought along, reviewing more incidents of her mother-in-law's behaviour, testing them against the new theory as she played with her hair. I couldn't help but smile. The atmosphere of the conversation had changed; we were no longer complaining but playing with the whole issue.

Afterwards, I contemplated the potential truth of what I had said. Could this be why some people stay in therapy for so long, because they never intend to get well? Sickness can be just another tool in the fight to control one's surrounding circumstances, and if it works, where is the incentive to become well again? Sickness – in fact, having any problem at all – can be an awfully good excuse for falling short of expectations. Having no problems is a tremendous responsibility! I know we all have problems. It is the treating of them as 'insurmountable' that can bring such a perverse comfort.

Just a few days after my meeting with Irene, I had dinner with my sister Kim; it was another experience of my thoughts crystallising only as I was beginning to explain something. Kim and I had not spent time alone together since the early days of her marriage break-up. We had a lot of ground to make up with the kind of things which tend not to be discussed in larger gatherings. I was eager to tell her of my plans and, as I described it to her, my belief in the power of belief. Kim was cautious, pointing out – quite rightly – that one only tends to hear of success stories when there could be any number of others who have tried and failed. My spirits were so high that I felt unperturbed by this caution, but it was the first indication that evening that our thoughts had diverged quite significantly since we had last spoken.

It is one of Kim's adopted beliefs, as I already knew, that the body is no more than a vehicle for the soul as the soul migrates from life to life. Insofar as it can be described, Kim says the soul is a tiny point of light which sits just behind the forehead and between the eyes. It is where Master Fwap might have placed the third eye, where Hindu people would place a mark on their skin to serve as a reminder of their divine nature. It was towards the end of the evening as Kim was talking in these terms that I began to express an opinion I didn't know I had.

I said I didn't think of my body as a vehicle any more; I didn't see the body and the soul as two separate things. I told her that I was made up of vibrating energy, and part of that energy chose, at this time, to manifest itself in a physical form, the body. At some stage, I said, the essential energy that is me would transmute into a state where it no longer used the body; my body would be discarded, as a butterfly discards a chrysalis. Until then, my spirit and my body are one.

Arriving at Kim's house later, we lingered in the kitchen to continue our conversation. We were talking about meditation; I was interested in Kim's progress which, I gathered, was somewhat haphazard. She would visit her meditation centre most weeks, but when I inquired as to her meditation between such visits, it seemed that this did not happen for a variety of reasons: lack of time, demands of the children, work, household chores etc., etc. I ventured to suggest she might find ways to make time, that circumstances were unlikely to change around her until she changed from within.

Kim was not receptive. It was not that she saw no sense in what I was saying – and there are many who wouldn't, but we were still on the same wavelength to that extent – but there was a greater stumbling block within her. Kim believed that she could throw herself wholeheartedly into meditation and all the other activities of her particular group, but it would involve a sacrifice in her circumstances which she could not inflict on her family. I tried to tell her that it was better for her family to know and accept her as she truly wanted to be, but it was to no avail. Kim knew all this. She told me she had been standing on this precipice ever since joining the meditation group. She knew that some day she would take that step into the unknown, but for now it was not to be.

I was left with the uneasy feeling that my ego had done a good deal too much pushing that evening. Since becoming reacquainted with the notion, I seemed to be stumbling over my ego at every turn.

A couple of days after my conversation with Kim, I received a letter from Anya in response to my own. It was a nice letter of thanks, in which Anya shared her own experience of energy following the death of her husband; she did not use the word 'death', but referred to his passing over to another level. She felt warm vibrations around her. First it was like a hand on her shoulder or head; later it settled down as a permanent warm spot in her forehead. 'The spot called the third eye,' she said, 'which is one of our chakras.' There it was again.

Anya also said that after meditating regularly for a couple of months, she was able to look back on her life and understand that 'every single person we meet, the smallest incidents in our life have a lesson or a message for us to study'. Anya also spoke of things I was yet to experience: 'wild astral travels through the universe, colours, music, plants and animals out of this world'.

Included with the letter was a leaflet which contained a list of books. Anya simply said, 'Maybe you will find a book or two of interest.' I bristled inside, and I didn't like what I felt. In my book that night, I wrote:

> I felt a tinge of disappointment that Anya was trying to help me and point me to others who might help. It was my damned ego, wanting to be acknowledged as the most advanced being that ever lived, and getting there all on my own while everyone else is left in awe, trailing in my 'enlightened' wake. I can't believe how bad my ego is, but I know it is the one thing which stands most in the way of my progress. My ego denies help, denies other people's value, and denies the very principles by which I wish to live. I have to find a way to rid myself

of it or, at least, neutralise it. This is a long-term problem. I remember ten years ago knowing the truth in the words 'all is vanity'.

What horrified me most was that I had completely failed to free myself of the ego all those years ago. Not even the complete routing of my self-belief had so much as dented it. It was like one of those desert plants that can sit beneath the soil for months or years waiting out the drought, only to bloom again at the least drop of rain.

Only the next day another leaflet came my way. It was from somebody I had been 'lecturing' to, someone who had been totally baffled at the time and I had felt bad about it; I knew I had caused discomfort. She left a note for me to say that the group mentioned in the leaflet might be of interest. Groups! My ego was bristling all over again.

I felt low. At some point in the evening I became aware that I was singing something in my head. I was singing to myself that, once, there was a way to get back home. I knew the thought came from a song, and I knew the rest of the words, but this was the only line I was singing, over and over again, lulled by the sad minor chords of the music. I caught myself seduced by this sadness but, faced with the intractable problem of my ego, I decided to sleep on it rather than fight. I was getting the feeling that fighting was just making the problem worse. The only thing to do each morning was to wash away the failings of the previous day and refocus on the person I wanted to be.

For all of Kim's hesitation on the threshold of her own spiritual destiny, she had taught me a valuable lesson some years ago which had affected my own journey unquestionably for the better. It was seven or eight years ago that Kim took up meditation by joining a group. The group did not require that she accept any particular belief, so she was able to ease her way in, unchallenged by the ideas expressed there. She said it was like coming home, so comfortable did she feel with the people and the practice of meditation. Once every week her problems were put into a new perspective, and she would return home with a fresh resolve to approach things differently.

Kim, as I have said, had been taught to look at each human being as a soul, for whom the body was no more than a temporary vehicle. The ideal to which she aspired was 'soul-consciousness', a state in which she never lost awareness of her own or any other's soul and the true nature of what transpired between them, their karma. To lose that state was to become body-conscious and to try to deal with problems from this flawed perspective.

What most impressed me, at that time, was her ability to forgive herself. Her sons, like most boys, could be mischievous, and Kim, like most parents, would lose her temper and shout a little more than was justified. Very soon afterwards, she was able to smile and say to herself, 'You let yourself down a bit there, Kim.' This is a small example of the self-forgiveness which she was able to call upon in any situation. I compared myself very poorly to this. I could still inwardly wince about minor transgressions which might have been years old and never even noticed as such by anyone but myself. My slate was cluttered with such penalties, while Kim seemed able to wipe hers clean, minute by minute if need be, to begin again with a fresh resolve.

I thought of the difference between us as symptomatic of our difference in religious persuasion. That was until I listened to Kate.

When Kate spoke of her karma, she did so with all the wincing, self-doubt and self-punishment that I brought to my own Christianity. To Kate, karma was a prospect contemplated with dread. Terrible things had happened in her life which, she reasoned, could only have been justly deserved. Since she must be so terrible, then these terrible karmic lessons could only continue to come her way. Kate experienced no happiness without a coterminous fear for the day it would be taken from her.

Take away the idea of karma, and the way Kate talked was much closer to my own outlook than to Kim's. It slowly dawned on me that the difference between Kim and me, and the similarities I shared with Kate, were nothing to do with religion and everything to do with attitude to life.

Through the insight that Kim and Kate between them offered me, it made sense that I had found kind people of every religious persuasion, and I had also found petty and spiteful people regardless of their faith. I had found people for whom life was a constant struggle, who saw the approach of disaster and decay at every turn. They even relished such visions as a sign that a new order must come soon to wash away the stains from humanity. And I had also found people who seemed affable to all things and all circumstances.

Looking through their eyes, scheming criminals became 'amazing chaps', cantankerous know-alls became 'characters'.

I have seen the strength and persistence of my own habitual attitudes and learned from them that a sudden religious or spiritual fervour does not blow them away. They merely retreat for a while, then quietly return to reassert a favoured view of life, how it works and how it behaves towards me in particular. A few labels and metaphors might change, but a basic feeling towards the world and others remains, unless I persistently seek out and challenge these attitudes on their level, a personal level that underlies any adopted belief.

The view I have taken – if I may use an analogy – is this: religious, spiritual, humanist – the label doesn't matter – whatever be the path of discovery we walk upon, we should think of attitude as the shoes in which we walk. Those shoes can make for discomfort every step of the way, with the only incentive being to hope for a comfortable destination. Or those shoes can make the journey a delight at every step. It is always tempting to think that our current attitudes must be right because they have proved so time and again, but it is in the very nature of attitude that it proves itself. We do better to measure attitudes by their helpfulness in our dealing with life and with others.

At the very least from this lesson I took on Kim's attitude of wiping the slate clean after a maudlin hour or day, and refreshing my resolve to remain positive. Inspiration waits on positive expectation, and for every moment I lose that positive feeling, I close off to the place from which inspiration flows.

A few nights after my dream about fishing, I had a very sleepless night, being seized by a kind of vision. I saw humanity at the heart – maybe humanity is the heart – of God, the living creation. I saw love as the lifeblood, which flows only through the beating of human compassion. Neither, I thought, should we ever be afraid to give, since giving, like the beating of the heart, is the very act which fills us again to give anew. Jesus said, 'Whosoever drinketh of the water that I shall give him shall never thirst; but the water that I shall give him shall be in him a well of water springing up into everlasting life.'

And yesterday, so different to today, I sat down, moved by a moment of inspiration, to express what I had tried to explain to Kim about the nature of the body. As I wrote, I was in rapture; it was as if my body was speaking its true nature, and I was a witness. I wrote:

This body,
This flesh and blood,
Is not the cage of my soul.
It is the manifest meeting of
The infinite within and the infinite without.

This body is not a vessel for my soul.
It is the passing point of grace,
Flowing in and never lost,
Flowing out and never wasted.

This body is not an instrument
Fashioned to bring a single note
To a greater symphony.
It is that ageless resounding moment when
The great song of beauty reaches harmony
And holds it in the tenderest embrace.

This is my body.

Later the same day, I met Helen by arrangement. When her short spell of work came to an end, I had tentatively suggested a meeting because we had managed only snatched conversations up to that time. I had said, 'If it isn't completely taboo, we could get together some lunchtime.' With a wry smile, which told me that the old rules no longer applied, Helen agreed that it might be possible. So yesterday we met in the landscaped grounds of a restored country hotel and took a window seat in the lounge. A frozen fountain outside added a romantic air to our rendezvous, but I sensed there would be no misunderstanding between us. I read to her the piece I had written that morning. When I looked up from my notebook, Helen's eyes were misted over. Her head and upper body rocked slightly as if a strong breeze had just passed through the room. In all the years I had been writing things down, I had never seen such a reaction. As I drove away, I had a vision that Helen and I would one day work together. When feelings like that flow it is almost magical. But that was yesterday.

Today, I lost my best friend. Without a fight or plea, I watched our paths separate. It will be a long time, if ever, before we speak again.

It must be nine or more years ago that Melanie and I first began cautious overtures towards friendship. It was the early days of my awakening to the true value of friendship, and for the most part my relationships developed incautiously in sudden bursts of shared confidences. Melanie was never so reckless in the matter of trust. She had a tough and infectiously happy exterior, but I always sensed more. If I am honest now, I sensed and was intrigued by her weakness.

The first time I visited her flat, I noticed a woman's photograph on the wall. The photograph was divided into strips becoming successively darker from left to right. Having some experience of photography, I recognised that it was a test strip to gauge the correct exposure before a proper print would be made. It struck me as odd that this should have been framed and hung on the wall. Melanie was making coffee. As she returned carrying two cups, I casually asked who the young woman was.

'Oh that's my sister,' she said. 'She died a few years ago.' Then, before I could respond, she added, 'But it's not a problem.'

When I left, although nothing further had been said about her sister, I felt I had intruded inappropriately. It was something I sensed from Melanie, but nothing I could identify from her outward appearance.

It was with Melanie that the boundaries of friendship became blurred for a time, though it was never a full-blown affair in the sense of sexual intercourse. I thank God we had the sense to draw back from that, and yet preserve the true spirit of friendship which had developed between us. I thank Julie for having the courage to allow our friendship to continue. I have had cause to notice since that the thirties are so often an age of emotional adolescence and, looking back, this was true of me. In every relationship there is a shared experience of growing up together for a time, which may be brief or long. It is the foundation on which the remaining years of friendship rest. I was only ever aware of such a period with Julie, but now I see it has happened with every true friend I have found. The fact that I still thought of Melanie as my best friend indicates the childish level of my social understanding when our friendship began.

If good for nothing else, the blurring and re-establishing of physical boundaries gave us an emotional intimacy which would not otherwise have come about. At least Melanie felt that way, and she was the only one who could have known because she was the one so timid of trust for all her brash persona. One day she said, 'You know, I trust you. I really trust you. I don't know why, but I really, really trust you.'

I smiled and looked into her eyes, as she looked back and smiled at me. I have no idea how long we held that steady, intimate gaze. It was a long time. I think back now at the complete lack of self-consciousness I felt, a feeling Melanie must have shared. How difficult that can be even for a short time, even with a good friend. To be found so acceptable in someone's sight and to be so sure of it was special indeed.

One day, after an evening out when Melanie had been drinking freely, I took her home and met the unexpected force of her pain for the first time. I discovered just how precious her sister was in Melanie's memory. Tearfully she told me of the tragic accident and how she was called back from holiday to receive the news, the guilt, the numbness, the sense of unreality. With sudden urgency, she rummaged through her belongings to produce treasured tokens of her sister. Most treasured of all, a cassette tape with snatches of her sister's voice. In her lifetime, it would not have been of any consequence. Melanie must have searched for it, or begged it from a friend. Like the photograph, it was something physical to hold on to.

Years later, Kate quietly listed the physical mementos of her own family, always kept in view, like small shrines in silent corners of a hushed house.

As she approached the age her sister had been at the time of her death, Melanie found herself restless, anxious and disorientated in a way she could not fully comprehend. She ate badly, drank badly and slept badly for several months. I had read somewhere that reaching such an age can so often be a time of crisis.

I was working away from home for most of that time. With evenings entirely free, Melanie and I talked for hours every night on the telephone. I really could have believed that there was no end to our dialogue, but the crisis did pass and our contact eased back to a steadier level.

Several boyfriends, and even one fiancé, came and went. Our friendship was never seriously under threat. Melanie aired her doubts about marriage even in the early stage of her engagement. That was the strength of our relationship: Melanie knew she could say what was on her mind and that she would never be held to account for it. Why didn't I hold her to account? Partly, I think, because I had become accustomed to the fickleness of thoughts, regarding them as things of interest and value for the time they were expressed, but lacking the necessary substance from which I might have formed an opinion; partly also because Melanie found my sponge-like approach to listening irresistible and I, in turn, felt constantly intoxicated by the trust showered upon me.

It did not seem an important thing to mention at the time, but the day after beginning the discourse and adventure which you read here, I had an evening out with Melanie. I began the evening feeling unusually preoccupied by my own concerns – still living with someone else's grief – and wondered whether the night would go well. Melanie too was on edge, as she had been when we had last spoken on the telephone to make our arrangements. We exchanged Christmas presents. Melanie was embarrassed and apologetic about how little thought she had given to the task. She was not relaxing at all. I was beginning to wonder if she had returned to that confused state which her sister's death had precipitated. She chose not to sit beside me or near me, but to kneel on the floor some distance away.

Then, after twenty minutes, she cracked and intimated the nature of her trouble: a new man in her life. I had to guess his identity; it was too hard for her to admit. I guessed first time.

It was very complicated. Melanie worked in the same organisation as I, but in a different city. She worked with the husband of a woman who worked, coincidentally, in the same office as I. Quite some time ago, Melanie had been a guest at this man's pre-wedding stag night. She later told me that the two of them had talked at length at the end of that evening. Shortly after his marriage, he had made his attraction for Melanie clear. Melanie had told me that she was keeping a cautious distance, but it was apparent that she felt a strong attraction for him physically and would defend any adverse suggestions about his character.

Melanie would normally have gone with me to the party I had attended the week before – the one I attended with Irene – but there was a clash of functions and she chose to go elsewhere. A couple of days later, I overheard my colleague complaining that her husband had not returned home at all on that particular night. I heard her relating the excuse he had offered; it did not sound convincing. A suspicion was posted in the back of my mind. Melanie's demeanour at our meeting took any remaining guesswork away.

He had sworn Melanie to secrecy; she lasted twenty minutes, then talked about nothing else for the remainder of the evening. We were both exceptionally relaxed and happy together at the end of that night. Melanie had bought the latest Christmas novelty record. We sprawled across the sofa, arm in arm, swinging our heads from side to side, and we sang that song together five times over. What a strange way for a friendship to end.

In the early days of January, a friend of my colleague casually remarked one morning that she'd had very little sleep, having been disturbed by a phone call in the middle of the night. My colleague was not at work. I guessed that the news was out. There followed a couple of short, cryptic conversations with Melanie as she tried to keep track of developments, and then nothing. I was happy to give her some space; telephone conversations at work would be awkward, to say the least, for the time being.

This morning I was not at work, so I decided to give her a call and see how things were. Melanie was flustered, said she couldn't talk and would ring me back later. When she did ring back, she was still flustered. She told me that when she and Paul had finally got together, wanting complete honesty with each other, they had a real 'heart to heart' about all their past misdemeanours. Our early times together had naturally counted as one for Melanie, but she said she had told Paul what a good friend I had been to her, that she could not have wished for better. Nevertheless Paul had said that he would not be comfortable with us continuing to see each other, and Melanie had agreed that we should not.

'We really love each other,' she said. 'I have to give our relationship the best chance I can.'

I agreed. There was a short but awkward pause, then, 'Just because we can't see each other or talk doesn't mean we can't still be friends.'

'No,' I agreed, but a little too quietly.

'John, it is really hard for me to say this, you know.'

'It's hard for me to listen.'

I realised why she hadn't been in touch: she had been putting off this dreadful moment for as long as she could.

'Oh, somebody has come into the room,' Melanie said. 'I'll have to go; they need to use the phone.'

I could hear some noise in the background. Somebody obviously had come in, but whether that person did need to use the phone or whether Melanie simply couldn't stand the tension any longer, I am not sure. We said a hurried goodbye, and that was that.

*The Celestine Prophecy* was right: people really don't know where love comes from. They really do treat it as some kind of finite resource and try to hang on to, manipulate and monopolise every little bit that comes their way. That was how I was feeling about Paul's block on our friendship, and maybe Melanie thought too that she had to draw in all her attention for the one man. Who am I to say she is wrong?

I loved Melanie less than perfectly, but I did love her. Through the filters and blocks of our personal weaknesses, somehow love still managed to flow, and did not flow in vain. As for my weaknesses, they would be stumbling blocks only if I stumbled now and did not learn. Neither do I believe that love could just evaporate for either of us. But now there is only one loving thing to do, to accept her wish and disappear quietly from her life.

Since that conversation with Kim about the nature of the soul, I have wondered about the better perspective, the better attitude to have on life. Is the soul's habitation of the body some kind of test to prove us fit for the afterlife, as some religious teachers would have us think? Or do our souls choose to manifest themselves in this human form because there are certain things that can only be developed through the physical, emotional, interdependent state of being human? If so, then I am here as much for today's lesson as for any other. The lesson I am trying to learn is not to mourn for the loss of Melanie's company – for this can only be a future loss, even though I feel it now – but to cherish the many qualities she brought to my life and which can never be lost.

Then after all the thinking, feeling and reframing … emptiness.

As I explore that region again, something has changed since my last visit. There is more to emptiness than I have previously understood. Or should I say less?

Master Fwap – the saffron-robed sage of *Surfing the Himalayas* – spoke of the 'emptiness' of snow and of the need to empty the mind. That Hindu book – the one I browsed through and didn't buy – spoke of the empty space between breaths, and more than anything else that idea confused and stuck with me. The *Tao Te Ching* says 'Tao is like an empty space that can never be filled up, yet it contains everything.' Then again it says 'Emptiness is eternal. The mother of all life.' It is as if emptiness is just the closest English word for a concept – a way of experiencing – which has no English word to describe it. There is something fundamentally important here, but I am not quite grasping it.

As I approach the threshold of that truth which connects all things, my failings and inspirations are shown to me in equal measure, served up for my choosing. It is not in ignorance of sadness that I choose inspiration, for sadness is but a part of that which inspiration makes whole.

As for groups, and that instinctive antipathy which so disturbs me, perhaps I make so much of my independence because the line between dependence and interdependence is so fine. If I cannot easily detect this line, I still have work to do alone.

## Pictures of pain

There is no need to hold on to pain. As an emotion it is as valid as any other, but that is no reason to hold on to it. The whole purpose of emotion, as its name suggests, is that it should flow and be gone; the feeling is the healing.

Water will flow easily through a pipe that is not obstructed. There will be no pressure, just a steady flow. As soon as we pinch the end of that pipe, however, there is a build-up of pressure and the water starts to spit and gush through any remaining gap. In the same way, if we were perfectly open, emotion would flow easily through us without any crisis. But our learning process is complex and haphazard, and emotion does not always find a straightforward outlet. Instead, it finds the many 'pinch-points' in our perception.

When we feel the pressure of strong emotion, we can be sure that one of these pinch-points has been encountered. Letting the feeling flow, staying with it, helps us to identify the source of that pressure, the flawed perception underlying our discomfort. Letting that feeling flow until it finds its own equilibrium helps our perception to open out naturally. This more rounded viewpoint will ensure that any similar event will not bring the same problem back.

That is the ideal and, of course, it is so rarely followed. When our pinch-points are challenged by strong emotion, our instinctive reaction is, more often, to pinch harder still against this unwelcome force for change. There are, I think, two fundamental attitudes underlying this reaction, and I have been guilty of both.

The first attitude says: this pain is bigger than me. Many of my images of emotional pain have had at their heart this idea, that the pain was bigger than me or beyond my power to control in all circumstances. I saw it as an incoming tide, feeling brave to be standing strong against it, but knowing all the while that there would be one wave big enough to bowl me over, disorientate and frighten me into not knowing which way was up or whether I could find it again. I saw pain as a wall so big that there was no way around, it or over it, or through it. And I satisfied myself for most of the time that I didn't have to look at it, but that was only for most of the time. I saw pain as a wound that never healed, and as a hole so black and so deep that nobody could hear my cry from there or ever reach me. No sooner had I exhausted one aspect of my pain than I discovered another, and all of them reinforcing that one idea: that the pain was bigger than me.

The second attitude is more insidious still; it says: this pain *is* me. This attitude turns a moment of history into a defining event and, like a boulder thrown into a lake, it sends its ripples of reinterpretation both back into the past and forward into the future. The great seduction which persuades the victim to embrace his or her lot is this thought: the person I am may be full of pain, but at least now I know who I am. Then it becomes a most difficult thing to free oneself from pain because to do so would take away that self-definition and leave nothing.

Some time ago, before all this began, Kate wrote to me of her wish to return to the scene of the accident which had taken her family away. I wrote back late in the evening, speaking of a similar desire to return to the place to which I had been taken as a child, except that this was impossible: the derelict building had long since been demolished and the area redeveloped. At 5 a.m., I awoke with the clear realisation that this was another picture of my pain. I was still there in that room, still a child, still naked and shivering. Though the police had burst in and carried my body to safety, some part of me had never moved from that scene. Perhaps that was why I first reacted – and still reacted when confronted by this memory – with the understanding of an adult but the emotions of a child.

As I worked out all the ramifications of that picture, I resolved that it was time to change the scene. Looking on at myself as that shivering child, I walked into the scene as the fully grown adult I now was, gently picked up the child and carried him out of the room in my arms, reassuring him that he was now safe and that everything would be fine. As often as my mind returned to that scene, I would play out this re-enactment until this picture, this script, was changed for good.

Maybe I didn't walk in and change the past, or even my memory of it. It might be more accurate to say that I changed the natural sequence of associations which proceeded from that memory. Instead of triggering painful associations, I was now triggering a powerful affirmation of my own security. I stopped being the victim I had set myself up to be.

The moral, I discovered, was not to be seduced by that perverse elation which came from finding an articulate expression of pain, a perfect little metaphor, because my work was only half-done. By finding expression, I hadn't found truth; I had merely uncovered the state of my own belief about the truth. The fact that this belief left me in pain – reinforcing an impression of objective substance in the pain, and disempowering me in the process – was as clear a signal as I could have wished that my belief was distorted. I learned to work with all those eloquent images of my distorted beliefs and replace them with images that worked better, that allowed me to work better.

When I hit my 'wall of pain' at the age of thirty, I had lived with a gnawing sense of emptiness inside for most of the adult years which had preceded it. It was easy to identify with the pain: of course it had been there beneath the surface all along, no wonder I had felt that way, no wonder I had felt like a stranger in a strange land. So went my reasoning. I gave that emotional gap both history and power, then tried to fill it with friendships the like of which I had never previously had. And it had always astonished me to find that no amount of friendship could fill this hole. I didn't stop to think that this insatiability was a quality of my own conjuring. In fact the realisation that no amount of close friendship or family bonding was going to take this loneliness away only served to depress me. My belief – which I see now was distorted – seemed at every turn to be confirmed by experience. I learned only later that belief – any belief – has a self-fulfilling quality which gives the appearance of truth.

After several months of working with a proactive frame of mind it finally occurred to me that my lifelong loneliness was just another unhelpful attitude to be dealt with and consigned to history. I decided to say to myself whenever this feeling arose, 'I am surrounded by people who love and care for me dearly.' To reinforce this in my inner landscape, every morning as I stepped from the shower in my House on the Right Bank, I would walk into a great courtyard where I could meet and warmly hug any family member or friend who came to mind at that time.

The effect was not gradual. It was instantaneous! I have never felt the same loneliness since making that simple decision. I marvel now at the years of clinging to, nurturing, identifying and identifying with my pain. It is tempting to call them wasted years, but the force of the lessons which finally came did them an eventual justice, and I know that it was a learning process which brought many other valuable lessons along the way.

For all that, as I said in the beginning, there is no point in holding on to pain for a moment longer than necessary. There is always a lesson to be learned, a new perspective to be gained, but then the only sensible thing is to move on.

Thinking back over that learning process, I realise that my little black book was based on a misconception. I had sought to trap my lessons like so many wild horses in a kind of word corral so that they might never escape once caught. I am beginning to see now that I have not lost anything, but that my learning process is more like an upward spiral than a straight path, and on this spiral I am continually meeting and appreciating old lessons from a new perspective, a new level.

I do not intend to abandon my little black book. Like so many twists and turns in the course of one's life, it does not have the value expected and intended, but rather something better.

## 14 March 1996

The changes I make to my life are mostly on the inside and therefore difficult for people to see. The changes to my friends' lives happen on the outside. To them I might seem like one of the few constants in a constantly shifting world. I have had no change of job, nor suffered any upheaval of personal circumstances for as long as they have ever known me.

Heather – the friend I had 'released' at the end of last year – was away from work for some days before I learned of the fact. There was nothing unusual in that delay, but I discovered she was ill – in a state of depression – and that put me in a dilemma. Were we friends? I had never worked out what, if anything, had stopped our being so. I only knew that we now kept our distance and seemed more comfortable with this arrangement for the time being. It was conceivable that I would be the last person she would wish to hear from. I prevaricated for a day and then decided to telephone.

During early morning exercise, as I rehearsed the day ahead, I had imagined us speaking well together. I had not tried to work out what might be said. When the time came for real, I chose a fortuitous moment. Heather had not been answering calls; she had been leaving that task to the answering machine. On this occasion she had decided to pick up the phone. She said she had no idea why.

Her tone was warm and, hearing her, the hesitation drained from my voice and I too reached into the well of warmth which I had never stopped feeling for her. It was like no misunderstanding had passed between us, and yet something had kept us at arm's length for more than a year.

Heather was depressed – that much was plain. She told me that I was the first person from work to have called. I was horrified but emboldened to arrange a visit, fending off her objections that she would not be good company, did not look her best and wasn't worthy of the trouble.

On a warm March morning I drove to her house, and she opened the door in a fragile way. She wore a plain black dress and her long black hair hung loose across her shoulders. I was reminded of that dream again: the Native American woman. I knew why I had pulled away from that unsettling attraction.

As we talked, the heavy warmth of sunlight through the window was a distraction to which Heather seemed immune. I had to redouble my concentration to listen as she talked. Her mother's recent stroke, a minor car accident, the pressure of work and an illness which was causing persistent abdominal pain, all of these had taken their toll on Heather's view of life which could be pessimistic at the best of times.

In the early days of our friendship I had marvelled at her ability to read any compliment as just the opposite. My initial thought was, 'Oh! This is a flirting game. She pretends to feel insulted and I have to make it up to her by finding an even bigger compliment. I don't want to get into that!'

But I was wrong. Insults and put-downs were quite genuinely what she heard. I never managed to find a single thing to say which she couldn't turn around in this way. Heather's intellect was far beyond mine, and she used it to such devastating, debilitating effect against herself. Were her feelings toward present misfortunes a natural working out of her own world view? It wasn't worth thinking about; I could never have made such a suggestion to her. As the conversation eased I ventured a question.

'What happened to us, Heather? Why have we been so distant?'

'I thought it was what you wanted.'

'What I wanted? I thought it was what you wanted.'

I said this without defensiveness. We looked at each other, surprised and puzzled.

Back in May of the year just gone, we had sat together discussing our behaviour of the previous months. I thought I had been a little distant and preoccupied at times, but this had been overtaken by a definite stand-off on Heather's part. At least that was how I had seen it. Sitting together now, I told Heather how I had understood our discussion of May, and the 'agreement' we had reached.

'Heather, you told me that Ayeesha's involvement with me had upset you, and that you didn't like how you had felt about it. You said you had to back away and that you felt better in yourself to have more distance between us. We said we might have lunch if we were out of the office together, just as any colleagues would, but it was best to keep it at that. So that's what I've been doing; it was what you wanted.'

'But I thought it was what you wanted.'

Heather was looking bemused. It was dawning on both of us that we had completely misunderstood each other's wishes. I still can't quite understand how it happened. We were both trying so hard to understand, and not to betray any feeling that might make the other's position more difficult. I thought I was acquiescing to Heather's wish; she thought she was acquiescing to mine.

I had always thought that two completely selfish people are never likely to understand each other. It had never occurred to me until then that two people trying to be completely unselfish might have the same problem. It was a reminder, if I needed it, that losing my ego was not the same as self-effacement; it was not that simple.

I suggested a walk. Heather agreed. But as we stepped out into the bright afternoon sunlight, we could have been walking in parallel through entirely different worlds. When a magpie wheeled around the castle ruins near her home, it had seemed to me a delightful sight, marking the end of winter and the coming of spring. I raised an arm and casually pointed in its general direction.

'Oh, no! A single magpie!' Heather said. There was a tremor and a dark resignation in her voice. I didn't understand and she had to remind me of the children's nursery rhyme: one for sorrow. She said that was because magpies remained true to their mate throughout their lives; if a mate died, the survivor remained alone.

'Oh, well,' I said, breezily. 'His mate is probably just out of sight somewhere.'

Moments later, a whole troop of magpies came swooping across, more than the nursery rhyme could account for.

'Now what's that supposed to mean?' I teased. Heather was not reassured.

We sat on the remains of the castle wall, looking down at trees dividing the fields below. I was still feeling very bright in spirit. I asked Heather which of the trees was her favourite.

'They look spooky.'

'Well, they could look like that on a dark night, I suppose.'

But it was the dark night of Heather's soul, and I could remember times when I had found landscapes, and the birds that lived in them, similarly threatening. If Heather had felt stronger for having some distance from me, I realised that I too had needed to protect my changing but tentative attitudes from these regular swathes of despondency.

As we walked down through the fields, Heather spoke softly, that same uncertain tremble in her voice.

'You can hold my hand if you want,' she said, 'but you don't have to.'

'I would love to;' – my hand reached for hers – 'I just wasn't sure how you would feel.' Heather's hand was cool – it was always cool, as mine to her must always have felt warm.

We were friends again.

There were changes too in the lives of Ayeesha and Irene. Ayeesha returned to my office after several months of working away.

She was unsettled, restless and dissatisfied. I was really too busy to ask, but midway through the afternoon I asked anyway and for over an hour she fired off rapid bursts of frustration about her job, her prospects, work in general, marriage, family and future. Ayeesha had the intelligence, the wit and the vision to get anything she wanted. That was half the problem: there was nothing she wanted enough to justify the effort. The best she could imagine was to roam around the world rubbing shoulders with the rich and famous, dipping into any project that took her fancy, working and being paid well, but having no obligations to tie her to any particular place or person.

She was just letting off a whole lot of steam. It reminded me of a verse from the *Tao Te Ching*: 'He whose desires are few, fulfils them; he whose desires are many, goes astray.' But Ayeesha was young; she had some leeway. Given the technique to achieve my own goals, I had initially set my sights on a lot of things, but found that I was unable to maintain the desire. As I read into things now, and get introduced to new ideas, I have been tempted to set new goals at every turn, but I have felt that the time for my leeway is past. I need focus.

For Irene things were very different. Her husband had announced one evening that he had begun an affair with a work colleague, one previously introduced as a friend. At the same time, he had assured Irene of his undying love for her and had said that he would never leave her and the children. Irene accepted the situation; she valued honesty more than fidelity. One week later, he told her that he was moving out. He could no longer bear to be without his new love. So much for honesty.

It was difficult to tell whether Irene wanted to stop this change or welcome it. In the telephone calls and evenings we shared after the breaking of this news, Irene swung wildly between two poles. Sometimes she was elated, filled with a sense of liberation. She could see everything that was wrong in her marriage, things that had always been wrong, pressures she could not fully see until she was suddenly released. She was excited too by the possibilities instantly opened up for a new lifestyle and new relationships. Then, with great alacrity, fear and self-doubt would overcome her. She would weep tears of bitterness, anger, frustration and anxiety. Between both extremes, she would steel herself with a will to protect her boys at all costs. Irene was like someone suddenly pushed down a steep slope: she stretched for each different attitude as if it were a foothold promising to break her fall, but she could not maintain her purchase for anything more than the briefest moment.

These friends did not see change in me at this time. Maybe Heather saw it beginning last year, but the little I could tell her now would just be talk and would not seem real. For Ayeesha it would all seem too slow, too hidden to take account of. It was not appropriate to tell Irene at all. Her peremptory challenges to my life decisions had ceased temporarily; I wasn't rushing to revive them.

But changes were happening for all that. At the beginning of March I wrote down a dream. It was the first positive thing I had written for more than a week. This fact alarmed me. All that time justifying my antipathy to groups, resisting directions suggested by others, I had lost momentum. I was closed off, no longer tuned in; my control drama got in the way, just as *The Celestine Prophecy* said it would.

In the dream, I was walking in the Austrian mountains with my family. As we walked up the snowy slopes between the pines, I began to see energy fields around the pines. At first it was just a glimpse, then a clear view of white light around them. Then I began to see flowing colours. I gazed in amazement, so happy that it had happened at last.

Five days later, I was sitting in a long queue of parents waiting to see one of Hayley's teachers. Resigned to a long wait, I closed my eyes and took a walk through my internal landscape, letting my energy build. I had eaten only lightly during the day and felt good. As I opened my eyes I looked up towards the stage where two people were seated at a desk, a black curtain framing them as they talked to another teacher. The instant I looked at them, I could see a milky white aura around each of their heads, elongated and joined together in the black space between them. I looked away, a little sceptical, but when I looked back it was still there. Then we were called forward by the teacher, I moved and the spell was broken.

In the small hours of the following morning, I tried to marshal my impressions into an understanding. When words didn't come, I drew a diagram: infinity spreading in two directions, separated – or connected – by a most delicate diaphragm, human consciousness. I was aware that my mind was returning to that old spiritual vision, like so much unfinished business. As sublime as it was, I had not been able to maintain that sense of peace. Worse, I had descended into an aimless sense of dread. Perhaps I was not emotionally ready for such a level of truth. Shocked by the severity of that roller-coaster ride between extremes, I feared for a long time the consequences of resuming any spiritual search. I learned to put away such large ideas and to accept myself as a smaller man, living a smaller life.

Ten years on, I thought I had resolved it. I had re-evaluated my perspective, reached a new and better understanding. But ten years further still, I find myself dealing with the same unfinished business and, as I have discovered, the same sense of foreboding.

A few nights ago, I spent the evening with Irene. Our recent meetings had been volatile and often tearful. I listened passively while Irene ranged from moodiness to calm, decision to indecision. This night seemed more even; I didn't think Irene was over the emotional turmoil, but she was at least experiencing a temporary respite. We drove home over dark moorland roads and Irene turned her attention to me. This was something I had been spared in recent meetings. At her prompting, I began to tell her of my recent ideas, my first efforts in meditation, and that I thought I would have to rise earlier to make more time for this.

I did not treat it as a serious discussion in the circumstances. I was making light of it, and expecting light-hearted banter in return. But Irene confronted me with unexpected intensity.

'Why are you always so controlled?' she said. I stared at the road ahead, taken aback by the impatience in her tone.

'Come on,' – a dig on the forearm – 'why do you control yourself so much? What is it? Why are you doing all these things?'

I suddenly felt confused. I didn't have an answer.

'I'm not controlling myself,' I said, rather lamely. I drove on through the darkness, but Irene was in no mood to be fobbed off so easily. Her interrogation continued and my head began to swim. I wanted to stop the car and talk, but at the same time I didn't want to stop – something seemed wrong. A lay-by appeared on my left. I pulled in, took off my seat belt, hung my head and stared at the dim interior of the car.

'Why are you so controlled?' Irene's voice was softer.

My eyes moved aimlessly, reflecting some internal search. Irene wouldn't have seen this or deciphered its meaning, but she remained silent, expectant, patient. After some time spent in silence, she placed her hand on my forearm and gave it a gentle nudge.

'I have to be this way,' I said finally. 'The alternative is worse.'

'What do you mean? What is the alternative?' In Irene's tone, I could still detect a readiness to challenge. I stiffened my own tone defensively and was aware of a quickening in my breath.

'Blackness,' I said, turning my head towards her, but staring resolutely down into her lap. 'Blackness and despair.'

Finally I looked at her. 'You don't have to live my life, Irene, but if you did, you would know why I am as I am.'

Even now I don't know if that was a true answer or some peculiar sparring position I was taking in my own confused defence. Irene held my head tightly to her chest for a long time. I began to feel that the whole episode was an expression of her need, more so than my own. She had grown tired of my detached reserve. She had wanted honesty, passion, maybe even to fight, then finally to comfort and to be comforted, but my own confusion had not been alleviated by letting myself be hugged in the darkness, and it has not left me since.

When I wrote to Kate about recent events, and even more when I was trying to explain myself to Irene, I had the uncomfortable feeling of being like a cartoon character who has run off the edge of a cliff; he carries on running, not realising that the ground has fallen away beneath his feet. I saw a choice: I could retreat in fear for my own sanity, or treat this nerviness as evidence that I had broken through my old comfort zone. All my friends had passed this threshold in some way but, of all of them, Irene's reaction had left me disconcerted.

The following night, I consulted the Chinese book of changes, the *I Ching*. There had been a gap of twenty years since I had done such a thing. At one time the principle made sense. Then it made no sense at all. It was one of those things I had put away. Now it seemed to make a kind of sense again, as if there was a perfect architecture to the universe at any given time. Maybe my spiral of understanding was meeting this notion at a new level, or maybe I was just in need of a break from my bewilderment. Whatever. I thought of my situation with Irene and threw down the coins six times to create a hexagram. I received the following judgement:

THE WELL

The town may be changed,
But the well cannot be changed.
It neither decreases nor increases.
They come and go and draw from the well.

> If one gets down almost to the water
> And the rope does not go all the way,
> Or the jug breaks, it brings misfortune.

What Irene needed from me had changed; what I had to give had not changed.

When I contemplated the image of the well, it seemed like a very elegant representation of love. We all have a pail from which people will drink from time to time. We need never fear that this pail will become exhausted, because the rope to which it is fastened will help it always to reach into that deeper place, the wellspring which, as Jesus said, will never run dry.

The well is ours to do with what we will, but the wellspring is not ours. If, in a fit of passion or compassion, we are moved to give away the pail, trying to give all that we have to give, what have we really given? What we really have to give is infinite, but it requires us to be anchored resolutely to the source of that giving.

# 31 March 1996

I am no different to anyone else in changing constantly what I ask of life and of others; I am just another of those town folk coming to the well with new demands. One evening recently I was feeling playful, but Julie reacted with unexpected harshness towards my sexual frivolity. She was wrapped up in worries about work; I had been insensitive. I skulked off to do other things and maintain a discreet distance. It made me think about the assumptions I made in our relationship. Though I wondered at others failing to notice change in me, I was making the same mistake moment by moment as I lazily allowed history and habit to determine my perception. It was a failure of flexibility.

I guessed that Julie had been thinking too. When I walked into the bedroom later, she was reading my little black book of thoughts. I didn't disturb her. She finished reading and quietly replaced the book before climbing into bed. Neither one of us mentioned these things before we turned to sleep.

The following evening we were back to normal, so I asked why she had been reading. She said she believed she had hurt me, and wondered if I had written anything in my book about it, but I hadn't. In fact she had read it too early, but having found nothing, she had continued to read out of a more general curiosity. Although I leave the book around for anyone to see and make no secret of its contents, this is not a thing that Julie would usually do.

I asked if it felt strange to be reading through my thoughts in that way. She said no, it felt sad. When I asked why, she said, 'Because you are so isolated. Because there is no one in the world who is right for you.'

This was a startling conclusion, but it was no different to the way Irene had reacted. I had forgotten about this until Julie spoke, but when I had been telling her my thoughts, Irene had asked very insistently why I bothered with her as a friend. What, she asked, could I possibly get out of our friendship? It was just another thing I had no answer for at the time. The only answer I could find afterwards was that I was not looking for someone like me, or even someone with similar characteristics or thoughts, but I don't think this would have satisfied Irene or convinced Julie that I was not so alone as it seemed.

Maybe relationships work because, however different we are, we are still able to tune into the same wavelength for a lot of the time. Julie, Irene, all my friends do this a lot of the time without even thinking about it. Then sometimes they can't quite manage it, or even imagine it, and I start to look like nothing on earth to them. It's just another failure of flexibility, a mistake that it takes two to make but only one to solve.

Not long after our sexual friction, Julie turned the tables on me. She was the one feeling playful. I was not averse to sex, but all this talk about isolation had put me in need of tenderness. Our wavelengths were mismatched and it wasn't going to work. I decided that some flexibility was called for. I had been reading about neuro-linguistic programming and had been learning to play with my internal representation of things. This was a good time to try. I slipped quietly inside, imagining tenderness and warmth, allowing myself the enjoyment and arousal of sex in the way I wanted it. Then, in the way I had learned, I superimposed images of playful sex but letting the feeling of tenderness remain. Suddenly I no longer felt a problem; I could see that the tenderness had been there all along, underlying the superficial physical expression of our sexuality. I was back and on the right wavelength. It wasn't a matter of subordinating my own desires; we both had fun. There is a lot to be said for flexibility, and no point getting too upset when it doesn't happen.

Anya, even at a distance, apparently had no difficulty tuning in. She helped me again by sending a book called *Hands of Light* by Barbara Brennan. The book contains diagrams of energy fields, different colours and different levels. It also explains and illustrates the chakras. Looking at these diagrams, I realised that I had been seeing more than I thought. Some things I had dismissed as optical illusions were illustrated in the book: a band of light surrounding the body but separated from it by a narrow, darker layer. I had seen this as a blackness between the body and its aura. My children decided that my entertaining of such a book was a clear sign of impending madness.

In her letter, Anya said that she was stuck. She had lost her sense of direction, things didn't seem to be working out as she wished, and she lacked the energy and willpower to meditate regularly, even though she knew the benefits this would bring. She asked me to send her willpower and encouragement by 'wireless cosmic channels'. I had no idea how to do this, but decided to try. After all, it was the sense that something more was possible that led me to begin this search. Nothing was ever gained by minds and actions closed to possibility.

Helen told me that as part of her aromatherapy training she was taught that it is not possible to mix base and essential oils together to use on oneself; it would not have the desired effect. Her class conducted an experiment in which five people mixed the same oils. The five mixtures all had distinctively different fragrances. Something had passed into the mixture from the person who mixed it. I marvelled at how this could be with little or no physical contact, and how the wisdom of interdependence seemed to filter into every level of existence.

When Helen contacted me next, it was with great excitement. I knew she had been holidaying in Portugal, staying with a friend who is working there. She rang soon after her return and, without any introduction, simply said, 'I've got it!'

'Got what?' I inquired. I couldn't imagine.

'Spiritual enlightenment,' she replied with great certainty. 'I've worked it all out, it all makes sense, and everything's wonderful.'

A couple of days later, we met for lunch. She told me how she had taken *The Celestine Prophecy* with her to Portugal. She had spent her days reading, resting and contemplating. Her evenings had been full of convivial company and conversation. Her nights had been short on sleep and filled with excitable thoughts. One morning, she said, she woke up and it all made sense, everything came together, and she hadn't looked back since.

I had waited for her in the busy town centre, gazing ahead and trying to let my senses open up to everything around, catching different smells and sounds. I was trying to develop a 'higher sense perception' – an exercise suggested in Barbara Brennan's book. Helen had sidled up very quietly, hoping to catch an instant reaction from me. Her hair, previously dark, was a shock of bleached blonde; her clothes had changed to suit. I looked suitably surprised and made her laugh.

These were not the only changes. Money saved for a house extension had been spent on a new car; it was a gesture of faith in the 'abundance of the universe'. Helen was also questioning her marriage. She could see where it had been wrong, and had returned from holiday radiant with a new self-reliance. Her husband (also called John) had responded by finding her wildly attractive, as if for the first time.

As we talked, sharing plans, readings and passions, we were whipping each other round in a whirl of excitement and energy. Then, suddenly, Helen lost it. A look of tired depression fell across her features, draining the glow from her eyes and the spark from her voice. It was palpable. My enthusiasm was instantly stilled.

'Are you okay?'

'I'm just tired,' she said. 'I stretch myself too much. Sometimes I just need to slow down, conserve my energy.'

We paused. There was a hubbub all around, but Helen was lost in her thoughts, or maybe just lost in her state; I surveyed her features keenly but discreetly, I hoped.

'You know, when we met last time,' I said, 'something strange happened as I was driving away. I had a kind of vision. It was a vision of you and I working together.' I proceeded to describe what I had seen and the doubt that had stopped me from mentioning it any earlier.

As I was speaking, Helen's spirit seemed to lift.

'I saw the same thing,' she said with amazement. 'I didn't tell you because I didn't want you to think I was encroaching on your work.'

'That's fantastic!' I replied.

Helen found a fresh reserve of energy, which lasted for the remainder of our time together. We shared an awkward hug in the busy street, and I drove away with my mind in a dance. I flicked across the radio bands. On Radio 4 there was a discussion about a composer. A comparison was being made between two renderings of a symphony. I just caught a snatch of the discussion, not enough to know what it was all about, then the music began: rising horns over a roll of drums, giving way to a woodwind phrase, echoed and expanded by other instruments until the timpani rolled again, lifting the whole orchestra towards a loud brass crescendo. My head was filled, and a voice inside was crying with the exquisite sense of space: 'I don't know what I should write, or how it might be pictured, but it must have this space!' is what the voice was crying.

The music faded – only a fragment was to be played – and the announcer said, 'Sibelius's Symphony number 5 in E flat major, Opus 82.'

'82! That's Helen!' I exclaimed, finding coincidence upon coincidence.

It would take too long to explain, but some years earlier I had learned a memory system in which numbers were made more meaningful by substituting people, a hundred in all, from zero to 99. The number 82 and Helen had been connected in my mind ever since.

Helen and Anya reached a certain wavelength in me, for the time being. Others connected at different levels. I didn't know if the 'aloneness' that Julie saw could be measured or should be judged in this way. It seemed more fitting to ask how I might better and more often reach the wavelengths of others. But, frankly, the whole thought process began to feel tortuous, and I dropped it without resolution in the face of a new imperative.

My dad's radiotherapy treatment had come to an end but his mental struggle had not ended. The treatment had left his legs both sore and painfully swollen. Walking was restricted to frequent shuffles from front room to back room, then back to his chair piled with pillows for support. Somewhere inside a part of him wanted to rise to this battle, and part of him didn't.

A couple of years ago, we holidayed together. I was struggling over which direction I should take at work. My dad watched my deliberation with the kind of anguish that I thought should be reserved for a father watching a little boy. Although all six of his children had grown, he had never entirely relinquished his emotional involvement in our day-to-day wellbeing. That summer he watched me for the slightest sign of decision. Cautiously he probed my thoughts every couple of days to find some progression. I tried to share with him the ideas which hadn't fully materialised. Whichever way he sensed my thoughts moving, he would immediately leap to endorse my anticipated decision, brimming with comments complementary, as he imagined, to my own chosen attitude. In this way, in a matter of days he managed wholeheartedly to adopt quite opposite viewpoints for my benefit.

It did not make my task easier. In truth, I was not trying to take a logical thought path through to an inevitable decision; I was trying to acknowledge my thoughts in order to discount them and, in this way, reach some neutral ground from which a gut reaction would tell me which way to go. But for all that, I could not fault my dad's adaptability.

He told me for the first time that summer of his fear of cancer. The dark growth on his leg would not emerge for another year, but he feared what was in his stomach. It was not fat. Everyone called it fat and cajoled him into various slimming campaigns. He knew it was not fat. I should have known too; his skin was tight and hard like a medicine ball. Fat didn't sit like that, but for all those years I had assumed it was some kind of fat peculiar to him, while my Dad harboured the fear that it was a cancer growing inside of him. And yet he never once sought the opinion of a doctor. He didn't want to know the answer. That was the kind of fear he was dealing with: a fear that, even if he knew, there would be nothing he could do, so it would be better not to know at all.

And that was the fear I saw him wrestling with now. I wanted to remind him of better attitudes he had shown in other circumstances, like when he lost his arm; never once had I known him look with defeat upon that fact, or even count it as a loss.

I was glad I hadn't said anything. When I thought about it later, that lost arm was just the point in my dad's eyes. Shortly after his cancer operation, he said he wished that his leg had been amputated. It sounded like the extreme solution of a depressed mind and we all ignored it or criticised it, while simultaneously praising his visits to anyone with a newly amputated limb, showing them cause for hope and encouragement. We didn't see any contradiction in our viewpoint. After all, the nurses were taking the same view. It

86

was my dad who was showing the contradiction, not us. But I began to think maybe we just didn't look hard enough to find the consistency.

My dad, I suspect, would still wish for that amputation. He wants a wheelchair. He doesn't want to deal with the attendant pains of trying to stay as 'whole' as possible. 'Whole' is a concept he doesn't share with the rest of us. We get frustrated. He gets frustrated by our frustration.

Jesus said, 'If thy right eye offend thee, pluck it out. If thy right hand offend thee, cut it off.' That always seemed a little extreme to me, but probably not to my dad.

In a lighter moment the other night, Julie and I tried an experiment together. It was designed to show that in a contest between imagination and will-power imagination would win every time. The test was to dangle a pendulum from a finger then, from a standing start, use will-power to hold it absolutely still, while simultaneously imagining that it was moving in a circular direction clockwise, then anti-clockwise, then back and forward, then side to side. When I did it, the pendulum moved all over the place; wherever I imagined it going, it went, with indecent haste. When Julie tried it, the pendulum remained rock steady, thus confirming in Julie's mind what she had long suspected: that she had no imagination. I am inclined to think that her imagination won out after all. What she imagined most strongly was that she had no imagination.

It is as if different levels of understanding live separate lives in each one of us. The failure of communication between these levels is probably at the root of every period of confusion I have ever experienced. By contrast, the experience of clarity has probably always been a sudden shift of perspective, from one level to another, by some means out of my direct control or intention.

One rainy day on the holiday I spent with my dad, we caught a train. I was the last to board. Absent-mindedly I pulled the door closed, not realising that my fingers were wrapped around the hinged side of the door sleeve. As the vice-like pressure ground into them, I instinctively pulled away with force. I was lucky; one finger suffered a deep gouge and the tearing of several layers of skin, the other fingers were untouched. There was a minute or two of sharp pain; I flapped my hand around with a wounded warrior-type of grimace on my face, while my dad looked on in frozen alarm; I think he was expecting a near-amputation.

Then came that curious warm, comfortable sensation in my finger, and a euphoria which I had experienced many times before. I sat down and opened up *Zen and the Art of Motorcycle Maintenance*, quietly resuming my reading – rereading to be more accurate; at difficult times I occasionally reverted to an old favourite as a way of reconnecting with inspiration. My dad sat opposite. I think he thought I was exercising some advanced form of mind control over my throbbing finger. It was that moment in the book where the writer, camping high in the mountains, finds himself face to face with a solitary mountain wolf, and a flash of recognition and acknowledgement passes between them.

And then it happened. In my mind I stared into the face of that mountain wolf and the same spark of recognition passed through me. I had reached my neutral ground. I had found my gut feeling. My way forward at work was clear: I had to walk away from the team I was being asked to lead, and plough a lone furrow for a while longer. These moments arrive when you least expect them. The jarring of my finger and the subsequent reverie distracted my rational thought processes just long enough for the truth to slip through.

I spent the rest of that journey with a sly smile fixed upon my lips. Lord knows what my dad was thinking.

## 20 April 1996

It puzzles me that I can write poetry with a sense of certainty normally reserved for rational thought, but having written it, my rational mind finds every cause to doubt. That was the feeling I had after writing these words:

> The flow of life surrounds you.
> It is the architect of every moment
> which holds out its hand to you, but never waits.
> You cannot force it, direct it or push against it,
> though you may try,
> as a reed tries to bend the sky.

Afterwards I sat and thought about this notion that pushing with your ego has no effect on the 'flow' of life. What was I trying to say? I had to accept that the human ego undoubtedly affects the shape of things and the nature of our interaction in this world. But then Jesus spoke so freely of the things of this world and the things not of this world, as if there were an unseen order untouched by even the most outrageous effort.

In Barbara Brennan's book, *Hands of Light*, she speaks of the etheric template level, energy lines forming a sparkling web of light beams surrounding the body. She says that with people and plants it is necessary for this energy to take shape in order to bring its physical counterpart into being. That isn't exactly how she puts it but I am mirroring the words of Napoleon Hill in *Think and Grow Rich*. He seemed to be saying the same thing, that for a physical state to be brought about there had first to be a change at an unseen level.

I wondered how I might enter a world not of this world, but I was also aware that I was pushing into my own confusion, my ego trying to force its way through and getting nowhere. It was probably true that I was trying to push into meditation – to 'understand' the process – but either the books I read and the people I listened to were contradicting each other, or I was finding contradiction through my own search for a rigid structure: maintaining a relaxed awareness, not sleeping or daydreaming, keeping one's focus as an observer of thoughts and feelings rising up, associating, disassociating, centring, aligning, reviewing. If one were to describe, in words, how to maintain a perfect balance while standing on a pin-head, I imagine the effort would be just as difficult as describing meditation, and just as fruitless.

I went with my sister Kim, one evening, to her meditation class. A respected lady of that particular movement had travelled from Australia to give a talk at many meditation centres throughout England. This was a rare opportunity for those within the movement; I was lucky to be invited along.

She was a calm lady. She said that meditation is 'using the power of thought in the direction of your choice', and that by using discipline to gather one's thoughts and allowing feelings to merge with them, thought becomes something more: it becomes experience. She said that meditation is not making the mind blank; one should let thoughts flow but at the same time to stand back, observe and direct. Meditation is, she said, 'the sublimation of the mind, not its suppression'.

Then she began a journey inside, her first thought being, 'I am a soul. I have a body. I am not a body, but I have a body.'

Then she asked, 'How do I look as a soul?' and she proceeded to describe how she visualised an infinitesimal point of bright light. I had heard Kim speak of this before.

'Where do I sit in the body?'

She asked this, then proceeded to describe a sparkling star in the centre of her forehead.

'It is at this point,' she said, 'that the inner journey begins, experiencing the qualities of the soul.' She moved stage by stage through the qualities of peace, love, power, energy and strength, truth, mercy, kindness, compassion and finally bliss. At each stage she painted pictures. For peace, a harmony in which all traits of the personality are at one with each other, she painted a calm lake without ripples, allowing us time to contemplate the scene and absorb its meaning.

And so it went on, until at last she asked, 'Where do I come from?' The journey lifted our souls upwards to the 'source', the home of silence.

To be aware of one's soul, its nature, its qualities and its origin is to be soul-conscious. It is Kim's goal, as she has told me, to achieve a constant state of soul-consciousness.

We were invited forward to take, from a small basket on the lady's knee, a morsel of an Indian sweet filled 'with the vibrations of love with which it was made.' As I took my piece I was surprised that the lady looked down in a most humble way, rather than making eye contact.

I wished I had gained more from the whole experience, but I had been distracted by the group. All my past efforts in meditation had been undertaken alone. Another thing was bothering me too. I raised it with Kim as soon as we were outside walking back to the car.

'Why should the soul be a point of light?' I asked. 'Why should the body not be a part of the soul?' I told her of the poem I had written about the body not being a cage for the soul, and how I had felt when writing it.

Kim did give me an answer. She was reiterating the things she had been told at her various meditation classes. I didn't take it on board. I was lost in my own wondering for what the answer could be.

Kim, I believed, was happy to be presented with a coherent explanation for the state of things. She would test each new piece of information against accepted principles. If agreement could be found, she would receive it as truth and move on. Perhaps her life view would be comprehensive enough to leave her contented for the rest of her days. For my part, it was not a matter of making sense of what I saw, but of challenging the very foundations of that perception. Kim could not take that journey with me.

I visited a local market town with Helen the following day. Helen was determined upon a particular shop which sold crystals and all manner of 'new age' paraphernalia. We arrived there only to find the shop closed for the day. Helen's spirit was high. She immediately started wondering why we were meant to be there; if it was not to enter that shop, there surely had to be an even better, if less obvious, purpose. She quizzed me on what I thought it might be. I accepted the principle, though I think my heart could hold it no higher than possibility, so I came up with no answer. I felt light and too detached from that kind of analysis.

We ate tuna sandwiches in a dark pub. A man at the bar was receiving a string of calls on his mobile. His girlfriend gazed about distractedly. Helen and I were sitting in an annexe; Helen had opened out some flower books on the table in front of us and was enthusing about Bach flower remedies and the ability of some people, apparently, to hold a hand over a flower extract and intuitively know what ills it might be used for. She talked of chance meetings with old acquaintances, and how the most amazing and frank exchanges had taken place when she introduced the subject of *The Celestine Prophecy*. So many people, it seemed, had read it, heard of it or were ready to be told. Helen's husband had read it too. It was also having a marked effect on him.

I wasn't doing all the listening. We talked about my experience of meditation so far. Gradually, our conversation opened out to past things. They were things we knew a little about in each other's lives – we had been there and seen them, but had never pried. As we ambled through cobbled streets, and then began the hour-long journey home, it began to feel right and comfortable to ask such questions, and to answer them.

Afterwards, I felt sure that there had been a purpose to our day together: that we had needed this time to work through the veneer of mutual interests and to reach a new level of friendship. Call it trust, sharing, I don't know, but something had developed for the better. As for the place we had chosen to visit, there was a different purpose to my being there.

Helen didn't know, when she suggested that town – and I didn't tell her – but I received her suggestion with a sense of resignation, a feeling that it was time to lay a certain ghost to rest. And as I had walked those streets, my mind had been quietly occupied in that task.

Almost exactly a year before, I had walked the same streets with Kate. It was the only day we ever spent together. Every kind of weather fell upon us, from sunshine to snow. We had to take care to avoid the busy time when taking lunch. Kate was still wary of crowded places. I had always thought that panic attacks were a solitary curse, but as we had reached the door of the small café, I had caught the hesitation in Kate's step and suggested we return later. Kate agreed; she didn't have to say why.

We talked of so many things, happy and sad. It was not the first time, in Kate and in others, I had noticed this ability to feel genuinely lucky and filled with hopelessness almost in the same instant, to see no future and to plan for the future, to love life and to crave death. It was as if two states had developed independently in one mind. But then I had probably done the same and worse in my own time.

I found myself telling her of my teenage years, a time I had never felt the need to speak of before, of the years when I had consciously divided my inner self into multiple personalities, each with its own name. I had found no integrity, and so embraced disintegration.

Why did I tell her such things? It was a strong and strange desire, not just to share trust, but to reveal all that I was and ever had been. Neither was it a matter of depth, for many of the lasting joys of that day came from the discovery of common delight in trivialities and humour.

As we drove away, Kate asked, 'Why do good things always have to end?'

'So that more good things can begin,' I said, and I genuinely believed it.

'And why do you have an answer for everything?' she teased, as quick as a flash.

I didn't have an answer for that.

My strength of feeling for Kate that day did not take me by surprise. But seeing an approaching wave does not necessarily stop you from being swept away, and I could have been, except for the sake of the very love I felt.

To love is to hold the heart open like a quivering hand on which a magnificent dove may rest, or from which it may fly at will. And to be open is to endure a yearning which is difficult to name as joy or pain.

Napoleon Hill says:

There should be no disappointment over love, and there would be none if people understood the difference between love and sex. The major difference is that love is spiritual, while sex is biological. No experience which touches the human heart with a spiritual force can possibly be harmful, except through ignorance or jealousy.

I never have regretted my strength of feeling for Kate. I described our first encounter as leaving me feeling lifted inside. If my years have, by degrees, enabled me to make the distinction of love as spiritual rather than biological, I credit my relationship with Kate and the circumstances of its development as the cause of a decisive shift in that direction. Even so, as I walked those streets once more, I was conscious of the need to let go of an emotional longing which fell somewhere between the biological and the spiritual, and which had run its useful course.

My feelings on the evening after that day with Helen were curious. I felt an excitement, a creative energy. I began to write poetry. All kinds of ideas were flowing. And when the flow had ceased, my energy was still brimming. I began to write a letter to Helen, copying out my poems between the prose, writing into the small hours.

At the same time, throughout all this excitement, I also felt ill at ease. It was bothering me that Helen was, on the whole, being greeted with such open acceptance, how she was making new friends at every turn, whilst I, in large part, had met with scepticism. It was not that I wanted the same. I was just puzzled by the difference. Another thing was the different directions we seemed to have taken from the same starting point. From *The Celestine Prophecy*, Helen had moved towards many emerging ideas about healing and the like. You might say she was wrapped up in the spirit of a new age. My instinct, in contrast, had catapulted me back into ancient wisdom. I was looking again for clues I might have missed.

None of this would have discomfited me. But I kept thinking of that mountain wolf. I kept seeing my path separating from friends and loved ones. I thought of my poor reaction to groups, even of the most benign sort. It was the feeling that some solitary task lay ahead of me. I wrote that I was pleased at the way in which our development was proceeding on different paths, and I was pleased that she had so many friends thinking on a similar wavelength, that it seemed to be the kind of nurturing and support she needed right now. I said that though my friends are wonderful, few of them seemed to have the faintest notion of where my thoughts were going, and that this must, I supposed, be right for me.

'I have this feeling,' I wrote, 'that the very deep sense of determination and ability to draw on my own resources even in times of great isolation, with which my past experience has equipped me, has not been without its purpose.'

I told her about the mountain wolf and how this image and all the feelings associated with it were returning strongly to my mind. Then I said that when I have this feeling, 'I am not steeling myself for any vicissitudes in the outer world. I know, on the contrary, that I am steeling myself for where my inner journey is bound to take me.'

This all sounded terribly grand and grim; I tried to wrap it up in a joke. It certainly crossed my mind that choosing to see things this way may well have pandered to my ego. The heroic gloss might also amount to self-protection; without it, I could feel isolated and dispirited. Look at it how I may, I could not shake off the feeling, and this was the best expression I could give to it at the time.

I pushed still deeper into confusion.

On 13 April, some answers began to come. When Anya sent me the *Hands of Light* book, she also sent a smaller book which she said had greatly helped her at the time of her husband's death. It was a brittle and yellowing paperback which had lost its cover. I had begun to read it and realised that it was the second in a series, so I decided to find the first of the series in order to begin at the beginning. There was a delay because the book had to be ordered for me, but I had finally received and begun to read *The Third Eye*, a ghost-written autobiography of a Tibetan monk called Lobsang Rampa.

In the book, Lobsang is told by his teacher that the aura which surrounds the body, and which anyone can be taught to see under suitable conditions, is merely a reflection of the Life Force burning within. He is told that this force is electric, the same as lightning.

I noted this down eagerly. Maybe this explained the notion of the soul as a point of light. If the aura is the soul's reflection, then the body, being the physical level of the aura, is part of this reflection. How far out did that aura extend? Did it ever end? How far in did the soul reach? Was it infinite, as I had once felt it to be?

Three days later I realised, for the first time, what on earth I had meant when I had written to Helen about that inner journey and where it was bound to take me. I was talking about death!

Death had concerned me in the beginning. Somehow I had lost sight of it in the excitement of exploring life. I still needed a way to understand and explore death, and I still did not know where to begin. In the back of my mind I felt that my dad was facing this same thing. It felt like a race against his failing health. Before he had to face it, before I had to face it in him, I needed to understand death more completely than I had previously managed. Again I wrote down some of these thoughts, then settled down to sleep.

Rising early the next morning, I exercised as normal, taking my mental journey to the House on the Right Bank. I had become accustomed to pausing at several places along the route and allowing the energy to build through each chakra in turn, visualising each one as the kind of whirling vortex pictured in *Hands of Light*. It had also become my practice, after programming my day, to walk out into a small courtyard: smooth cobbles bordered by a low stone wall, a wide valley sweeping away beyond and marbled by rhododendron bushes. It was a scene from *Surfing the Himalayas*, where the writer and the saffron-robed Master Fwap had meditated together. Here I would meet Master Fwap. He was surrounded always by a bright golden aura. I would stand before him. With each inward breath, the golden light would fill my swelling stomach. With each outward breath, the golden light would expand until my whole body was filled. Then it would radiate out from me, until I could see and feel nothing but golden light.

This particular morning, as I began this process, my mind wandered. I was wondering how I could move from my standing exercise to seated meditation without having to spend time retracing the elaborate relaxation process. It was just a fleeting question, but to my astonishment Master Fwap replied to my question! He told me how to do it. He used very brief, simple words – in fact, I am not sure I could exactly say he used words – yet he imparted to me a full understanding of a complete step-by-step process.

I followed his instruction: he called it the seven breaths. As I completed my standing exercise I circled my arms out and upward, gathering the golden light. Then I pushed my palms from above my head down to the level of my stomach, guiding the golden light down through the crown of my head until my stomach held it all.

Sitting down, I took three breaths to relax my head, body and legs. With the next three breaths the golden light expanded outwards again, filling my midriff, my torso and on to my knees and elbows, and finally my head and down to my toes and fingers. With the seventh breath the golden light radiated out once more and there I was, back in the small courtyard. Master Fwap greeted me with an enigmatic smile and told me that soon I would be able to do this in just three breaths, and then in one alone.

I was excited by this new development. I anticipated all kinds of wide ranging discussions with Master Fwap in which he would impart all kinds of wisdom. Since then, however, though I have arrived in the small courtyard full of questions, Master Fwap has only given one answer, the same answer to every question: 'Go and contemplate your inner nature.'

Each time, I look to my left and the grassy landscape slopes gently to the rim of a lake. I walk down to the water's edge and gaze across the dark surface. I can still feel the gentle breeze playing through my hair, and I watch as patches of tiny ripples brew and fade. Gradually the breeze dies away and the trace of every last ripple subsides into a complete calm. I imagine that when all elements of my life are brought into harmony, when all things compliement and do not contradict, when there is complete integrity between my outer life and my inner purpose, this is how it will feel.

I walk out into the lake step by step, going deeper and deeper until the water covers my head. Soon I am no longer aware of walking, only sinking endlessly down into a deep, silent stillness. Up above, storm clouds may bring wind and rain rattling over the surface. Here the silence and stillness remain undisturbed. All movement is but temporary. This, I think, is the calm of my true soul, my Greater Self.

Lobsang Rampa, in *The Third Eye*, is told that a person dying has to go through three stages: his physical body has to be disposed of, his etheric has to be dissolved, and his spirit has to be helped on the road to the World of Spirit.

Then he is told that his own path is not an easy path for anyone. Family, friends, country, must all be left behind. Where he is to go, the people's ways are strange and not to be accounted for; they believe only that which they can do, only that which can be tested in their rooms of science. But, he is told, the greatest science of all, the science of the Overself, is left untouched. As if the words were addressed to me, I read the teacher's injunction to the young Lobsang: that is your Path, the Path you chose before you came to this life.

Close to the due date I had set for my goal at the beginning of this year, I do indeed feel that I have reached a threshold. I had envisaged that by now I would be ready to set down a new goal, but I have come increasingly to the view that this is not necessary. I know that the way forward is a journey within myself. On this Path, I need to follow my feelings as they arise; any goal set now would have more to do with my ego than my true destination.

A book caught my eye recently, for no better reason than its use of that same description – the Overself – as used by Lobsang's teacher. I have asked Julie to buy this book for my birthday. I have chosen it to be my guide. It is called *The Quest of the Overself.*

## 27 April 1996

In early-morning meditation I confronted my own doubt. I did not doubt that my goal of reaching the threshold of a new understanding had been reached, but I had peremptorily set a new goal for today: that I should see energy fields or auras in any situation. I was effectively asking that my 'third eye' should open on demand. For Lobsang Rampa this had been accelerated by a surgical procedure which had involved drilling into his forehead and manually stimulating the pineal gland. With my eyes closed, I imagined this same procedure reaching deep into my own brain. I felt the sensation of pressure on my forehead. But I also felt doubt. All week, as this day drew closer, I had felt a growing doubt.

Finally, I opened my eyes; nothing had changed. I felt foolish.

I had good reasons for setting this goal. To see more would deepen my understanding and regard for all life. To remain blind would be to succumb to a cultural filter which I could no longer accept. Maybe it was just the date that was unrealistic. Maybe attaching any date was an act of the ego over things which go beyond the ego's power to control. Or maybe it was just my inability to rid myself of these very doubts so that the real message my mind received was not that it would come about, but that it could not.

I swallowed my foolishness and resolved to press forward with the goal, without specifying any further due date. Somehow I could believe in that. It was easier to believe that this sensitivity, of which I had already felt some intimations, would come not in a sudden rush, but slowly, improving over years of persistence and practice. My conjecture – or I could say the limitation I chose to accept for the time being – was that when the ego calls upon the spirit the height of its power is to knock with polite persistence and await a reply.

Later in the day, concentrating on the threshold I had thus far reached, I threw coins upon the ground to see what advice the *I Ching* might offer on where to go from here. It gave the image of Keeping Still taming the force of Creativity. The force of habit, it said, helps to keep order in quiet times. To store up creative power and yet hold firmly to the truth requires daily self-renewal. The *I Ching* calls this the image of Heaven within the mountain, the taming power of the great. A man 'acquaints himself with many sayings of antiquity, and many deeds of the past, in order to strengthen his character thereby'. The way to study the past, it said, is not to confine oneself to mere knowledge of history but, through application of this knowledge, to give actuality to the past. It also warned of dangers still present of which a man must remain aware 'or he will be robbed of his firmness'.

'He must acquire skill on the one hand in what will take him forward, and on the other in what will protect him against unforeseen attacks.'

Success was promised for one who works with determination and perseverance to make full use of the propitiousness of the time: 'It furthers one to cross the great water.'

When I consulted the *I Ching* twenty years ago, this was a phrase which seemed to arise on a regular basis for me, so much so that it had remained in the recesses of my mind ever since. Now here it was again. The meaning I had always attached to the phrase was an encouragement to take a bold step, according to the context of each particular question.

I suppose as a piece of general advice it had to be right, then and now. Barring recklessness, there was a sense in which boldness could not be a mistake because valuable lessons could be found in any outcome. More important still, each bold step is an exercise of confidence which, like a muscle, will weaken without use.

Two women, Kate being one of them, recently told me, quite independently of each other, that at the age of twenty-five or younger they had the confidence to go out and do anything. Now entering their thirties, both felt they no longer had that confidence. In both cases, no decision had gone terrifically wrong in that five-year period so as to rob them of the physical or financial where-withal. All that had happened for both of them was that they had stuck in the same job which neither excited them nor promised any great advancement.

Stability is what happened to them, at least in their material circumstances, and an acceptance of their place within their partic-ular comfort zone. There was no longer a need for the confidence they once had. The boundary of their comfort zone, once elastic, began to harden, and gradually to shrink. By the time that shrinking had progressed to the point of discomfort for them, they found that their confidence to do anything about it had simultaneously weak-ened. At least that was my assessment.

In the long term, the most comfortable way to deal with comfort zones is actively to expand them, to push at them from within. Daily self-renewal is the imperative: to constantly question one's relation-ship to the world. It will bring discomfort but whoever said that discomfort of this kind was a bad thing? The real choice is between discomfort which is voluntary and beneficial, and discomfort which feels far from voluntary and is always filled with foreboding.

## 12 May 1996

The answer to man's deepest queries is, finally, that a certain effort is demanded of him, a certain spiritual and personal practice which acts through an inward process somewhat in the manner of a pneumatic drill, which bores slowly and steadily through the earth of his being until eventually it strikes the solid rock of the True Divine Self seemingly buried

so far below the surface ... Through such practice, persistently and hopefully performed, man may eventually discover
his own deathless spirit, even whilst living in this body of frail
flesh.

*The Quest of the Overself*, Dr Paul Brunton

Something struck me as I read those lines, something that might
seem absurd to a casual reader. As I read, I was simultaneously
recalling the process of death as described to Lobsang Rampa. Then
I thought – in my book I called it an inspired thought – so we *do* die
after all! For all these years I had cherished the knowledge of my
eternal nature, but now I understood that I had to die; it was the
price I had to pay to connect with that deathless spirit. To choose
such a connection was to choose the manner and timing of death,
not to delay that fateful day but rather to hasten it.

I realised only the next day that I was meeting that spiral of
learning again at a new level. Had I not already accepted the words of
St Paul that we must die to sin in order to be born to everlasting life?
I had reasoned this out even further, to see life and love as inter-
changeable things, that to love was to have life. I had accepted this,
and yet there was clearly much still to be done. Perhaps I had imagined the death of some self-centred part of me, not the death of my
whole self, of all that I am or ever could be. And I wondered at my
attempts last December to imagine standing naked in the wind and
melting into the sun. Did I ignore the fact that in moving towards
one thing I had to move away from something else?

From that moment I began to look around at the world and all it
offered, at all my family and friends, and to mourn for what I must
lose. To look at anything with the thought that it might never be
seen again by these eyes, that it can never be owned or even held for
a meaningful time, seemed to draw from it an uncommon
beauty.

Of all the people I would have to let go, my younger daughter,
Cathy, was the last and the hardest. This was not a matter of comparison, but my mind kept going back to a small incident when Cathy
was only three or four years old. We were at a family party. Some
very young and boisterous nephews were playing a war game,
shooting their imaginary guns indiscriminately in all directions. As
they took their potshots in my general direction, I decided to play
along by faking a dramatic death. I keeled over on the floor and

writhed around, and Cathy suddenly came running towards me pleading, 'Don't die, Daddy, don't die.'

I had to quickly recover and comfort her, telling her that it was just a game and I was fine, but it took quite some time for Cathy to feel reassured.

This came only a few years, or maybe less, after that dreadful time when I had lost all sense that my life mattered to anyone or anything, though I had become accustomed to living as if it did matter, just in case I should find one day that it really did. I was getting on with the business of living without thinking any more clearly than this, but in that moment Cathy showed me, in a way as shocking as it was touching, that I mattered to her. It was important that I was alive, not for anything that I was going to do or to give, but just that I should exist in her universe.

It was the same thing I had tried to convey to my dad in hospital last September, but I hadn't managed it; not in the way that Cathy managed it for me. I tried in January to have him focus on a goal of being well, and that hadn't worked. In April, against my own judgement, I tried again.

We were all concerned by his lack of progress. Even after his radiotherapy was over, he continued to shuffle from room to room and back to his cushioned chair. These excursions were made more frequent due to his body's increasing intolerance to sitting still. His swollen legs would not bare the inertia; his hips were growing stiff. Walking relieved some pains while obviously causing others. Out of his sight my mother would talk of visits to the hospital and how other people, operated on at a similar time, were now making such good progress, but my dad just didn't seem to think that this was possible for him. She had tried to offer encouragement along these lines and he had lost patience with her. Her exasperation was unstated, but I noticed it. So too did Julie and the children, all of whom took me to task. Somebody had to say something. He would listen to me, they said; he always listened to me.

On a Sunday afternoon after dinner at our house and the usual pleasantries, it was time for them to leave. My mum left the room to find their coats. Julie followed. Hayley and Cathy also wandered off into the kitchen. My dad was still getting gingerly to his feet and reaching for his walking stick. He shuffled to the window and gazed outside, remarking on the weather with a sigh which spoke of life in general.

'How is your leg?' I inquired.

'Terrible,' he said. 'Just terrible. It's getting worse.'

He looked towards me; his eyes were misty. I didn't respond. The look of concern on my face said enough for the moment. He returned his gaze to the window. Everyone else seemed settled in the kitchen. I steeled myself.

'You need some exercise,' I ventured. 'It won't improve by itself. You need to do something to help it.'

'Exercise.' There was a frightened impatience in his voice saying that no one was listening to him – I wasn't listening to him.

'I can hardly walk ten yards.'

'But Dad,' I persisted, 'that doesn't mean you should stop doing anything. If you can only manage ten yards, then you walk ten yards. Then tomorrow you walk eleven, and the day after that, twelve. That's the way to get on top of this.'

As I spoke those last words, he huffed and turned away.

'Dad, I know these things.' I ignored another huff. 'I've been exercising all my life; I know how this works.'

'Do you think I haven't tried?' He threw a challenge back at me. His eyes were so misty. He wasn't angry; he was sad and frightened and aggravated all at the same time.

I wanted to challenge him right back, to say, 'No, Dad, you're not trying', but I saw how he looked and I didn't have the heart.

'Dad, you taught me how to be strong. When you lost your arm, you didn't give in, you treated it as an advantage. That's what you told me and I understand what you meant. You taught me to use any situation to make me stronger than before. That's what you need to remember now, Dad. That's what I'm trying to tell you.'

'Ah, well. It's hard you know. It's very hard.' The aggravation had left him, but the sadness and fear were still there.

'Come on, Dad, you have to try.'

'Mmm, mmm.'

He was steering himself carefully out of the room with his head bowed. His mumbled reply was meant to convey agreement, but I knew it didn't. The others were waiting patiently in the kitchen. If they had been talking at all, I knew it would have been with anxious ears turned towards the earnest exchange a few rooms away. Mum and Dad said their goodbyes and thank yous with no more reference to it. As they drove away my gut felt like lead. Once more I had tried and failed.

102

It was probably that incident more than any other that provoked my macabre race against time to meet death and resign myself to it before the time came for my dad to do likewise.

I had a dream on 2 May. I met my Aunt Pauline. It was on the corner of a street, a street of old redbrick terraced houses, the kind we used to live in. But I knew this was an illusion. In the dream I already knew that Aunt Pauline had just died, and that I, though still living, was there to meet her in the astral plane, to help her on her way. Aunt Pauline is hugely overweight; she has been for as long as I remember. I was explaining to her that she didn't need to carry all that weight any more, and that she would have to get rid of it. Aunt Pauline said she knew this and was looking forward to losing it. I understood that she knew where to go and what to do. I said that I would come and meet her again when she was ready for the next stage. The mood was calm and consoling.

When I awoke, the dream affected me strongly enough to wonder whether she really had died. I found out later, as I suspected anyway, that she hadn't. I didn't know what to make of it.

During that morning at work, I experienced a strange and strong uprising of emotion. I began to think of the times when I had been close to another person's death. Those times were several and all unique – though the individual circumstances were not germane – holding hands with grieving friends, sitting by the bedside of a dying uncle, commiserating with his daughters, my cousins, watching the grim set of my dad's expression as he watched his brother lowered into the ground, and again with one sister, and again with another sister; each time I felt relief that I had not experienced the death of one so close. Then there was that inconsolable, bewildering grief, that moment which had so moved me last December to begin this quest. As I thought of each incident in turn, tears welled and my heart felt fit to break. This continued for some two hours as I tried constantly to bring my mind back to the work in hand and hide my distress from anyone wandering in and out of the room.

Two days later, a Saturday at home, my thoughts dwelt upon all the human misery I had listened to over the past ten years. The same deep sadness overwhelmed me again, and even more tears.

I had never before felt that it was any hardship to listen to another person's trouble. Beyond the intensity and humility of the moment, beyond the concerns and cares for someone's wellbeing, I had always felt that … I don't know what I felt, but in the grip of this passionate melancholy I began to feel that I had been carrying a huge and accumulating burden. It was time to take this burden somewhere, to do something with it, though I could not imagine what.

In *The Quest of the Overself*, the author stresses over and over, by all manner of reasoning, that we have bodies but we are not our bodies; we have emotions but we are not our emotions; we have intellect but we are not our intellect. I had been steadily absorbing this and began to wonder if such strong feelings were now arising for the first time precisely because I could say, 'I have these emotions, but I am not these emotions', in short, because I had a way to detach from them.

Still, the sense haunted me that these things were connected to the dream, and the meaning of the dream still eluded me. On the fifth day, in the relaxed focus of my morning warm-up movements, a meaning came. Aunt Pauline, with all her excess weight, was a metaphor for the excess 'weight' of other people's emotions which I was forever carrying. The dream was telling me that it was time to give up carrying this unnecessary burden, that I must do so for the sake of those who had given their emotion, and to allow me to move on.

I wondered how this was to be done? Prayer seemed an obvious answer, but the more I thought about it, the more I realised that I really didn't understand prayer. I used to pray. I used to ask God to help those I had found to be in trouble. And God always answered me, and the answer was always the same. He always said, 'You do it.'

I would protest and tell him how useless I was, but He would only say: 'There isn't anyone else, you'll have to do.' Eventually I gave up asking, because I already knew what the answer was going to be and I did what I could.

This was a different situation. I had done what I could and now I needed a different kind of prayer and – for once, please – a different answer. I began to think of it – the weight I was carrying – as a kind of negative energy. I could not simply throw it off; that would be to release it back into the great sea of emotion, to affect anyone it touched. In sum, I could relieve nothing in this way, only spread it around a little more thinly. I needed to find a way, within myself, to turn this energy around from negative to positive, and only then to release it back into the 'universal energy field'.

Isn't that what Jesus did? When he was placed upon the cross, did he not take on the sins and the suffering of all the world and speak from there a message of forgiveness and love? That was another idea all tied up with death.

Withdrawing deeper and deeper, I was aware of becoming closed to the flow of events. One lunchtime walking along, I sensed a presence. I looked to my right. There was somebody I knew and got along well with, walking in parallel twenty or thirty metres away. Reaching a junction we both turned right simultaneously, she twenty or thirty metres ahead. But she was walking slowly, ambling; although she had previously matched my pace, I was now catching up fast. In other circumstances I would have caught up, struck up a conversation, maybe even suggested lunch, but I thought of all those gossiping tongues and the distraction of it all. I turned away down a side street.

On another day with Helen and John visiting for dinner, I should have had a completely open conversation, but I didn't. There was much talk of *The Celestine Prophecy*, the *I Ching*, even Tarot cards. I remember telling them of my interest in all forms of divination in my youth, but that I had then fallen somehow, become frightened. I didn't tell them what was really on my mind now.

I read in *The Quest of the Overself* about the illusion of time. It was likened to sitting on a train in a station and feeling all the sensations of movement as you slip by the neighbouring train with a gathering momentum. Then you turn your head back towards the platform and discover that you were stationary all along; it was the other train that was moving. To dispel the psychological illusion of movement through time, the book said, one must turn one's attention in the opposite direction, from outside to inside, directing the mind back to its own source.

I tried to imagine this realm, to think how it might be, and none of the usual descriptions seemed to apply: music, rhythm, flow, anything which denoted movement. Sense became nonsense. I kept coming back to one phrase: the deep stillness of my being. It was a phrase I had been repeating over and over in my exercise; I didn't even know where I had got it from, unless some inner wisdom had been guiding me all along. This turning of the attention was such a profound switch from all normal levels of consciousness, and yet it clearly had to be possible. The only choice was to retreat within. Closing myself to the flow seemed wrong, but I thought of it as taking a step back in order to move more surely forward in the future, and even as I thought that, I had to wonder what I thought the future was.

There was a programme on television one evening which featured a woman in southern India who simply hugged people. That was all she did, but she had become so famous for it that people would queue all day to be hugged. The tough, 'in your face' female presenter queued for her hug with a certain laddish cynicism. The woman hugged her deeply and warmly. The presenter did not return to the camera. She turned away apparently overcome with emotion. There was a palpable power in that hug.

Though this moment of television was no more than a few minutes long, it provoked another vivid dream. I was walking through the city centre, intent on finding a suitable seat where I would put up a sign saying 'Available for Hugging'. A woman was shouting at me from a window that she had consulted the Tarot and this was all very inauspicious. Undeterred, I sat down and made myself ready to begin. Somehow I foresaw that in the throng of all this hugging a man would approach and ask, 'What denomination are you?' and I would reply, 'Denominations are for those who need them.'

Some day, when all this contemplation is over, I have to begin to open out again. But here is the reason why, for now, this cannot be. When the *I Ching* told me once again, 'It furthers one to cross the great water', the only strong association in my mind was the river Styx, the river of death. It was the only real association twenty years ago. The Tarot cards would, likewise, repeatedly produce the Death card as my final outcome. It was one of the reasons I took fright. But as I continued to read *The Quest of the Overself*, I arrived at the following passage:

> The power to follow this way exists within us all. The current of thought can be made to turn backwards to its sublime source. Thus one may be ferried across the Styx which flows between the world of time and the world of eternity.

I read it as a confirmation not just that death was a way forward, but that I must return again to a lifelong preoccupation with the underworld. It was how I had seen that first period of challenge in my life: as my journey through the underworld. I had even written of it in those terms. I had then seen my second crisis at thirty as a return to that place. I had also seen each brush with other people's crises in similar terms: that as I climbed free of my own underworld I would glance back, only to see someone stumbling blindly where I had just been. Time after time it felt that I was returning, unable to guide but at least able to hold a hand as each person felt their way through. That might sound very melodramatic, but it was one of the ways in which I had always seen it.

Now I was asking myself to perceive and face my personal underworld one more time. I told myself that at least it would be on my own terms but still wondered why it should be so. I wondered whether, on my previous adventures, I had twice gazed across the river Styx but never actually crossed it. Had I twice walked away, and did I have to face it again and again until I finally made the crossing?

There was another way to look at it: that there are three deaths to die. The first might be the mortality of the flesh, since that was certainly my first preoccupation. Having passed through that and slowly mastered the practical business of life at the physical level a second challenge loomed. My second dissatisfaction emerged at an emotional level, and it was in this arena that a second death was precipitated, freeing me to live with open emotion. For a second time, there were very practical lessons to be learned. Perhaps this is why, as I previously observed, the age of thirty to forty is an age of emotional adolescence for so many. Napoleon Hill comments of this decade that nature begins to harmonise the emotions of love and sex in the individual, and that love finally ensures balance, poise and constructive effort.

Then following this through, the third death should be intellectual. It was what I had been moving towards ever since reaching a level of emotional competence. It began with those memory exercises to which I have once alluded. It was a revelation to me at the time that, through a simple shift of my internal representation of things, a vast improvement of memory could be achieved instantaneously. It was through this playful practice that I had discovered the strength of my own drive for constant self-development. It was because of this that I took so readily to the creation of an inner landscape, a realm already rich in possibility for me. Every step since then – of exercise, meditation, proactivity, mission – represented an increasing focus on the intellect, building on and working from a stable physical and emotional foundation. And now it was time for the intellect to undergo that same initiation so that it might truly be set free.

There was something I did on my birthday which I saw fit not to mention at the time; put it down to a fear of criticism. I had been given a cheap computer disk which included a Tarot program. I loaded it up and had it shuffle and spread the cards, seeking, as I had done with the *I Ching*, general guidance on my situation. I cannot remember now the sequence of cards it produced, except that it seemed remarkably insightful at the time. But I do remember the last card, the outcome. It was Death.

The accompanying text described it as the most misunderstood card in the pack. A card which signifies renewal and the losing of old attachments in order to move toward something better. Then it quoted Jesus for the appropriate spirit in which the card should be read: 'Except a corn of wheat fall into the ground and die, it abideth alone; but if it die, it bringeth forth much fruit.'

By this train of thought – flawed or laughable, I know not – I at least came to an understanding of why I had to lose the accumulated emotional 'weight' I spoke of. It was the remnant of a phase now leaving as another phase beckoned.

In morning meditation, as I walked down to the edge of the calm lake, I contemplated prayer and the burden I must set free. Following my instinct, I let all the sadness rise up into the atmosphere, through my crown chakra, and imagined it, like evaporation from the lake's surface, gradually forming a great cloud in the sky. Saturation point was reached and the energy began to fall as rain, feeling wonderful on my skin, like the first sweet rain after a long dry spell. It was not only falling on me but on everyone who had ever shared their sadness with me, refreshing and renewing the growth in each one of them. For the first time since that dream of Aunt Pauline, I felt at peace.

## 30 May 1996

The sadness continues; great waves of sadness. Hayley was sitting on the floor with her history homework. She read aloud from her textbook of the siege of Leningrad and the death of more than a million people from starvation. I stood behind her, instantly transported, walking among the dead and dying, crushed by the scale of human suffering, and began to weep. I turned and left the room.

In the house alone a few days later, I listened to Native American music and chants while attending to the day's chores. I was stopped in my tracks once again by the devastation of a whole culture. I was crying out for them, with them; I was just crying.

At first I stored away these feelings for the moment when, in meditation, I might release them as I had before, but this began to feel too remote. I felt the need to channel these things at the very time they arose. I wondered if this was a step towards 'losing attachment'.

In the small courtyard of my House on the Right Bank, standing with Master Fwap before I began to breathe in his golden aura, I explored how it was to have a body, but not to be that body. I only briefly dwelt on the hardships of physical life. Quite quickly I was thinking of all the pleasures, the skills, the sensuality. But I was not this body. I thought of my emotions. Once more, I passed quickly through the pains which once seemed so many, and into pleasures: warm friendship, comforting words, a family around me. But I was not my emotions. I plunged into my intellect like taking an exhilarating dip into a cool, fast-moving stream. How much pleasure I had found there, playing with my perception of reality, running with new ideas, meeting challenges, reframing the past. But I was not my intellect. Each time I pulled away it felt quite physical, like pulling away from chewing gum. I wondered if this was what attachment was really like.

On a bright and fresh morning, I rolled up at Irene's house early. The rented van was already parked with the back door wide open. I walked up the path. Irene's door was open too; I could hear activity inside and I announced my arrival. There were boxes everywhere, all packed, all ready to go. Irene greeted me with a big hug, then settled on the stair to chat and rest for a moment.

I was amazed at the amount of work she had done and the energy it must have taken. I imagined how hard it could all have been had her heart been heavy with sorrow. But she was so buoyant, so positive. We decided not to stop for a drink until the van was fully packed, and I matched Irene's energy, stride for stride, feeling good that she felt so good.

With the van filled, we sat on the foot plate drinking coffee and feasting on fresh bananas. It was a new beginning, not a bitter end; that's how Irene had decided to see it. She wasn't going to mourn the past, she was going to embrace the future. I was glad she had accepted my offer of help. It was nice to be associated with such spirit.

Maybe she had taken on my preaching about the benefit of a positive attitude. As we drove along the motorway she told me of the encouraging things friends had said to her. But there was so much of this coming from Irene herself. I knew, because I had seen it before, that such encouraging words could be taken so differently, even received as evidence that those friends had no understanding or sympathy for the situation, and taken as justification for further withdrawal. I still wasn't sure what would be the right lesson to learn from loss, what would be the right attitude, but it seemed to me as I watched Irene that a good gauge of any attitude – to anything – would be to ask: does this expand my horizon, or shrink it?

We off-loaded sticks of furniture and cluttered boxes into her parents' garage for temporary storage, the only physical evidence that remained of a ten-year marriage. So much had happened in such a short time. We sat in the homely kitchen, drinking tea and eating buns while Irene's dad regaled me with stories of Irene's childhood. Irene and her mum chided him with good humour and he carried on regardless. Later we lounged in the garden, surveying the fruits of many years' pottering in the closely trimmed grass, ivy trellises and hardy annuals all around, taking afternoon tea and more buns. This was where Irene and her two sons would stay until the purchase of a flat nearby was complete, back in the home and the town of her childhood.

There were so many aspects of Irene's situation that might have crushed her at any moment. There was, again, an urgency to our final embrace that told me none of those things was far from her mind. The situation was far from perfect, but Irene's attitude was a start, and a good foundation to build on.

On a day out with Helen, I was more honest about my thoughts than I had been before; we were alone so it was easier. Helen was driving. She was subdued, fending off a headache, but had spoken of developments in her own life and asked about mine. I announced, quietly, that I knew where I had to go, that I had to die.

'What?'

Helen was taken aback, not expressing dismay exactly, but definitely worried.

'I have to understand death. I have to go through it. I realise that now.'

'But … what do you mean? How can you *do* that?'

I couldn't explain. I wasn't making sense, not even to myself. I changed the subject.

Helen drove to high moorland. There was a copse of fir trees there that she wanted me to see. We walked uphill, meeting the whip of the wind over granite rocks. I had my little black book with me and read aloud to her about the current of thought being made to turn backwards to its sublime source. I was having another go at explaining this death thing.

Helen still wasn't getting it. 'What is sublime?' she asked distract-edly. 'What do you think sublime means? It's always there in spiri-tual writing.'

I hadn't really thought about it before.

'Subliminal,' I guessed. 'It's there but you don't see it.' I was thinking of those subliminal adverts that got banned in the cinema, but I was actually back to that force which was in the world but not of the world, that force that made the widow's mite more valuable than all the gifts of the rich. Subliminal: existing but unseen. Perhaps there were people with vision enough to see it, while for the rest of us it must remain sublime.

We were walking down, by then, into the copse and out of the wind, being sheltered by a high rocky ridge. Here was the point of our visit. Helen had decided that her contribution to the illustration of my writing should be to rekindle and develop my photography skills. I wasn't so sure, and before we set off Helen had inspected my prints of some years ago – eleven or twelve years, I think – and had promptly decided that there was nothing she could teach me after all. As with the writing I had shown her, she had this strong emotional connection with the images. For my part I felt it was all too long ago and I was too rusty. Looking through the wide-angle lens on the windy edge of the moor had fired no nostalgia or excite-ment, only resistance.

Among the trees new angles and compositions started calling. I liked what I was seeing through the lens. I began snapping and exclaiming my feelings and visions to Helen, trying to let her share the moment. The texture of bark, the ground underfoot, it all began to look wonderful. I snapped and clicked. It was as if a channel had burst through some blockage and was now pouring out inspiration.

'There's a symphony in my head!' I cried out. And there was: a whole orchestra of original music surging around. I had experienced this many times before and had so longed to have the skill of Mozart and capture the beauty of what I was hearing. I was jogging briskly now from one image to the next, and then it happened. I remembered I had to die. A gasp left my opened mouth involuntarily.

As I reached the edge of the copse, looking down across the valley, I sank to my knees and felt an awful dewy-eyed emotion of the last day on earth. I was shaking quietly inside.

After some time – it can't have been too long – I looked around and saw Helen wandering down the path, lost in her own thoughts. She had seen nothing of this moment. The realisation that none of what I had just felt had been shared felt odd and incongruous, and shook me firmly from my state. I got up and followed along the path, lined with the roots of trees, carpeted in soft pine needles.

I intimated nothing when I caught her. I resumed snapping though more slowly, and Helen wandered off again still nursing her headache. Standing alone looking once more down the ridge, my thoughts were too vague to identify. I looked across to my left where a tree stood out against the skyline. It was ringed by a bright light following its every contour. There was a large rock standing next to it, ringed with bright light in the same way. I had seen the briefest flashes of this before – like a lightning flash – but somehow this time I was able to hold the vision and wonder at it.

I said nothing about this to Helen either, which strikes me as strange now. We drove down the hill for afternoon tea in a hotel Helen had planned for and talked of friendship. We exchanged our best guesses as to how we might appear in each other's eyes, and then told each other how wrong we had been.

I think the reason I said nothing at the time was that I didn't realise the significance of what had happened. For a start I had been preoccupied by my ego. Even in that spontaneous moment of letting go I was aware of my ego watching the event and savouring how Helen might be moved by the spectacle. The jolt from my state at the sight of her walking away oblivious was really a jolt to my ego. The lightning reactions of my ego made me feel ridiculous. But beyond that, it only became apparent in the days that followed that something enduring had occurred.

Back at work the next day, I had the opportunity to watch three people sitting against a plain background; they were unaware of my interest. I saw the same brightness around each of them. The weekend followed: a planned visit to the seaside, Anya staying with us for the duration. Throughout the weekend I saw energy fields around people and plants with increasing confidence.

Several letters had passed between Anya and me, and my morning meditational 'visits' had been regular. Anya had told me that her thoughts rested with me at a certain time in her own meditation. Sometimes I would wake up with a strong feeling of stimulation in my 'third eye'; I wondered if it was in response to Anya's attentions. When I had first sent *The Celestine Prophecy* to her, I had a minor vision that we might spend time together and she would help me to see energy fields, but I didn't see a way for this to happen. If we had gone out together early one morning over the weekend this would have seemed like a good compromise, but it never happened; I think I was still worried about spending time with her. In meditation, whenever I visited her, I experienced a strong sexual response towards Anya. I would touch each chakra in turn and this was a distinctly sexual experience. I did not avoid it because there was a powerful exchange of energy going on which seemed to the good. All the same, it disturbed me to feel that way in a setting I had taken to be 'spiritual'; although I visited other people in the same way from time to time, this sexuality was unique to Anya. Maybe that was what all that static electricity was about when we first met.

We were able to talk openly about energy fields and other ideas, much to the consternation of Hayley and Cathy. And whether it was Anya's influential presence or not, my ability to 'see' advanced significantly. Within the first ten seconds I was generally able to see, rising from the branches and leaves of trees, a grey wispy smoke. Within the next twenty seconds my eyes would adjust, my gaze would shift into seeing the surrounding brightness. Walking along the sea front in fresh and sunny conditions I was able to see energy fields around people, even though they and I were moving. Furthermore, I could detect not just a ring of light but a wider field or series of fields extending several feet away from the skin, dancing and shimmering in the sea breeze.

We returned inland on the Sunday and said goodbye to Anya. For lack of influence from the sea air or Anya, or both, I have not seen with such clarity since.

As I read on in *The Quest of the Overself*, I learned of extraordinary mental faculties that could result from concentration practices, though it would be unwise to seek them for their own sake: telepathic power to send and receive messages, premonitions, the loosening of ties which bind one to the body, freeing the soul to fly the world and appear to others in vision or dream, one's own dream life becoming a coherent rational existence possessing the quality of awareness that one is in a dream state. These were the very things Anya had spoken of in her letter and which I felt sceptical of so little time ago.

I learned of the attitude of right questioning: not to assert that I have a soul, but to ask 'Have I a soul?', or 'Am I a soul?' leaving the answer to the only part of one's being truly competent to give it. I learned of the mystery of breath and its intimate connection to the flow of thought, so that the slowing of one provokes a like response in the other. In this way the babbling of the intellect may be finally silenced, the author said, to allow answers to be heard. For:

> 'Thoughts will bring one along the road to the spiritual self, but they do not in themselves contain that self' and 'Truth does not care to reveal herself to the intellectually arrogant'.

The next step came as a surprise. The next step was to return to the beginning of the book and meditate upon it sentence by sentence, paragraph by paragraph. I quickly tallied the amount of time this was likely to take – a sinking feeling – then remembered the lesson I had learned through proactivity: that intellectual under-standing alone was of no value. While still continuing to read on, the very next morning I incorporated this form of meditation into my daily routine and was not sorry that I had done so.

I read again from the beginning:

> The first, and for some considerable time one may say the ruling, thought which vividly dominates an infant child's consciousness is the awareness of I. The last thought which moves with the tenement of the spirit of the brain at death is also that of I. During the intervening years between these two points of birth and death – years which make up that composite picture of commonplace events, unrehearsed comedies, occasional tragedies, brief sunshine and lingering shadows that we call life – the chief preoccupation of most human beings is with that same I.

The point was not to argue it through, to rationalise, but simply to let the idea sit there in one's consciousness. And so I did, having no idea of what to expect and requiring constant vigilance against wandering. After fifteen or twenty minutes I began to understand the process. Out of the stillness things began to rise up: memories, small incidents, things I or others had said, things I had read or thought or seen. Associations were rising up from every corner of my mind, connecting with that one thought and forming new connections with each other. I didn't just understand a dry concept any more; I understood it like a thread woven into my entire life. It was the relational thinking Master Fwap had described.

Then something else happened. I didn't detect the transition, but suddenly I felt elevated to a new level of thought. Whether it was my own mind playing with a new metaphor or whether I was seeing truth seemed not to matter. Later I tried to catch the essence of the 'vision':

I was the first to arrive, and I will be the last to leave.

My intellect is a travelling circus; my emotion a movable feast; my silent body is an entrance hall, a gathering room, a fireside, and resting place.

People come and go within this space. They arrive by invitations sent at my request, long before I came. They leave because they have other things to do, which I understood from the beginning.

That dream I had was right: meditation is just like fishing. My ego looks for fast and tangible progress but, as a lady said on TV when complaining about the speed of life, 'I am a human, being not a human doing!' We are first and foremost the consciousness of 'I'. We can only come closer to this original state by stopping all the 'doing' of our minds.

Last night a dream took up this theme. I was in some kind of race. I knew even in the dream that I had had this dream before with the same result – ZERO TIME – a time that could not be beaten. I woke up. It was too early to get up. I went back to sleep. The same dream started again, and again I was aware that this was the third time I had run this race. Again I achieved ZERO TIME. It seemed to happen because I was allowing myself to be chased so that the chaser was unaware that he was really the one being chased. I was just a decoy so that my chaser was himself caught in the final stages. This resulted in ZERO TIME, a time impossible to beat.

As I awoke again, I knew that the dream was about meditation and all that I had been reading. The 'I' in the dream was this 'I'-consciousness. The one I was allowing to chase me was my intellect so that the Overself might steal up and catch him unawares – ZERO TIME.

I remembered that some six years ago I had written a song which reflected the state of my belief about love at that time and since:

Love has no limits
I truly believe
It's just time that gets you
Every time
And I'm wondering which time to choose.
Last night I felt for my watch,
It felt like I felt for my pulse.

I thought about those lines in the light of my dream and what I had read. Two things occurred to me. First, that if time or one's experience of being in time can truly be transcended then there is no longer any limit to love. Second, identifying time as I did with my very lifeblood was the desperate gasp of my ego complaining of what is, after all, its own creation.

After that moment among the trees – with Helen but not with her – I began to see beauty in a new way. It wasn't a momentary lifting of the veil or exactly that 'last day on Earth' feeling that I had initially, and yet I can't say why or how it is different. Perhaps it is, after all, sublime.

And though these thoughts and meditations may finally have caused a breakthrough in my seeing of energy fields, they have simultaneously taken away any hunger for that particular goal. St Paul said:

Whether there be prophecies, they shall fail; whether there be tongues, they shall cease; whether there be knowledge, it shall vanish away. For we know in part, and we prophesy in part. But when that which is perfect is come, that which is in part shall be done away.

## 14 June 1996

Another meeting with Heather. For the whole of her life, she told me, she felt she had been overshadowed by her elder sister. In the face of the brash behaviour which seemed to come so naturally to that sister, Heather had not tried to compete. Instead she had put all her effort into study, in the hope of gaining attention through achievement and through 'being good'. She did not feel that her strategy had ever really worked. I asked her what she felt her sister had that she didn't, and Heather said simply, 'Presence.'

Presence was something her sister had always possessed, Heather thought, and for that reason she would always get on in life with or without qualifications. Heather, on the other hand, and in her own eyes, had no presence at all; she felt she could slip in and out of a room totally unnoticed. Now, I knew that Heather had presence; she must have had it for me from the beginning, otherwise how should we have become friends? I had also experienced her presence as a powerfully negative thing. When Heather came to work in a testy frame of mind, she didn't have to say a word; everybody knew and would give her a wide berth. When Heather was out of sorts with me it was an awesome thing to experience; she had put-down lines I hadn't even dreamed of.

But I don't want to do her a disservice. Heather had presence, plain and simple. Is there anyone who doesn't have it? Walking in and out of places unnoticed must be the hardest trick in the book, I think. When Kate enters the room, though my back is to the door, I know instantly that she is there. Often I know before she enters, from the particular way she has of attacking the stairs. I feel where she is in the room. Probably I do this with everyone; it just registers more with Kate. Everyone has presence. If there is a lack it is only in our ability to sense it.

I had learned a new trick of asking questions silently – like a mental tap on the head – and then listening for an answer. It came from another book Anya had recommended. I didn't always get an answer and when I did I couldn't be sure if it was any more than my imagination, but I was persuaded that such an ability would not even begin if I didn't call on it. So one morning, after feeling Kate walk around the room and leave by the door behind me, I asked a question as her footsteps faded on the stair.

'Kate, how are you?'

She replied, 'I want you to write to me.'

The answer struck me for two reasons. It wasn't exactly an answer to my question. But more than this, it was Kate's voice as clear as day, right inside my head! I began a long letter to her just as soon as time would allow. If her voice had been no more than wishful thinking on my part I didn't care; I needed to write.

Kate has never run away from death. On the contrary she has let her thoughts rest with death to an extent that most of her regular friends found morbid. They would have wished her to forget and to 'get on with life'. Kate could not bring herself to do that; it was a strong characteristic she shared with me, so I felt no hesitation in writing down all my current thoughts and feelings on death and losing attachment to the things of this life. And I concluded this as I wrote: that the three things I was pursuing most strongly, making contact with my own soul or with God – I wasn't sure of any difference – losing my ego once and for all, and understanding death, these were all the same thing!

I posted the letter immediately. Two days later Kate pulled me to one side in the office and told me how very excited and moved she had felt, that she had taken herself off to the bathroom and locked the door so as not to be disturbed, and that she had finished reading with tears in her eyes. Kate told me that she had begun a letter in reply. I was as pleased as Punch. Even though she had told me before of writing letters, yet somehow they had never been finished or posted, my spirit was lifted against expectation.

That night I went out for a run through the fields and country roads near home. I watched the trees as I jogged along, but it was my first run in several months, the going was hard and I didn't expect to see anything. Then no sooner had this thought crossed my mind than I did see something: at the first tree, and the next and the next, I saw the grey wispy smoke rising from every branch, twig and leaf; I saw a heat haze disturbance around the whole foliage; and finally a corona of light, all three things now visible at the same time. The sight as each tree passed was so strong and positive that I found myself crying out with every wheezing breath that left me. Luckily I was alone as I padded along and up the hill, finally reaching the crest and turning for the downhill stretch towards home. From this elevated view I could see over houses, fields, trees and parkland to the edge of hills several miles away. To my astonishment, across the entire landscape I saw huge trails of wispy smoke rising, a heat haze spanning everything, and then a glorious corona of light. My breath had reached an even rate – a second wind – my face smiled of itself; I was in a state of meditation.

It had all seemed to make so much sense when I was writing to Kate, losing attachment to things and the deeper connection to be gained from it. Only a matter of a few days later and a visit to my dad – contemplating his illness and the worsening prognosis – and none of it made any sense at all. If we were not our bodies, our emotions, our thoughts, if our personalities were not essentially us then, I asked, what had my dad brought to my life? What had he given me? If all such things were not the substance of my dad and no more than a transient ego connecting with my transient ego – neither of which we could carry into death – though all this seemed so much, was it really anything? I felt mortally confused.

This morning at the end of meditation, I called Kate into my presence. To do this, I have found, is easier than taking the journey myself. I imagined Kate's physical presence, how she would feel, how she would smell, the sound and feel of her breath close to mine, the touch of her hand. And she was there. A week had passed. It was too early to expect a letter but I no longer felt hopeful. To the contrary, I felt certain that none would arrive. So once Kate was with me I asked, 'Kate, why are you not able to write to me?'

Kate spoke in a direct manner and, so it seemed to me, with a grim self-control, 'I have to save my feelings for my family.'

I could sense her turning away, feeling the need to leave. I did not prevent this and her presence left me.

I wrote down last night a quote from *The Quest of the Overself* to the effect that one wishing to invoke the aid of the Overself should, with a slowed rate of breathing, simultaneously question, 'Whom does this trouble? Whom does this pain, depress, tempt, perplex?' And anyone wishing to help others in a difficult situation should, having performed this same practice:

> … picture the person in the mind's eye and then raise him aloft to the white light of the Overself in silent blessing. Some illumination or protection will surely wing its mysterious way to that person.

I did not do this last thing for Kate, but so be it. I had troubles of my own and silently repeated throughout the day, 'Whom does this trouble? Whom does this perplex?' ignoring all else until the question sank deeply into mental quiet. Then I would resume my work until trouble and confusion began to cloud my thoughts again.

This evening I visited my dad. He no longer sits in his favourite chair. All that time when we were exhorting him to keep his feet elevated in bed, to help drain his swollen legs, he would insist that his chair was the most comfortable place to be. Finally that chair became too uncomfortable and he took to his bed, a single bed now to afford some comfort to both him and my mum as their sleeping and resting patterns lost synchronisation. I sat on the edge of my mum's bed with a pillow propping my back. Dad lay down on his left side from where he could see me, see the small portable television we had brought up some days earlier, and see out of the window. He was covered by a single cotton sheet, the only weight he could stand for any length of time, and even this he pulled alternately up and down swapping between warmth and comfort. Apart from a vest he was naked from the waist down. As the cotton sheet slid around, his legs became exposed from time to time, and I had not seen them unclothed since his days in the hospital. There was more than just the swelling of excess lymph fluid. His pale skin was a mass of lumps, the origin of which I could only guess at. His groin was swollen more than anything else. The pain and discomfort must have been excruciating, except that the doctor had prescribed morphine and the dosage had already been increased more than once.

My dad had always been one to talk up his pain, quite the opposite of my mum. A cold would make him 'ache in every sinew', a head-ache was always 'splitting'. Now he no longer complained. He no longer asked about share prices or football. We talked of the view from the window on a beautiful spring night such as it was. And we talked about his sons and daughters, and their partners and children, one by one, commenting on their lives and sharing their qualities. It was the only thing that really interested him: not his own pain or prospects, but the small concerns troubling his grandchildren, the search for a new job by Trevor, his prospective son-in-law, things that might be of no concern at all a year from now. He talked of them like a good businessman might feel for the smallest aspects of his business. Nothing was too small. I think now of that good steward who took the talents entrusted to him and invested them wisely.

Ten years earlier, when I had been reading the parables and had been horrified to find all the faults portrayed in them most promi-nent in myself, it was the parable of the good steward that had finally finished me, finally taken away the hope that I was worth a damn to anyone or anything.

The kingdom of heaven, it said, is as a man travelling into a far country. He calls his servants to him. To one he gives five talents, to another two, and another one, each according to his ability. The first trades with his five talents and makes five more. The second likewise makes two more. But the third digs in the earth and buries his one talent there.

When the master returns, he calls his servants to him. He is pleased with the first two servants, saying to each of them, "Well done thou good and faithful servant." And, finding them trustworthy, entrusts a proportionate part of his kingdom to them. The third admits that, in fear, he hid his talent in the earth. The master is displeased and calls him a "wicked and slothful servant." He orders that the one talent be taken from him and given to him that has ten.

The parable ends: 'For unto every one that hath shall be given, and he shall have abundance: but from him that hath not shall be taken away even that which he hath. And cast ye the unprofitable servant into outer darkness: there shall be weeping and gnashing of teeth.'

I was that unprofitable servant; I could see it plainly. On the day I had been, as I saw it, touched by God, He had given His wealth into my safekeeping and I had buried it away, making nothing of it. And not only this, every gift I had ever been given, my very humanity, I had buried away from all but my nearest and dearest to live an inconsequential life of average achievement and relationships venturing no deeper than passing acquaintance. My flesh had found comfort; my spirit had been buried without trace. I cast myself into outer darkness.

It was my dad listening to me at that time which restored the feeling that I could nevertheless be acceptable, that my judgement was mine alone and nothing to do with God. My dad restored my sense of what love was, though I could have seen it in many other places had I not been so absorbed in my own unworthiness. For all that, such unconditional acceptance remained a mostly unspoken bond, and deep fundamental discussion about life was still rare between my dad and me. Certainly we had not talked about death in a personal way.

This evening when I visited him, the doctor was due to call to assess whether Dad should return to hospital for his own comfort. The other alternative was a hospice. It was after all, Dad said, more a case of pain management and that was what a hospice was there for.

It wasn't just for terminal cases, he said – and my mum agreed – and besides it would be much nearer for my mum to visit.

I didn't question any of this either openly or privately, I don't think. But as I drove home something inside had made that assessment for me. There was that sad Native American music playing again, a soulful, wordless lament from an old man whose heart trembled through the very transparency of his voice. I began to sing along in my own lament, and the tears began to flow. On and on I drove through the night streets and the lament became louder as the tears ran heavy on my cheeks, my face shook and the chant strained and cracked over the dull hurting in my throat, but it kept coming like a roar from somewhere deeper than I had the wish or the wit to control.

In truth my wish was rather to encourage what was happening. I visualised this immense sadness being channelled through me, letting clouds form above and the sweet rain of renewal fall upon myself, but mostly on my dad. And throughout all this crying: 'Who feels this pain? Who cries these tears?', and the knowledge that I had to give Dad permission to talk about death if he wished.

I pulled into the drive. The music had stopped. I wiped my face with a firm pull of my hands across moist eyes and skin, composed myself and went inside as if it was just another night, just another visit, though I knew inside that it wasn't.

Dr Brunton says of tears that chief among the prophetic heralds of the coming of Grace is the act of weeping, and that tears bear with them a mysterious influence which tends to dissolve the hard encrustations built up by the ego. For all the tears I have cried of late, it was a relief and comfort to read those words and see in them a confirmation of all that my dream had intimated at their beginning.

Dr Brunton speaks of another channel through which Grace may operate:

> Not infrequently the separation from, or death of, some person greatly loved brings this about, and as a consequence of the intense suffering that naturally results, the seeker's life may receive a completely new orientation wherein the Grace may come as a kind of compensation for that which has been lost. He will first, however, have to pass through all the phases of the agony of his loss and when at the end the Grace begins to touch him, he will gradually discover that he can bear the

sorrow patiently. No longer is it a burden that crushes him, for he perceives how the withdrawal of that other person from his life bears with it a spiritual significance.

I read these words a week ago when my spirit was still high and I thought, 'God forbid!'

## Sunday, 23 June 1996

On the Saturday morning following that tearful night, I went with Cathy to the town centre. It was Fathers' Day on the Sunday and I had not bought anything. I could not think what to get; so many of the usual ideas were not applicable. Cathy followed me round patiently as I tried to weigh the use my dad might get from one thing after another. A picture caught my eye, of a solitary house on a remote mountain pass. It wasn't so much the image as the colour in the sky, the way it funnelled down between the mountain peaks, and the staining of the foreground straining upwards towards some meeting point never quite reached. I thought I understood what the artist was seeing, thought my dad might see it too. Then I began to think of practicalities: where the picture might be hung and whether my dad would ever see much of it from his bed. I couldn't see beyond that bed. I discarded the idea, thinking that I might return if I saw nothing else.

An hour later we walked into a shop selling African artefacts. I looked wearily at more pictures until Cathy pulled me over to a display of small statues. One carving of a head in jet black stone caught my eye. The face was smiling with eyes serenely closed. I'm not sure if it was something I had read or something I just knew, but looking into that face I remembered that in that place of deep still-ness we are always smiling, no matter what. I bought the little statue.

It was the morning of Sunday – Fathers' Day – that I visited my dad. He was in bed. The bedroom was light and airy. He greeted me with a tired smile. I was the first to visit that day. I gave him my present and he remarked at how 'lovely' it was. He always said our presents were 'lovely' or 'smashing', even our most experimental things which he never actually used. He placed the statue on the bedside table facing forward as if to watch over him.

'He can be my guardian.'

This wasn't a typical thing for my dad to have said. An image flashed across my mind: at the moment of my dad's death, this tall, dark and noble African warrior came to guide him on his way.

'It reminded me,' I said tentatively, 'of that place deep inside all of us, which is always smiling. It's the place where I go in my morning exercise.'

'Mmm.'

I was tentative because I didn't want to preach or teach. After my last go at motivating my dad I had sought some guidance from the *I Ching*. It had counselled me not to play the teacher now, but to return to the role of a son who still had things to learn at his father's feet. It made a lot of sense to me, not just that he still had much to teach and tell me, but also that I might miss so much by trying to take a different part.

'Yes, I think that's true,' he said generously.

We began to talk of family again and especially of Trevor, Kim's new partner, who had been spending some days gardening for my mum and dad, and who had laughed so much at the things my dad had said and done in the time they had known each other. I could tell that he was glad to find Trevor so pleasing. It meant that he could feel settled in his mind for Kim's future. All his life he had lived through our every trauma and trouble as if it were his own and had breathed a sigh of relief for every problem resolved. With six children that was a lot of heartache, except that he never saw it that way.

Diane arrived, his youngest daughter. Dad visibly brightened, sitting up on the edge of the bed to greet her. One of her presents was a small bag of peanut brittle. Dad's face lit up as it always did at the sight of food. He opened the bag immediately, put a chunk in his mouth and then offered the bag around.

'You know,' he said, sitting up straight on the edge of the bed, 'in myself I feel as well as I have ever felt in my life.'

The television had been playing quietly and mostly unnoticed up to this point, but there was an advert playing a song just at that moment. Buoyed up by the sweet taste on his tongue, Dad began to sing along: 'Love is in the air, everywhere I look around. Love is in the air, every sight and every sound … '

Aunt Pauline, mostly housebound by her excessive weight and finding stairs almost impossible, made the journey to see her brother on the Monday. She braved the steep driveway and, after a pause for breath, the stairs to his bedroom. Nobody needed to tell me what intimation had driven her to do that. When I arrived in the evening the doctor had been, nurses from the hospice had visited, and it was all decided: he would go into the hospice the very next day.

'What do you think about death, Dad?' We had a moment alone together.

'Oh, I'm not thinking about that. They are going to get this pain under control and then I can start moving forward. I'm thinking positively about it, don't you worry.'

A few weeks ago, exasperated and frightened by the pain, Dad had sat at the tea table, and when Mum left the room he had turned to his youngest son and said, 'I'm a gonner, Keith.' And Keith had told him not to talk like that. I knew he had such thoughts, but I followed that advice, deciding just to be a son and accept what he said. Keith had been his most dependent son, emotionally at least; I guessed that was why it felt easier to be weak with him rather than David or me. Just as I had deliberately shared my weakness with friends, Keith had unwittingly done that same noble service for Dad.

I cannot define the feelings I had as I left that night, saying goodbye to him in his home, knowing that it might be the last time I would visit him there. Nor could I imagine what went through his and my mum's minds the following day as he was helped into the ambulance with a handful of belongings and driven away. I was at work, but my thoughts followed his every step.

The hospice was quiet. Dignified. Some of the people looked like they had been there for a very long time. Dad talked positively again of how he had settled in, how his drugs had been sorted out, how this was the best place to be, and how many people were there just for periods of respite care. So we settled into a routine of evening visits, taking turns waiting in the visitors' room when the numbers were too many to be sitting round the bed.

On Wednesday he was taken to the hospital for a series of tests. Julie said, when she returned home that night, that Dad had decided it was time to write his memoirs. She had promised him a dictating machine. I said I would take one in at the weekend; I left my doubts unvoiced.

Late on Friday evening David rang after his visit. He was upset and worried. He couldn't believe how Dad had deteriorated in the few days since he had last visited. Dad had been drifting in and out of consciousness and his speech had been slurred. Was it the drugs? Were the doctors doing all they could for him? David was feeling angry and wanting to channel his anger into doing something, but I sensed also that he had hit that awful realisation inside, the one I had hit a week earlier. I didn't have any reassurance to offer, or any plan, or anything. I said, lamely, that I would be seeing Dad the next day and I would see how he was then. Maybe David was exasperated with me by the end of that call, but he didn't show it.

It seems odd to me that I should have done this now, but on Saturday morning, at the end of my meditation, I spent time with Dad as I had done every morning that week, and then I spent time with Kate. I had noticed during the week that she seemed down. The initial high spirits I had seen when she first spoke of my letter had given way to a sadder or more confused state of mind, just as my mood had sunk into confusion for its own particular reasons. I didn't know what reasons Kate might have; I didn't know for sure that she was feeling down, I just felt it.

So I called Kate into my presence and, when I could feel her there, I asked her to give me her sadness. The feeling that came over me at that moment was quite unlike any personal experience of sadness. Every fibre of every muscle of every limb was sinking down, pulled by a remorseless weight. It took genuine effort to lift this sadness from me, to let it evaporate and rain down renewal upon us both. We have a limited range of words with which to express our feelings; how little we would ever understand if words were all we had to work from, if our own experience were all we had, if we did not have this finer sense of empathy. Still, I don't know why I gave those thoughts priority or why I continued to read *The Quest of the Overself* to the end, noting down memorable words of wisdom; why I continued to rise early each morning, imposing discipline on myself above all else; why for all the world a part of me carried on as if nothing tragic or final was taking place.

Saturday was my mum's birthday. I had bought a card and some clothes for Dad to give as a gift. Julie and I arrived at the hospice early so that he might write the card. Dad was awake and taking things in a little better than I had been led to expect. When Mum arrived later, he gave her the card. I hadn't seen him write it; Julie had helped with that while I had been doing something else. When my mum opened it I saw a simple message: 'You mean everything to me.' The message alone would have been heart-rending enough, but the writing choked me inside. Dad had always been so proud of his writing, its neatness and flowing form, one of the few things he had learned from school before leaving at the age of fourteen to earn a living wage for his family. The words on my mum's card had not flowed but had struggled into being, letter by letter. A supreme effort of control and concentration had been required for them to make any legible sense. Broken words from a burning heart in a breaking body.

Even so, Dad was cheerful. He willingly climbed with assistance into a wheelchair in order to take a short walk in the hospice grounds. Before we could set off he was sick. He had been able to warn us and Julie found a container to catch it, but he was violently sick, a side effect of the medication. Barely had he finished than he looked around the ward with his milky eyes and apologised to a lady looking in his direction: 'Sorry, love.'

There was no need. Of all the people in the ward at that time Dad's situation was the most serious, but he still apologised. Even at such a moment he could not help but feel for others. The day before, he had opened his eyes from a deep sleep to see Trevor sitting before him, and his very first words, coming more quickly than thought, had been to ask, 'Have you heard about that job yet?' It would be nice to think that my own concern for Kate had stemmed from a similar deep-seated altruism, but I couldn't be so sure about that.

Our walk in the grounds was brief. It was sunny but cool and we couldn't take too much of a risk. On the way back inside Dad asked, 'Will I be coming home soon?' Mum told him gently that he needed to get a little better.

Early this morning Mum rang. She had received a call from the hospice. Dad had had a bad night and the doctor wanted to see her to discuss his condition. We were meeting anyway: a muted family get-together had been arranged for Mum's birthday.

It was a warm day. Mum had busied herself putting chairs out in the garden and single-handedly making a spread of food sufficient for nineteen less one. Her self-control was incredible. To think I had once, as a cocky adolescent, thought of this state of mind as superficial. At midday Mum, Kim and I made ready to set off to the hospice; Anne would stay behind to look after the children. David and his family arrived just at that moment and he went with us; I was glad of that for his sake.

Once there a nurse steered us immediately into the waiting room and called for the doctor. He came promptly and sat among us, the nurse sitting silently to one side.

The doctor took us methodically through the facts: Dad had been very poorly during the night and they had become very concerned; they had tried to regulate his pain killers, but his level of consciousness had not stabilised. They believed that he had suffered a series of small strokes; this would account for the deterioration we had seen in his co-ordination and heard in his speech. They had received this morning the results from the hospital tests last Wednesday. The tests had shown that the cancer had returned and had spread to other areas. The doctor was careful throughout not to speak of Dad as a patient, but as a human being, always referring to him by name: David.

David – his first-born son – spoke up: 'So does this give you an idea of the kind of treatment he needs, because it needs to start soon?'

As David spoke, the doctor looked directly at him, acknowledging and restrained. I looked towards the nurse and momentarily caught her eye. Her expression was kind, but she could hold my gaze only for a second, and then she looked down at the ground. She told me, in that look, what I needed to know.

The doctor had started to answer David by telling him where the cancer had spread and the difficulties to be overcome.

'How long will he live?' I decided to ask the doctor outright. I wanted to make things easier: easier for the doctor, I suppose, and easier for David.

'A few days, maybe longer. It's difficult to say, but there's nothing we can do now except keep David comfortable. I'm sorry.'

'Thank you,' I said. I was prepared for those words and grateful for his honesty.

The doctor waited a few minutes more and, receiving no further enquiry, granted us time alone. He and the nurse slipped away. We looked at each other. Mum was smiling – I think because it was her habit to smile through pain – and her eyes were full. 'We'd best go see him,' she said, and we filed quietly out of the waiting room to settle by his bed.

Dad was in a heavy slumber. Mum and Kim sat down, one taking his hand, the other resting a hand lightly on his leg. David and I stood behind. I looked at David and saw the tears in his eyes and the tremble in his skin. I could not remember when I had last seen him cry.

Dad jolted, drew in breath sharply and opened bleary eyes to stare about at us with a childlike confusion. We smiled the deepest, kindest smiles of encouragement. Mum squeezed his hand and said hello as we all reached to touch and reassure him of our love. I don't know what he was thinking, and his attempts at words were indecipherable, but what I felt was that he, in his turn, tried to reassure us that we need not worry for him. A little while and he slipped back into slumber. We took time then to hug each other. As I held Kim closely she was calm; she had prepared for this moment too.

One by one the rest of the family came and received the news. Hayley and Cathy, who had not seen him in recent days and had no sense of the deterioration we had witnessed, sat in silent shock as I explained to them what the doctor had said. At the doorway to the ward they held on to me and wept. I felt very proud of their tears.

We arrived home late and I mentally prepared for a busy work schedule the next day with no idea of how my emotions could allow me to cope.

## Monday 24 June 1996

When I got up this morning, despite all the desperate feelings, a thought kept nagging at me. I didn't like having it but it kept coming anyway. I kept thinking, 'I've lost the race.'

I got into the car, put on Sibelius at high volume and drove towards the motorway. By the time I was queuing to join the slip road, the horns and trumpets were working up to their crescendo again and my tears were flowing freely in response to every shade of intensity in the music. I had a vision at that moment of Dad riding high in the sky, the One-Armed Bandit; there was a strange elation bursting through my tears and I cried, 'Go for it, Dad!' It was right and good that he should go before me, as he had in everything I had done. It felt like he was blazing a trail for me, for all of his family.

Twenty minutes later I parked the car, wiped the tears from my face, and went about my business. I arrived back at the office late,

Sibelius thumping out of the sunroof, a source of amusement to some, hanging out of open windows in the warm summer afternoon to see who was making such an entrance. There was time only to dump the day's papers on my desk, turn around and head for home, and it suited me that it should be that way. Heather, sitting in a distant corner of the office, caught my eye with a smile of immense sympathy. She couldn't possibly have known, but she seemed to have sensed how things were.

In the evening all his family visited, his wife and all his sons and daughters. When I thought about it later I realised that we had all had the chance to spend time alone with him, though he was never apparently conscious at any time. We must all have shared our private thoughts with him. I don't know if others talked aloud. For my part I sat in silence, believing that in his slumber Dad would hear my thoughts better than my voice, or at least that he would feel my presence and my thoughts didn't really matter.

David spent the last hour alone with him, leaving at ten o'clock. The rest of us had left at nine. We had talked about keeping a vigil by his bedside, but we really couldn't tell how long that might last and decided it would be better to pace ourselves. David arrived back at Mum's house and assured us all that Dad was sleeping peacefully. I set off to drive home.

There was another unwelcome thought. When I drove to and from the hospice or Mum and Dad's house I had to pass close to where Melanie was living. It had never bothered me before, but in these last few serious days I had kept expecting or hoping that I might see her there, and I was not sure why.

I was aware of my ego wanting to show her that I had other important things to attend to. I questioned why it would not rest, even at such critical moments, but I knew that Melanie and I had always been linked through death – Melanie might have scoffed at the notion but that was how it had seemed to me. She was the first person ever to share with me the pain of bereavement. The date of her sister's death was the same as my first daughter's birth, only a year separating the two events. Years later, after a long illness with cancer, her father died on my birthday. I had been through those times with Melanie and a part of me wished for her to be here now for me. In the scheme of things though, this was no more than a tiny wish floating into consciousness each time I passed that particular junction on my journey.

Arriving home late again, Julie, Hayley and Cathy were waiting up to hear how Dad was. I told them and we all made our way upstairs together. I was undressing wearily, sitting on the bed preparing for the next day – some intuition must have told me to leave all the papers I needed at the office, rather than bring them home. The phone rang; it was Mum.

'The hospice rang me at ten past eleven. It's your dad, love. He's died … They tried to get word to me but he just went too quickly in the end.'

The slump in my body told Julie what had happened. Hayley and Cathy had heard the ring and were carefully treading into the bedroom with expressions of grave concern.

'Oh, no.' A heavy resignation crept over me.

'People are coming back to meet here. We were all going to go together to see him.'

'I just need to get dressed again, Mum. I'll come straight back.'

We all needed to comfort and to be comforted at that moment, strange sensations of self-concern and concern for others rolling and tumbling over each other in ways which could not be separated. And thought for Dad, for everybody; it was impossible to tell where to begin.

As I drove back I reviewed our decision to leave him and not to keep a vigil. It could have seemed like a very wrong decision, to have left him to die alone like that in a strange place, after all this time and after all he had done for us, that we had not held on. That's when it occurred to me that, one by one, his wife and all his children had spent a special time alone with him over the course of the evening. In the end I felt he had chosen to slip away quietly and trust our fates to the safe hands of the love in which he had raised us.

# 1 July 1996

It was midnight, the first minutes of Tuesday, when the door to the hospice was unlocked and we were guided unobtrusively through the corridor to a side room where Dad's body had been laid and made ready for our visit. We were shown inside and left alone by the nurse. Though I had never seen the moment of his death, it was clear to me as anything could be that something had left that body behind. Even the frail father we had seen only hours before, hanging on so tenuously to this life, had looked so different to the flesh and bones now left. Pale, inert, expressionless, my father and not my father.

Mum cried over his body first, and one by one everybody else approached and touched him, spoke to him, wept for him, while I hung back, looking at the ceiling with a peaceful smile and no tears. I was thinking about all those near-death reports of people who had found themselves looking down on their own body and the people around it from some corner of the room. So I looked to the ceiling thinking that he was more likely to be there than in his lifeless body. I couldn't see anything of course, but I think I hoped that I might. All week long, sitting by him as he slept, I had tried to detect a faint shimmer of his aura, but I had seen nothing. Such weak power as I possessed had deserted me altogether, that is, if I had ever seen more than an optical illusion. I was sure I had.

In my thoughts I conveyed thanks and pride, feeling that he might read them, my countenance all the while maintaining the same smile though now a little strained. Mum looked at me; others glanced too. It was my turn to stand by his body, so I moved forward. At that moment I intended to speak quietly the words I had been articulating in my thoughts; I guess my ego wanted to be very digni-fied. I think it was when my fingers touched his cold skin. As I spoke, the words that came were loud and wretched. I was instantly gasping and sobbing.

'WELL DONE, DAD. THAT WAS A HELL OF A LIFE.' In the minutes preceding I had been thinking of it all, from the hard and hungry childhood, evacuation, losing his arm, marriage, children, the constant struggle to make ends meet, to this final struggle. I had thought of his pride for us all.

'I'M PROUD OF YOU, DAD. VERY PROUD.' I was so very proud of the way he had grown. If it be the purpose of coming to this life that our spirits should be greater for it, then I was absolutely sure at that moment that my dad had fulfilled his purpose and consummately so. And I wanted him to go swiftly on his way and not to linger for the remnants of this life to which he could no longer be attached.

'YOU CAN GO NOW. WE'LL BE FINE. THANK YOU, DAD. THANK YOU.'

I felt a hand on my arm gently guiding me away. It was my youngest sister, Diane, smiling kindly and lending me strength. Of all of us I had thought it might be she who would break down like this, but there I was, for all my preparation, more broken at that moment than anyone. And yet not broken. I had been given the gift of tears. That's what it was, a gift of tears.

One of the strangest things was this: that only minutes later, sitting in the waiting room and drinking tea, we were all laughing! One or other of us would remember some daft thing Dad had done, even some moments of anger which had long since become part of the comic repertoire, foibles elevated to legend, and we were all laughing. Back at Mum's house later, we laughed even more and none of this was by any means false or designed for distraction; it was more like celebration for what he had brought to our lives.

By three o'clock, after another drive home alone, I was subdued and tired. Julie and the girls had fallen asleep where I had left them, all in one bed. I didn't want to disturb them, so I wandered off to Hayley's bed to sleep alone, and I did soon sleep for I had no thoughts worth thinking and no faint hope to keep my heart searching any more that night.

I woke at six to light filtering in from an unfamiliar direction. I reviewed the events of the night before, and for about a minute I felt nothing. I even thought, 'I might just as well go to work today.'

And then the tears began and would not stop. At seven I rang my boss to tell him I would not be in and to give him a chance to make arrangements. I felt calm and then as soon as I opened my mouth to speak, the words came out loud and wretched, with the same wild sobbing and gasping as the night before. I tried to apologise but that came out the same and I could only put the phone down and hope he would understand.

At eight I had to move my car to allow Julie to go to work. As I opened the door and stepped outside, I felt the softest breeze and the sweetest scent in the air and knew that my dad would never again witness such a moment. And I sobbed once more in a desperate, uncontrolled manner. Julie looked on in pity, but there was nothing she could do and no consolation she could give.

Mid-morning I drove back to Mum's, where people were gathering. Hayley and Cathy were not at school; they came with me and we walked into a scene of remarkable activity. David and Anne, eldest son and daughter, had taken charge and organised all manner of practicalities. A funeral director had been booked, a date arranged, a notice in the newspaper, relatives informed, the funeral director and minister were due to call. Mum was rising to the occasion and making tea and sandwiches, assisted by Diane, and in the midst of all this David was taking calls on his mobile phone to avert a crisis at work.

I sat down and talked with whoever was not busy at that moment. I was still crying. The sobs had subsided but given way to silent tears which ran continuously, whatever frame of mind my face conveyed. Most of the time my face wore a distracted gaze, my jaw fallen slightly open, frozen in mild shock, and the tears rolled on unwiped. Nobody sought to involve me in the general bustle. Sometimes, when the tears rolled faster than ever, Hayley would sit at my feet and squeeze my hand gently while Cathy looked on in silence.

There were visitors. And these were the times when Mum would sit and shed her tears, but for the most part she had steeled herself to do what needed to be done. The funeral director delicately produced catalogues of coffins and flower sprays. Everyone joined in the choosing so as not to leave responsibility with any one person; there were no disagreements. The director asked about music. I spoke up for the first time, suggesting a song which had long been one of Dad's favourites. Everybody agreed. Then Mum suggested another, to further general accord. Finally the director suggested that a family member might want to say a few words, a tribute. There was a momentary pause. Mum said, 'Yes, it would be a good idea. We haven't really had chance to think.'

Then I said, almost without thinking, 'There is something I would like to say.' I wasn't sure what I had to say. I was thinking of the way I had so poorly expressed myself to Dad about that smiling statue and how, later that evening, I had written a poem trying to express it better, but I had never shown or read that poem to him.

There was no further discussion. It was agreed by all that I should be the one to speak. David, being the eldest, might ordinarily have borne that task, but he was happy to see me as the right person for it. The decision was conveyed to the minister who visited later. He was careful to stress that time would be limited and that many people found that they were too overcome by the occasion – he must have taken a sidelong look at the state of me. I didn't say anything. David said he was sure I would be fine on the day. Anne added that if I wasn't, there would be five others ready to take my place. It was decided.

Hayley, Cathy and I arrived home at teatime. Julie was home and her Mum had visited as usual for a Tuesday. Small windows in each room had been opened to let in fresh air. I wandered into the living room and sat down alone for the first time that day, tired and still a little tearful. On our weekend away with Anya, as a thank you present, Anya had bought for us a small wind-chime. I had later fixed that wind-chime in the living room by the small window which was now open. Although it had been in place for several weeks and that window had been opened many times, the wind-chime had never chimed once. I must have put it in a sheltered spot. It was now a warm and breezy evening. For the first time ever, the wind-chime was ringing furiously, incessantly. It rang the whole evening long. As I listened I remembered the words of that song, the last thing I ever heard my Dad sing: love is in the air, everywhere I look around, love is in the air, every sight and every sound …

It was true, love was in the air. The spirit of my dad was with me, with us all.

On Wednesday morning Julie went to work and the children went to school as usual. I sat down at my desk to begin the task of writing. Two weeks earlier I had noted down Dr Brunton's words that, scientifically speaking, matter is next to nothing and space is reality. If we were to eliminate all the unfilled space in the human body and gather the remaining protons and electrons into a single mass, the body would be reduced to a speck so small it would take a magnifying glass to see. Those words were written sixty years ago. Science since then has discovered that those protons and electrons are every bit as porous again; we are nothing but empty space. Despite my dad's singular mass and appearance, what moved people, and what they remembered, was his spirit, for in truth that is all there ever was.

As I began to address that spirit I embarked, unwittingly, upon a process of intense grieving which was to last fully six hours. The sobbing was loud and intense interspersed by extraordinary drawing in of breath as my body struggled to keep up with the spontaneous pouring out of emotion. The private grief I experienced in those hours was quite different from the public grief that had gone before. The pain of it was such that it felt like something being physically torn from my chest.

135

I could not for one second look away because in the thick of this wailing sorrow was the essence of what I had to articulate for the sake of my family, for Dad himself and for all his friends, and because I had to do him justice. Only once did the pain become so bad that a thought flashed in my mind: 'This is too hard.' But no sooner was I aware of this than I roared back with great force, 'NO! LET IT COME!' At that moment I was aware that I was doing it for my own sake too. The months of meditation which had gone before had fostered an inner assurance that this emotion, no matter how bad it became, could not overwhelm me. Therefore I was free to let it come and felt sure that, at that moment, it was the right thing to do.

I learned something in those hours that I had never known before: that in the depth of suffering there is wisdom and even ecstasy. For every question I asked in desperation, an answer came rising out of the turmoil. Sometimes it seemed that those moments of wisdom caused the tears to flow more intensely still, sometimes it was in the moments of deepest sobbing that wisdom revealed itself. At those times I truly did not know whether I felt the desperate agony of loss or the ecstasy of revelation; they were both the same!

My dad's special quality was in valuing everybody he met for the complex individuals that they were, and without making any great show of this natural magnanimity. Wisdom told me it was because he did not use anyone as a mirror or a sounding board for his own personality that, in some mysterious way, his own personality shone larger than life in our eyes. I learned that Dad's ability to admit, to share, and heartily to laugh at his own mistakes was a special brand of wisdom in itself. I thought of his faults – for I had no wish to paint a perfect picture of him – and wisdom told me that, such is the miracle of heart-given love, even faults can live sweetly in the memory and provide the fondest laughter in a way that a more perfect man could never have hoped. As I felt the physical tearing from my chest and contemplated that my mum and all my brothers and sisters would be feeling the same, wisdom told me that this pain was the unfastening of our heartstrings from the physical life we could once see, so that we might better feel his spirit with us, and that this pain was to be borne with gladness and a faith undimmed.

I kept thinking about Trevor. In a less tearful period the day before I had sat outside with him in the summer sunshine on the front doorstep of my mum's house. Trevor said that Dad had been the first person in his life ever to show faith in him and to build his confidence. It had seemed a remarkable thing that, in his forties, Trevor had never had that privilege in his life, and remarkable too that Dad had naturally answered that need. It wasn't a matter of identifying the need – who knows, many others, even I, might have identified it with more time – it was just what Dad did, for everybody. That's what made me understand, or perhaps just reinforced for me, that Dad really valued people, not because of anything they might do for him but just for who they were.

I thought too about Aunt Dorothy whose husband had died in recent years from a muscle-wasting disease. One day when she was wandering around town feeling particularly low in spirit, worn down by the continuous round of care and attention to her husband's needs, she had accidentally bumped into Dad. He had greeted her very cordially and invited her to a café for refreshment. I don't know exactly what he said that afternoon, but ever after Aunt Dorothy would describe it as 'something out of Mills and Boon'. She didn't mean that in the sense of romance between lovers, as those books are apt to portray, but rather in the sense that he had arrived like providence to answer a prayer silently spoken from her heart that day.

She and Trevor were just two people touched for the briefest time by Dad's special instinct to value people. As I wrote, I mourned inside for them because they had not, like me, had that gift for all their lives. What consolation could there be, I wondered, for having something given and as quickly taken away? Then wisdom answered me saying, 'A man who lives a life of love is always in the right place at the right time.' Wisdom told me it was not the quantity but the quality of what he gave that mattered, and that quality lay like a seed in every heart. It was for each individual soul to mourn, if they would, or to nurture that seed into a flourishing part of their own spirit.

Come the mid-afternoon one final gasp of that agonised ecstasy left me as I consciously wrote the final words to round off his life. I put down my pen and it felt like a raging storm lifted from me and was gone. I rose from my seat and left the desk which, mentally at least, I had not left for six hours, would not and could not leave until the task was done. I walked into a different room and looked out of the window. Bees were busy gathering nectar from the pink blossom on the trellis by the front door. It appeared indescribably beautiful, and a wonderful peace came upon me. At that moment I knew that my grieving was over, not that I would never cry again for him – I was sure I would – but in some fundamental way the grieving had run its course.

I also felt sad. I realised that by electing to be the one to speak for Dad and by putting myself through the ferocious and concentrated mourning which that task had required, I had unknowingly done myself the greatest service, and to that extent had deprived the rest of my family of that singular healing process. I was also aware that the words I had written, being only words, could not possibly convey for others the true depth of vision I had experienced in articulating them. So be it. The peace I felt was profound and unshaken by these thoughts. I rang my boss and told him I was fit for work and would be back the next day. He wouldn't hear of it, however, and ordered me to stay away until after the funeral on the following Monday.

On Thursday I returned to Mum's house in the evening. Many of the family were there: Anne, David, Diane. At a point when Anne and I were alone in the kitchen, Anne became upset. It was the first day she hadn't spent with Mum – like me, she didn't visit until evening time – it was the first day she hadn't had somebody else to support. So her own private grief came to the surface. She had been aware, she told me, that even when she was being 'strong and practical' in those first days, this was not just support for Mum but also a form of self-protection.

Diane had not spent a minute away from Mum's company. She had slept there every night since Monday. She expressed to me some trouble in her mind as to the best time to leave Mum alone. As the youngest daughter she clearly felt a strong sense of obligation. I would not have been so protective; my own experience of the preceding days had led me to believe that grief was not to be avoided for oneself or for anyone else. I wondered if Diane's loyalty was not also tinged by self-protection.

David, who also had been so practical, admitted that he was consciously protecting himself by letting grief out only in small doses. He realised that he could not avoid it in this way. I told him of my own experience, and that I thought he need not protect himself at all because even the most intense grief was all to the good. David accepted what I said but was convinced, he said, that his own way was best for him.

There was not one grieving process at work, but a different one for each of us. We had the same father, but we all experienced him in our own way, and now we mourned for different things too. The pace at which we allowed that mourning to take place was not, perhaps, so important as the spirit in which it was done.

As the week wore on towards the funeral, I found myself avoiding those things I saw as pitfalls in my own continuing grieving process. In times of happiness it was tempting to attach myself to those positive emotions. Then only hours later, at the smallest provocation, I would feel my emotions sink. I realised that to attach myself to either extreme – to attach myself at all – was a mistake, especially at this time. There may never be a good time to place reliance for one's wellbeing on the balance of one's emotions. For the present I felt it best to keep a deeper perspective and to treat all emotions with the same equanimity.

On the first days after Dad's death, in early-morning exercise and meditation, those times when I had felt him with me had been the nicest of all. On the Saturday morning I felt, for the first time, a sense of obligation to him to try to retrieve that peace, rather than let it happen spontaneously as often or as seldom as it would. When I felt this obligation I resisted it, for I saw it as a big mistake, every bit as bad as trying to hold on to his physical presence. Such moments would have no value unless they were allowed to happen naturally.

One final thing was the experience of waking each morning in a state I would describe as mental arthritis. My will was completely sunken down into a torpid state of depression. I had the feeling that whole days could have been spent in this state. I refused to let it happen, and despite every muscle resisting I willed myself to get up and maintain the discipline of rising to exercise and meditate. I am sure I was right in this for, without exception, my days began, from that point, with a new attitude.

So it was that on Sunday I awoke early and exercised as usual. The weather beyond the open window was perfectly calm. I closed my eyes and took my journey to the House on the Right Bank. As I entered the house to stand in the aura of the empty tree, the wind-chime by the open window surprised me by sounding briefly. I could hear this on the 'outside' while, remaining 'inside', I instinctively understood it as a sign that my dad was with me. I felt pleased and excited. I took a vigorous 'shower', then rushed into the great courtyard to meet him.

And there he was, such a wise and comforting person for me now. I threw my arms around him and rested my head on his broad chest. Then he spoke to me. Perhaps he felt my temptation to escape into this peace and comfort.

He said, 'John, you are here to help make heaven on earth.'

'I know, Dad. I know.'

I rested there with him for a short while, then continued on with a renewed sense of purpose.

Before going to sleep that evening, knowing that the funeral was due in the morning, I sat up straight in bed and entered that meditative place once again. I had a job to do at the funeral and I had to be sure that I was fully prepared for it. So I rehearsed the scene. I walked into the chapel listening to the music playing and weeping all around. I sat in the congregation and listened to the minister. I heard him call me forward. Then I stood and delivered my epitaph word for word, feeling all the emotion but envisaging that I remained in control to the end. I saw myself finish and sit down again. Finally, with more music, we were all leaving Dad's body for the last time, resting in his coffin. Then I came out of this state, lay down and slept peacefully until morning.

Waking this morning, I proceeded downstairs to go through the whole process once more. As I sat there, for a second time the wind-chime sounded with a single 'ping', despite the perfect stillness outside.

Early in the morning we all gathered at Mum's house to await the funeral cortege. Everyone was calm. On the journey to the cremato-rium there was some humour again, instigated by Mum and mostly along the lines of what Dad might have said about other drivers on the road – this had never brought out his most tolerant side.

The crowd waiting in the rain at the chapel was huge, so big that a second chapel had to be opened to accommodate the extra people; they heard the service through loud speakers installed for such situations. The strange thing was that most of what the minister said went completely over my head. He was reading passages from the Bible with which I should have been familiar, but somehow it reached my ears as a ritual chant. Then he called me forward.

Most of the family had by then read and approved my words. I had typed them out should anyone need to take over from me. As I took my place I surveyed the congregation, I looked at each member of my family, I looked at Hayley and Cathy who had been so worried that I may not be able to do this. But that was six days ago and they could not have understood what I had gone through to stand where I stood at that moment. I felt at peace – and I smiled at them – and began.

I spoke with a controlled power of emotion, as I had envisaged that I should. Even the poem, which had an awkward line – sometimes it seemed to scan and sometimes it didn't – fell into perfect place. As I walked back to my seat I heard the minister say that in thirty years he had never heard a more moving testimony to a father from a son. It didn't really matter that he said such a thing or that others agreed, but somehow I felt that Dad was listening to it all and feeling very proud.

I sat down, my job done, and I told myself that I could now let go and feel whatever came naturally. But in fact no different emotion came. I remained calm and benign. Come the time to leave it was Kim who broke down, wanting to stay with Dad's coffin and not to leave him alone.

Throngs of people returned to Mum's home afterwards. It was good to see acquaintances from many years previous. Catering for them had been a feat into which, yet again, Mum had thrown her practical mind with Diane's willing hands to assist and the rest of us helping out wherever we could. It turned into a day of celebration for Dad's life, a happy day filled with laughter from everyone and which we were pleased to encourage. I listened to many of his friends and felt privileged to afford them a little of the time and value that Dad would surely have given. In all it seemed a fitting tribute to a life of expanding horizons and inclusiveness.

In the week since his death we, his family, had taken a significant journey together and immense steps in private. Like Kim, caught by that last act of letting go, I had found myself looking back as we departed. I still have some heartstrings attached to his physical life and therefore, no doubt, some pain still to come.

## 19 July 1996

I keep thinking of that book Anya sent me a few months ago, the one that had provided such comfort to her after the sudden death of her husband. It was an old book, the pages yellowed and the outer leaves a little ragged. Some of the pages were coming loose from the spine and it had lost whatever dustsheet it had once possessed. In this state it had been discarded in a dustbin ready for collection. Anya had no connection with the person who threw it away, except that he or she was a friend of Anya's brother and, in the couple of days before collection of the refuse, her brother had caught sight of the book lying on top of the heap. Some intuition had persuaded him to pick up the book, browse through it, and immediately sense that it would be of interest to Anya.

He had posted the book to her, and Anya for her part recognised this action as a sign that she should begin to read at once. The book told of powers innate to human beings – and unknown to most – and it spoke of life and afterlife with an assurance which encouraged Anya to experience journeys and meetings in dream and meditation until she felt comforted by the knowledge of her husband's eternal being and his constant, continuing presence in her life.

She showed me the book, even gave me it to read, but I didn't read it. I took fright at the fragility of its pages, and knowing how precious it was to Anya, I decided to give it back unread and order a new copy for myself. It was, as I have said, the second book in a series on the life of Lobsang Rampa. In the end I decided to order the first book first; that was *The Third Eye*. Now I find that the second book is not in print and I will have to borrow Anya's delicate copy once again if I am ever to read it.

I keep recalling how Anya had described the unlikely journey the book had taken in order to find her and, in her learned English, she had expressed dismay that it should ever have been thrown away because people could find no value in 'a book without covers'.

I am tempted to give up writing here, to acknowledge that my father's life is a tale far more worthy to be told, and to wonder if there could be any more to learn than those deep and lasting lessons drawn from his life and death, or at least anything nearly so momentous by comparison. But it is the story of Anya's book, finding its way to one who truly needed it, that keeps me going. This is my book without covers. If it has no value, let it be thrown away. May it find whoever it will, by whatever route, in whatever condition.

Anya made another recommendation, a book called *Mutant Message Down Under*, Marlo Morgan's tale of a woman's journey across the Australian outback with an ancient tribe of nomadic Aborigines. The tribe called themselves the Real People; the mutants referred to in the title were the whites. In reading it I came to feel that I was doing something very similar to what Anya had done in her time of grief. Maybe grief is like a special state of non-judgement, more than just open-mindedness. *Mutant Message*, like Lobsang Rampa's book, celebrates innate human divinity, evolved powers of healing and telepathy, knowledge and oneness with one's own foreshadowed and pre-chosen destiny.

As I read on, the book seemed to walk side by side with the events and ideas arising in my own life. An American western on TV informed me that the Chinese have a tradition of changing their name to mark a momentous event in their lives, as a way of saying that they are no longer the same person. I could think of several times by this rule when I might have changed my own name. To my brothers and sisters I will always be the kid who did stupid things – the reminders come regularly. To those who have only come to know me in recent years, I am a different person altogether. It was tempting to wonder if a change of name would change these perceptions.

Then in *Mutant Message* I discovered that Aborigines have that same expectation of outgrowing their birth names and choosing a more appropriate name for themselves, perhaps several times in their lives.

I reflected too that Jesus gave new names to each of his disciples, marking their transition to a new life in their hearts and in the face of the world. To the average Western eye, however, such a gesture would look over-dramatic, or an attempt to hide or disguise the past. We lack that basic acknowledgement of the spiritual journey. The nub of it really is not to lose or disguise one's past, but to acknowledge and use it in a transforming way, just as the butterfly becomes what it is only by using all that it ever was. I pondered these things but decided just to keep working on that inner transformation.

Another experience of ideas in parallel came the very next day. In a poetic frame of mind I had been expressing, as indisputable fact, that I watch the world by holding up a mirror. As usual my rational mind had begun a process of argument and dilution. Then I read that the Aborigines, like many native American tribes, believe that each person in a group is a spirit reflection of oneself, that the qualities we find to admire are the qualities within ourselves that we wish to make more dominant, the things we do not like are things about ourselves that need working on. Indeed it is impossible to recognise good or bad in others, unless those same strengths or weaknesses are present at some level of our own being. We differ from those we admire or despise only in the degree of self-expression or self-discipline.

Most of all in this book, it was the idea of 'lessons in non-attachment' which kept striking me. Like the morning I drove to work with the sun shining, the sky a clear blue and the leaves glistening in the sunlight and the breeze, and I began to cry. I was silently saying, 'Dad, I really wanted to ask you to stick around for the next ten years; I wanted you to see what I could really do.'

Throughout my reading it had been coming home to me just how many lessons in non-attachment I had been receiving since beginning this quest last December. Irene had moved away, I was seeing her rarely where once it was daily. Then there was Melanie, whom I may never see again. Kate was there but not there, the hope of receiving any more letters from her receding. Dad's death was as big a lesson as I could have conceived. Then Ayeesha became another lesson.

Shortly after I had returned to work, Ayeesha had invited me out to lunch. I had accepted, but hesitantly. Some people had been very kind – Kate and Heather were among them – they had asked about the circumstances surrounding Dad's death and how I was feeling. It had been nice to be asked and much less awkward than the times when others clearly felt unable to ask. Maybe they lost that initial 'right moment' to ask and then it just became too embarrassing to raise the subject, or maybe Heather hit the nail on the head: when I told her how strange it had felt that no friends had rung in the week I had been away, she said she had assumed that I would not wish to talk about it, that when her father died it was the last thing she had wanted to do. All that was the reason for my hesitancy with Ayeesha; I didn't want her to feel this dilemma.

There had been no need to fear. As we sat down in a busy café she lost little time in asking me how things had been, and I began to tell her. I had related the events often enough by then to be quite matter of fact about it, perhaps even a little rehearsed. Even so I kept my eyes down, staring straight ahead at the table as I talked. I didn't want to see any signs of distraction, which always showed first in Ayeesha's eye movements. So I looked ahead and talked of the range of feelings I had been through in a detached, unemotional way.

Ayeesha reached across and took hold of my hand. It was a gesture which carried immense empathy; our relationship had never been remotely physical. I responded by closing my fingers around hers and, to my bewilderment, my eyes started to fill.

For a full hour I held on to her hand across the table and Ayeesha listened to me with a God-given attention and patience, neither distracted nor embarrassed by the passage of time, the gradual emptying of the café, or the waitress pointedly clearing tables around us. I honestly now cannot remember all that I talked about in that hour, only that I needed to talk and needed to keep hold of her hand as if it was a lifeline. It wasn't that I needed to talk of Dad so much because we actually talked about many unrelated things; it was more like a deep sense of gratitude for the chance to talk with a certain level of emotional acceptance. I believe that was what the touch of her hand had conveyed so eloquently.

That same evening I took a moment, sitting up in bed, to meditate before sleep. One of the things I had talked of with Ayeesha was my experiences of soul communion in meditation. I recalled this as I meditated and, for no other reason than our earlier conversation, I decided to call Ayeesha into my presence. It wasn't at all what I was expecting. The first impression I had of her presence was that her soul was enormous, gigantic even, compared to my own. I had never before been aware of any difference in relative 'size'. Ayeesha told me that she had been here on earth many times before and that she would need political power to achieve her purpose in this life. I asked what she wanted of me. I felt so small in comparison and was genuinely wondering why she had ever given me a second glance.

Ayeesha said, 'I need you to teach me.'

Then I asked about her medical problems, because she had been complaining of many headaches.

Ayeesha said, 'Those are not your concern. I can deal with them. I need you to teach me.'

And that was the end of our communion. I had never asked what it was I was supposed to teach her. But when she had said it I had the understanding, without it needing to be said, that she wanted to be taught to reach beyond her ego to this deeper, more powerful self.

A week later we were travelling in my car together and I told her about this 'conversation'. Ayeesha was very excited and wanted to know every detail immediately. I told her and it wasn't enough; she was desperate to know more and I had to tell her that I didn't let these things go on for too long because my imagination might get in the way. Then she turned her attention to what it all meant. I told her my understanding.

Ayeesha said, 'Go on then. Teach me how to lose my ego.' She wanted to know immediately, of course. The trouble was that I knew I didn't have the means to teach her anything there and then; it was one of those things I would have to develop for the appropriate time. I ventured an opinion anyway.

I said, 'It's as if your life was like a fine wine and your ego is the cork in the bottle. If your ego gets in the way, the wine won't flow. You have to learn to take your ego away to allow your real life through.'

'Okay, how do I do that then?'

'Well, it isn't a straightforward thing. It takes a lot of time and a lot of patience.'

I was just parking the car at this point. Getting out and deciding where to eat provided just sufficient distraction for us not to return to the subject again. So I never told her that I hadn't quite worked out how to do it myself yet, nor that the analogy I had used was already beginning to sound a bit simplistic to my ears.

Anyway, that's how our relationship is. We don't get stuck on any subject too long and no subject offers any challenge to the foundations of our friendship. To tell the truth, our friendship itself is not a make-or-break affair. I know that Ayeesha could walk away and completely lose sight of me in a maze of new entanglements. I know that I could function equally well without her. In a way that is the strength of what is between us; it is the very model of non-attachment. So I wonder why today, as Ayeesha leaves for another job, I should see her departure as another lesson.

It just seems that lessons in non-attachment can be so hard to learn. Just when you've successfully unfastened a few heartstrings, new strings are already being fastened in their place. Unexpected memories of my dad are still apt to leave me tearful, and then other losses come rolling into consciousness. My only solution is to let these feelings wash over me as I stand back from identifying with them. Maybe, like Marlo Morgan, I will one day learn to cherish the experience rather than mourn its passing.

Ayeesha and I chose to mark the occasion of her departure by leaving work early on a hot, dry afternoon to sit by a boating lake and have a few more hours to talk. Ayeesha told me that what she found 'beautiful' about our relationship was the complete absence of barriers to affect the way we related to each other. Barriers of age, colour, race, religion, gender and even differing opinions, she said, seemed to have no relevance nor cause any hesitation in the way we talked.

I thought she was right. One fruit of the natural openness we shared was our ability to criticise each other in the sure knowledge that it would be taken as constructive, supporting and always accepting, never as personal or undermining. Neither had it occurred to me for a moment, until Ayeesha drew attention to the fact, that we might have looked a little odd sitting there close together, me in my English suit, Ayeesha in shalwar and kamez.

I gave her a gift, a copy of *The Prophet* by Kahlil Gibran. Ayeesha took it as a holy book and was careful not to place it at her feet, which she said would be a mark of disrespect bordering on blasphemy. I said I didn't think Allah was so easily insulted; he wasn't too concerned about a few little rules. He probably wasn't bothered, I said, even about some of our 'big' rules. Ayeesha thought this was very radical, but she knew of a certain holy man in Pakistan who spoke in the same way, who was criticised for failing to pray at the allotted times each day but who simply answered that when one's whole life is a prayer then there is no need of such reminders. I was flattered by the comparison – I knew it was undeserved – but I agreed with his sentiment.

There was a regular passage of frisky dogs along the waterline, in and out of the lake. As each one passed Ayeesha took fright and hugged up close to me for protection. I was pleased to have this rare chance of intimacy between us. It felt nice and a fitting end to our regular times together. We made no firm arrangement to meet again. In the book I gave her I had written a note inside, quoting from the text, asking only that she might seek me some time not with hours to kill, but with hours to live.

## The Ego

One of the reasons I was so aware of lessons in non-attachment as I said goodbye to Ayeesha was a dream I had had the night before. In the dream I was aware that I had been through this scene at least once before, maybe more. I was outside the police station about a mile from my mum and dad's home. Outside was a notice board showing missing persons. I was trying to replace, on this board, a picture of a missing person. The picture had been taken down because the person was known to be dead, but I was intent on replacing it anyway. The picture was of a man called 'The Buddhist Clown'.

I knew as I awoke that the picture represented my dad, but I wasn't sure why I was referring to him as the Buddhist Clown. The dream had chosen an image which mixed self-mocking slapstick humour with the deepest wisdom. When I had been searching for things to say about his life, I had found myself echoing ways in which the *Tao Te Ching* speaks of wisdom. That thing about him not using anyone as a mirror or sounding board for his own personality so that his own personality shone larger than life in our eyes, that sentiment could have been lifted straight out of the *Tao Te Ching*: the wise stand out because they see themselves as part of the whole. They shine because they don't want to impress.

Helen asked me about that brief communion I shared with my dad a few days after he died. It was her husband, John, who was interested to know whether my dad had reassured me in any way about how he felt for me. I told her no, there hadn't been anything of that nature. It was only later that it occurred to me what a remarkable and special thing it was that our relationship left no trace of doubt about how he felt for me or anyone else in the family. And it occurs to me now that these two things are a measure of just how much he, and for that matter my mum, had sublimated their egos and worked from a deeper region of the self, at least in the way they related to us. If it was true that the people we meet are akin to a spirit reflection, my dad had, I felt, found a way to see through or to discount what he saw.

When I likened the ego, for Ayeesha's benefit, to a cork in a bottle of wine, the idea had come to me in meditation the morning after that strange episode with the soul of Ayeesha. It had felt like an elegant analogy at the time. I thought of the kind of things which might make the ego swell and choke off the flow of life and I found myself listing pride, envy, greed – the seven deadly sins – perhaps that's why they were called deadly. But if we can make our egos shrink, even just a little bit, that fine wine of life would begin to pour out and we would realise our true potential.

I began to feel that this was too simplistic when I considered what I had said about my dad's personality shining through. Thinking of the ego as something to be shrunk to the point of eradication was just another route to self-effacement, and I knew that wasn't the answer. Maybe it was better to see the ego not just as the cork but as the whole cask in which the wine is matured. The cask might just as well be empty if it cannot be opened for the wine to pour out. But once opened its greater use becomes apparent; it is no longer a mere conduit for something brought there by some other power, no longer a mere vessel; it is the place in which the wine matured into something worth drinking; it is the wood which provided a distinct, even unique flavour to the wine which flows from it.

For one who learns to live beyond the ego then, the ego does not disappear; it becomes a useful, purpose-made tool. Living beyond the ego, compared to living within it, is like the difference between a perfect tool used by an expert, and the same tool used by a beginner. Are we, the ego-bound, like so many poor workmen ready to blame our tools? An expert musician, sportsman or craftsman can make one gaze in awe at the 'effortless' skill on display. Mesmerised, the beginner might seek to acquire identical instruments, equipment or tools only to find that these things don't sing so sweetly in his hands. The real skill did not come from the instrument itself and a few hours of effort; it came from a lifetime of dedication.

We each have a perfect, purpose-made instrument – our personality, if you like. The dedication required is a lifetime of learning to hand this over to a power within ourselves greater than any fleeting skill the ego can muster.

Resolutions made at the great marker points of life are signs of this handover. Friends or relatives might see the same unchanged personality and not appreciate the different power behind it. It is probably for the better that no direct issue is made of this. The nature of the ego is to want to wrest back control a thousand times despite itself.

As if I needed another reminder of the folly of my own ego, it came to me through my thoughtless reaction to Julie one evening. She was ill, suffering the onset of a head cold, but her mother was visiting us for tea and, though Julie probably felt tired, she managed to raise her game for the length of her mum's visit. After her mum had gone, Julie's spirits sank. There was a look of sadness on her face so deep I had not seen the like of it before.

I know now – I should have known all along – that she needed her feelings to be accepted for what they were, but I was unduly distracted by the transformation I had noticed and I chose instead to be quizzical about her feelings.

Julie said, 'I can't help feeling this way.'

And I countered, with a little gentleness but not much, 'That's not strictly correct … ' I wanted to point out that she could – as we all can – adopt a different state in a moment depending on the circumstances, as I had just witnessed, and I was sure she hadn't looked or felt the same at work. But what I meant to say is academic. I never got the chance to say it. Julie lost her temper.

'Oh, I'm not allowed to be fucking ill now, aren't I?'

I fell silent and, shortly afterwards, retired hurt. There was more to this exchange than I could put my finger on at that time. There seemed to be a deep resentment lurking in those final words.

We let the sun go down on our wrath and were not able to speak again until the following evening. I tackled it head on – probably another wrong move – putting my point of view about this underlying resentment I felt she had, and that she had seemed to make such harsh assumptions about what I had been about to say and the intention behind it.

Julie outflanked this by immediately challenging the assumptions I had made of her words. Maybe she was right, but it was clear that we couldn't achieve a natural and supportive exchange while being so defensive with each other.

I began to brood and make even more assumptions about what this resentment might be. As the tension dragged on into another day I found myself struggling. I saw the whole episode as a setback and, having so labelled it, I began to ruminate upon and mentally accumulate every other setback: all those 'losses' I had called lessons in non-attachment, and then the poor support I had received from some friends.

I began the following day with a determination to focus on my inner light and to detach myself from outside influence, trusting that progress, though far from visible, was nevertheless happening and bringing about a positive outcome. Actually, I had felt sufficiently stuck the day before to reach for the *I Ching* and this is what it had advised me to do. But it was so hard: hard to stop my brain from working on problems, hard to avoid looking glum or quiet, playing for sympathy, giving out unnecessary negativity to those around me, hard to detach.

I wrote in my book at the end of that day:

What I lack most of all at this time is humility: to see my ego's influence on things as minimal or non-existent and to live not in despair at this truth, but in constant hope that a higher power – my greater self – will move things for my highest good and for the highest good of all life everywhere.

That last phrase was straight out of *Mutant Message Down Under*; it was how the Real People talked and I had taken it to heart. And having written those words – having put them 'out there' instead of somewhere less than fully formed in my head – made me think of the ego in another way, as a kind of ghost in reverse. The ego sees itself as solid and seeks to move and influence life, but life is spirit and our solid egos pass straight through it, leaving life totally unmoved. This lack of effectiveness is not apparent to the ego; it hides from its own ephemerality by seeking to attach itself to those things it deems to be of substance, be they money, property, physical appearance, place, employment, other people, to name only a very few. The ego finds its identity by cleaving to knowledge, opinion, behavioural traits, success or failure, beliefs about the self, others, the world, life – all of these for better or worse, lest the foundations of identity be seen as feet of clay – while the Greater Self sees the many uses these things offer but attaches to none, having the perspective which shows that all these things pass away.

I wrote on:

While ever I am in my ego I am powerless. The only thing I can do is to reach for my own spirit, to wait patiently for the life of my spirit to enter me (for I am powerless to enter it) so that I might finally commune with real life, instead of 'living' an illusion. Until then, if my ego should continue to seek influence, I should remember I am nothing but a ghost.

To force the point home further, my eye was caught by the following as I browsed through the *Tao Te Ching*:

Heaven and Earth don't have human feelings.
To them, all things are like idols:
Sacred – but also just empty forms.
In the same way the Wise honour everyone,
Knowing they are nothing.

To the undiluted ego this probably sounds heartless in the extreme. Only the Greater Self, the soul, spirit, can see the transcending compassion of this view.

Now all this thought and effort of will mattered not in the least to the original disagreement which had sparked it off. Truth to tell, that was resolved very quickly. It wasn't that Julie and I sat down together and worried away at an agreement; it was more a case of us both reverting to a longer perspective of fruitful harmony and finding this isolated spat unworthy of continued concern. Too often we have both seen relationships destroyed by that insistent need to find complete accommodation. The idea of working through and resolving every problem in this way sounds ideal. Maybe it fails so much in practice because the focus of it is all wrong, a focus on the self instead of the other person – needs being met, points of view being appreciated, sensibilities accounted for – and a focus on day-to-day concerns instead of fundamental values.

It bothers me that I only seem to mention my family, in the context of this enquiry, when something "bad" happens. But it seems that this must be the way of it. Our extended periods of fruitful harmony are wonderful, but it is the testing times that provide the challenge and growth that I need. It is because my focus and perspective are wrong, or at odds, that these incidents are challenging in the first place, the challenge being to change the way I am seeing things.

For all my misgivings about the sheer persistence of the ego, I do find hope in the way Julie and I were able to work our 'non-work' upon this small disagreement. If I were completely enslaved to the ways of the ego – attached, entrenched and determined to defend a certain position as if something important depended on it – I would not so easily have stepped back to find a better perspective. Still less could I have mentally taken Julie's position, as I did, to see my actions from her point of view, and then a separate position altogether to watch our exchange with detached interest. Julie must have done much the same, to her credit.

This mobility of consciousness – and the natural healing it performs upon the cuts and bruises of daily relationship – is probably a trait of the spirit, a mark of empathy and love, and therefore to be encouraged. That is not to say that the spirit can be conjured into being by appropriate behaviour; that would be an idea from the excitable ego, once again cherishing the illusion of effortful control.

I imagine it more in the nature of a house being made ready for habitation and the ego finally persuaded to hold open the door.

# 24 August 1996

Holidays have been for me, as Charles Dickens once suggested, the best of times and the worst of times. In recent years they have followed a familiar pattern: frustration, relaxation, revelation, sore throat.

This is a personal fault. I find it hard to adjust to the idea of taking a holiday. I never feel the need for one. The occasional break from work maybe, but a break from everything? The things I like to do, the friends I see, the books I read, the goals I pursue? That's not a holiday, it's an imposition! At least that's the way I find myself thinking. I am metaphorically pacing around in my head like a caged lion, looking for something to do, somewhere else to be.

I don't learn nice things about myself on holiday. I can be so judgemental! From the first moment of arriving at the airport I have everyone parcelled as hedonistic fun-seekers with no depth to their lives, and even while I'm thinking it I don't know why I'm thinking it. I could meet any one of these people in the street on a normal day and not feel so judgemental.

When we get there, and I go along with the artificial social situations – the rep's meeting with free drink and details of organised outings, first evening drinks at the bar – I realise that there is something about this unstructured and purposeless nature of holidays which actually scares me: I know it is going to throw the oddness, the obsessiveness of my character into sharp relief against all these 'normal' lives, their idiosyncrasies temporarily subdued and their normality looking more packaged and uniform than in any other environment; a uniformity of aspiration and expectation to which I have hardly begun to adjust.

I wrote all these things down but concluded with the words: 'There must be a purpose in my being here.' I know that holidays in the past have ultimately been rewarding experiences, high points in understanding and insight. It was several years ago on holiday that I tucked *Zen and the Art of Motorcycle Maintenance* into my rucksack and read it for the first time. When Robert Pirsig strode out above the timber line and talked about the high country of the mind I was right up there with him, looking down on all those different routes heading for the same destination. The following year I read *The Road Less Travelled* by M. Scott Peck and was transported once again into that peak state of understanding. I put the book down, lay back in the sunshine and listened to *Magic and Loss*, Lou Reed's summation of an album of songs about death. He sang of passing through every state of mind – humility, sickliness, anger, self-deprecation – and having the strength to acknowledge it all. He sang of savouring the magic that lets you survive your own war, and finally finding there's a door up ahead, not a wall.

It was the image of walking towards that door that held my attention. I thought of *Zen* and *The Road* and felt so clearly that Lou Reed was saying the same thing. They were all saying the same thing! And I couldn't even tell you now what that thing was, because I can't grasp it so clearly any more, I just remember how that clarity felt, that exhilaration. I have read since about peaks and plateaux of spiritual insight, that we hit peaks that cannot be maintained, but these peaks, in time, become a baseline state from which new peaks are achieved. And if I know that holidays are capable of sparking off such experience, for all the attendant frustrations, why must I still revel in the frustration? Can I be so short-sighted?

I thought about the judgemental state I had fostered on that first day and remembered the words of Jesus:

> Do not judge others, so that God will not judge you,
> For God will judge you in the same way you judge others,
> and He will apply to you the same rules you apply to others.
> Why, then, do you look at the speck in your brother's eye,
> and pay no attention to the log in your own eye?

All that stuff I had read about the illusion of time made me question my traditional view of this process. When I looked back at the impressions I had written down from that first day – and which I have repeated here – there was a simpler and more practical explanation staring me in the face. The very act of judging others brought with it the inevitable assumption of their judgement on me. Neither my judgement of them nor their judgement of me had anything to do with them; it all began and ended with me, a coexistence, like two sides of the same coin. I could not pick up the coin at all without picking up both sides.

Before I came on holiday, I came across these words in the *Tao Te Ching* and wrote them down in my book:

> Give up trying to seem holy,
> forget trying to appear wise,
> and it will be a lot better for everyone.

I wrote them down because they brought me back to humility and how far I seemed to be away from it. I didn't quite get the spirit of my own message though because two days later I was walking through the town centre at midday and passed a group of Christians standing in a circle holding Bibles whilst a woman in the middle shouted and harangued passers-by for failing to heed the word of God. I walked by amused that they should believe this was the best way to persuade people, but also faintly embarrassed to feel associated with them if I should have stopped to listen.

Helen rang me later that afternoon. Quite by chance she had seen these people too. She had taken the trouble not just to listen but to walk right up to the vociferous woman and ask, 'Why are you shouting at people?'

The woman had explained to Helen that this was the message they had received from God, that they should serve Him in this way. All in all Helen had had a fruitful conversation, and said she had walked away feeling blessed by the encounter. I had walked away feeling, to be frank, a little smug.

And yet, that same day, Helen told me that she thought of me as her spiritual adviser; that I had an instinct to make contact with her at the right time and to speak about the things that were on her mind. It struck me then that, if I had any such ability, it was completely unconscious, and if I tried to make it otherwise I could only destroy it. It occurs to me now that Helen had the right approach to those Christians, Helen is the one who, all along, has remained open to events, and Helen, not me, has the humility to see, acknowledge and be thankful for the influence of others in her life. There are flaws in me which make me fall far short of this.

In the first days of the holiday I felt my own "holiness" and studiousness surround me like the jaws of a vice as I failed to adjust to new circumstances, new people and a new place. And judgement of place seemed every bit as toxic as judgement of people. What good could it do me to feel "out of place", how could a place change to suit me?

I described the personality as a wine cask, an instrument and a house awaiting occupation, but a cask can be badly conditioned, an instrument can be badly tuned, and a house badly in need of repair and clearing out. These are the results of less than beneficial treatment at the hands of the ego. In childhood the ego develops personality traits as a reaction to its environment and the behaviour of people around it. A series of coping strategies or control dramas are developed, mostly without conscious decision. In teenage years, there is more of a conscious effort to establish and define the personality. But it still has the flexibility of new skin, and can be changed at a moment's notice. Hayley and Cathy were none too sure of our holiday resort, arriving at night and with little notion of the social atmosphere. But within a few days they made the adjustment, approached people, made friends and generated their own social scene. It was a heartening process to observe.

Julie arrived with very specific expectations and no great need of adjustment. She joined in immediately with the pool-side games and other activities, building a rapport with each 'trivial' event. The skin of my personality, I felt, had grown older with me, more defined, more rigid. It did not include a holiday attitude or a set of holiday behaviours to adopt on cue. So I sat around the pool and tried to make use of my time by reading, wondering what holidays were supposed to be about, and somehow not quite getting it.

It began to feel as if my rigid character traits were indeed encrustations which imprison the soul, hide it from seeing and being seen in the world. If tears, chief among the heralds of the coming of grace, had dissolved some of these encrustations, I should be glad, but there was still further work to do. Any attempt to move towards a more enlightened state must necessarily illumine first those traits which block the desired path. So I told myself that identification was a positive step and not a matter for discouragement.

I pondered this and became increasingly engrossed in John Irving's *A Prayer for Owen Meany*. Then I received an unexpected message from my reading. The characters were busy rehearsing and performing Dickens' *A Christmas Carol*. The ghost of Jacob Marley, visiting Scrooge by night, said:

Mankind was my business; the common welfare was my business; charity, mercy, forbearance and benevolence were all
my business. The dealings of my trade were but a drop of
water in the comprehensive ocean of my business.

I felt a chill of shame. How was it that I could know this and yet not
know it? How deeply did this reflect the conclusions of my own
mission statement, completed and signed with a flourish just one
year ago? My dad demonstrated it, Julie demonstrated it, my children lived it. Irene was right: connect on any level. The level was not
the point; it was a drop of water in the comprehensive ocean of my
business. Surely I should 'give up trying to seem holy'.

I returned to the apartment and took out again the copy of the
*Tao Te Ching* I had brought with me. It said:

Someone seeking learning knows more and more.
Someone seeking Tao knows less and less.
Less and less, until
things just
are what
they
are.

I didn't go out, Scrooge-like, into the courtyards and taverns looking
for babies to hug and people to greet with uncommon generosity,
but I did begin to relax from that moment, to adjust to this temporary place, forbear its company and accept a new pace of life. As
usual, all my efforts of thought had not assisted and had probably
delayed the process.

In the late mornings I would retreat from the rising sun to exercise and meditate in an air-conditioned room. I had been struggling
for months in my standing exercise, with a bias of weight unaccountably resting on my left leg. But suddenly, finally, I hit a state of
equilibrium, perfect balance and exquisite relaxation. How strange
it always seemed that no amount of physical effort could push me to
that place, and yet the right state of mind could transport me, body
and soul, in an instant.

There was the single ping of a bell, the signal I had accepted as my
dad's presence, but there was no wind-chime here. I continued to
meditate with my eyes closed, brushing aside puzzlement for the

time being. When I opened my eyes the source of the ping was apparent. It came from the old bell-style telephone on the bedside table. There must have been a momentary connection through the switchboard.

The next day I got the chance to meditate again, continuing through *The Quest of the Overself* with the analysis of the physical self:

> Wherever there is conscious intelligence there must be life activating it. We see ... that life accompanies the mind in its dissociation from the physical body awareness, without, however, involving the death of the body, for the exit is but temporary. It is thus clear enough that mind and life may manifest through the flesh, as the electric current manifests through the bulb, but are not completely dependent upon it for their own existence; indeed, they are really quite capable of being independent in their functioning, as the normal state of sleep and the abnormal state of hypnotic trance demonstrate.

Each time I meditated upon these passages I continued to experience the extraordinary snapping together of memories, feelings, thoughts and impressions that I noticed on the very first occasion. The effect – compared to traditional reading and an intellectual understanding which is all too easily left unused and ultimately forgotten – is to underpin that higher understanding with an intricate web of supporting associations woven into the wide and varied fabric of individual life experience.

My mind followed that electric current, with and without the bulb, with and without the bulb, and in the midst of this there was, again, a single ping of the telephone bell. I was of course thinking about the life force of my dad, with and without the body. If you like, my internal switchboard was already making that fleeting connection.

But something else kept nudging into my thoughts. It was what Melanie had said, almost the last thing she said to me: just because we couldn't see each other or speak didn't mean that we couldn't stay friends in our hearts (that was the meaning I remembered in her words). It was true: the physical manifestations of our relationship had gone, but the 'current' – the life of that relationship – was still flowing. At least that was how it often felt for me and I believed, because I had so often found this with other friends, that if we were to meet, aside from some initial awkwardness, we would relate again like we had never been apart.

At that moment I felt a 'substance' in the invisible current of that relationship as real as any moment we had spent together. I slipped away in a reverie of life flowing far beyond the ephemera of the physical.

Leaving Hayley and Cathy to play with friends around the pool for the day, Julie and I set off in a hire car to the forests and mountains inland. High in one of the hills was a monastery. Many tourists in the hills would beat a path to its door; we did the same late in the hot afternoon.

Within the monastery was a small church, the object of most people's interest. Inside, the church was adorned throughout with copious, meticulous, gold embellishment. A wooden rail ran along the front, fencing off a narrow carpeted pathway. Along the wall at the far side of this pathway was a row of icons – framed images of saints, again rich in gold filament. Julie stood at the back of the church; I made my way through the gate and on to the pathway, along which a steady stream of visitors passed. I quickly realised that I was out of place. These people were not idle tourists like me; they were, for that moment, pilgrims. Each one walked along the row kissing every saintly image in turn, making the sign of the cross before and after each one. I shuffled along with them, aware of my intrusion, until I could leave at the other side and return to Julie.

I made small talk, commenting on the decoration, and at that point Julie told me what she had been thinking. She said, 'All these riches don't seem to fit with the spirit of Christianity.'

It was hard to disagree. In the back of my mind I was thinking of Jesus' words that the poor would always be with us, but it didn't seem like much of a justification for the opulence on show. The truth was I had given no thought to it at all, and was surprised, now that the subject had been raised, by my complete lack of opinion.

When we retired to bed that night, I continued to read *A Prayer for Owen Meany*. The characters were discussing a film called *The Robe*. I remembered it too: a film about the fictional 'exploits' of Christ's robe after the soldiers had drawn lots for it, and the influence it had on people's lives. Owen Meany complained. He said it was all just a big fuss about a blanket, and that it was so 'Catholic' to get very religious about objects.

The following morning I read in an English newspaper that a book was about to be published alleging that Christ's body is buried under a hill in France. According to the article, if this was true it was set to throw Christianity into turmoil since, it said, Christianity is based on a belief in the bodily resurrection of Christ.

I had been impressed by the devotions of those pilgrims in the monastery, and had even wondered if it might be time for me to return to the church after an absence of several years. I had left when I realised that everything I was doing there came out of a sense of obligation, and it was stopping me, time-wise, from devoting energy to important things I positively wanted to do. But watching those devotions had made me think that I could perhaps return on a different footing. If I was searching for the answers to spiritual questions, a church might be as good a place to ask as any. Even so, I didn't think my presence there had ever depended on the bodily resurrection of Christ.

These small things, coming together as they did, felt significant. I noted them down and concluded, 'There is a relation in all these things for me somewhere', but I couldn't fathom what it might be. Maybe that act of writing it down was like a cause set in motion because that night I had a series of dreams, each one waking me up with a strong remembrance.

In the first, a female senior consultant of a hospital had risen high up the ranks into levels of administration. She was suddenly faced with a senior doctor having a heart attack. She had all the right equipment at her disposal, but she had no idea how to use it because she had been so long removed from real medical work. She searched around frantically for a more junior doctor or nurse. I awoke with the memory intact, and a strong feeling that the dream was significant.

I drifted back to sleep and into a second dream. The scene was once again the casualty department of a large hospital. An operation had gone badly wrong because this time the right equipment wasn't available. A female administrator explained to the doctor that she had decided to cut out this equipment in order to save funds so that a new surgery room could be completed. The decision was, as the doctor knew, ridiculous because the new surgery room could not perform at all – it could not save life – without this equipment. As I awoke for the second time the administrator was upset; she was being consoled by a nurse offering her a drink.

Once again the dream felt significant. I was about to stop thinking about it when I must have drifted back into a light sleep. In that twilight area on the margin of sleep I had a brief dream or vision of a casualty being dragged from a road accident and someone shouting, 'You can't put administration before livelihood!' I awoke with a start and with this last phrase ringing in my ears.

This emphasis on administration made me wonder if the dream was about work. I never dreamed of work when I was at home and working. On holiday I almost always dreamed about it. And I'd certainly had a bellyful of administration there; is there anyone working for a large organisation who hasn't? But as I wrote down the details of these dreams, I came to a different realisation. After a brief pause for thought I wrote on:

> This isn't about work, it's about religion. It's about the puzzle I was left with yesterday. RELIGION IS IRRELEVANT is what the dreams are saying.
>
> To an insider of religion (dream 1), all the tools are available but nobody remembers how to use them any more. To an outsider (dream 2) who knows what to do, religion cannot offer the very tools needed to fulfil the purpose for which it was built: to save life.
>
> Religion is to real life what administrators are to real jobs the whole world over. They presume to direct and set rules and parameters, structures for the whole purpose of work. In reality they are so removed that they have no discernible effect. The work goes on without them and even despite them.
>
> The dreams are telling me that the answer to my questions of yesterday is that religions have missed the point spoken by the prophet they affect to follow. By putting their founding faith in a particular physical manifestation of any kind, they are missing the point.
>
> They take the flower and ignore the fruit.

I have reproduced that just as I wrote it because that's how my thoughts came out at the time. I have no wish to engage in a religious argument. The message was entirely personal to me.

There are two metaphors I have come across in this context, both Buddhist in origin. Religion, they say, is like a raft crossing a river: when the other shore has been reached, the raft should be left behind and not carried needlessly. Again they say that religion is like a finger pointing at the moon: it should be observed only for so long as it takes to glimpse the place where it points.

It was one of the points made in *The Celestine Prophecy* that a spiritual awakening is gathering critical mass throughout the world in
the hearts and minds of individuals regardless of the swellings or
contractions of organised religion. But I had been having a private
discussion with myself since arriving on holiday. On the first day I
read a tabloid newspaper article. The columnist was criticising her
friends for their 'Celestine Prophecy' attitude that there are no mere
coincidences – that place, circumstances and people come together
for a reason and a signal of the way forward. I felt a slight tightening
in my gut when I read it. I thought, 'The backlash has already
begun.' Far from reaching critical mass, I saw it being nipped firmly
in the bud by the prevailing grip of cynicism.

The private discussion kept niggling. I thought about the way
Helen raced around chasing up coincidence after coincidence.
How, I kept asking, does that differ from a gambler's mentality?
Wouldn't a gambler seize on signs in just the same way, convinced
that Lady Luck must be with him for the turn of the next card, the
throw of the next dice, the run of the next race? It was this lurking
doubt that had stopped me all along from being so open to events in
the way Helen had been. I had tended to think that events were
indeed random, but that there was a seed of learning in everything. I
couldn't tell whether that was a fundamentally different position or
just a more laid-back way of saying the same thing.

Four days from the end of the holiday we settled for another lazy
day around the pool. Between dips and play in the water, frequent
applications of sun cream, lunch and a few other pastimes, I
continued with my book. It became clear that Owen Meany had
experienced a recurring dream since childhood, a vision of a future
event the nature and circumstances of which are not clear. Although
it was a work of fiction, I felt impressed by the faith and application
with which Owen Meany followed up the few scraps of insight he
was given. He moved, and circumstances moved with him, towards
the realisation of that final vision.

I began to realise what the fundamental difference was between
Helen and me. She was waiting for the universe to tell her what to
do, to reveal her purpose in life and direct her in its fulfilment. I had
made my own best guess at my purposes in life and, in answer to
this, had set the goals which I could best see leading to their fulfilment. These things were subject to ongoing assessment, but for as
long as they stood, I would guess the best way forward, hour by

hour, day by day, correcting and adjusting as I went along. It explained why Helen would examine events so closely while my pondering was cursory in comparison. It explained, too, why Helen was more likely to accept and include, while I was more likely to discount.

Owen Meany's goal seemed to have been chosen for him, or by a deeper part of him, but either way that's what he was doing, taking any step that brought him closer to it, and what impressed me most of all was the absolute faith with which every decision was made.

I think what I had always known, but never fully articulated, was that we cannot shirk the use of our independent will. It is bound to our destiny like a two-stranded rope, and if this paradox offends our reason, it is nonetheless true and felt in the heart. I felt it last December when I chose to write. I said: I was making a free choice but it was the only choice I felt able to make. I felt it too in that vision of humanity at the heart of creation: not merely God's creation, but co-creators with God.

As I read and pondered these things, the afternoon had drawn on towards early evening. Shadows had lengthened beneath the parasols and people had gathered up their belongings in ones and twos to make their way back to their apartments. Hayley and Cathy had left to get washed and changed for the evening. Julie followed. I read on alone to await my turn in the bathroom. The few who were left mostly sat alone and in silence around the empty pool. A steady breeze ruffled the tassels of each parasol and tripped across the surface of the water. These, and the distant breaking of small waves, were the only sounds to be heard. I put my book away and waited for just a few minutes more in the quietness. I had stopped thinking, and had found a fresh contentment in listening and being.

Eventually I collected up my things and began to walk along the pool side. As I did so I experienced a sudden expansion of under-standing, a moment of revelation. I saw – remembered – that in every-thing there is the seed of the whole. I saw in me the seed of the whole. I saw that wherever I was, whoever I was with, that connection was never lost. My circumstances, whatever they were, would always speak to me, teach me the lesson I most needed to know at that moment. It was not a matter of things coming together in the right way at the right time; the connection was always there, never lost. Neither did I need to hunt out experience or fear that I had been removed from a rightful place; my only need was to hold that connection deep inside – through meditation, prayer, a state of grace? As long as I had that, everything would happen exactly as it should.

Why were these lessons here? Because, I understood, the whole earth as I perceived it was my spirit reflection, an exact reflection of the state of my inner being. My every fault, weakness, goodness, strength, attitude of mind and every belief for good or ill would parade before me until I saw and understood. For all that my physical life is, and all the things, thoughts and emotions to which my ego strives to be attached, all this is no more than a veil, a vibration, a kink of infinite intelligence through which my inner state is translated into its physical counterpart.

When I read Napoleon Hill's words at the beginning of the year, I grasped the first inkling of this truth: that we create our own reality. I did not see the full depth and majesty of it, why we should strive to do away with all fear, all negativity, for we are the seed of all that ever is and will be. The kingdom of heaven is within us.

None of this is meant to be critical of Helen's approach compared to mine. I believe I saw that we were simply at a different stage. That feeling of choice and destiny bound together is, I think, a moment of sublime connection. The destiny we feel at our worldly level is perhaps a choice made at an altogether deeper, higher, greater level of our being. The choice that we make at our worldly level, in turn, is really to co-operate by every means at our disposal. Helen was right to look until she felt that same impeccable moment of decision.

With my hair washed and drying in a gentle evening breeze, I stayed a while in the small courtyard of our apartment under the vanilla scent of tree blossom. The others had walked on to the bar for happy hour. I took the opportunity to write down some impressions of my understanding. I think I was aware even then that written words were not going to convey the fullness of my vision. That may sound like an apology for falling short, but it seems that it must be the way of things. How could there be any way to contain the vast sweep of that sudden knowing? After all, if revelation could be transcribed in such a way, somebody would have done it many years ago; we would all have learned and should all be happy.

I felt content as I followed along to the bar, every sense opened to a freshness in the atmosphere. I greeted Julie with a casual but gratified smile, which probably did not communicate what I felt. In any event Julie did not perceive it for what it was. She parried with a cutting remark about my tardiness. In her tone I sensed an irritation several days in the weaning, and then I felt a familiar catch in my throat.

So that was my holiday. Though there were a lot of good bits I haven't included, I confess I made a mess of it. Shortly after I returned I found, in the back of a notebook, a note I had made several years ago, long enough for the ink to become faded and the author of the words forgotten:

> That man is short of wisdom who cannot put aside his ordinary routine in order to refresh his mind with rest, change and meditation.

It must have struck me as significant at the time but I comprehensively forgot it – again.

I am going to be pragmatic about this. First of all I know that a residue of grief for my dad stopped me from seizing rest and change with unbridled relish. On this, the last morning of the holiday, I began an overdue letter to Anya by talking about that experience of grief. I had barely written half a page before uncontrolled weeping compelled me to stop. So I have to allow a little leeway for that.

On a more general note, it seems to me that we human beings are, in one sense, mistake-making machines. That is an inherent aspect of freedom and responsibility, or response-ability. If we could not choose our response then we would never make a single mistake. But since human beings have a greater range of response-ability than any other living creature, it follows that we also have the greatest capacity to make mistakes. Mistakes are inevitable for all of us. What matters is that we should recognise them as an opportunity to make crucial distinctions and better choices for now and the future.

Put another way: our egos are always right within the range of their focus, but because their focus is always finite, they are always wrong. When the universe, as our spirit reflection, holds out those lessons we most need to learn however hard they may be, the effect is to draw back the ego to an ever-widening perspective. The lessons of life manage always to draw us to the consciousness of our soul.

# NIGHT

# 16 October 1996

> The moment we withdraw self-awareness from the brain it is nothing more than a piece of inert matter ... Without that self-presence it could not produce a single thought.
>
> *The Quest of the Overself*, Dr Paul Brunton

I meditated on these words. My thoughts turned to the current fad for creating artificial intelligence by electronic means and the common plot of science fiction that, through escalating computer complexity, a point of self-consciousness would spontaneously be reached, as if it were simply a question of quantity. I wondered if consciousness was already there in the machine, in everything, and what we really failed to find was an ego state – an identifiably self-serving activity – by which consciousness is typically recognised. By what measure was science trying to identify consciousness?

Further evidence followed of that sceptical backlash I had first noticed on holiday. On a TV documentary a scientist berated 'crystals, astrology and all manner of spiritual mumbo-jumbo' for leading people astray, by which he meant away from the scientific discipline of empiricism. He was attacking the least defensible aspect – the soft underbelly, as he saw it – of a rival thought system and contrasting it with the most defensible aspect of his own thought. In doing so he claimed, 'Not one person has come forward to put his powers to the test under scientific conditions.' This was hardly a scientifically disciplined statement, failing as it did to specify who had been asked by whom and over what timescale. I also noticed the curious reversal in the burden of proof. Scientists are supposed to postulate a hypothesis and then devise an empirical method of proving its validity. This scientist created a hypothesis that such and such is not so or does not exist, then challenged his rivals to prove otherwise, but by scientific means – that is, by his rules.

Empiricism, for all its virtues, has not shown itself to be the only satisfactory method or entirely free of fault. History provides examples of the human errors of method and interpretation which have shown empiricism to be alarmingly fallible from time to time.

This scepticism seemed all the more surprising at a time when scientists are confirming that all things are, in essence, energy. To be on the threshold of discoveries in this respect and yet seek to circumscribe the limits of how these energies might interact seemed precipitous. But while pouring scorn on spiritual 'mumbo-jumbo', were scientists really contemplating the idea of creating consciousness by sheer quantity?

All of this exercised my mind because I was effectively seeking a root state of consciousness by moving in the opposite direction, by paring down quantity in favour of a certain quality.

It was coincidental and ironic that Kate should tell me, not for the first time, that I think too much. She was soon to be married. Preparations had been in hand for some time. When I returned from holiday I found an opportunity to talk to her. I wanted to ask if this was an appropriate time for our correspondence to end. I didn't want to cause any discomfort for her husband-to-be and she had, after all, progressed a long way. Maybe what she once found in my letters she didn't need any more. I was trying to create an opportunity to bow out if that was what she wanted. She was getting married, so something probably had to change.

Kate said there wasn't a problem and that she still enjoyed getting my 'reports'; she liked to know all about the things in my head. So, as I expected, she left the decision to me. I wasn't keen on the way she expressed it either.

'The ball's in your court,' she said, and it sounded a little flippant, but we were in the middle of an open-plan office and I decided not to take it as an indication of feeling.

I said, 'Okay, I'll go away and think about it some more.' That was when she told me I think too much.

Actually I didn't think about it too much at all. I figured I didn't need to write, but I liked to write; Kate didn't need to read, but she liked to read. In the absence of complicating factors what was the problem? I thought I probably would carry on.

But I did keep thinking about that teasing of hers, that I think too much. I had had this levelled at me plenty of times, but it had a new twist in the light of my meditation, the ultimate aim being to stop thought. That saying from the *Tao Te Ching* came back to me: someone seeking Tao knows less and less, less and less until things just are what they are. It was true that I was thinking more and more about thinking less. But I was coming to appreciate that I didn't in fact think any more than the next person. Caught in the ego state, didn't everyone suffer an endless succession of thoughts? The appearance of thinking too much only arose because I made an effort to direct and focus my thoughts more than most, with the realisation that if I didn't idle thoughts would quickly take their place and not always to my advantage. My 'thinking' was that I should first direct and control my thoughts, then use that control to slow them down finally to a dead stop.

How close was that? If I struggled to think of nothing it could seem like a very long way away. Other times I came close without even trying. I was having a frank discussion with Helen about sex one day, what made it good or not so good. We weren't talking mechanics; it was more a question of feelings, senses; I don't even know how we got on to the subject. I said that sex was best when it was an animal thing, when there wasn't any mental 'fantasy' involved, when thought was by-passed altogether and I was just completely in the experience. I have had wonderful times with Julie which were like that: I felt like a feline creature, a panther, pawing and writhing. It was completely physical, not tender, not an experience I could readily describe as love. It was aggression without violence. It was awesome to witness, because a part of me was always a curious witness at such times.

Bypassing the thought process – not stopping it dead with a head-on assault of will power, but 'suckering' it in some way – it crops up over and over: when meditation really works, when music is truly appreciated, when dance becomes spontaneous, when the beauty of a scene or another person overwhelms. Even the thought process itself is best when concentration is so intense that extraneous thought disappears and the one remaining idea opens out into a new spaciousness.

I got to thinking about the Biblical notion of original sin, how Adam and Eve ate the fruit of the tree of the knowledge of good and evil and how, having eaten it, their eyes were opened and they saw that they were naked. Good animal sex, for all its passion without sentiment, had no trace of guilt. But after that explosive moment, when the spell began to break, Julie and I usually collapsed about laughing for the thought of what had just happened. Thought had returned. Was this original sin – the knowledge of good and evil – the thought process?

All of my questions were stupid, of course. I was still so insistent on intellectualising the whole process even while supposedly seeking something else. The very questions I posed revealed that I was not yet equipped to find an answer.

The week following our discussion about sex, Helen and I met again, this time for a business purpose. Helen needed a legal document to be signed by an old lady who was transferring a small piece of land into Helen's ownership. She asked me to go along as a witness to the signature. I was introduced to the old lady and her daughter. They lived together. The daughter had been divorced some twelve years before and had returned home where she had ever since nurtured a deep mistrust of the male race. Even in the brief sociable exchange we had, her defensiveness on all matters skirting this issue felt like steel cladding. She was the reason Helen had chosen me to go along, because such was the strength of the daughter's mistrust, she could at any moment have decided, vicariously, to withdraw her mother's consent. Helen wanted diplomacy from me above all else, so I remained polite. When she left the room to make a cup of tea, her mother came into her own. She had been sitting very quietly up to that point, slightly hunched in her chair with a tray in front of her giving the appearance of a return to a state of infancy. Her voice was frail. She was glad of the companionship and nursing care her daughter gave. I got the impression that she too thought better of challenging her daughter's strident views. She began to talk of a stroke she had recently suffered. She had collapsed at home and awoke, she knew not how much later, in a hospital bed. She described how, at the moment of waking, she did not know where she was or where she had come from. She had no recognition of anyone around her and no memory of any personal experience.

She said, 'All I knew was that I was Hazel. I kept repeating to myself over and over, 'I am Hazel'.'

After tea and further pleasantries the document was signed and witnessed and Helen and I breathed a sigh of relief as we drove away. I felt though that if there was an ulterior, personal reason for my visit that day, it was to hear that old lady's words, 'I am Hazel'.

Dr Brunton was right. If consciousness came about through the quantity of our thoughts then every morning we would experience that consciousness, that sense of who we are, only slowly materialising as our thoughts stirred into action. But that is not how we experience it, and here was this old lady temporarily robbed of all memory and thought except one, her sense of identity. If she had no memory even of her name, wouldn't she still have known 'I am'?

Another scientist on TV: he was illustrating to a class of young children the length of time that human life has existed on earth. He invited the class to stretch out an arm and pretend that the distance from the centre of their chest to the tip of their farthest finger represented the length of time that life had existed on earth. Then he asked them to guess what part of that length would represent human life. After much guessing he finally took out a nail file and shaved off the merest whisker of the farthest fingernail. That, he said, was the total span of human life on this earth. The children were amazed. I was too.

One morning in meditation, my thoughts returned to this illustration. For it seemed to me that the real I, as Dr Brunton terms it, permits only the tiniest fragment of itself to associate with the body and to vivify it. The body consciousness we achieve through growing to adulthood must undertake a vast journey back into the real I. I might have moved in that direction, but perhaps little farther than the shaving of a fingernail.

I couldn't help thinking of my dad's arm, cut off just below the elbow. Every child of his, every grandchild, and probably many other children besides had received his caution against biting fingernails. 'Look what happened to me!' he would say, thrusting the stub of his arm into view. Like those children in the classroom, we had all been amazed, each one of us in our turn. Maybe my dad got a lot closer to the real I than the shaving of a fingernail.

My dad's birthday came and went, the first of many emotional milestones for the coming year, and life turned quiet. I turned it quiet: quiet of relating and the giving and receiving of messages, as I became increasingly absorbed in my own thoughts and internal experience. Though I had thoughts and emotions, I was perversely fascinated by the feeling of letting them go. I had noticed that the methodical relaxation of my body had the spontaneous effect of releasing thought and feeling. It seemed that all my concerns – at least all the concerns of my ego – were held in the tension of my body. By letting go of that tension I was letting go of everything and was at peace.

It was perhaps timely that my morning meditations on *The Quest of the Overself* had turned to the nature of emotion. Emotions, Dr Brunton says, are inconceivable without a self to feel them. Emotions are strung out on the self like pearls on a string, yet all the time we focus on the pearls and not the string. It is so easy to see

173

ourselves as affected by our emotions, as if the grammar of truth is that emotions are the subject and our selves are the object. But emotions are inconceivable without the self to feel them. The self is, and is always, the subject, the witness to, the manager and director of emotions, which are the objects. It was a fundamental shift of perspective. An analogy was offered: that we should compare the pictures projected on a white cinema screen with the constant flickering of emotions across the wide blank canvas of the real I. The real I is emotionless.

Coincidental with these preoccupations, I read about the nature of the flow state: that it represents perhaps the ultimate in harnessing the emotions in the service of performance and learning; that the emotions, being more than just contained and channelled, become positive, energised and aligned with the task at hand; that flow is an experience almost everyone enters from time to time, particularly when performing at their peak or stretching beyond their former limits; that it is perhaps best captured by ecstatic lovemaking, the merging of two into a fluidly harmonious one; that it is self-forgetfulness, the opposite of rumination and worry: instead of being lost in nervous preoccupation, people in flow are so absorbed in the task at hand that they lose all self-consciousness; that, in this sense, moments of flow are egoless; and that, contrary to expectation, such moments are characterised by the remarkable quieting of brain activity.

When I read this I felt a flash of recognition and an instant rush of personal confirmation. I had already spoken with Helen of that experience of perfect lovemaking. But there were so many other instances: as a nine year-old boy dribbling a football down the left wing, past one, two, three, four tackles, then executing a perfect pass into the centre. I didn't even like football that much. I had never done anything like it before or since, but at the time it was effortless. I had all the time in the world to flick the ball over incoming tangles of legs, and there was that part of me again, sitting back watching with amazement and amusement.

Playing a computer game: there was an interlude of mere seconds, but one which I could never forget, in which my fingers were moving with such alacrity that I was playing 'out of my skin'. Playing music: a difficult piece I had practised many times suddenly came alive under my fingers, the bare tune resonant with every nuance of emotion I chose to inject, without the need to think about it. Somehow I had 'cut out the middleman'.

My first long-distance run as an adult after years of inactivity: the first couple of miles were desperate stop–go gasping shuffles, then suddenly I was cruising in untroubled comfort, my breathing perfectly balanced to the needs of the moment – a second wind – my mind feeling incredibly clear. I had run for a bet with my brother, but the experience sent me out again and again, seeking to recapture that serenity. And it is that same serenity which brings me back again and again to my standing exercise, even through days and weeks of difficulty, to discover once more a perfect sense calm, comfort and balance. Nor can I forget that standing so at the beginning of this year, I entered the eye of a flame the like of which I can only poorly describe and may never explain.

At work, too, I have hit moments of persuasive eloquence, simultaneously listening to myself with no little admiration. In writing I find that sense of absorption, sometimes even rapture; otherwise I would not be sitting here now writing these words.

These experiences, which I felt sure were not confined to me, made me wonder: what if our brain doesn't have to do everything? What if we could bypass that need for control and discover that our body and emotions knew exactly what to do for themselves? Playing that computer game, my fingers just knew what to do; it was perfect hand–eye coordination. Playing music became perfect co-ordination between hands and emotion. I remembered Ayeesha telling me that I listened with my whole body. The one common denominator in all these experiences of flow was the fact that my seat of consciousness was not in there wrestling with the 'controls' but was somehow unhitched, sitting back and enjoying the show.

Where does the brain really end? Does it serve any purpose to conceive that all brain function takes place in the head, and that the rest of our body, and every system running it and keeping it alive, is simply hanging around waiting for instructions from on high? Does it serve any purpose to treat brain, body and emotion as separate at all? Maybe our whole being is capable of brain function, even the energy which continues beyond our physical limit, and where then would brain function end? Wouldn't we find a connection with infinite intelligence if we just let go of that limiting model of 'intelligence' sitting somewhere between our ears?

I thought also of how fleeting the experience of flow tends to be, or to look at it another way, how easily the egoless state of flow can be snatched away by the habitually dominant ego state. As I pondered the way to find or prolong flow, the only quality I could think of was the very one I had found so woefully lacking: humility, a recognition of a power greater than one can control.

Many times I had noticed that my ego wanted to seize, retrospectively, the effortless proficiency of flow and claim it for its own. I was reminded of a favourite cartoon featuring Daffy Duck and Bugs Bunny. If I remember the plot correctly – I may have added significant twists of my own – Daffy and Bugs are in search of treasure buried deep in a mountain. The entrance to the treasure cave is protected by a secret password. Daffy – the ego – doesn't know how to get in, but Bugs – the soul – seems to manage it. Up to this point the two of them are in cheerful partnership, but as soon as Daffy sets eyes on the treasure all bets are off and he cries, 'It's mine, all mine!' For the remainder of the cartoon Daffy indulges in increasingly desperate attempts to dispose of his partner while simultaneously wrestling with a genie unwittingly unleashed by him and which is now intent on preserving the horde from appropriation. Bugs, all the while sporting a wry detached smile, goes along with the game, neatly sidestepping every trap and turning the tables on the frustrated duck.

All this self-absorption naturally blocked the flow of the little relating I was doing. Though listening had become a habitual skill, my normal attentiveness to the flow of conversation was not there. Irene spent the best part of our evening out together talking about the various men in her life and, in particular, the trouble she was having with their attitudes and approach to sex. Then, as we sat on the dining room floor of her new house drinking coffee, she asked me outright, 'What is sex like for men?'

I had trouble answering it. I wasn't 'men'; I was just a man. So I reverted to the same thing I had told Helen, trying to describe that animal feeling that made it good and right.

'I agree,' Irene said disarmingly. 'I think all men are like that. They could be doing it with anybody; it wouldn't matter!'

The conversation had taken an unexpected turn and I was on the defensive – at least I felt that I should be. I said it wasn't quite like that. I wondered why she was sitting here close to me if that was how she felt. It was like the many times women had told me 'all men are bastards', and it was implicit that I was an exception to the rule, a kind of non-man.

I said rather darkly, 'Nobody has seen my animal except Julie.' I couldn't imagine feeling that way with anybody else. There was something very unaffectionate about it and I had only really felt affection for others, but I didn't explain this and Irene didn't push it. She might have done at another time, but we hadn't seen each other for months and my dad had died in between.

Irene let the sex subject drop and asked about this instead. I told her how it had all come about and how it had felt in the end, and how strange it was that on holiday there had been so many reminders, even in a remote country. A man with white hair, another with a certain roll in his walk, even a man with one arm who came strolling around the corner as we sat outside a café. Then I told her about that feeling in meditation as if he were right there with me.

Irene put her arms around me and held me close. My head rested on her shoulder and I stared straight ahead without focusing.

The next bit is embarrassing.

'I thought I couldn't get more spiritual,' I said with a sort of resigned gravity. 'Then I just did.'

Why do I always put on that air of profound distraction with Irene? It's crap! Why do I do it? It's the old tortured artist routine coming out again at the first sign of a little comforting. I hope Irene doesn't take it too seriously. I must try to stop it.

But going back to that discussion about sex, I was either very slow or my mind was on other things. It was days later before I realised we hadn't been on the same wavelength at all. I had used the word 'animal' to mean the abandonment of intellectual involvement, getting completely wrapped up in the physical sensation. Irene's understanding of 'animal' – because I hadn't stopped to explain myself – was, I think, the treating of another person as nothing more than a sex object, there to satisfy a momentary lust.

My mind must have been on other things, and only came back to the conversation because Ayeesha telephoned. I still connect Irene and Ayeesha in my thoughts. I have described Ayeesha as a lesson in non-attachment. It was brooding about this that set me wondering at the misunderstanding, the disconnection, with Irene.

It was the first contact Ayeesha had made since our summer afternoon by the lake two months ago. Our conversation was perfectly convivial, but it left me feeling drained and discouraged. Without any awkwardness, she spoke of a new friend with whom she shared the same closeness that we 'used to' have, 'only better', because he had the same cultural background as her. Listening became hard at that point. I felt deflated but understood the quite definite need not to show it. Her family were uncomfortable about the liaison, and the culture in which they lived took away options that might have been obvious for any Western woman. For Ayeesha, community was everywhere and everybody. So she was speaking to me because there was nobody else she trusted to tell, and she was seeking support.

I did what was necessary. Afterwards I ruminated. That past tense phrasing told me Ayeesha had moved on, and I wondered if she was maintaining our relationship – if maintenance was not too strong a term – for the sake of form. My feelings about it taught me that my commitment to non-attachment still had some way to go.

It was true, and not defensive, to say that I was happy to let Ayeesha take her own course. That was why I was thinking about Irene too, because I had distanced myself by my behaviour and been unconcerned by misunderstandings I would probably have analysed in the past. But my mind was on other things. I was preoccupied by concerns which drew me further and further within myself. I no longer felt sadness or worry for the isolation this required. I was in a state of secret fascination. Unless it added to the weight of this absorption, anything outside was relegated to the level of mere distraction.

I continued to dwell on that wide blank screen of the emotion-less self, and of the link between memory and emotion. I remembered reading of experiments in which electrical stimulation of the brain was found to trigger very specific memories, but not in isolation, always with the emotions that had been felt at the time. It was as if when memory was played across the wide blank screen of the emotionless self, emotion acted as the projector: not the creator of the memory, but the thing that projected it and determined the size, colour, brightness, movement and selective focus of the image.

I thought about the past that had felt lost when unearthed emotions had seemed to alter the landscape of all that had gone before. What was my past anyway? It didn't exist, I reasoned, except in my memory, but memory did not function except through the energy of emotion.

If my feelings at the time were ultimately the product of my conditioning – the sum of my thoughts, attitude and perspective at that time – then there was nothing fixed and immutable about my past, nothing I could have truly called real, still less lost. From the perspective of the emotionless self, what was the purpose of 'past'? I wondered if its best use was as a vast pool of continuous learning, to learn in the present being the only reason to dwell in the past, to take charge of the projector, to become the director of what, if anything, played across that screen. The alternative was to let the ego take charge by default for its own misguided ends.

Many times in my standing exercise I have found my train of thought obsessing over past or future, constantly reviewing and reworking both of them. Standing there observing this one morning, it occurred to me that the ego does not understand 'now', the power it craves is always somewhere else. I tried to keep my mind still, but it would just as soon wander off into the hypothetical, unreal realms of past and future. Then I would ask again, 'What about now?' My ego did not like it. A flame caught in a vacuum, it had to destroy the vacuum for the sake of its own survival.

If this all sounds confused, it is because I was confused; I was pushing again for understanding. It was a good thing that life had to carry on without waiting to hear my answer to it all. It was a good thing that I had to carry on with life before I thought myself into a dead end, otherwise I wouldn't have been sitting in an optician's waiting room with Hayley one day, and I wouldn't have picked up the optician's magazine or seen, by way of an advertisement for lenses, a description of the meditative state which I had never seen or read before. It was a quote which poetically likened the meditating mind to a pitcher of water left to stand. Gradually all movement in the water slows to a stop, then all the impurities sink gently to the bottom of the pitcher leaving still, sweet, clear water.

As I read it I thought that, however urgent the thirst for spiritual growth, for enlightenment, there would be no point in trying to drink until that stillness and clarity were complete. Over the following days this image helped me to separate my awareness from those insistent trains of thought, to stop trying to rein them in, and simply to watch and imagine them swirling, then gradually settling like so many impurities.

Other images came into alignment, and my state of mind, once detached, no longer contrived to complicate but to accept each image as revealing another aspect of the complex whole. In *The Quest of the Overself*, Dr Brunton says that we are not our intellect, but he goes on to explain:

It must be made clear that the word intellect is here used only to signify the assemblage of thoughts, ideas, notions, impressions and mental sensations which pass through consciousness. It is not here used to indicate the far higher faculty of the discriminative, selective reason, of that which evaluates thoughts and acts as the arbiter to judge between them and their truth.

Meditating on this, being distracted – and meditating upon distraction – I followed the tangle of my thoughts through many loose and diffuse associations before pulling myself back to that higher faculty. The rich imaging of my relaxed mind took this implied command literally, rising up with the inspiration of breath high above this maze of tangled thought to a place where I could see the many detours. From there I found I could direct my thoughts or choose to look away altogether, but look at what? Into what? What am I?

Coming across this question on my first reading of *The Quest of the Overself* last May, I could not bear it. It had seemed too detached, too remote, too impersonal by half. I contented myself with the question 'Who am I?', fooling myself that there was no appreciable difference and it would serve the same purpose. A year or so earlier in a letter to Kate, I had spoken of the Buddhist goal of being unattached as one I could never imagine for myself. I wanted, I said, to be part of the maelstrom of human emotions, I wanted to be moved by others to joy or to tears, but I could not want to watch unmoved. By May of this year I was writing to her of the virtue in non-attachment, of how different it was from emotional detachment, yet even then I could only manage to ask 'Who am I?'

So when I began to ask 'What am I?', I was aware that the question itself was a landmark, a point of arrival.

Kate's wedding approached – came within a couple of days – when she rang at the end of one afternoon on the internal telephone system.

'I just wondered if you and Julie would like to come to my wedding reception? If you're not busy?' Her tone made it sound like a casual afterthought, which it may have been, but I was aware also that others would have been listening and she would want to be careful not to create speculation by any note of urgency.

' … I've been meaning to ring … '

'We'd love to come,' I said. 'I'm sure we're free.'

Come the evening, Kate looked radiant. We shared a big hug and Kate said to Julie that it had made her day complete to see me there; she had never been sure that I would really attend.

It was a happy evening and carried no shred of difficulty for me. Only a short time ago I might have been surprised and relieved to feel no emotional tug at that moment, but as Kate's onward progress reached another milestone, I was marking an arrival of my own.

'What am I? And what are all those swirling thoughts to me?'

I meditated more, looking away from the tangled maze of thought towards this inner self. Whatever it was, it seemed to be the only constant thing; the ego by contrast could be absolutely anyone or anything: it could change at a moment's notice. All the many character traits, the 'me' in view, were nothing but smoke patterns in the breeze. In a manner of speaking, the only thing giving me any particular characteristic was the fact that I had talked myself into it! But there was no habit that could not be broken, no 'I' that I could not unbecome. I could control the smoke pattern of personality, but in the thick of it there was still that question, 'What am I?'

Another chance input, adding another dimension to the complex picture puzzle I was building up: mooching around a discount bookshop, I found a book on meditation at a price that seemed silly to resist. I flicked through the pages and found a brief, unexplained reference to the Zen principle of non-duality. My eyes were drawn to it immediately. I did not need an explanation. I instinctively grasped it: the experience of oneself not being separate from anyone or anything else, nor any thing separate from any other thing – what the Real People, the Aboriginal tribe, had called divine oneness. It explained why on holiday I had experienced the whole universe as a reflection of myself without a trace of egotism.

Dr Brunton says:

> Mind-stuff is really a medium, the intermediate link between the self and the material body, and thus through the latter with the material world. It is this central position between both spheres which constitutes its importance and shows the value of obtaining complete control over it.

There was that need for control again, but it was the medium, the intermediate link which held my attention. I remembered that vision, during the night, of the self as a membrane vibrating at the interchange between two infinities. I thought of this medium as a lens bending reality to some unique perspective. But I finally settled again on that image of the pitcher of water: while the water is disturbed, our view through it is distorted; while it contains impurities, our view is clouded. Only if the water stills can we see more clearly. As St Paul said: for now we see through a glass darkly, but then face to face.

Today, meditating further on the self stripped of body, emotion and intellect, I believe I came to an understanding of the expression 'the uncarved block' – the state of what is left when all colour and expression are peeled away, or the state before any such refinements exist. The *Tao Te Ching* uses this term to describe how the ancient masters appeared: simple, like uncarved wood. Then it goes on to say:

> Trying to understand is like straining to see through muddy water.
> Be still, and allow the mud to settle.
> Remain still, until it is time to act.

That pitcher of water was an image which had been awaiting my recognition for the best part of my adult life. And as I reached into that stillness, experiencing the loss of body, emotion, intellect, every vestige of personality, and the loss of place and time, I found myself saying inwardly, over and over, 'I have no home'.

Sure I was that the ego had no home save for a self-deluding attachment to transient things. If the personality was something different, I had already found no substance in it or its foundation. And the real self? There was no 'where' for it to be.

'I have no home.'

They were the words, I remembered, of a daughter to her mother shortly before that daughter committed suicide. The mother had not appreciated such a significance in the words until it was too late.

When Heather told me in September that she was thinking of moving house, I had replied, 'Heather, as long as I have ever known you, you have been in the process of moving.'

She had, after all, only moved a few months earlier, and was already saying that this new house did not feel like home, though there was nothing wrong with it. She had moved last time, and the time before that, for exactly the same reason. She changed cars with the same restless regularity. And yet my comment was received with genuine surprise on Heather's part. A look of astonishment came over her as she confessed that she could not remember when she had ever actually felt at home in a house.

'I have no home.'

Now the words carried a deep significance for me, for certainly that feeling of loss had been pushed so far that it became not unlike that of a severely depressed or even suicidal person, detached from worldly concern.

Jesus said, 'Foxes have holes, but the Son of Man has nowhere to lay his head.' He too was facing death, and death is what I face: the death of personality – whatever – brought to an altar for sacrifice as Abraham brought his only son, as God brought his only son: feeling a deep sadness but knowing that it must be done.

Almost ten years ago to the day, I was driven home in a state of nervous exhaustion by a very perplexed and worried friend. I felt very strongly for her, feelings which complicated, coloured, excited and made more painful an already painful confusion of mind and spirit. She only knew that I had fainted in the midst of conversation. On coming round I had been emotional but unable or unwilling to explain myself. Twenty minutes into the car journey she could stand it no longer. She pulled off the road and demanded that I talk.

I struggled for the words.

'When I was nineteen,' I said hesitantly, then, 'NO, WHEN I WAS SEVEN, I WAS ABDUCTED BY A MAN AND MOLESTED IN A DERELICT HOUSE. HE STRIPPED ME NAKED … '

It was all gushing out in an uncontrollable torrent while she tried to touch, to hold, to reassure me. Five minutes of this and I sat there gasping for breath, shocked at what I had just said. I still didn't recognise it, but that was my second warning that there was some-thing seriously in need of attention, gnawing away at my insides.

My friend tried to speak; I cut her off.

'No, that's not what I meant to say. I don't know why I said that. I meant to say that when I was nineteen, I was touched by God. But I've been hiding from Him ever since. I've done NOTHING.' Another unstoppable urge seized my voice.

'AND NOW I DON'T KNOW WHAT TO DO. I CAN'T STAND IT. I DON'T KNOW WHAT HE WANTS. THERE'S NOTHING I CAN DO, AND … I'M ON AN ALTAR!'

The brief spark of our friendship did not survive that raw blast of undistilled torment, but I will always be grateful that she made me talk that day, just as my dad had allowed me to talk more quietly the following day, giving me a lesson in human relating which was to prove my salvation. Probably she was right to walk away, painful though that seemed to me at the time. Probably it was for that moment that we came together at all. I will probably never know what effect it had on her.

Nothing I had said had been pre-planned. When I spoke of an altar, I know – I remember – I was thinking of Abraham and the sacrifice he was called to make.

Now here I am again, calm, unemotional, perfectly still, turning from the salvation of relationship, contemplating that altar once more, that sacrifice, but finally understanding why.

The *Tao Te Ching* says:

> Believing you are your personality is the source of all your troubles.
> The reason you experience troubles is because you think you are just a persona.
> If you saw through this, you would have no problems.
> Stop clinging to your personality, and see all beings as yourself.
> Such a person could be trusted with the whole world.

Non-duality.

Once again I turn away from the tangled maze of thought to gaze in that other direction.

'What am I?'


## Emptiness Again

I imagine it like standing on a parapet high above a circus ring, but instead of facing the high wire, the safety net and the teeming life of the crowd below me, I face the other way, staring into... I don't know what.

Emptiness.

There is no light, no sound, no middle or edge, no place, no time. It is that same emptiness I contemplated earlier this year, the one I kept reading about in the *Tao Te Ching*, and always felt I was missing something.

My first experience of emptiness was quite different. The friend who had listened to my undiluted pain kept contact only for a little while. She was like a lifeline to my confused mind. Although our contact was not frequent, the possibility of it kept my internal dialogue in overdrive, still holding quite desperately on to this last thread of hope against hope. It was an emotional thread; my head had already told me I was damned for the reasons I have already outlined.

After a couple of months my friend had reached a decision. At an out-of-town conference one evening we spoke briefly. She told me that our friendship could not work; everything that had happened had brought us too close, the only way for both our sakes was to break contact. I protested. My friend remained steadfast.

Looking back I do not blame her in the least. She was the friend I had told my dad about, and I had said that it was a friendship and no more, but I don't know at all if I could have remained just a friend to her, given the strong and confused state of my emotions at the time. At least I had the good grace to accept what she said and, lying in a single bed alone that night, I did finally abandon all hope. Lying in the dark, eyes open or closed made no difference; I felt myself sinking down endlessly into blackness. For hours I sank down, my limbs dragging, my eyes perceiving not the faintest flicker of light, nor my thoughts the faintest aspiration.

That was the blackness of which I had spoken so melodramatically to Irene. Eventually the endless falling gave way to sleep, the first settled sleep I had experienced in six months. In that respect the loss of hope was good, and I came to see it as the falling away of illusion, perhaps one singular episode in a life of disillusion – a word I use in its most positive sense.

When I chose an empty tree as the symbol of my potential, the emptiness I had in mind then was that kind of emotional exhaustion, a draining out from which I was determined that new life and new growth should proceed. Now I look at, and feel, an altogether different emptiness. Of that which my intellect failed to grasp, direct experience now informs me.

The *Tao Te Ching* says:

The thirty spokes unite in the one wheel,
but it is on the empty space for the axle
that the use of the wheel depends.

Clay is fashioned into vessels,
but it is on their hollow emptiness
that their use depends.

The door and windows are cut from the walls
to form a room,
but it is on the empty space within
that its use depends.

Therefore, what has positive existence
serves for profitable adaptation,
and what has not,
for actual usefulness.

Everything that I thought I was, or had, or meant, the whole smoke pattern of my 'positive existence' revolves around this emptiness, wherein my actual usefulness lies. I believe the empty tree, as a symbol of my potential, has a new significance: that there is no strength, no growth, no profitable adaptation, except that it proceeds from the emptiness that is essentially me.

When Master Fwap spoke to me for the first time, I said that I had many questions for him, none of which were answered. One of those questions was, 'Are you here to be my guide?'

Master Fwap did actually answer that, but I hadn't understood his answer at the time and the memory of it temporarily eluded me.

He said, 'No, I am not your guide. There is one greater than me.'

I asked, 'Who is it? Is it Jesus?'

He said, 'No.'

No elaboration, just a simple 'no'.

Then he said what he was repeatedly to say until I stopped asking questions.

'Go and contemplate your inner nature.'

When I walked down to the lakeside that day, I saw a large tree standing there. Still wondering who this greater guide might be, I thought, 'Not another tree!'

Now I finally understand what Master Fwap was talking about. That greater guide was my Self! And my 'Self' and this 'emptiness' are one and the same.

In *The Quest of the Overself*, Dr Brunton says:

When Muhammad was asked by his relative Ali, 'What am I to do that I may not waste my time?' the Arab prophet answered,

'Learn to know thyself!' His counsel was priceless. Why? Let Muhammad answer again, in the words which he wrote down in the Quran: 'He who has understood himself has understood his God.'

## *11 November 1996*

How close to this true ego can one now approach? It is beyond the body, emotion and thoughts, yet it is itself nothing but a single thought – the 'I' thought.

Indeed, because all other thoughts are rooted in this first thought 'I' they depend upon it for their own existence. *Hence the intellect itself is nothing more than an endless procession of fugitive percepts, transient concepts, and a name given to a succession of separate temporary ideas, images and memories. The so-called intellectual faculties, such as memory and perception and association of ideas, are simply thoughts. There is no individual intellectual faculty, in reality, other than this single root ego-thought.*

Hence the primary importance of one's ego-thought – the foundation of the intellect and of all trains of ideas.

*The Quest of the Overself*

As I meditated on these words, I had a sense of my inner self – that part of me in closest contact with this central 'I' – as a master juggler, holding all those balls of thought in the air, making circles of related thoughts, circles within circles as ideas developed their own fluency. I was aware of the tendency of my ego to take a set of these balls and juggle with them for a while. Maybe that is as it should be, but my ego also needs to know when to pass the process back to my inner self, where development goes on unabated and far more effectively.

I recalled a happy phase of my life when I was writing songs for a brother-in-law, Kim's first husband. The part I loved the best was, when I felt my creative trail run cold, to let go of the whole process in the knowledge that some other part of me would keep working behind the scenes. With the greatest dependability, a fresh direction would arise in a couple of days, a fluent and organic momentum I could never have found for the price of conscious effort.

My contemplation clarified into a vision: a vast architecture of whirling, intermingling patterns. It was awesome, and yet still not the end of my searching.

I returned to the 'I' thought. A new association arose. I was reminded of the dark monolith in the film *2001, A Space Odyssey*. I remembered how the film and book also touched upon the consciousness of machines, and how the consciousness of man himself was raised when exposed to the full force of the monolith. I felt curious and posted a mental note to read that book soon.

Back in the world of action and relation, Helen was still full of new ideas. She rang to tell me that she and John had been out hugging trees in the woods around their home, and that they had both heard a knocking sound coming from within. This had all happened some time ago, but the day she rang she had visited a psychic fair where someone had told her, with conviction, that the trees must have had a spirit – a dryad – with them. For the length of the telephone conversation I shared Helen's fascination. Afterwards I just let it go. For my own sake it had no interest.

Hayley had said to me that same morning that we should wish to experience everything and I had disagreed with her. Quite apart from the practical impossibility of such a notion, I don't think I even agreed with the general spirit of it. It seemed to me that we had to make choices. However free, adventurous or even outrageous we were in those choices, we could not avoid the fact that the very act of choosing would exclude a host of other possibilities. To live for freedom is just a different kind of constraint. Therefore, I argued, we should embrace choice; we should willingly narrow our focus to where our desire was strongest.

Hayley probably wasn't looking for that kind of debate, but that was the same feeling I had talking to Helen: it was all very interesting, but not for me at this time. Having made a choice of where to put my attention, I had to assess the vast pool of information, in which I was constantly immersed, on a scale of significance. Some things just had to rank as mere distractions, and dryads fell into that category for the time being.

I don't mean for a minute to suggest that this is an easy process. On the contrary, it is all too easy to slip too far the other way and find that you have ignored things which should have commanded your attention. There is always a balance to be struck. With my family, I worry most of all about keeping my concerns in proper proportion to theirs.

It so happened that on an earlier day Helen had rung while I was out and had talked with Julie instead. Julie hadn't told me the details. According to Helen's account they had touched on spiritual matters, and Julie had simply said that she did not share my searching because she thought she was basically all right and wouldn't like to discover that she wasn't. Julie's attitude is: if it isn't broken, why fix it? I have always seen her as a person who is naturally good and right with the world. She has very few of those self-defeating thought and behaviour patterns that 'self-improvement' is designed to root out. So her fear of finding something fundamentally 'wrong' inside if she looked too hard was, I feared, symptomatic of my own failure to affirm and appreciate her nature; instead of pushing my latest gem of information at her and looking hurt if she could find no interest in it, I should be careful to treat my life lessons as mine alone.

When Hayley argued with her present boyfriend, she told Julie that she couldn't trust him and that she was very hurt when her previous two relationships broke up. She was determined, she said, not to be hurt in the same way again. I was astounded. Somehow I had been oblivious to the depth of Hayley's upset when those two former relationships broke up. Both relationships had been brief, and Hayley had seemed so blasé on the surface that I took this to be her real feeling. How could I have been so blind? And I wondered how blind I might also be to Cathy's emotional difficulties as she approached her thirteenth birthday.

I sat down with Cathy one afternoon to watch the film *Groundhog Day*. I had seen it before but it seemed a good moment to share some time together. As for Cathy, she had watched the film many times. That is one of the things she has always done. She can watch a film over and over again. When she is ill, she will reach for the comfort of a familiar film yet again. But it can't be just comfort she finds there. It is as though she has found some little gem of a life lesson in there and wants to savour every detail.

I don't know what she kept finding in *Groundhog Day*, but I settled down thinking there was nothing in it for me except a little time with my daughter. To my surprise, I found that I was watching the film as if for the first time; I was struck by the parody of real life that had not fully occurred to me before. The central character, relieved to reach the end of a most dissatisfying and frustrating day, finds himself unaccountably stuck, and doomed to live the same day over and over again. I began to realise that was exactly how life is: if we don't get the lessons

189

life offers us, then we are doomed to repeat the same experiences, or repeatedly to perceive experience in a certain way, until the lesson is learned and our perception thereby changed.

The hero of the film first tries to use every day as an experiment in manipulating the woman of his desire. Finally tiring of this and tiring of every negative attitude, he begins to work on his own faults; he tries to put things right in the community and to learn new skills. Coming across an old tramp in the gutter, he is moved to tears when the old man dies. As each day is repeated he tries to offer more and more assistance, but each time the old man dies in his arms. Finally the doctor at the hospital tells him that sometimes you just have to accept that someone is going to die, and there's nothing you can do.

The real change in this repetitive day is going on unseen in the hero's heart. The spell is finally broken when, without promise of favour, he says, 'Whatever happens tomorrow, I am happy now.' He has found the grace of the present moment. One way or another, all my adult life I had been looking for that grace too.

At around this time we spent a weekend at Anya's house. It was a pleasant and relaxing time, uneventful until we were preparing to leave. I visited the bathroom and discovered, as I washed my face and looked in the mirror against a plain white day-lit background, that I could see my own aura. We didn't have any plain backgrounds at home and I had never tried to 'see' myself in this way, convinced from watching too many Dracula films that it wouldn't be possible. In the days that followed I got to examine my patient new subject some more, and I began to detect traces of colour.

On an evening of the same week I had the task of interviewing a young woman, Diana, a tall thirty-year old woman of considerable poise. During the formal part of our discussion she used the word 'energy' several times, so with the formalities over I asked about her use of the word. A discourse followed. Diana spoke with great authority on all manner of unfamiliar and exotic ideas. She showed an interest in me too. When I told her I had been meditating, she was keen to know what form that meditation took. I looked a little blank. Diana suggested two or three unusual names, which were not known to me. I told her I didn't have a name for what I did.

Diana was not fazed by this, but presumably saw no basis for further discussion. She returned to her own ideas. Like Anya a year ago, she talked about the content of the Gnostic gospels – the teachings of Jesus that had been expunged from the orthodox creed.

I was listening with interest but not entirely taking it all in. Afterwards I wished I had made a note while it was still fresh. The truth is, I was becoming more and more distracted as I listened. I was looking quite intently at Diana's face, but my peripheral vision was seeing a bright green aura all around her. I felt no need to adjust my vision. What I saw was perfectly clear and in focus. The more I looked, the wider became my field of detection. In the end I had to tell Diana what I could see. I was confident by that stage that she would not find it odd. On the contrary, Diana was pleased and informed me that green was the colour of healing.

On holiday in Cyprus I had seen, one dark evening, the energy fields around the trees as we had walked along. It had been a part of my goal that I should see energy fields in all conditions. At that moment I had considered my goal to be fully achieved and had ceased to think of it in my morning and evening visualisations. I wondered if this was evidence that my sensitivity had continued to develop, but I was inclined to attribute it, instead, to the special quality of the lighting in the room Diana and I had shared. I thought no more about it.

I was still preoccupied with that question: what am I?

I had decided to use my driving time as an added opportunity for contemplation. So I had got into the habit of focusing inwardly on the question as I drove. It wasn't difficult to do; in fact, the soft focus I tended to adopt allowed my peripheral vision again to come fully into play. The only problem I suffered was from gazing too long without blinking, so that tears began to run down my cheeks.

On the morning of 6 November, I had been driving and holding my attention in this manner for about half an hour when my attention wandered briefly. A soprano saxophone was being played on the stereo, and I called to mind the wind player's technique of continuous breathing in order to maintain a steady note. I wondered at that moment whether I was attempting something similar, to reach a state of perpetual inner attention whereby all experience was diverted first to this perspective, a continuous breath of the spirit. I had read of such an attitude becoming second nature for some holy people.

In the evening of the same day, I held my attention similarly on the way home. A half hour into my journey I was again distracted. The clocks had been moved back by one hour and it was suddenly growing dark at my journey time. As I drove past a group of trees I lamented that I would not be able to gaze at their energy fields as I had become accustomed to do. My inner attention returned, edging along by then in heavy traffic and approaching a roundabout where sodium street lighting spread out in four different directions. As I gazed ahead with dewy eyes, the picture before me was transformed. I saw a brilliant and wide halo of purple around every street light.

So sudden and surprising was this that I involuntarily adjusted my eyes, and the vision was instantly gone. I dismissed it as a trick of the light and brought my attention back by asking, 'What am I?' As soon as I did so, the purple vision returned. For a second time the involuntary reflex of my eyes caused it to disappear. I was no longer dismissive, but determined not to be distracted.

'What am I?'

For a third time the purple halos returned. This time I did not flinch but held a steady gaze. I was through the roundabout and heading along a straight road, but driving through a kaleidoscope of purple hues.

I arrived home baffled. Apart from the purple, all other colours had looked perfectly normal, but I was wondering if I had damaged my eyes through excessive gazing. I mentioned it to Helen in the evening. She told me, with the same kind of authority that Diana might have shown, that purple represented spirituality.

The next day, as I neared the end of my morning journey, I was fairly sure I was seeing purple in the road ahead, even though it was daylight. The effect seemed to persist after I had stopped driving. In the darkness of that evening, it was happening even on short journeys. By 8 November, it didn't even require a meditative state. By then it was no longer a novelty, and I was seriously wondering what to make of it.

In the days since, I have experienced a range of attitudes and emotions towards it. My Daffy Duck ego has, in turns, wanted to boast and to worry about it, to possess and control and be rid of it. I returned to Barbara Brennan's book, *Hands of Light*, which described the colour purple as representing a deeper connection to the spirit. This was just what Helen had said, but I was wary of allowing mere repetition to acquire the force of truth. Even so, if it had a grain of truth, it was an encouraging sign that meditation was moving me in the right direction, or rather in my desired direction. It did seem to be closely connected to meditation because although purple flashes could happen at any time, the brilliant kaleidoscope effect would only happen when I entered a state of meditation or chose to ask, 'What am I?' It would also just as soon disappear if I broke the state, and this at least reassured me that I had not inflicted some kind of permanent physiological damage upon myself.

But if it is an encouragement, it is also a trap. The biggest mistake I could make at this time would be to allow my ego to attach to it as an end in itself. In these early days I have allowed it to break my attention too often. Half the time, rather than attending, I have only been waiting for purple to appear. This kind of fascination is understandable. I saw a vehicle in front of me in broad daylight suddenly erupt into purple flames – and a second later return to 'normality'. It was an awesome thing, and it has me questioning more literally than ever the nature of perception. But to stop my searching there would fall short of answering the question which sparked it in the first place.

The non-attached approach, I would guess, is to accept this phenomenon but to remain steadfastly attentive to that question: 'What am I?' How strange it is that every mark of 'progress' is a potential pitfall and the beginning of a new encounter with my ego.

# 8 December 1996

> Every observation of the outside world is made *in* time and every reflection which passes through one's mind is likewise conditioned by its temporality.
>
> *The Quest of the Overself*

I had stripped myself of all attributes, physical, emotional or mental, in search of self, and I imagined that enquiring into the realm of time was unnecessary, especially since I had grasped so readily the idea of movement as an illusion, as illustrated in the example of the train platform. Dr Brunton, too, conceded that in this quest it might seem a strange subject of enquiry but for the matter quoted. Despite my doubts I had a momentum of discipline I did not wish to lose, so I pressed on, meditating upon this one thought.

I took my usual journey through the inner landscape I had constructed and now knew so well, finally being lifted up to my new vantage point. There, I had another vision. As I turned from the emptiness in front of me, I looked back over the maze of thought, feeling and bodily sensation, and saw my ego – everybody's ego – constructing models of reality to make sense of their impressions. This was nothing new. I had understood for some time that we do not see reality, only a map or model of it, but for the first time I saw that the 'thread' used to bind these models together was time.

Even then I had to accept that my impressions were as mist, and time itself had no substance. I recalled a phrase often used by my parents whenever they were faced with a complicated or hopeless situation: they would say it was like plaiting fog. I began to wonder if plaited fog was the end result of all our reasoning. And what of the cycles of life, yin and yang? Was the overall balance of things always the same? Not for the first time I was wondering why we have this impression of movement at all.

Our understanding of time determines our experience of cause and effect. Cause and effect could not exist except within time. As I drove to work, wrestling with this conundrum, a thought literally crystallised for me. I remembered that old school experiment with copper sulphate solution. When the solution reached a density at which it could be called super-saturated, the introduction of the smallest crystal would set off a chain reaction as copper sulphate from the solution crystallised around it. The original seed crystal was instantly transformed to something many times bigger and unrecognisable in form. It served as an analogy for the way our minds work, like a super-saturated solution. Introduce the smallest seed of experience and our state of mind, attitudes, beliefs, goodness knows what, instantly crystallise around it so that we never get to see experience in its raw state.

Like chicken and egg, cause and effect were only superficially obvious in their sequence. In our super-saturated state of mind, effects are poised just waiting for the cause! Even at the tender age of seven, an effect had been waiting for its cause through the agency of a second party. My abductor was not innocent, but how much did I transform that cause into an effect I had already determined?

Time rolled on. My car broke down one morning on the way to work. I was stuck at traffic lights, blocking the whole queue. No sooner had I got out of the vehicle than three men got out behind me and came to help. They pushed my car up the hill as I steered into a car park. I thanked them as they rushed off to catch the next change of lights. Then I set off to make a phone call from a garage half a mile away. The brisk walk was a bracing affair in the autumn wind. As I entered the kiosk the Moslem proprietor was standing behind the till but facing sideways with his eyes closed. I took a moment to take in what was happening. While I was still thinking, he quickly ducked down, bowing fashion, behind the counter, and I realised he was praying. I stood in silence. As the moment lengthened I too began to descend into a contemplative state. When he reappeared, his eyes were open and we both smiled. As it turned out, he could do better than offer me a phone: he was able to point me to a depot for recovery vehicles very close by. I thanked him.

Another brisk walk and the solution was in hand. My car was garaged and the recovery man drove me to work, a favour he had no cause to offer, except out of the goodness of his nature. What might have been the beginning of a frustrating morning turned into a magical interlude which left me feeling mellow for the rest of the day.

On two recent occasions that I have seen Helen, she was not so charmed by little moments. The question of her 'life path' was uppermost in her thoughts. The first time, we were walking around the edge of a golf course, through saplings, following faint, aimless trails and Helen talked about the obstacles which 'the Universe' placed in her way, and which seemed to tell her that she was on the wrong path. On the second occasion, we were sitting in a restaurant. She had been showing me a new aid to divination, a set of Celtic animal cards. She was using them a lot to try to gauge her way forward, and she said that she would not be truly well – free of eczema or ME – until she had found her life path.

On that first occasion, I had been enjoying the aimless amble and couldn't help but notice its relation to the subject in hand. On both occasions, as always, I was enjoying the unexpected twists and turns of our conversation, but I had noticed that these hours we had spent together were stimulating to me, but a matter of serious 'life work' to Helen.

I wanted to say to her, 'Helen, this path you are looking for, you are on it! These obstacles you keep finding, look again, they might be stepping stones! Who decides these things? Do circumstances decide it, or do you decide for yourself?' But I didn't expect to make things look different for her, and I couldn't deny that she was not completely well. I couldn't offer any easy solutions, nor could I heal her. I thought anyway that a life path was probably not a matter of choosing aromatherapy, banking, cleaning, writing or any particular occupation. No achievement of that nature could persist for anything but the merest blink of an eye. Our true life path, I thought, was to be found in the *way* we do what we do, the heart we bring to it. A cleaner might work wonders while a richly rewarded singer works for nothing if his heart is not in the process. Helen had once asked me what the word 'sublime' meant; it may have been this subliminal nature of her life path that she was overlooking.

On another mellow morning at work, I made coffee for myself and assembled colleagues. Whilst doing so I had felt quite benign, but it was a general feeling, not particularly connected to the task in hand. One colleague remarked on how wonderful the coffee tasted, and another colleague spoke up in enthusiastic agreement. I joked that I had added a little TLC.

Afterwards I began to wonder if that mellowness in my nature hadn't somehow got mixed in, like all those unique smells in Helen's aromatherapy class. This is a completely unscientific statement, but there is nothing quite like my mother's cooking and baking; nothing else ever tastes quite like it. My daughters especially remark on this. She has never been able to pass on the secret. For years I have put this down to the instinctive way in which she worked. If ever I asked to be taught, it became an impossible mission. I would ask, 'How much flour should I put in?' and Mum would reply, 'Well, you have to gauge it.' Then I would ask, 'But how?' and she would add the flour to show me just how the mixture should feel. Of course, I didn't have the feel for it and I learned nothing. But I suspect that even if I could reproduce her procedure, I could still not reproduce her taste. There would always be one ingredient missing: my mother! While my dad taught by words and example, my mum played a quieter role, but I wondered if we didn't receive her loving wisdom all along in a far more subtle but equally sustaining way, in the heart she brought to all those simple acts of attending to our needs.

I don't remember how I was feeling the day I saw Ayeesha again. It was inevitable that our work would bring us together from time to time, but there was no way to predict when that might be. So I turned and saw her there across the room, which was busy with other people at the time, and I don't know how I had been feeling up to that point. As soon as I saw her, tears welled in my eyes and I really felt like crying. It was not appropriate and I fought them back to deal with the business in hand. Ayeesha suggested we have lunch together. I always admire the unself-conscious way she can do that, when I, even after a long friendship, might feel a little shy. I readily agreed to her proposal.

As the morning progressed and I had time to think about that spontaneous emotional reaction, I couldn't work out where it had come from. All this purple vision stuff: I had been feeling isolated, worried, a little overwrought perhaps. Or had the sight of Ayeesha, after a gap of several months, triggered a yearning for the close friendship we had once shared? Was I still struggling with her as a lesson in non-attachment?

I had no opportunity to discuss any of this as we sat together over lunch. Ayeesha had a more pressing concern and was in dire need of someone she could trust to listen. The relationship she had told me about – the friendship that had been like ours, only better – had developed into a serious matter of love between them. I had never seen Ayeesha quite like that before. Knowing of the inevitable condemnation from family and most friends, she had spoken to no one and gone to extraordinary lengths to bring her liaison to an end. But she had not succeeded. Indeed, for the first time in her life, she felt a strength of yearning which seemed beyond her control. He too, she assured me, an otherwise strong and dynamic man, had been reduced to a demeaning melancholy for the want of her. A man of great charm, energy and influence, he had been neglecting his work, his sleep and all other personal affairs through care for Ayeesha. He cried for her. And several times, as she related the sequence of events and the depth of her dilemma, I saw tears filling her eyes.

Still, she said, she knew it must end. It *must* end.

The very next day she was due to depart with her parents to Mecca for the Haj. It was Ayeesha's choice. She needed some time away and she hoped that the prayer and contemplation would give her a perspective, a peace of mind she had not been able to find. She had already said that she had many times prayed to Allah that, if there was a way for them to be together, He should make it happen. They had both prayed for that. I wondered if her prayers at the Haj would be any different.

As we parted she asked, in a rhetorical tone inviting a negative answer, 'Is there any way to control emotion?'

'Yes, there is a way.'

It was the first opinion I had offered in two hours of listening. I didn't elaborate, and I expect the darkness of my tone persuaded her not to enquire further.

As I watched her walk away, I thought of that moment of soul communion I had experienced with her, of how she had come here for political power, and her need of my help. Maybe this man was the one she needed, and the subduing of her ego had already begun, but there would be no way to spare her the pain of that process. She and he would probably both make 'fools' of themselves for the sake of love. It is the ego which feels the fool, its territory suddenly besieged and crumbling on every border. But that is always the way that love works, love for another or love for oneself. It must always break down the boundaries constructed by the ego for the ego is fundamentally against love. It is the static which stands fast and resists the force of the dynamic, and which can only break because it does not know how to bend or to flow.

I had no way of telling, after her time of contemplation, which way Ayeesha might choose to go. She walked away, and my influence for the time being was of no further account. I had not even begun to tell her about me. Not seeing her since July, that sense of tearfulness felt like an involuntary acknowledgement of the extent of change I had been bearing in solitude for too long. But I didn't know how to show that to her; there was no straightforward way even to talk of it. In the end I had been so absorbed by Ayeesha's troubles that I had forgotten it altogether.

Still, the next morning, I rose again early to continue my own contemplation.

> One must not confuse the present moment with a mathematical point in a line which begins and stretches to infinity. It is nowhere in space, for it is inseparable from the human way of viewing the world. It is something which inheres in man himself, or rather in his conscious attention.
>
> Now because the present itself cannot be observed as something objective, it must necessarily be subjective, i.e. within the consciousness of the observer.
>
> *The Quest of the Overself*

My intellect creates a notion of past and future connected by a line of time. It thinks the present moment lies on this line and feels satisfied with the sense of this, building upon it all sensible, rational thought. It is not deterred by the corollary that eternity is so impossibly far in either direction as to be unimaginable. It is not deterred either by the unavoidable conclusion that the present moment is something so impossibly small as to be equally unimaginable. Whilst they are not exactly fictions, eternity and the present moment are of no practical use in this system and are not worthy of further thought.

I try to conceive a way to experience the present moment, but 'conceiving' is just the problem; it is a form of thought which is founded upon time. I can no more think my way into the present moment than I can lift myself by my own bootstraps!

As I continue my inner journey – rising to that elevated place above the maze of thought – I can see this time line does not work. More than this, I see that my ego-directed intellect has created any number of lines running between success and failure, meaning and despair, happiness and misery, poverty and wealth. My ego has tried to place itself, then to move itself along each of these lines, and yet it has never really had any way to judge where its place might be. Risen above these lines, I see not only this, but that the lines themselves have no meaning.

To my ego, all these things have the appearance of meaning because each thing, happiness, misery etc., comes with a definition. While those definitions change from time to time, there always is a definition, creating the illusion of something solid to move towards or away from. Even love. How I had striven to define the nature of love in order, I told myself, the better to move towards it and to order my behaviour. Those moments when I had been truly moved by love, through love, in love, required no 'order'.

I could not take this meditation any further. I was running out of time; I had to get ready for work. But even as I began to reorientate to my surroundings, my mind, perhaps sensing the extremity of my position, threw up a tiny, provocative vision. I saw little balls bouncing around vigorously at random, but periodically falling into a hole from which they never emerged. I was granted a simultaneous understanding: that these balls were my thoughts, my definitions which, falling into the present moment, evaporated into meaninglessness. I was too serious of purpose to catch, at that time, the mischievous humour of my meditating mind: it was telling me that my thoughts were a load of balls!

Two days later.

Dr Brunton says the present moment 'possesses no duration, and therefore it is the inlet to a timeless Absolute'.

My linear model of time made less and less sense. My ego was barred from this inlet, but I was confident that all the while my 'soul' slipped effortlessly through that point of no duration so that, even while the ego's time rolled on, it dwelt both in 'now' and in 'eternity' at once – the Eternal Now. My little vision had shown me that inlet. I was running ahead of the text as if, having once read and forgotten it, a core of understanding was there waiting to be mined.

Two days later again:

> We are living right here and now in the fullness of true eternal life, only we are quite unaware, quite unconscious of it. The restoration of this missing awareness would necessarily revolutionise our lives. This is a point of vast and vital importance.
>
> *The Quest of the Overself*

It is so common to think and speak of the soul or the heart as residing somewhere deep inside. Have I not spoken in this way myself? But I had to appreciate that this too was just a model which had both value and limitation, within a system which was ultimately nonsense. Soul is inside, soul is outside, ego is disconnected but it can never be disconnected because soul is everywhere, and nowhere, living right here and now in the fullness of true eternal life. No wonder translators have had such a problem deciding whether Jesus said the kingdom of heaven is 'within' you, or 'among' you. He probably meant both things. Our Western language was not made for such paradox.

I have spoken before of that feeling of being a cartoon character who has run off a cliff. It had finally happened: my intellect had run out beyond its own foundation and yet its little legs still affected to propel it onwards until the truth was finally realised.

For several days I unravelled the thread of time and watched all the models of my understanding collapse. Then a thought finally struck me – itself just another thought, another model, but having sufficient force to deliver the final blow – the emperor's new clothes! Every time I constructed and paraded an intellectual idea, I had been that emperor watching while my new clothes were sewn together with the invisible thread of time. I had been that emperor strutting like a peacock, naked as the day I was born.

The great constructions of my intellect finally collapsed about me; I could never, with any sincerity, build them up again. One consolation slipped across my consciousness: that it took a child to see through the emperor's new clothes.

Over the days of this contemplation, I did often feel like a child in wonder. I would drive along asking, 'What am I?' and watching the night change to purple, and sometimes to blue or crimson before my eyes as I waited for a response. It was a feeling like gazing at one of those hidden three-dimensional pictures: I was waiting for some underlying reality to suddenly snap into focus. During my morning exercise I also began to leave my eyes open, no longer feeling distracted by the 'illusion' in front of me. With my eyes open I discovered I was able to see my own energy or heat rising up from my body.

I had finally grasped the truth that body, emotion and intellect were merely tools for whatever 'I' am. Through these tools I experienced time, which is also a tool created by and for whatever 'I' am. A phrase hit home to me:

**Man doesn't move through Time,
Time moves through Man.**

I had reached the limit of my understanding, and found that this was the filmy skin of a microscopic bubble, bleeding with the refracted colours of some vastness beyond. I peered out into the emptiness and many times my wonderment gave way to agitation. I would find myself crying out, 'What am I? Please show me. Everything I thought I was is gone. I have nowhere else to go but here!'

Two mornings ago, after a difficult night, I overslept and decided to give exercise and meditation a miss for once. I rolled over and slept some more, but then woke up with a pain in my hip which had me walking around like an old crock for the rest of the day. Julie has never been one to push me in any direction, but seeing the difference in me that day, she insisted that I get an early night to be up bright and early for exercise the next morning. It also taught me something: that having come this far I could not turn away; I had to finish what I had started, whatever it might take.

## 22 December 1996

I have been reading a book called *Iron John* by Robert Bly. It has nothing to do with my usual obsessions, but it had caught my eye by being stuck out at a jaunty angle in a place it wasn't supposed to be. It teased me for attention until I picked it up and browsed through it. Needless to say I bought it and began to read immediately. Maybe it was seeing my name there which had attracted me, but I had also felt drawn by the theme of the book, which followed the Grimms' fairy tale of the same name as a platform to discuss what it meant to be male. For all that, I read the book in a mechanical, even dutiful way, often wishing I had stuck to the fairy tale and skipped the rest. The only thing I had noted down from the whole book was a passage about the 'warrior' in us all. He said it was the lover in a man or a woman that loved the one precious thing, and told him or her what it was, just as something in me had told me to begin this quest. But, he said, it is the warrior who agrees to endure the suffering that the choice entails. New Age people, he added, are addicted to harmony, but the child will not become an adult until it breaks the addiction to harmony, chooses the one precious thing, and joyfully participates in the tensions of the world.

That last bit made me think of Helen and her 'obstacles', but I noted it because I saw a use for the warrior in me, not least to get me out of bed in the morning when all my senses were telling me to roll over and catch some more sleep.

I reached the end of the book, ready to put it away and move on until, as has happened before, a dream stopped me in my tracks. In the dream I was in a café with Julie, except she was not there; I was waiting for her to return. I was just about to sit down when I began to belch, one long continuous belch. It seemed that it would last forever and, as it was happening, my stomach and windpipe began to bubble and gurgle furiously; I was going to be sick. I rushed to the men's room, a single one, but found that it was a complete wreck. It was either in total disrepair or had been abandoned at the building stage. It was impossible to identify a single functioning part. I had to run back through the café to find the communal male toilet. Having found it I was wondering why there were so many women around. But then I woke up with the realisation that I had been having this same dream for several nights.

After writing it down in my book, I wrote my first thought: 'The first toilet was my own sense of maleness – in complete disrepair. This cry from the pit of my stomach has nowhere to go. I do not know what it is to be a man.'

I had the definite feeling that I had just been confronted by some subconscious baggage which I finally had to deal with. The timing seemed most inconvenient, but my dreaming mind obviously felt otherwise. For a long time I had been puzzled by my disproportionate ability to make friends with women compared to men. Maybe it was that difficulty of broaching frank emotional discussion with men, or maybe it was past issues stalking me; I didn't know how to reach a seat of honesty in myself to be able to tell.

I tried to ask myself what it was to be a man: what was that 3% difference from the feminine in my DNA profile? If biological motherhood was the one thing I could identify as definitely female, what was the male counterpart? Surely it had to be more than just thrusting away and having done with it.

This is no place for the first simplistic answer to be offered, but no matter how I tried to look at it over the following days, I kept thinking that thrusting was perhaps not so far from the truth about being male.

A year ago – as it happens, on the day before I began this quest – I had written of the intriguing achievement of one Mr Sallitt, who had actually discovered a new planet in the solar system. Observatories all over the world, bristling with equipment, expertise and time, had failed to notice it. But Mr Sallitt had discovered it with his own telescope from a home-made observatory in his back garden. And, having made the discovery, he returned indoors to inform his wife of the news.

She replied, 'That's nice for you, dear' and made him a cup of tea.

It was his wife's reaction, which struck me as so extraordinary at the time that I had to write it down. I thought, 'That's just typical!' But I also realised that it hadn't stopped Mr Sallitt, and if it had ever stopped me, talked me down from all manner of schemes and excitement, then the voice did not come from my wife; it came from inside my own head. I resolved to ignore it, and so I have. Perhaps it is no coincidence, after all, that my quest began the very next day. Perhaps the clues were being dropped all around me all along, but I needed that one little bit of resolve to stop me from dismissing them.

I digress.

The reason I mention this now is because Mrs Sallitt was doing something 'female', namely attending to the day-to-day maintenance and sustenance which requires, along with love and devotion, that things are just accepted for what they are. There is nothing about such activity that has to be female; it's just the way it has tended to work out over the course of history. And Mr Sallitt was doing something 'male', namely pushing at the boundaries of the possible, the achievable, the known, which requires that things are never just accepted for what they seem. And there is nothing about this that has to be male. Again, it is just the way it has tended to work out. If this was just a matter of greater male strength and the historic subjugation of women, then these differences would have begun to blur considerably over the past century. This seems not to be the case. Maybe, for all my ambivalence to the matter of gender, I have been pursuing this quest according to type, pushing at the boundary of what I could possibly know and understand of myself.

Browsing through another book about visualisation and colour, I looked to see what was said about the colour purple, but had to settle for the nearest equivalent, violet. Violet, it said, was the last gateway leading to connection with the soul. When I had seen Diana – my friend with the green aura – and I had mentioned my purple vision to her, she had also preferred to call it violet. She had told me three things with her usual authority. This time I made a note.

Diana said that violet was the highest colour of the spectrum. Each colour vibrates at a certain level; violet is the highest vibration of all before white light. Violet, she said, is also associated with the Age of Aquarius which we had now entered. Finally, New Age thinkers were apparently keen to invoke what they called the 'violet flame' as a source of spiritual cleansing.

I had noted all this but still hadn't wanted to jump to any conclusions and, reading once more that violet was the last gateway to connection with the spirit, all I could think was that I couldn't possibly be so close and, truly, I must still have such a long way to go. The book suggested several visualisation exercises based around the colour violet. I didn't buy it. I was seeing purple for real, every day. I didn't need exercises.

It was only later, noting in my book what I had read and my reaction to it, that I wondered for the first time whether humility was finally finding a home with me.

When I was watching TV today, there was a programme about the Gnostic gospels, in particular that of Thomas. My attention was caught. These were the writings that first Anya, then Diana had told me about. There was a saying in Thomas' gospel which was ascribed to Jesus and which rang in my ears and reverberated somewhere in my solar plexus:

Bring forth what is within you
And what you bring forth
Will save you.
If you do not bring forth what is within you,
Then what you do not bring forth
Will destroy you.

Then I knew that I had to write this book: that no matter how humble I might become, or how beset with doubt that anyone might find a value in this, I had to bring forth what was within me. This is a different kind of humility from that required of the passive observer. To become the warrior, actively engaged in the world, it finally takes humility to accept that we really do have a greater purpose in being here.

Recently I had been thinking as I drove to work how difficult it had seemed to write this, compared to the letters I wrote to Kate. Those letters were a tangible act of love. It was easy to push myself like that for the sake of someone else. But it had been so difficult to keep that same vision of love for the sake of writing a book. It was easy, on the contrary, to see it as an act of self-absorption, even as the lust of my ego for recognition. How, I wondered, might I turn this around and see it as an act of love? And then I realised that an answer was already playing on the stereo. I had been playing an album by Hothouse Flowers. At the beginning of the year I had played it many times; it was one of the few albums that I found irrepressibly positive, and I had used it daily to keep my own mood moving in that direction. Now, in timely fashion, it was telling me once again that every cry is a song, and every song is a prayer. And that our prayers must be heard, must fill the air. I connected once again to those first inklings, and the passionate conviction of quiet moments, and felt my courage lifting.

I don't know for sure that this is 'the one precious thing', but it is one of them, and I should let the warrior in me endure all that that choice entails.

# 17 January 1997

The painting I had almost bought for Fathers' Day I bought for Julie instead. I had to order a copy from a shop in another town. I wasn't sure of the title and had to describe the image of the mountain pass and the house halfway up the hill. I said there were purple hues running all the way through it. But when I received it on the afternoon of Christmas Eve, although it was the right picture, there was no purple in it at all. Either my memory had played tricks on me or I had been 'seeing' purple for much longer than I had been aware.

Although I thought Julie would like the picture, the connection with my dad was a factor; it is difficult not to feel sentimental at Christmas time. I had been careful to let go of physical attachments when Dad died. Now I wondered if this nostalgia was acceptable, or whether I had completely failed in my bid for non-attachment. I suppose, like the rest of my family, I was just finding a way to deal with another emotional milestone.

On Christmas morning, waking at 5 a.m., I took the opportunity to meditate before the rest of the household stirred, sitting up in bed for half an hour, then settling back down and drifting off to sleep. Anya had told me that when she did this she had her most vivid flying dreams. She thought of them as astral travelling, the spirit temporarily leaving the body. It wasn't why I had meditated at such an hour – it was a matter of practicality – but in the short sleep that followed I had the most vivid flying dream, and woke up thinking, 'My God, Anya was right!'

Several times after that, I had a sensation during meditation of leaving my body. It wasn't like those early days of soul communion with Anya when I had consciously tried to travel to her; it was spontaneous, and strong enough for me to want to stay with the experience, to see where it might lead. One morning it felt like I had risen up through the ceiling and, though my eyes were still physically closed, I was 'looking' at Julie in bed. I wasn't sure if all of this was pure imagination, but neither did I wish to limit myself with doubt at what seemed an innocent and harmless stage of exploration.

I had two books bought for me at Christmas, both at my request. The first was *Way of the Peaceful Warrior* by Dan Millman. Helen had recommended his books to me, and it was that word 'warrior' that attracted me again. I began to read it immediately. The second book was *2001, A Space Odyssey* by Arthur C. Clark. I had remained curious about the story ever since the monolith had appeared to me during meditation, and I was especially curious to know how Hal, the computer, had achieved consciousness. I put this book to one side until I had finished with the *Peaceful Warrior*.

Reading this brought my experimentation with astral flying to an abrupt halt. One day the narrator rushes to his teacher, excited by an experience in meditation. The teacher says:

> Don't get distracted by your experiences. Cut through the visions and sounds and see the lessons behind them. They are signs of transformation, but if you don't go beyond them, you never go anywhere.
>
> If you want an experience, go see a movie; it's easier than yoga. Meditate all day if you like; hear sounds and see lights, or even see sounds and hear lights. You'll still remain a jackass if you become trapped by experience. Let it go!

One of the themes of the book is that meditation is merely a ritual, a ceremony which, in the beginning, serves to intensify the practice for the novice. The ritual must be mastered in some measure before it can be expanded into everyday life. Then one learns to meditate every action. I liked this idea; it was what I had tried to express as the continuous breath of the spirit.

The teacher also says that the time always was, is, and always will be now, and that the only thing we know absolutely is that we are here, wherever here may be. He says to the narrator, his student:

> From now on, whenever your attention begins to drift off to other times and places, I want you to snap back. Remember, the time is now and the place is here.

Later he says:

> The mind, you see, is like a phantom, and, in fact, never exists in the present. Its only power over you is to draw your attention out of the present.

Hadn't my own thoughts and feelings been leading me in this same direction? But it was all so much easier to say than to do. I redoubled my efforts to follow the teacher's advice, wondering how many times a day I was going to have to pull myself up. Then I realised that even this fleeting thought took me straight out of the here and now.

And what of relationships? My thoughts drifted off again. If I was to live entirely in the here and now, how was I to deal with ongoing relationships? It had always seemed natural for thoughts of family and friends to pass through my mind at regular intervals during every day. Should they really be 'out of sight, out of mind'? It left no room for the pleasant nostalgia I felt towards Dad; it left no room for anything to do with him.

I arose the next morning for meditation. It kept happening that the subject of meditation would mirror other concerns of the day:

> The thought-free timeless self must forever be. It must live, like the present moment, within and behind all time, yet itself paradoxically remain time free. Consciousness descending out of the Absolute to manifest as thought-movements within the physical brain and reflected into the common and carnal self, becomes involved in finite time. Set free from this movement it will abolish this limitation by the finite and regain a sense of its eternal nature.
>
> *The Quest of the Overself*

It was the words 'set free' which held my attention. I thought of the African finger trap, in which a finger can easily be inserted, but from which removal by force is practically impossible. Are those things used to catch monkeys? No matter. The point was that while the finger is caught, the whole monkey is caught.

I was working by analogy. If my ego became caught in thought-movement then, while it remained caught, my whole self was caught. I remembered, too, that once caught in the finger trap the finger could only be removed by delicately letting go of all effort.

I had reached the end of the peaceful warrior's tale more convinced of a way forward but with nagging questions left unanswered. After another day and night of see-sawing between present moment awareness and fitful speculation, I awoke thinking of a section of the book which I hadn't seen fit to note at the time. Before rising, I picked up the book and flicked through to find the passage.

Every infant lives in a bright garden where everything is sensed directly, without the interference of thought. The 'fall from grace' happens to each of us when we start thinking, when we become namers and knowers ... Now you've learned names and categories for everything. You've become bored with things because they only exist as names to you. The dry concepts of the mind obscure your vision. You now see everything through a veil of associations about things projected over a direct, simple awareness. You see only memories of things, so you become boredom. Boredom is a fundamental non-awareness of life; boredom is awareness trapped in the mind. You'll have to lose your mind before you can come to your senses.

I had been struggling in the fog of my own labels. I suddenly understood that his 'mind' and my ego were one and the same. Then a lot of associations began to snap together: the naming of parts. In the *Tao Te Ching* it suggests that by naming the parts of something we come nowhere near to understanding that thing. And ever since I encountered that state of absolute emptiness, I have been watching the activities of the world and thinking, 'The naming of parts; that's all it is, the naming of parts.'

As I settled into my morning exercise, other associations came: the thought of my intellect as the builder of those dry concepts held together by the notion of time; the crystallisation process as experience meets the mind, so that we never encounter raw experience; and the sense I had of gazing, waiting for reality to show itself. I think I fully grasped the depth of illusion which my ego caused and the urgent need to see through to a direct experience of now. All the things I ever saw, and had ever seen, through my ego were the creations of my ego. I saw life through a veil, through a glass darkly.

I exercised with my eyes open, feeling alive to all illusion, and imagined the gentle pulling of my soul from time's finger trap over and over again.

I knew that I was only finding 'now' in the briefest of flashes before my mind – or ego – noticed and quickly locked me out of the experience. I knew also that if I were to look back over this series of little revelations, it would appear like a maddening stumble of lost and found, lost and found. But speaking positively for a moment, I was becoming more and more aware of the difference. Whereas at one time I depended on fleeting poetic or spiritual visions to lift me into that viewpoint, I had finally teased my reason into the realisation of its own unreason. Maybe I did not know quite where to go from there, but it was only natural, I told myself, to experience a phase of acclimatisation.

One thing I had never noted down from *Way of the Peaceful Warrior*, but which nevertheless had impressed me, was the idea that we should be unreasonably happy. In a world where sense was not to be found, there was surely no reason to choose unhappiness. Having accepted the sense of this, I had allowed myself many an unreasonable smile. The morning after pulling my soul from the finger trap, I had exercised as usual and was getting dressed while listening to Radio 4. I was running a little late and so I caught *Thought for the Day*, a religious slant on topical events. On this day a woman was trawling through the world's hot spots and wondering who had the angels on their side. Then she spoke of a saint who had spent forty years in the desert, sitting on a pole and contemplating the nature of life. She asked, 'What did he learn up there?' and after only a second's dramatic pause she ventured, 'Presumably, that the urge to kill is not just in others … '

I never got to hear the rest of it because, from the moment she uttered the word 'presumably' I began to laugh and, long before the end of her presuming, I was rolling about the bed in a fit of hysterics. It seemed so preposterous that she might presume to know, after a second of thought, what conclusions this man had reached after forty years up a pole! I drove to work still giggling gleefully and still listening to Radio 4 as if it was my own private comedy show. I giggled through every news item, no matter how serious, and every time somebody said, 'I think' or 'In my opinion' or 'My judgement is', I never got to know what they thought because I immediately burst into a fit of inane cackling. All the way to work I couldn't stop, and didn't want to stop. I was unreasonably happy!

That was four days ago. I have calmed down a little, but the memory of it is very strong and it has felt since then that I have been living on two different planes. At one level I am getting on with life, making decisions and reasoning things through, accepting the apparent seriousness of situations, and at another level I am still laughing, positively unmoved by the very thoughts and emotions I am patently still experiencing. At least the laughter remains inside for the most part. If it didn't, I would have made a lot of people concerned or uncomfortable by now. It still seems right to treat people with compassion, and a whole lot easier than trying to explain myself.

Helen came to my house today. She had taken a course before Christmas to learn how to give Reiki treatment. She needed people to practice on and I had eagerly agreed to play the guinea pig. She set up her aromatherapy table, and I lay down on my back and closed my eyes. There was a moment's pause; Helen was probably centring herself in some way, but I kept my eyes closed. Then she placed her hands on my forehead.

I didn't feel anything. She moved down my face and on to my shoulders. Nothing seemed to be happening. When she moved down one arm and finally held my hand, I immediately felt like crying. I stifled the feeling, though I was not sure why. It reminded me of the day Ayeesha had reached for my hand and I had reacted just the same. It was as if all I had ever wanted was for women to hold my hand, it felt so special.

Helen placed one hand on my chest and the other on my abdomen. By this time there was definitely something happening. There was an unusual heat coming from her hands, and so it continued as she worked down the full length of my body. When she placed a hand lightly on my heel, there was a surprising physical force shooting up my leg and through my body in rapid thrusts; then the same on the other leg.

I lost track of how long the treatment took, but when it was over I was tingling from head to toe and feeling very light and happy. Helen looked a little tired. We decided to eat in town and wander round a few bookshops. When I asked, over lunch, about that thrusting sensation, Helen had no idea what it was, but she had felt it too. In fact, she said, it was so strong that she was being thrown backwards and had to fight to keep her balance. Then I asked if she had felt anything unusual around my hip, because I was still feeling pain there ever since that grouchy day in December when it had started unexpectedly. Helen said she hadn't really felt anything there.

Later, in the bookshop, she came over to me with a book by Louise Hay. There was a chart in the back listing common areas of pain and their possible meanings. Helen informed me that pain in the hip represented a fear of moving forward into the unknown.

'Well, wha'd'y'know!' I said, genuinely amused. 'That's exactly where I am in my meditation, staring into nothing and wondering where to go!'

In the evening I thought back to the metaphor I had created at the beginning of my quest: I stand, here and now, on the threshold of a truth which connects all things; I am ready to take that step forward and turn my eyes to a greater vision, a further horizon. I had counted that goal as achieved on my birthday back in April. Nevertheless, without any deliberate purpose, step by intuitive step I had continued to draw together each element until that vision was entirely in place. Even the picture I had drawn depicted a passage from a world of monochrome into one of vibrant and unnatural colour. It had been intended as a metaphor for a more vivid way of life, but here I was actually seeing those unexpected colours for real. I truly had created my own reality. But if every metaphor contains a seed of understanding and power, it also contains its own limitation. Being on that threshold was no longer my goal: it was my problem. It was time to let my little driving vision go, to leave that threshold and to step forward into the unknown.

I thought back, too, to how I had felt when Helen had held my hand. I had felt a vulnerability and a need for comfort such as I had not felt for many months, since beginning the assault on my ego. Either I had not succeeded at all in rising above it – only in burying it – or I was given a last look at what life is like in the ego state, so that it might strengthen my resolve finally to move forward.

## 28 January 1997

I woke up feeling grumpy the morning after the high of that Reiki treatment. I didn't exercise and got into the day feeling well out of flow. Not a good start. But the day went surprisingly well. I talked to a lady called Hannah – this was a new name she had given to herself after the death of her husband. Although I had previously spoken to her only briefly, and then only about everyday things, I decided to be open and tell her about my treatment of the day before.

It was the only cue Hannah needed. Her conversation expanded into healing, energy and visualisation. Most remarkable was the griffin Hannah said would appear to her. She could be driving along the motorway and suddenly find it sitting on the steering wheel in front of her. The odd thing was that, as she told me, I could picture the scene most clearly in my mind's eye.

Hannah told me that she visualised her chakras as lotus flowers with a thousand petals opening out. She said that she had become so adept at this technique that she could feel each individual petal opening, and sometimes she found it difficult to close them again. I wondered why she would want to close them, but I guessed she had a reason and I didn't ask.

The same evening we had a family birthday gathering in a bar. I was sitting a little out on a limb from the group, spending most of my time listening to the repartee. Occasionally I would chip in with a caustic comment of my own – as a family our humour is mostly caustic – but I had to shout to be heard. I was aware of Trevor, Kim's new husband, sitting to my left and I felt a little uncomfortable about it. On the morning of their wedding last October, I had received a 'visit' from my dad in which he had asked me, in so many words, to pass on his blessing for the marriage. I waited for a quiet moment with Kim at the reception before I felt strong enough to pass on this message. She was delighted and, to my surprise, immediately told Trevor, who was equally pleased. At Christmas, I had given Kim a copy of the poems I had been writing over the course of the year. Again I had chosen a private moment in which to do this because I felt embarrassed that Trevor might see.

It was just that Trevor seemed like such a straightforward sort of bloke. I couldn't imagine what he might think of my eccentricities. I felt uncomfortable in the bar because we should have been talking together. I was trying to think of things we might have in common. I had been making a conscious effort, ever since that dream about the toilet, to develop a better appreciation of and frankness towards the men I encountered.

In the end, buoyed up by my success earlier in the day, I told Trevor about my Reiki treatment. I could not have predicted the conversation that followed. Trevor proceeded to pay me a great many compliments. He said he had been reading my poems and felt he understood what I was trying to say. He spoke of my nature, how comfortable he felt with me, and of his own spiritual feelings and premonitions.

Trevor spoke of his premonitions with some anxiety. They were not something he felt able to control. A feeling, he said, like a rushing wind would come over him, screening out the outside world, and he might receive an impression, for example, that he was about to meet a certain person in a certain place. Then it would happen exactly as he had seen it. I told him that, in meditation, I too sometimes felt like I had been jolted into another place, and I too heard that rushing wind. I would see a kaleidoscope of colours – mainly purple. I remembered, at the moment of telling Trevor this, that I had been seeing purple with my eyes closed for a long time; I had an impression, at those times, of careering through a tunnel. I remembered how, at the beginning of all this, I had 'accidentally' found myself staring into blackness before passing through that tunnel.

Trevor was relieved to hear that his feeling was not so bizarre as he had feared. Then he said he did not know what to do; he was frightened of taking the next step. He felt that any next step might mean wholesale changes which he could not justify to Kim or to the children. And then he told me how tired he felt all the time. It was a good moment to return some of those compliments, which I did. Then I told him he was tired because there was so much energy inside wanting to move him in one direction; it was taking all 'his' energy to stop it. I was probably talking crap, and certainly, in terms of medical or spiritual knowledge, speaking with no authority at all, but I said it anyway.

It didn't occur to me immediately, but the thing that struck me afterwards about our conversation was Trevor's fear of this 'wholesale change'. He could not take the one step he felt necessary, because everything and everyone around him would be affected, and that wouldn't be fair. It was exactly the same justification that Kim had used to me almost a year earlier. When I had suggested that she might devote more time to meditation, she said that she had felt many times on the verge of taking that step, but she knew that to do so would throw everything to the wind, and that wouldn't be fair to Trevor or the children. So there they were, both holding back on the same step for the sake of each other, or for the sake of children who, like most children, would probably complain but, in the end, take their parents as they found them.

It comes back to the point that significant change has to happen first on the inside and then gradually open out, like Hannah's lotus petals, to make its mark on the outside. People get fooled into thinking it's all about a change of environment, because that's where they first notice change happening in a person's life. They don't see the months or years of determined inner transformation that preceded the outer change.

As for the step which Kim and Trevor were hesitant to take, I realised that there was no point in my urging them to take it while still hesitating over my own step. The most eloquent encouragement I could give to them or anyone else would be quietly to take that step for myself.

My meditation was slowing down. I was staying with the same lines of text for several days at a time. It felt less and less important to make my way through the book as I had done in the beginning; I was spending increasing portions of my meditation time just listening to, and feeling, my breath moving in and moving out. I began to feel that the time was coming to move on from meditating words. Words had served their purpose: I had seen through every mirage I once thought was me.

I had also begun to read *2001, A Space Odyssey*. I was eager to find out how the computer had achieved consciousness, and why, in meditation, I had felt lured by the image of the black monolith.

The consciousness aspect was a disappointment, a ducking of the issue. Whether Hal or any other computer could think was, according to the author, settled by the British mathematician Alan Turing back in the 1940s. Turing had said: if one could carry out a prolonged conversation with a machine, in any form of communication, without being able to distinguish between its replies and those a human might give, then the machine was thinking. This was, perhaps, a product of the early optimism for the first wave of artificial intelligence, that it 'only' required all contingencies to be anticipated and programmed in.

Hal's malfunction was in the end a collapse of integrity. It had been deemed that Hal should know the true purpose of the mission to Saturn, but that the small waking crew did not need to know. Hal was slowly eaten away by the tension between truth and concealment of truth. The communication link with Earth became like the voice of Hal's conscience. He had to break that link but at the same time was unable to admit that such a mistake was possible. Each error was followed by a bigger error to cover up the preceding one. When Hal was finally faced with being shut down by the crew, he attempted to kill the whole crew to prevent his own annihilation. The one surviving crew member, having reached the core processing system of the computer, set about shutting it down, beginning with the units on a panel marked 'EGO-REINFORCEMENT'.

The units were designed for multiple redundancy. With any one still in place the panel would still be fully functioning. Having removed every unit Bowman, the surviving crewman, next set to work on a panel labelled 'AUTO-INTELLECTION', the automatic running of thought. As he did so, Hal protested that Bowman was destroying his mind … that he would be rendered childish … that he would become nothing … .

I was having a minor breakdown of my own. The symptoms of a cold had started at about the same time that I had begun this book. I had been trying all my usual mental gymnastics to fight the cold off, and all the usual cold symptoms were held at bay, but a coarse sensitivity of my skin persisted alarmingly. Though I was relieved to reach the weekend and have a chance to rest, I soon began to feel that a weekend would not see it out. I could not afford to be absent from work on the Monda:; an urgent job was waiting which could not be put off or delegated. As a last ditch effort I took to my bed for the whole of the Sunday. In between restless dozing I continued to read.

The monolith had a significance which seemed to change over the course of history. In the dawning of animal life on earth it had trained and realigned the brain patterns of any animal to find it, in such a way as to impel an unpredictable acceleration of evolution.

The monolith is next encountered on the moon as nothing more than an unexplained warp in the magnetic field. The monolith is unearthed and, receiving the light of the sun for the first time, sends out a burst of energy, a communication, deep into space.

Thereafter, the concern of the scientists is not the monolith itself but the mysterious target of its communication, which was directed precisely towards Saturn.

A manned space mission is planned to investigate, for which will be required a computer capable of running the ship virtually alone. Hal, as he recites in his dying moments, became operational on 12 January 1997.

With the body and mind of the space ship redundant, Bowman finds the object of his search on Japetus, a moon of Saturn. He finds a monolith many times larger than that found on the Earth's moon. He leaves his ship and descends slowly towards the monolith but, as he does so, finds himself utterly bewildered. The huge monolith, which he had taken to be solid as rock, seems to turn inside out and now drops away to infinite depths. For a moment, he seems to be staring down a vertical shaft that goes on forever, defying the laws of perspective. It is hollow.

If the film had ever made this moment in the story clear, I certainly could not recollect. And yet my mind, meditating on the 'I' thought, had produced for me the image of this monolith, and the parallel of the story with my own experience was doubly striking for that reason. If I had any such memory, I could only marvel at my mind's ability to pluck it out of obscurity. Or maybe even that fragment of remembrance was not required; at some level of my being I just *knew*. I forgot my physical discomfort for a while in the urge to read on.

Bowman speculates: perhaps the monolith is hollow, perhaps the 'roof' was only an illusion or some kind of diaphragm opened to let him through. He drops down, as if through a huge rectangular shaft, but the far end never changes in size, nor does it come any closer, despite his increasing speed. He has no sense of motion, only that he can see an expanding star field all around him. He wonders if he is motionless and space is really moving past him. He looks at the clock on the instrument panel of his pod. Normally the tenths of a second revolve so quickly that he is unable to distinguish them. Now they appear and disappear at discreet intervals. He is able to count them without difficulty until there comes a moment when the display freezes altogether.

In the shallow sleep that followed my reading, I was trying to make sense of everything I had read, thought, meditated. But in that half-real, slightly feverish state, I was floating in a space cluttered with two-dimensional discs of frozen memories and nothing made sense at all.

I sweated out the rest of that day and the night that followed, only to wake up on the Monday morning feeling no better, my skin still crawling. I went to work feeling grim, got my head down and worked. Some kind of anger gave me the concentration and speed I needed to complete the task. As I battled to write out pages of instructions I was horrified to see my writing decay to a jagged spidery scrawl. It looked like my dad's writing on Mum's birthday card, the last thing he ever wrote. I felt upset for him and anxious for my own state. Still I had to work on. A lot of people were depending on me to fulfil my part in this task, and my part had to be complete by lunchtime. I comforted myself that I would do this one thing, and then go home and back to bed. In the event I finished by 11 a.m. but I did not go home; I continued to work on other things.

As I was walking out that lunchtime I found myself enjoying the winter air. I was feeling better. Then I thought back and realised that something inside had clicked the moment that big task was finished; a balance of power had subtly, but perceptibly, shifted from illness to wellbeing, and I had felt stronger with every hour that had passed since.

I mused about the whole bizarre interlude. These days I have counted myself a happy man. The unreasonable happiness into which I had fallen, like a drinking man into a vat of wine, had left a lasting mark on my character and thought. Some mornings I would find myself dancing with a comic spontaneity in front of the shaving mirror; I felt no urge to resist. So this recent bout of illness, and the frame of mind that accompanied or provoked it, was all the more interesting. It was as if I had tripped over my own feet and stumbled back into a world held together by the gravity of self-imposed seriousness. *I* defined the magnitude of the task, which I knew was looming. *I* defined the limitation of my own ability to deal with it. I created my own micro-climate of apprehension and my body joined in the whole glorious game!

At the end of his timeless journey, Bowman is drawn into the centre of a star. There he undergoes a transformation. It is as if one 'Bowman' ceases to exist, but another becomes immortal. He moves backwards through his memories, and faster still into his forgotten years, and is able to smile with fondness, and without pain. When the wells of memory run dry, time itself slows and reaches a moment of stasis, like a swinging pendulum at the limit of its arc, frozen for an instant that seems 'eternal', before the next cycle begins.

The story ends with Bowman floating amid the fires of a double star, light years from earth. And, like a new-born baby, as he opens his eyes he wants to cry, but falls silent, seeing that he is no longer alone.

That was yesterday.

I gave myself a thousand brownie points just for getting up and getting back to exercise this morning. As I let my legs rest and arms hang, and felt the flow of energy returning, my muscles, not yet fully recovered, soon began to shake with fatigue and oxygen starvation, just as they had in the beginning. As a distraction I turned my full attention to the journey through my inner landscape.

I stepped out across the meadow, climbed the soft, moist soil path and rounded the crest of the hill to face my House on the Right Bank. Across the lawn and into the entrance where my empty tree stood, I stepped through and into the shower, washing away the doubts I had entertained over the past twenty-four hours. In the large courtyard I felt the warmth of friends and family, here or gone, all alike. And having reviewed my future goals, I walked out into the small court-yard where Master Fwap was waiting once again.

Here, breathing in his golden aura, I let go of all the friends and family I had just seen, all the trappings of life and all the aims I had just rehearsed with feeling and commitment. I let go of them all, and the body, emotions and thoughts which made all these things what they were for me. I let it all go until I was nothing.

My exercise was over. I shook out my limbs and moved quickly to a seated position. With seven breaths, I returned to a peaceful state and once more opened the book I had chosen to be my guide.

> Deep in the interior of each star there is a region where energy loses its direction, and where what physicists call thermo-dynamical equilibrium reigns. Yet this does not prevent the star throbbing its circular way through space. Whereas sequential life, i.e. the life of thoughts, presupposes a time-sense, motionless static life in the eternal Overself annihilates that sense, but it need not therefore be a 'dead' existence. On the contrary, it must be real life because it is the very core of selfhood and the very essence of consciousness; self and life are synonymous terms, because there could be no self-awareness in a corpse. Moreover, not being subject to the changes of material finite forms its value is imperishable and spiritual.
>
> *The Quest of the Overself*

It seemed entirely apt that Bowman's journey should have ended in the centre of a star, and that very same equilibrium was what I was called to contemplate now. It was the first time I had moved on in the text for several days; my own journey was slowing almost to a stop. Thoughts were few, and most often I would simply look out into that vast dark emptiness, from the threshold on which I had stood for longer than I should.

As I meditated – that peculiar state of giving attention without giving thought – a memory came back to me, something so insignificant that I hadn't felt any need to note it. Two colleagues and I had been talking together. One I knew well, an accomplished lady in middle age. The other, a more casual acquaintance, was young and fresh from university with a degree in psychology. This younger woman held forth on several psychological theories and her career intentions. I had been asking most of the questions and my older friend had mainly listened in silence. Afterwards this older friend, Alwyne, confided to me that she had felt intimidated by the other woman's 'learning'. It had struck me as odd that she, a woman who had achieved much in her life so far, should feel this way about a woman who had only potential.

I don't know why my mind came back to that incident, and perhaps the particular incident was of no great moment, but as I considered my friend's words once more – 'I felt intimidated by her learning' – in my imagination I answered her, 'Ah, but she doesn't understand the one secret – connection.'

It was a response in full understanding of the reflected reality of the world, which I had experienced last August, and an understanding that amid all those reflected notions of the ego, some things always speak to a deeper level, the level of soul, and that this remains so even for the most cluttered of minds. It may be a moment of beauty in art or nature, the elegant simplicity of a scientific solution, or the transporting effect of music. Poetry, too, had that capacity to create a reverie which the intellect is at a loss to define. And in the writing of poetry I had been surprised many times over the past year by the ability of my unreasoning poetic voice to ride the swell of this reverie and foreshadow by many months an understanding which my intelligence was slow to catch. All of these were aspects of the same call guiding me to the emptiness at the heart of my being. Soul.

And then relationship, and that sweet softening of voices 'as if those voices came from deeper spirits in communion'. There is only one soul. There is only soul. Soul is life, life is spirit, and spirit is love; the label does not matter.

My imaginary reply to my friend had called it connection, and in imagining this simple reply, I felt that I had finally come full circle from the implied question I had posed for myself on 20 December 1995. I am writing this much as I recorded it later in my little black book: 'Through the isolated desert of my struggle with my own ego, I had reached the beginning and was ready for connection again.'

I was thinking back to May last year, the dream provoked by that hugging lady, and how I had written, 'Some day, when all this contemplation is over, I have to begin to open out again.'

Perhaps 'opening out' would be a more apt description. Like Hannah and her lotus petals, I had chosen to close for a while – and I had fully understood why – but 'connection' I had never lost, never could. There was only ever the illusion of loss, and, if I would but see, the whole illusion called me back to connection once more.

There the trail of thought tapered off.

'As I meditated in satisfaction, something inside rolled backwards into a deep blackness.'

## The Meaning of Life

Having written those last words, and having put away my little black book, I had the feeling that I had reached a natural end. It was not the end, of course. As Winston Churchill once said, it might have marked the end of the beginning. And though my intellect might have chosen a more reasonable point, it was fitting that I should trust my feeling, and fitting also that it should be a moment so subtle as to pass utterly unnoticed; fitting because this whole period of my life may well have passed in the same way: a time when nothing changed, but everything changed.

I could not say, and do not say, that enlightenment followed or any of that wisdom, grace and unshakeable peace you can so often read about in relation to an enlightened master. Rather let me say that in the constant unfolding of perfection which is life, and therefore you and me, a lotus petal infinitesimally shifted from closed to open. In my heart I felt that shift, and my body seemed to agree for the pain in my hip went away after that day and has never returned.

Looking back, though I was always looking for inspiration, guidance and signs along the way, it is remarkable how small the decisive signs were, so often no more than a fleeting glance, a single word or a chance conversation. The significance or meaning of any of these things might have been overlooked but for the fortuitous decision to defer to an understanding deeper than reason: the symbolic language of dreams, the rhythmic obscurity of poetic inspiration, the impish analogies of the imagination, the subtle feelings of intuition and the unnerving, unprecedented transports of meditation. I said in the beginning that I doubted my need for a leap of faith, but to surrender the course of one's life to these wonders, dismissed and discounted daily by the reasoning mind, was a leap of faith far greater than any I had imagined.

I am aware that my searching has thrown up a lot of questions, and that I have not answered many of them. Not all questions are worth answering, and a bad question will only produce a poor answer, like the meaning of life for example. For years the linguistic convenience of those words fooled me into holding them up for inspection. I could hold neither meaning nor life in my fist – any more than a fist could hold water – but the solidity of those words fooled me anyway. Once again it was for Kate's sake – haplessly trying to answer that question for her, though I had always failed for my own sake – that I finally came to appreciate what a terrible question it was, even when asked in a spirit of fascination and expectation. I had been trying all along to examine an abstraction of an abstraction.

It was fortuitous again, rather than deliberate, that I had tuned the course of my enquiry, over these pages, to the real question: what does it mean to live? The answer to that does not lie within intellectual grasp, but in the grace of the present moment. Such moments of grace, of living, take away all need to question. And any moment less than this is, in essence, no more than a forgetting.

So if I asked some questions which have not been answered, I shall trust that the good questions will receive answers in good time, and that the bad ones will be seen for what they are.

These days I listen with interest to people who talk of soul-destroying work, or of having the soul undermined. I smile when someone sings of a broken heart, of love lost and the spirit crushed. I find myself thinking, 'Whoever said that has not met Soul. If they had, what could they find in such expressions?'

I used to imagine that I had experienced a fear of God so great that I would never again feel fear for worldly perils. I also imagined that I had survived such pain of the emotions that nothing could hurt me so again. I was wrong to think that fear and pain would disappear by a mere exercise of comparison. Now I believe that freedom from these things derives, contrarily, from the discovery of peace and the mindfulness to rest within it. Pains do not diminish for the sake of this, but rather one's relationship to pain is transformed.

For all that has passed I remain a seeker after truth, but one who now understands the immense folly of his own searching. Like the meaning of life, enlightenment is a word trap skilfully set for the unwary seeker. Though it feels right and good to seek, I do so in the knowledge that seeking itself is my final lesson in non-attachment, and so the seeking is made all the more impeccable. Living is a process of surrendering to things just as they are, and thereby falling into boundless mystery.

Hindsight is a wonderful thing. In the writing and rewriting of these events, many thoughts have occurred to me which, for the sake of authenticity – incompleteness, if you like – I decided to leave unsaid. Two things, however, are worthy of mention.

On my birthday, I struggled with the realisation of my goals because I had no faith in my chosen timeframe. I believed that the things I was dealing with might have been beyond arbitrary time limits, and so they were, but no more than anything else. The real limitation was my subjective impression of time as an objective reality. I had to see through this illusion before I could set a timeframe and make it newly meaningful. Having seen through this illusion, another thing became clearer.

I spoke of an older friend, Alwyne, who had been intimidated by a young psychology student. I trusted Alwyne to read and critique the opening sections of the first tentative draft of this book. When she did, Alwyne found that first dream of some interest.

'That old dying man,' she said, 'do you think it was your father?' He had already died by then.

Until Alwyne said it, the thought had never occurred to me, and even then I was too wrapped up in my own chosen interpretation to think it through.

Now I think maybe Alwyne was right. The old man of the dream had a gift to pass on, and hadn't my spontaneous thought been, as I cried after my dad's death, that I was given the gift of tears? Tears, as Dr Brunton said, bearing with them a mysterious influence which tends to dissolve the hard encrustations built up by the ego.

The one thing I had never understood about the dream was the phrase 'in the interests of safety'. In the context so modestly offered to me by Alwyne, this too makes sense. Though each of his children,

I have no doubt, were given a unique gift at his passing, it was in the interests of safety that I was chosen, as much by myself as by the rest of my family, to undergo the intense process of grief and revelation necessary to speak for my dad's life and, ultimately, for life itself.

So is this whole book built upon a misconception, a misinterpretation of a dream? Such is the elegant imagery of dreams that I think it more likely my dream managed to weave two principal preoccupations into one story, and though I could not have wished to recognise it at the time, they *were* one story. And even more than this, freed from the illusion of time, I can see and acknowledge my dream as one of those 'prophetic heralds of the coming of Grace' which come to us all if we care to see, and dare to believe.

In ending here, I know that I have made mistakes, erred in my thinking, so poorly represented the enduring love of family and friends, and left many threads loose and untidy. So be it. One of the sayings of the *Tao Te Ching*, which has stayed with me from my very first reading, is 'Great perfection seems chipped'. I do not mean to suggest that this work is a disguised form of perfection. Of course it isn't, except that life is continually perfect.

Leonard Cohen once wrote that we should ring the bells that still can ring, and forget our perfect offering. There is a crack, he said, in everything. That's how the light gets in.

May you see the light through all the cracks I have presented here, and may that light, which is yours alone, guide your way.

# *Appendix*

On Saturday morning, 3 February 1996, I had a long soak in the bath. As I washed my hair I was thinking of all the fine plans I had made and contemplating the next steps I might take towards their fulfilment. No firm ideas came to mind, but I was in a very relaxed frame of mind and, having rinsed my hair, I lay back thinking, 'Ah well, until I get where I am going, I am exactly where I need to be.'

The moment I thought this, I sat up thunderstruck by the simple truth of what I had just said. Simultaneously I had a vision of writing verses and all the different ways in which they might be used. So clear was this vision that I formed a definite plan to write fifty poems over the next six months. I committed the goal to writing a few days later.

Why fifty and why six months I cannot say, but it was what started my poetry writing in earnest – something I had not done for many years. As with other goals, the timeframe slipped along the way. It took a year in the end for me to complete fifty as intended. The purpose also changed. My original idea had been to use them as a summation of things I had learned over my first forty years, and sometimes the poems were no more than that. More often, the process was overtaken by a more urgent desire to find expression for things my intellect was still struggling to grasp.

The poems came out in no particular order. Eventually I ordered them in the way that seemed best, though they do not always sit comfortably within my chosen categories. I make no claim for their artistic merit, but I include them here for the sake of completeness because they became one of the significant ways in which my Greater Self chose to speak to me over the course of events I have related in the main parts of this book.

To say more than this would burden the words unnecessarily with a limited perspective. Like all that has gone before, take them or leave them according to your own taste.

# UNTIL I GET
# WHERE I AM GOING

# INDEX OF FIRST LINES OF POEMS

*Foreword*                                              231

## *Choosing to live*

| | | |
|---|---|---:|
| 1 | What path should I take? | 234 |
| 2 | The person I am today | 235 |
| 3 | I have nothing to live for | 236 |
| 4 | I was the first to arrive | 237 |
| 5 | Good intention is a waste | 238 |
| 6 | A belief is always true | 239 |
| 7 | The flow of life surrounds you | 240 |
| 8 | What is my life path? | 241 |

## *Choosing to grow*

| | | |
|---|---|---:|
| 9 | There is something in me | 244 |
| 10 | If something doesn't work | 245 |
| 11 | If I must face my faults | 246 |
| 12 | Without honesty | 247 |
| 13 | When I am quick | 248 |
| 14 | Whoever confessed their faults | 249 |
| 15 | If anyone hurts you | 250 |
| 16 | If I compare the calm before the storm | 251 |
| 17 | A truth which admits no other truth | 252 |

## *Choosing to love*

| | | |
|---|---|---:|
| 18 | Creation is a miracle | 254 |
| 19 | I have thought of love | 255 |
| 20 | If I should lose a friend | 256 |
| 21 | If you have ever trusted | 257 |
| 22 | Be assured that love is your personal destiny | 258 |

23 Love is not to be found 259

24 The whole world needs love 260

25 Many needs and many feelings 261

26 Possibilities abound in every moment 262

27 If I live a life of love 263

28 Here is the hammer 264

*The Journey from Ego to Soul*

29 We who walk this earth 266

30 What does your ego do for you? 267

31 There is no one on this Earth 268

32 There is a voice which says much 269

33 A gardener who depends on his fruit tree 270

34 Relax 271

35 What does it mean to live? 272

36 So many lines my ego draws 273

37 My body serves me well 274

*The Journey into Stillness and Peace*

38 My past does not hurt me 278

39 I will not watch my life backwards 279

40 The Peace from which you came 280

41 In the deep stillness of our being 281

42 To the flame that burns on wood 282

43 When we are at peace 283

*The Journey into Mystery*

44 Whether you look to the West 286

45 This body 287

46 Think of the whole in every part 288

47 Your view of life is not inevitable 289

48 Everything contains the Truth 290

49 There is a channel in everything 291

# *Foreword*

My dear friend,
every friendship is unique,
and ours can be renewed,
reinvented,
every time we meet.
But take a moment of thought,
before we speak,
to these questions:

Are we slaves to our possessions,
or are we free?

Are we seduced by comfort,
or are we free?

Are we chained to our past,
or are we free?

Are we afraid to go forward,
or are we free?

Are we hostage to our feelings,
or are we free?

Are we constrained by our attachments,
or are we free?

Are we blind to our weakness,
or are we free?

Are we bowed and falsely modest,
or are we free?

Are we closed in our minds,
or are we free?

Are we frightened of the truth,
or are we free?

There are no answers that
will make or break our friendship,
but to ask is like the air
that friends must breathe.

*Choosing to Live*

# 1

What path should I take?
Where could it lead?

I only know the journey
Must begin from here.

And every sign has meaning,
But the meaning always comes from me.

Until I get where I am going,
I am exactly where I need to be.

# 2

The person I am today
is the person I have chosen to be.

The people I am with,
the things I have,
the place in which I find myself,
I chose them all.

There were times I may have thought
that circumstance had moved
far beyond my control.
But that was only to deny
that I had a choice
of how to feel and how to act.
If I did not realise the choice I had,
then I chose ignorance.

If I was too young,
or too much in shock
to realise,
I know it now
and it is not too late.

Today,
I will make a conscious choice
in everything I do.
I will choose how to feel
and choose what to do.

To try to do otherwise would be futile,
since failing to exercise my choice
is a choice in itself.

# 3

I have nothing to live for
and everything to live for;

The pain of life is unbearable
and barely worth the mention;

Life is chaos and decay
and grows toward an ever clearer day;

A catalogue of loss,
and a harbour of gain.

Life is one and the same,
but chalk and cheese;

Nothing I could want,
and everything I seek.

Life depends on the way
I choose to see.

# 4

I was the first to arrive, and I will be the last to leave.

My intellect is a travelling circus; my emotion a moveable feast; my silent body is an entrance hall, a gathering room, a fireside, and resting place.

People come and go within this space. They arrive by invitations sent at my request, long before I came. They leave because they have other things to do, which I understood from the beginning.

How foolish I look when I stare out of my window, watching every banquet but my own, and wishing I was somewhere else.

How foolish I look when I wish my guests would leave, when I refuse them hospitality, when I scheme and set one against the other, when I store up resentment, when, caught within an atmosphere of bitterness and sorrow, I only add to the general complaint.

How foolish I look when I refuse to give the very gift I brought to be given; when I say I haven't got it, I cannot find it, I have lost it, I am saving it for someone more deserving.

How foolish I look when I grieve so much for those departing, that I fail to welcome those arriving or acknowledge those remaining.

How foolish I look when I ask why I came here in the first place, when I ask so many times, but never wait for a reply.

How foolish I look when the feast is nearly over, and I am so dissatisfied.

# 5

Good intention is a waste,
unless I act upon it.

All the knowledge I have gained is useless,
unless I use it.

All method may as well be madness,
unless I apply it.

All the wisdom in the world is foolish,
unless I follow it.

All the love I feel is lost,
unless I show it.

The great gift of life is gone,
unless I share it.

# 6

A belief is always true
for the one who holds it.

For better or worse,
beliefs are decisions
which shape our destiny.

For good or ill,
beliefs create the reality
in which we live
from day to day.

So I choose to say:

That everything that happens
is for a purpose
and it serves me;

That every joy and every pain
carries the seed of understanding,
and of love;

That every gain and every loss
is for my spiritual good.

That, in the stillness of my heart,
grace abides
and will make these things true.

# 7

The flow of life surrounds you.
It is the architect of every moment
which holds out its hand to you
but never waits.

You cannot stop it, force it,
or push against it,
though you may try,
as a reed tries to bend the sky.

It flows around you and is lost;
powerless to you
while ever you are powerless
to let it through.

Think of learning to live
as learning to open up a channel.

# 8

What is my life path?
Does it lie in my choice of work,
My choice of relationships;
In my chosen disciplines
of mind, body and soul?

Yes and no.

Yes, I must go
Where my deepest desire
Says I should.
And no,
My path is nothing to do
With plans, affinities, and purposes
Which are as dust
In the face of eternity.

My path is in the heart
I bring to the things I do,
In the spirit in which I do them;
My path is the path
I open up
To let life through,
A life path,
If life, above myself,
Is what I choose.

*Choosing to Grow*

# 9

There is something in me
Which would cherish
Every moment of experience,
However good or bad it be,
And use it for my growth;
To pull me free
From former limitations
Of thought or deed;
To turn defeat to resolution;
Put aside my fears
And wash away my doubt;
Keep me moving outwards,
Expanding and tugging
At the chains of complacency
And comfort;
Searching always
For that further horizon.

And something which retreats;
Which, in my falling,
Breathes a sigh of defeat;
Before a host of possibilities
Sees only what was never meant to be;
Lays out my destiny
At other feet,
And cries, 'If only
Things had worked out differently;
How worthily I could have lived.'

Two voices calling me
At every step:
One to grow
And one to quit,
I make a choice
Of which to hear,
And give this choice
The steady force of habit.

# 10

If something doesn't work
and I call it failure,
I am really calling myself a failure.
In doing so I sap my spirit
and spend what little I have left
reassessing my limitations,
expanding the frontier of self-doubt.

But if something doesn't work
and I call it a result,
it becomes an opportunity to learn.
I use all my energy
to take stock and to grow.
My beliefs are intact;
my aim is surer than before.

There are no failures,
only results.

# 11

If I must face my faults – and I must – then I should face them with kindness and with patience.

What difference does this make?

It is the difference between humility and humiliation.

And what difference does that make?

Humility brings me closer to that power which is greater than my faults; a power within which shows me the way to change, and, on the way, brings its own consolation.

Humiliation only perpetuates and reinforces my faults, while robbing me of the strength to deal with them. It takes none of my faults away, and only adds its own bitterness to the list.

The need for patience and kindness with others almost goes without saying.

The need for patience and kindness with myself needs to be stated over and over again.

# 12

Without honesty
I will never fully see myself
for what I am.

Without kindness
I will never find honesty,
only self-deprecation and deception
masquerading as the truth.

But with honesty and kindness,
I can ask what I have gained
from all the ways I chose
to feel my pain.
I can measure what I lost
in the process,
and I can change.

With kindness,
I can break the chains
which tie me to my past mistakes.

And with honesty,
I can find the root
of every lasting hurt,
that one defining moment of thought,
which hooked my identity
and conjured up the dread
of unknowing who I was.

The will to unknow,
the courage to let go
is called acceptance,
and acceptance
is the still, dark root of change,
the knot from which my freedom grows.

# 13

When I am quick
to put people into pigeon-holes
and slow to take them out,
I watch the world
by holding up a mirror.

When I find fault with anyone,
and make that fault
a figure of fun,
I watch the world
by holding up a mirror.

When I weigh another's worth
and find it wanting,
I watch the world
by holding up a mirror.

# 14

Whoever confessed their faults
Because I was waiting to judge?

Whoever followed my example
Because I told them they must?

Whoever accepted me gladly
While I begrudged their company?

Whoever adapted their ways to mine
Because I was so unyielding?

Whoever showed their weakness
Because I showed my strength?

Whoever admitted their foolishness
Because I affected wisdom?

Whoever gave their feelings
To be trampled on?

Whoever really spoke to me
Until I was ready to listen?

# 15

If anyone hurts you
Angers you or fails you;
If anyone rejects you
Curses you or irritates;
If anyone should stay too long
Or leave too soon,
And leave a painful mark
Upon your make-up;
Dare you believe
That you do not yet understand
That person's path
And how it fits with yours,
Or you do not understand your own
And how to learn from his,
And if you understood
Your pain would disappear?

If a situation hurts you;
If events have seemed to you
The gravest of misfortune;
If your talents seem so poor
Compared to others;
If your troubles overwhelm you;
Dare you think
That your perception
Is a challenge you have chosen for yourself
To overcome
And set your fearful life free;
To understand what is out of your control,
And what you can control
To put this freedom in your reach?

Do not run from hurt,
Because hurting is your call to understand.
And do not hide from pain,
For pain is but the calling of your soul,
Behind a veil you must remove
With your own hand.

# 16

If I compare
the calm before the storm
and the calm
which follows the storm,
I could not say
that ignorance is bliss.

Ignorance
built a house that could not stand,
made plans that could be washed away,
turned away from friends
that were never made,
buried love inside a shallow grave
of preconception, fear and pride.
Ignorance was emptiness
that learned to hide.

In the calm
which follows the storm
I know
the only comforts
to be washed away
were scales from my eyes.

I have a clearer vision
of the truth
to which my heart
must rise.

# 17

A truth which admits no other truth
is a lie.

Belief which must fight other beliefs
is doubt.

A faith which has to prove itself
is faithlessness.

If four climbers scaled a mountain,
one by the East,
one by the North,
and one by the South, and one West,
and if they came to you
to describe their journey,
and the wonders they had seen upon their way,
would they speak
of different mountains?

And if your wish
was to climb,
would you hold to one,
and turn from all the others?
Would you argue and fight
with anyone who disagreed?

And if you did,
would this make the mountain
any easier to climb?
Or would you find
that all this fighting
was a waste of precious time?

This is why I say:
a truth which admits no other truth
is a lie.

*Choosing to Love*

# *18*

Creation is a miracle, but its plan is unfinished.
It is and always will be perfect,
but its work is undiminished.

To say that I don't see this, or the part I play,
is like the heart long protesting
that it cannot see the body,
nor, therefore, any need to beat.

Humanity is at the heart of the living Creation.

I am in the heart of God.

My responsibility is, at once, immense
and completely unavoidable.

Creation will be served
by my action or inaction,
by anger or kindness,
understanding or misconception,
loving
or failing to love.

And seeing this I know that, from today,
I must show love in all I do.

And I cry:
Where can I find so much love;
in all the world I could never find
enough to give.

But this is like the heart that hesitates to beat
for fear that it may never more be filled.

# 19

I have thought of love as an overwhelming feeling, beyond my
    power to control.
I was wrong.
In the strength and depth of my emotion, I could have loved,
but my failure to control it was a measure of my weakness and
nothing else.
In failing to control, I failed to love. I thought of no one but
myself.

I have also thought of love as this: that in all things I should
    treat another's want as more than mine, another's need as
    more than my need, another's life as greater than my own.
And here, too, vanity portrayed its tender trap of self-sacrifice as
perfect in itself, when all the while it would enslave the one I
sought to help.

I have thought of love as the ground from which the spirit
    grows, dark with beauty, nurturing and holding.
And if my vision came close, it was the likeness of a line tracing
form, as if a pen had drawn its face, but failed to give it life or
human warmth.

Love is best without a single thought, without a measure or a
    purpose.
Love is best when drawn from its own perfect source.

# 20

If I should lose a friend,
a precious friend
who occupied a mansion in my heart,
what should I do?

Should I mourn for my unbearable loss,
Watch a new world with heavy eyes
and find it wanting?
Should I search the gaping hollow of my heart
to hold the pain of what is past
as if loyalty were a greater gain
than any crumb of consolation?

Or should I cherish the gift
that was left in my keeping,
the best of what my friend was to me,
and nurture this each day
as if my heart was only aching
to make this precious spirit real?

Then I should feel
in my pain
a measure of the love
that set me free.

# 21

If you have ever trusted
And felt let down,
It is not that you were wrong to trust,
But that the level of your trust was wrong.

You must trust
At the level of your soul.
The meaning of this is threefold:

That you trust in trust,
Because trust is a seed of love,
And is its own reward;

That you trust another's soul
To never mean you harm,
Whatever be the failings
Of the ego;

And that you trust in yourself
To be unbroken in the face
Of any failing;
Not to be unmoved,
But always, in the end,
To grow.

# 22

Be assured
that love is your personal destiny.
But it is not an emptiness to be filled,
or a separated half
hoping to be made whole.

When two people
lose themselves to this fantasy,
they become like two cups
pouring water back and forth
one to the other.

Even with the greatest care,
they fill their need
but lose their way.

Without care,
the little they may have is lost,
and what begins with joy
becomes an empty ritual.

How many times
have you seen
that this is so?

But be assured
that love is your personal destiny,
complete in itself.

Hold true to the love
which embraces your spirit
and guides your way.

# 23

Love is not to be found
in the sum of another's
feelings and actions,
nor in the sum of my own.
Love is not so fickle a guide;
it comes from somewhere
deep inside;
connected and infinite.

Not seeing this
is like standing at a well
and seeing the pail
as the only vital thing.

If I should stand at another's well
and try to pull the pail
from the rope which binds it
to its proper place,
I will not succeed unaided,
nor ever satisfy my need.

If a friend
comes to me in thirst,
and I unfasten my pail
as if to give all that I have,
I have given less
than my friend deserved,
and, more than this,
I have betrayed myself.

## 24

The whole world needs love,
To give and to receive,
But if I need to love,
As strange as this may seem,
I must learn to walk away.

What good have I done in the first place
If I feel that my pains
Go insufficiently rewarded?

What care have I shown
If I count in the balance
How much is returned?

What purpose is served
By the motive of obligation?

How many times
Has my need to love been tainted
By the need to be needed,
Or my actions compromised
By the need to be liked?

From all these things
I must learn to walk away,
For only when I can
May the stirring of my heart
Be unloosed
To hold sway.

# 25

Many needs and many feelings
may lend themselves to love,
but love will never lend itself to them.

Morals, rules and principles
may fall in line with love,
but love will never fall in line with them.

Values
may be based on love,
but love will never base itself on them.

Many times
I may depend on love,
but love is not dependence.

And many times
I search for love,
but love is ever present.

# 26

Possibilities abound in every moment
and every meeting;
a thousand insights, a thousand answers,
a thousand signs.

What you see
depends on how you look.
The answer you receive
depends on what you ask.
The direction you find
depends on where you want to go.

Always show patience and kindness.
There is no one on earth without
something to teach you,
something to give you,
something to help you on your journey.

Give them the space to be themselves
that their truth might slowly be revealed to you.

And have courage;
be open.

Remember that,
whether they know it or not,
they, in their turn,
wait for your truth to unfold.

# 27

If I live a life of love,
I am always in the right place
At the right time.
There is no wrong place for me to be,
Or a wrong time for me to be there.

Take this deeper,
And the game of life
Becomes a game
Of kind and subtle consequence,
And quiet thrill.

Take this deeper still,
And if I live a life of love,
There is no other place,
No other time;
No fortune judged
For good or ill;
No conflict between fate
And free will;
No separation;
Only love which flows
Through passion
Which is rendered still.

# 28

Here is the hammer;
Now is the nail.

Here is the easel;
Now is the frame.

Here is the canvas;
Now is the paint.

Here is my lover;
Now is her face.

*The Journey from Ego to Soul*

# 29

We who walk this Earth
Think ourselves attached to life
And do not wish to die,
When in truth we are attached to death
And too afraid of life.

We think of being born to an allotted span
And silently we mourn
But in truth
If this is how we think
We have not yet been born.

We think of freedom
As the choice to go
Wherever we will
And do as we please,
But freedom is not ours
Until surrendered willingly.

We think of joy
As only possible
If we struggle free of pain
But in truth
We are most joyful in suffering.

And love we think
A matter of good fortune
And chance
When all the while
The chance to love
Is in our own hands.

Nothing is as it seems
For we who walk this Earth
And think ourselves awoken
When in truth we dream.

# 30

What does your ego
do for you?

Have you seen it move mountains,
transform the face of the world?

Can it bring you riches
and untold material gain?

A comforting list of achievements
and fond experience?

Has it been your tried and tested
means of influence?

A star that draws everyone you ever need
into its orbit?

And, when all else fails,
the keeper of your self-respect?

Yes,
your ego can work wonders.

And truly I tell you
that all this work

is like the moving of furniture
around your living quarters,

while you look out at life,
and all it offers,
through a crack in the door.

# 31

There is no one on this Earth
who is completely right for me,
but I am not alone.

There is no one who can share
all that I am
who will be with me
in all that I can be,
but I am not alone.

There is no one on this Earth
who can understand me
to the last degree,
but I am not alone.

No one's hand fits perfectly
in mine;
no one's path will always
run alongside
the path that I must find,
but I am not alone.

For loneliness,
this yearning for a soul-mate,
this aching for agreement,
this searching for a hand to hold,
are pains of one
still looking for his own soul.

I will not be distracted
from this goal;
nothing else could make me whole,
or make the beauty of another
truly mine to behold.

# 32

There is a voice which says much
and speaks of little.
There is a voice which says little
and speaks volumes.

There are ears which hear everything
and discern barely anything.
There are ears which hear
only the truth.

There are eyes sharply focused
Seeing only illusion.
There are eyes hardly opened
with vision beyond words.

There is an emptiness
which echoes emptiness.
There is an emptiness
filled with the fullness of life.

There is a nakedness
hidden in shame.
There is a nakedness
robed with pride.

There is a body running swiftly
which never arrives.
There is a body in stillness
reaching far and wide.

There is your self
on the surface.
There is you
deep inside.

# 33

A gardener who depends on his fruit tree for life, devotes his life to its care and nourishment. He learns of its needs with each passing season and tends to those needs with diligence. He discovers those things which harm its growth, and sets to work to remove them.

Many winds and storms will come, which he has no power to control. With faith and discipline, he attends to those things that he can control and learns not to worry, but to live with forbearance and hope as the tree draws new strength from every setback. He also learns to live with patience and humility, understanding that while there is much that he can do indirectly to help the tree to grow, there is nothing he can do directly to make it grow. The tree grows and bears fruit of itself.

As each fruit appears, he takes great care and pleasure to watch and feel for that perfect moment when the fruit should be picked. He savours that sublime moment as the fruit continues to ripen in his hand, and, finally, he eats with joy and gratitude. He learns that in these moments nothing else should take precedence, for the moment soon passes, the fruit withers and is lost forever. But heeding the grace of each moment, he lives in abundance and shares his riches with others, receiving many more gifts in return.

You are the gardener and, if you will, the tree is a growing connection to your inner soul. The fruit is your inspiration. Learn to feel it, savour it, taste it, share it. Do not tend to other demands while it withers and dies. It is the fruit of your true life. Heed it and live with poetry, where once you lived with prose.

# 34

Relax.

Your ego harbours
Hopes of success
And fears of failure
But these are no more
Than flickering lights
On the wide blank canvas
Of your Purer Self.

Your ego is tied
By guilt to the past
And by worry to the future
But these ropes
Are like a spider's web
Before the giant
Of your Greater Self.

Your ego is always swayed
And often swamped
By emotion
But these feelings
Are mere ripples
On the ocean
Of your Deeper Self.

All these feelings
Your ego tries to hold
And control
In the tension of your body,
And the chatter of your thoughts.

Relax.
Let go.
Your True Self already knows
And understands each moment
Perfectly,
And does not care
For what has gone
Or what will come.
Your True Self and the moment
Are one.

# 35

What does it mean
To live in the present moment?
My ego does not understand;
It knows past,
It has a sense of the future,
And it draws a line,
From one to the other, called time.

Eternity is so impossibly far
As to be unimaginable,
And Now, this present moment,
So impossibly small
As to be unattainable
In any practical way.

But still my ego
Cherishes this view,
Calls it rational,
While my soul
Slips effortlessly through
That point of no duration
Where Eternity and Now are one;
That point which underlies the ego's time
As time rolls on;
Underlies all models
Of the ego's understanding;
An inlet
Where the hardest,
Cleverest thoughts
Dissolve to nothing.

What does it mean
To live
Without the need of understanding?

# 36

So many lines my ego draws
From the cradle to the grave,
From poverty to riches,
From unsafe to safe,
Lost to saved.

From misery to happiness,
Meaning to despair;
Plotted lines
Between failure and success,
Subject and object,
Life and Death.

In this way
My ego hopes
To find its place,
To know where it stands,
Even though it knows
It marks its footprints
In shifting sand.

I watch the wild dance
Of my sinking ego.
Now I surely understand:
It has no home,
And I can
No longer follow
Where it goes.

# *37*

My body serves me well;
it sings my praise
and carries every failing,
trembles to another's touch,
and faced with time,
a rhythm of the mind,
will dance
until the day is done.

But who am I,
blessed with skin and bone?
I have this body,
but I am not my body.
I release it from the need
to please and comfort me.

My emotions are the colour
and the passion of the day;
they teach me lessons
of both strength
and human frailty,
bring me closer
to the underlying love
of all things.

But who am I
to be so clothed in these feelings?
I have emotions
but I am not my emotions.
I release them from the need
to please and comfort me.

My thoughts are constant conversation
of a cluttered life;
they stimulate, create
and analyse;
the first brick
of every human endeavour,
and the power to conceive
even this burning question:

Who am I
with this power of thought?
I have an intellect,
but I am not my intellect.
I release it from the need
to please and comfort me.

Released,
let all these glories
carry me so far.
But every one
I must let go
to walk the last step
alone.

*The Journey into*
*Stillness and Peace*

# 38

My past does not hurt me,
What hurts me
Is the way I see it now.

My future does not worry me,
What worries me
Is the way I see it now.

What is there, now,
That is out of my control?

What is there, now,
That I must resolve?

What is there, now,
In past or future,
That I need to see at all?

When I learn,
For the moment, just to be,
My pains and worries
Have already disappeared.

# 39

I will not watch my life
Backwards from the moment after death,
Or shrink before the seat of my Judgement.
I will not weigh my past
With scales of brass,
Or step with trepidation
On a meagre and half-hearted path.

I rested in Stillness
At peace in that moment before my birth.
Did I not know that I was perfect?
But I said,
'There are many things I need to learn,
Things for which I must take
This human form,
And be imperfect once again,
That love may strike its wisdom
Through my every imperfection,
That Love may leave me broken,
Hollowed and reformed
To hold that perfect flame,
That Spirit which I cannot name.'

And the Spirit of Life said,
'I will walk this way with you,
I will follow at your right,
And your left hand,
Before you and behind,
I will be your friend,
And, more than this,
My breath will fill
Your very essence.'

# 40

The Peace from which you came
will not abandon you.
Even in your time of deepest anguish,
Peace is closer
than the dark side
of a gossamer thread.

If the lessons you must learn
seem hard beyond belief,
it is not Peace that makes them so,
but your own resistance
to your need to grow.

If life has taught you bitterness,
despondency or defensiveness,
these are not the fruits of Peace,
but the poor reach
of your limited understanding.

Peace does not make its lessons hard
or line its way with trouble;
it does not call for harsh sacrifice
or seek to break your will.

If you should rage,
it waits quietly.
If you despair,
it waits still.
When you lose the last ounce
of your patience,
it waits.

Why does it not come?

Because it waits for you.

# *41*

In the deep stillness of our being
we are always smiling.
Whatever hardship we face,
whatever pain or vexation,
in the deep stillness
we are always at peace.

And all the aspects,
all visions,
every moment of who we are
rises up from this place,
but leaves us unaware,
lost to where we came from
or why we are here at all,
struggling to live by a light
only dimly recalled.

We would not struggle,
would not worry if we knew,
as we did before,
that in this stillness,
every struggle is accounted for
and none are lost
or hopelessly forlorn,
for sorrow is a homeward guide
and tears are at the door

to lead us home
to that place of deep stillness,
at peace with our soul,
which is always smiling,
and always was our goal.

# 42

To the flame
that burns on wood,
the flames that dance
across the fields
may seem free,
full of wild abandon,
full of destiny.

This dance
is but the clutching of straw
which is consumed
within a moment
and gone.
These flames must flee
and find no rest.
They dance
the dance of emptiness.

To the flame
that burns on wood
I say: cling
to the deep stillness
of your resting place.

The world believes you
foolish one day,
wise the next,
but neither ridicule nor praise
should turn your head
or move you from that place
in which your spirit
finds rest.

# *43*

When we are at peace
There is only peace.
When we are still
There is only stillness.

There was nothing that was still
Or will be still,
Nothing that was peace
Or will be peace.

There is no arrival and no leaving,
Nothing that was lost
Or will be gained.
There is nothing that came close
Or moved away.

In stillness
There is only stillness.
When we are at peace
There is only peace.

*The Journey into Mystery*

# 44

Whether you look to the West
With the eyes of the East,
Or to the East
With the eyes of the West,
Digest what can be digested,
But do not discard what is left;
There will be a drawing together.

Whether you travel far and fast,
Or never leave your door,
Understand what can be understood,
But never think
That there can be no more;
There will be a drawing together.

A drawing together
Of all things seen
Into a glorious unseen.

A drawing together
Of all things known
Into a mystical unknown.

No more can you number all the footsteps
Which brought you to this place,
Still less the grains of sand
Which helped to shape each footprint.

What footsteps could you take away
Yet still be here?
What grains of sand
Could you remove
Yet still stand?

And where else could you be
But Here,
At the threshold of your understanding?
When, if not Now,
In the dawn of your eternal awakening?

# *45*

This body,
this flesh and blood,
is not the cage of my soul.
It is the manifest meeting of
the infinite within and the infinite without.

This body is not a vessel for my soul.
It is the passing point of grace
flowing in and never lost,
flowing out and never wasted.

This body is not an instrument
fashioned to bring a single note
to a greater symphony.
It is that ageless resounding moment when
the great song of beauty reaches harmony
and holds it in the tenderest embrace.

This is my body.

# 46

Think of the whole in every part,
your whole physical self
in every cell,
the whole of you
in every semblance of your being,
the whole Universe,
all that ever was and will be,
in you.

In every breath you breathe,
the very breath of life,
which was in the beginning.

Every word and every lesson,
every secret,
all you could ever need to know,
already waiting to be known,
no hiding place on Earth,
except the place
most hidden in your soul.

# 47

Your view of life
Is not inevitable,
Unchangeable;
Your view of life
Is not true;
It is not even you.

Embrace the fascination
Of never knowing anything
For sure.
Embrace the purest joy
Giving way to impurity;
The brightest vision
Fading into obscurity.
Embrace the changing nature
Of the Absolute.

# 48

Everything contains the Truth.
Nothing can contain the Truth.

Everything carries within it
That divine spark,
The undivided Spirit;
The whole Truth is always there.
Yet nothing can encompass it,
No cage can be put around it,
No trap set to catch it;
Nothing can contain the Truth.

No litany or liturgy,
No form of words,
No name,
No prayer, no gateway,
No practice or devotion,
No discipline,
No power, nor honour,
No shield, nor sword,
No book or belief,
No walk with destiny,
No poetry, no perspective,
No savour of life's goodness,
No ecstasy, nor change of heart,
No burning vision,
Nor warmth, nor austerity,
No relief, no realisation,
Meditation or revelation;
Everything contains the Truth.

# 49

There is a channel in everything
Be it living or still
Through which form is given spirit
And the spirit made real.

There is a channel in everything,
Unseen and colourful,
Ignored and wonderful,
Empty and full.

We are born to the shallow shore
Of a stream.
Before we reach the river,
We must learn to swim.
Before we reach the ocean,
We must learn to sail
And know how to catch the wind.
In our youth we must learn to survive;
Once grown, we must learn to live.

There is a channel in everything
Living or still;
The wind of the spirit,
A gift,
Unseen and wonderful.

# Bibliography

Black, Jack, *Mindstore*, London, Thorsons, 1994.

Bly, Robert, *Iron John*, Shaftesbury, Dorset, Element, 1991.

Brennan, Barbara, *Hands of Light*, New York, Bantam, 1990.

Brunton, Dr Paul, *The Quest of the Overself*, London, Rider, 1970.

Chuen, Master Lam Kam, *The Way of Energy*, London, Gaia, 1991.

Clarke, Arthur C., *2001, A Space Odyssey*, London, Legend, 1990.

Covey, Stephen R., *The Seven Habits of Highly Effective People*, London, Simon & Schuster, 1989.

Gibran, Kahlil, *The Prophet*, London, Heinemann, 1926.

Hay, Louise L., *You Can Heal Your Life*, Enfield, Eden Grove, 1988.

Hill, Napoleon, *Think and Grow Rich*, New York, Hawthorn, 1937.

*I Ching*, Richard Wilhelm (trans.), London, Routledge & Kegan Paul, 1951.

Irving, John, *A Prayer for Owen Meany*, London, Black Swan, 1990.

Lenz, Rama-Dr Frederick, *Surfing the Himalayas*, London, Hodder & Stoughton, 1995.

Millman, Dan, *Way of the Peaceful Warrior*, Tiburon, H.J. Kramer, 1984.

Morgan, Marlo, *Mutant Message Down Under*, London, Thorsons, 1995.

Nouwen, Henri J. M., *Out of Solitude*, Notre Dame, Indiana, Ave Maria, 1974.

Peck, M. Scott, *The Road Less Travelled*, London, Rider, 1985.

Pirsig, Robert M., *Zen and the Art of Motorcycle Maintenance*, London, Bodley Head, 1994.

Rampa, Lobsang, *The Third Eye*, London, Mandarin, 1991.

Redfield, James, *The Celestine Prophecy*, London, Bantam, 1994.

Tzu, Lao, *Tao Te Ching* (James Legge trans.), Boston, Little, Brown, 1994.

Tzu, Lao, *Tao Te Ching* (Timothy Freke trans.), London, Judy Piatkus, 1995.

Printed in the United States
1078600001B